SILENT
JOE

T. JEFFERSON PARKER

SILENT

JOE

HYPERION

NEW YORK

Copyright © 2001, 2002 T. Jefferson Parker

All rights reserved. No part of this book may be used or reproduced in any manner whatsoever without the written permission of the Publisher. Printed in the United States of America. For information address: Hyperion, 77 W. 66th Street, New York, New York 10023-6298.

Hyperion books are available for special promotions and premiums. For details contact Hyperion Special Markets, 77 West 66th Street, 11th floor, New York, New York, 10023, or call 212-456-0100.

MASS MARKET ISBN 0-7868-9003-7

FIRST MASS MARKET EDITION

10 9 8 7 6 5 4 3 2 1

For Fritz and Flo,
who have known me longer than I've known myself,
but still invite me into their home and meadow

Acknowledgments

I'd like to thank the men and women of the Orange County Sheriff-Coroner Department for their help with this book.

In particular, thanks to Sheriff Michael Carona, Assistant Sheriff Rocky Hewitt, Lieutenant Terry Boyd and Deputy Mike Peters, all of whom gave of their time and experience. Especially Mike, who taught me to watch my back and showed me the secrets of the plumbing tunnels.

Also, thanks to Rex Tomb, Matthew McLaughlin, Mark Hunter and Carl Swanson of the Federal Bureau of Investigation.

These are outstanding men. The truth is all theirs and I'm glad they're on my side.

Like so many of my books, this one began with a phone call to Larry Ragle, retired head of the Orange County crime lab, who opened doors for me—many of them jail doors—that I could never open myself. Thank you Larry, *again*.

Thanks also to the staff of Orangewood Home for Children. And not just for helping me, but for helping hundreds of children every year.

Former assistant DA Chris Evans answered my questions with experience and good humor and for this I am grateful.

Byron Brenkus answered by fast-car queries.

Lastly, thanks to Jonathan Lethem, whose writing inspired me to try this book.

Chapter One

"Drive hard, Joe. Mary Ann's blue again, so I want to be home by ten."

This from the boss, Will. Will Trona, Orange County Supervisor, First District. Mary Ann is his wife.

"Yes, sir."

"Talk while you drive. Are you carrying?"

"The usual."

Will was on edge again. Lots of that lately. He sat down beside me like he usually did. Never in the backseat unless he was in conference. Only in the front, where he could watch the road and the gauges and me. He loved speed. Loved coming out of a turn with his head thrown back against the rest. He'd always ask me how I did it, go that fast into a turn and keep the car on the road.

And I always gave him the same answer: "Slow in, fast out," which is the first thing they teach you about curves in any driving school. A good car can do things most people think are impossible.

We headed down from Will's home in the Tustin hills. It was evening in the middle of June, the sun hanging in a pink haze of clouds and smog. Lots of new mansions up there, but Will's house wasn't one of them. Supervisors make a decent salary, plus some perks. Orange County is one of the most expensive places in the country. Will's place was a tear-down by the new standards of the neighborhood. Just old and plain, nothing wrong with it besides that.

In fact, it was a good house. More than good. I know because I grew up in it. Will's my father, kind of.

"First stop is the Front," he said, checking his watch. "Medina's finally peeking out the windows again."

He talked without looking at me. Leaned back his head, eyelids half down, but his eyes moving. He usually looked like he was disappointed with what he saw. Like he was judging it, trying to find a way to make it better. But there was also something affectionate in his expression. Pride of ownership.

Will reached down between his feet and snapped open his leather briefcase. He took out the black calendar, set the briefcase back on the floorboard, then started scribbling with a pen. He liked to talk while he wrote. Sometimes it was to himself, and sometimes it was to me. Growing up with him since I was five, working nights for him since I was sixteen, I've come to know when he's was talking to me or talking to himself.

"Medina's getting a second chance. He registers five hundred illegal aliens to vote, they tell a *Times* reporter that they're illegals, but they're allowed to vote in a United States election. Allowed to, because Medina told them they could. And they all voted for me, because Medina told them to. Now, what am I supposed to do with that?"

I'd already thought about it. I checked the rearview as I answered. "Distance yourself. Five hundred votes isn't worth the scandal."

"That's shortsighted, Joe. Mean-spirited and stupid is what it is. I get the whole Latino vote thanks to Medina, and you think I should toss him overboard? Who taught you to treat your friends like that?"

Will's always teaching. Testing. Revising. Arguing it out. Saying things to see how they sound, to see if he believes them or not.

I've learned to see some things Will's way. Other things I'll never learn. Will Trona made me what I am, but even Will can only do so much. I'm less than half his age. I've got a long way to go.

But one thing Will taught me is to make up your mind fast and put the whole weight of your being behind that decision. Instantly. Later, if you have to change your mind, put all your weight behind *that* decision. Never be afraid to be wrong. Will hates only two things: indecision and stubbornness.

So I said, "You need the Latino vote to carry the First District, sir. You know that. And those votes won't go away. They love you."

Will shook his head and wrote again. He's a handsome man, good build, strong in the neck and deep in the chest, with hands that got strong and dark working summers in construction, helping himself through school after Vietnam. Black hair combed back, gray on the sides, blue eyes. When he looks at you it's the same expression he gets in the car, head back a little, almost sleepy, but the eyes are alert. And if he smiles, the lines of his fifty-four years frame it in a way that convinces people that he knows and likes them. Most of the time, he does.

"Joe, pay attention to Medina tonight. Mouth shut, eyes open. You might actually learn something."

Mouth shut, eyes open. You might actually learn something.

One of Will's earliest lessons.

He closed the calendar and slid it back into the briefcase. Clicked it shut. Looked at his watch again. Then he leaned against the headrest and lowered his eyelids halfway and watched the white middle-class boulevard of Tustin become the barrio of Santa Ana.

"How was work today?"

"Quiet, sir."

"It's always quiet in there. Until there's a fight or a race riot."

"Yes."

By day, I'm a deputy for the Orange County Sheriff's Department. I work the Central Jail Complex, as do all new deputies. I've worked the jail four years now. Another year, I'll qualify for reassignment to patrol and start becoming a real cop. I'm twenty-four years old.

I became a deputy because Will told me to. That's what he was, until he got elected supervisor. Will told me to become a deputy because he thought it would be good for me, and because he thought it would be useful for him to have a "kick-ass son" in the sheriff's department.

Down on Fourth Street, not far from the jail where I work, there's the Hispanic American Cultural Front. It's Jaime Medina's outfit. HACF does good things—distributes money and goods to the Hispanic poor, offers scholarships and stipends for needy students, expedites immigration, shelters families in crisis, all that.

But because of this misunderstanding about when Medina's almost-citizens could vote, the DA is considering closing down the place on charges of conspiracy and election fraud. They raided the HACF building last week for records. Front-page picture of guys in suits lugging cardboard boxes to a van.

Will shouldn't have been going there, with an investigation pending. And he's good friends with the DA, Philip Dent—one more reason to keep his nose clean while the investigation played out. But Will also represents Medina's district on the

Board of Supervisors, a district you can't win without the Hispanic vote and Hispanic dollars. Another political pinch, one of
the thousands in any supervisor's life. Sooner or later he'll have
to take a stand, because, as Will taught me early on, politics is
action.

"Joe, Jennifer is going to have something for us. While I'm
talking to Jaime, put it in the trunk and lock it."

"Yes, sir."

I turned left off the boulevard, checking the mirrors again,
looking out at the *zapateria* on one corner, the bridal store on
the other with all the white-laced mannequins in the window. I
studied the cars behind us, the people on the sidewalk. I was a
little nervy myself that evening. Something in the air? Maybe.
Maybe nothing that obvious. Even with the windows up and
the air conditioner blowing you could hear the Mexican music
jumping from the *discoteca*. A polka on mescaline. A dark-
faced man in a white cowboy hat and boots stopped at the curb
to let us turn, maybe recognizing Will Trona's car, maybe not,
his face a walnut deadpan that had seen everything and was no
longer impressed by any of it.

Then into a dirt parking lot in the shade of a huge pepper
tree, facing the back door of the HACF headquarters. We
stepped into the pleasant heat and Will, dressed in his usual trim
dark suit and carrying his leather briefcase, led the way in.

The back doors were locked so Will rapped hard.

"Open up, Jaime! *La Migra!*"

The door cracked open, then swung all the way.

"As usual, you're not funny," said Jaime. He was a slender
young man with stooped shoulders, tortoiseshell eyeglasses and
khaki trousers that looked two sizes too big. "The racists raid
me and you run away."

"So now I'm back. Let's do business. I'm in a hurry."

Medina turned and walked down the hall, Will following, then me.

They went into the office and Jaime shut the door behind them, acknowledging me for the first time with a hurried nod as the door shut. I'm used to being ignored, prefer it. With a face like mine, you don't want people paying attention to you. One of the first things Will taught me was that people were far less eager to gawk at me than I thought they were. He said that most people were afraid to even look. He was right. That was nineteen years ago, when he first took me into his home.

I went down the hall, through a set of saloon doors and checked the work room. There were six stations: desk, phone, stacks of papers, and three chairs at each for clients. American flag on one wall, Mexican one on the other, travel posters, soccer posters, bullfight posters.

Quiet.

No clients since the raid.

No workers since the raid, except Jennifer, the assistant director under Jaime.

"Good evening, Miss Avila." I took off my hat.

"Mr. Trona. Good evening."

She came over, offered her hand and I shook it. She's a black-haired beauty, thirty, divorced with two. Smooth fingers. Wearing a man's white cotton shirt tucked into her jeans, small waist, nice straight shoulders, black boots. She changed to an apple red-lipstick a few months back, after a year of cinnamon brown.

"Will must be here."

"They're in Jaime's office."

She looked past me down the hall, just a reflexive glance, then walked back to her desk. Jennifer is taken with the boss. This is one of the many secrets I'm not supposed to know. The world is layered with them.

She said, "That thing for you is over by my chair."

"I'll get it, thank you."

It was a U.S. Open tennis bag, a big black one with a blazing yellow ball on it. Heavy. I carried it back out to the car and set it on the asphalt while I disarmed the alarm and opened the trunk. Then I set it in and spread a blanket over it, locked the trunk again, set the alarm.

Back inside I got a magazine from the lobby, then rolled a chair into the hallway and sat outside Jaime Medina's office.

Medina: *You've got to talk to Phil Dent, man. . . .*

Will: *I know him, Jaime. I don't own him.*

Medina: *Right . . . that's not your job, my . . . friend. . . .*

Jennifer walked past me, fresh with scent, and leaned into the office without knocking.

"Coffee, beer? Hi, Will."

"Coffee, please."

She whisked by me without a look, then back again a minute later with a couple of mugs in one hand and a carton of milk in the other.

She went into the office. Will muttered something and all three laughed. She came out and shut the door and looked at me like I'd just gotten there.

"Anything for you, Mr. Trona?"

"Nothing, thank you. I'm fine."

She walked past me and back to her station.

I spread the magazine across my knee but didn't look at it. My job is to watch and listen, not read. *Mouth shut, eyes open.*

I heard the traffic on the boulevard. I heard the air conditioner hum. I heard a car go by with a subwoofer that you could feel in your chest. I still felt a little wrong about things, but I didn't know why. Maybe it was just Will's mood rubbing off on me. I often catch myself adopting his feelings. Maybe be-

cause he adopted me as his son. I heard Jennifer dialing a telephone.

Medina: *There's all that tobacco settlement money, man . . .
like a billion plus you're—*

Will: *That billion isn't mine, it's the county's, Jaime. I can't
hand it over in a pillowcase. Didn't the ninety help?*

Jennifer: *Get Pearlita.*

Medina: *Every bit helps. But what am I going to do when it's
gone? Sit and watch this place go straight to hell? We need the
money for operations, Will. We need it for job training, for lawyers, for food, man, we need it for . . .*

Jennifer: *Okay, okay. Yeah, he's here right now.*

Medina: *. . . we can't even do anything when some poor
pregnant Latina gets run over and killed a block from her apartment. We can't do anything when a Guatemalan kid gets shot to
death by fascist Newport Beach cops. We're handcuffed, man,
dead in the water.*

Will: *It's awful what happened, Jaime. I know it is.*

Medina: *Then help us find a way to help them, Will.*

I heard Jennifer put the phone back in its cradle. She turned
my way but I didn't look up from the magazine.

Will: *You helped me find Savannah, so maybe Jack will take
care of you. And the Reverend will put in a good word for you
and the Front. I have already.*

Medina: *We need more than good words, Will.*

The office door opened. Medina, face pinched, led us down
the hall and shook hands with both of us at the back door. Jennifer walked us outside, left the door open behind her.

Will gave me a nod. I went to the car, started the engine and hit the air conditioner. I could see them in the side mirror, Will in his dark suit and Jennifer in her jeans and boots and crisp white shirt, standing in the light of the open door. They talked for a while. Will set his briefcase on the asphalt.

Then he shook her hand like Will's shaken a million hands: an open-palmed reach and clinch, the left hand coming forward to enclose yours while he leans his head back in a posture of welcome and possession as he smiles at you.

"I love you," she said.

I couldn't hear anything over the air conditioner, but it was easy to read her apple-red lips.

Will reached into his pocket and handed her the money that I'd counted, rolled and rubber-banded for him, about the size of a half-smoked Churchill: just a couple of grand to help out some of her friends.

"I love you," he said back.

We drove out of Santa Ana and into Tustin. Will directed me to Tustin High School, had me pull up alongside the tennis courts. Not much tennis action by then, just two of the courts being used.

"Joe, fetch that tennis bag out of the trunk and take it over to the middle court. Leave it on the bench."

"Yes, sir."

When I got back we sat in silence for a minute or two. Will checked his watch.

"What's in the bag, Dad?"

"Silence."

"Is that an answer or an order, sir?"

"Reverend Daniel at the Grove," he said.

The Grove Club is never called the Grove Club by its members, just the Grove. It's hidden in the south county hills, off the 241 Toll Road, then up a winding private drive and past a gate staffed by two armed guards, usually moonlighting deputies. You can't see the Grove from any public road. A canopy of enormous palm, sycamore and eucalyptus trees obscures aerial views. It has never been pictured in a newspaper or on the TV news.

I took the first few miles of the 241 at ninety miles an hour. The electronic marquee said "Take the Toll Road—Because Life is Too Short!" The marquee was the only light out there in miles and miles of dark hills. Just a couple other cars in sight.

Politically, Will fought all four of the toll roads because— although the public has to repair them, maintain them, and pay exorbitantly high tolls to drive on them—they're privately owned. The profits go into the pockets of the Toll Roads Agency. TRA sounds like a public outfit, but it's not—it's a consortium of extremely wealthy developers who are raising buildings along the toll roads before the asphalt is even dry. In south Orange County, you can watch half a city go up over-night.

There's more to the story. The TRA guys got the State Assembly to stop maintaining certain public highways in Orange County. The highways go unrepaired and unimproved through the year 2006, which guarantees customers for the toll roads because the unrepaired highways are dangerous and clotted with traffic six hours a day.

Anyway, Will lost that battle but was half glad that he did, because you can drive seriously fast on the spanking-new toll roads. We use them all the time, due to Will's hatred of traffic and love of speed.

Once I got past the first toll plaza I opened her up past one-twenty and Will leaned over to get a good look at the speedometer, then sat back.

He chuckled. "Yeah, Joe."

Six months ago Will and his fellow supervisors voted themselves a car-allowance increase of two hundred percent, which allowed him to lease a BMW 750IL. The stock engine gets 330 horsepower out of 12 cylinders. It's a good car, fast but not quick, wakes up at sixty, stable at 160 mph, corners beautifully for a big sedan. Off the line it's not going to blow your hair back—a Saleen Cobra clobbered me at a traffic light last week.

"Ah," he said quietly. "This feels good."

I pushed the throttle through the kick-down switch and the car hesitated for a fraction of a second, then barreled up to one-thirty-five, then one-forty. This model was built with a kill switch at 155 mph, but Will had me install a Dinan chip to override the governor. The chip also brought the horsepower up to 370. Will likes to listen to the muffled shriek of that engine under full acceleration, and so do I. When the German horses are running hard, nothing beats them for an honest ride.

"Son, sometimes I wish this road was ten thousand miles long. We could just drive for hours. Away from the Grub. I loathe the Grub."

Grub, for Grove Club—Will's contraction. He checked the time again.

"I know," I said.

Even though he loathes the Grub, the boss is a member because he needs to be a member. As a man who isn't afraid to piss on the flames of free enterprise for the occasional good of the county, Will Trona is not Grove material.

But as a politician who votes himself a stupidly expensive car to be driven at criminal speeds on semi-work-related business, he becomes Grove material.

Obviously, as the supervisor of the powerful first district, he helps run the government, and the government can influence the business interests that dominate the Grove, so the Grove needs Will, too.

Will told me he pays two grand a month membership dues,

all of which is covered by patrons. Dues for public servants are "nominal" because no honest one can afford the usual costs of membership. Most of the money goes into the Grove Trust, then into its Research & Action Committee, a nonprofit 527 Organization that operates free of both the FEC and the IRS.

Every year the trust coughs up several undisclosed millions for the causes and lobbies it thinks are vital to its interests. Its interests are profit and power. But they're interested in more than those things, too. Last year, for instance, the Grove Trust donated $60,000 to the Hillview Home for Children. That's enough for two mid-level salaried positions, for one year. I think highly of Hillview, and the struggle they go through for money. Hillview was where I spent most of the first five years of my life.

Two off-duty deputies logged us in and raised the gate. The Grove sat one mile in, tucked in a valley between the hills. It's an enclosed hacienda-style building, built around a large courtyard. The rounded archways of the colonnades are brick and adobe, wrapped by purple bougainvillea. The courtyard gardens and fountain are illuminated by recessed lights, and they glow from a distance like an emerald wrapped in tissue. The building itself is kept mostly dark on the outside.

I parked the car and followed Will to the entrance, where another off-duty cop wrote our names onto his sheet. He was about to ask me my name when I tipped back my hat to let him see who I was. I have notoriety because of this face. It's unmistakable. What happened to it was a big story when I was a baby.

Will led the way into the dining room, shook a few hands. I stood back, folding mine in front of me. An average night at the Grub: half the tables were couples, mostly older, lots of gray hair and diamonds set off by dinner jackets and dresses. Three major developers—one commercial and two residential. A building industry lobbyist who had formerly served as supervisor. Two assemblymen, a state senator, the lieutenant governor's top aide. A four-top of venture capitalists. A table of thirty-something guys made billionaires by the NASDAQ back in ninety-nine.

We went up the stairs to the lounge, which is a large room with an island bar, billiards tables and booths around the perimeter.

Will took his usual booth. I chose a cue and racked the table nearest the booth, where I could entertain myself and eavesdrop without making Will's guests nervous.

I glanced up at the third floor. I could see the wide burnished staircase and the closed door to one of the hospitality suites. A waiter knocked. Hush-hush stuff, up in those suites. Rich men and their dull secrets. I've spent time in all of them.

I got a good break, watched three balls clunk into their pockets.

The Reverend Daniel Alter, dapper and gray-haired, arrived exactly on time. He touched my arm on his way by, but didn't say anything. I watched him shake hands with Will, slide into the booth across from him, then draw the privacy curtain.

The Reverend Daniel runs an enormous "television ministry." The broadcasts originate in his multimillion-dollar "Chapel of Light" here in Orange County, and they go worldwide. You've probably seen him on TV. Daniel's sermons are upbeat and optimistic. On his show he sells Christian products—from compact discs and inspirational videos to Chapel of Light keychains that really light up. The money that floods in is tax-free and no one knows where it goes, not even Will Trona. That's what he tells me, anyway.

Reverend Daniel: *Here's this*.
Will: *Good-good*.

Reverend Daniel: *The bullpen is killing us.*

Will: *Then score more runs. I got the bag from Jaime.*

Reverend Daniel: *Do you have her?*

Will: *I know where she is. But I'm not so sure I trust those people with her.*

Reverend Daniel: *What could you mean by that?*

Will: *We'll see what.*

Reverend Daniel: *You've done a wonderful thing, Will. And Jack's done his part. It's all going to work out.*

A long pause then, while I banked the two ball across the felt and into a corner pocket.

Reverend Daniel: *I'm counting on you. Let God work this miracle for me through you.*

Will: *I don't think your God wants to do any miracles for you, Daniel. You've gotten about a thousand too many as it is.*

Reverend Daniel: *Don't be pissy, Will. I thought this was your kind of thing. Is everything set?*

Will: *It's been arranged, Dan. Don't worry.*

Reverend Daniel: *You know, Will, the Lord really does work in mysterious ways.*

Then the Reverend Daniel slid back the curtain and they both stepped out. Daniel glanced at the table, then looked at me with his half smile.

"I'd recommend the six," he said. "With plenty of follow."

Will clapped him on the shoulder and Reverend Daniel headed for the bar.

Will checked his watch.

"Let's go, Joe. We're picking up a package, making a delivery, then calling it quits. It's been a ball-buster of a day."

As we left the lounge, the Reverend sat at the bar next to a woman with shiny black hair and watched us go.

* * *

The fog rolled in as the night cooled, big swirls puffing in from the Pacific. Par for June. Down at the coast they call it June Gloom. When we got out of the hills and back into cell range, Will's phone went off.

He said, "Trona," then he listened a moment. "You got her, right?"

Listened again, then flipped the phone shut.

"Joe, we've got a package at seven thirty-three Lind Street, Anaheim. Flog this pompous piece of tin and get us over there. Boy, I'll be glad when this day's over."

"Yes, sir." I checked the mirrors, hit a hundred in less than ten seconds. "What's in this package, boss?"

"We're trying to do a good deed."

When we hit the Tustin city limits Will's phone rang again. He answered and listened. Then he said, "Things are lining up. I'll do what I can do, but I still can't turn coal into a diamond."

He flipped the phone shut, sighed.

We were almost into Anaheim when he dialed out.

"Looks like we'll be there on time," was all he said.

It was an apartment backing an alley in the ugly part of Anaheim. Will told me to park in the alley. It was so narrow another car couldn't get by unless we moved. There was a row of carports to our left, and to our right a cinder-block wall wild with graffiti. Not a creature stirring, just the fog easing along.

"Be unfriendly," he said. Which is what he said if he thought there could be trouble, or if he just wanted me to intimidate people.

Will stood behind me as I knocked with my left hand, my right up under my coat lapel on the grip of one of the two forty-five Automatic Colt Pistols I usually carry.

"Yes? Who is it?"

"Open the door," I said.

The door cracked. A woman's face, fat, squinting until she saw my face, then her eyes opened wider.

I pushed past her and stepped inside. Her hands were empty and there was no movement behind her, just the sound of a TV.

She looked at my face, then I gave her a look at what was under my coat. Her eyes moved from the gun to my face, then back again. Trapped between two horror shows. She raised her hands slowly, deciding to look at the floor.

The apartment smelled of bacon and cigarettes. Bedsheets for curtains, carpet worn to the padding, padding worn to the plywood.

"I don' know anything about this, mister. They say come and watch a girl, I come and watch a girl. I don' know—"

Will, then: "Be calm, *señora*. She's okay, son. Where are they?"

She nodded toward the bedroom. "She here. He no here. Watching television."

"Stay put," I said to her. "What do I do, Boss?"

"Go get her."

The girl stood up from the floor when I walked in. She was small, blonde, pale. Blue jeans and a Cirque du Soleil T-shirt, white sneakers. Twelve years old, maybe.

She studied my face. Children will do that sometimes, just stare. Often, they'll make a face, sometimes cry. Sometimes they run. I saw her eyes go afraid and her chin tremble.

"I'm Joe."

"I'm Savannah," she said very quietly.

Then she stepped forward and offered her small, quivering hand. I shook it. I pulled the brim of my hat down a little more, to help her.

"How do you do?" she asked.

"I'm not sure. Please come with me, though."

She slung a Pocahontas backpack over one shoulder and led the way out.

Going back down the stairs to the alley, I held the handle of my weapon. Will held the girl's hand.

I opened the passenger-side doors for them and waited while Will took her backpack off, strapped her in, adjusted the shoulder restraint for her small frame, showed her how the armrests tilted out of the seat back.

Of all the things that he is—husband, politician, agitator, manipulator, dreamer—I can forget that he is a father, too. An adoptive father, maybe the most generous fathers of all.

He had his hand on her shoulder, talking quietly, one foot dangling out the open door.

Headlights swerved toward us and I heard a car engine down the alley in front of me. No hurry, no threat, probably a renter heading for his carport.

"Sir, let's get going."

"I'm talking."

I heard another car coming up from behind, saw the headlight beams crawl up the shiny black trunk of the BMW.

I moved closer to the open rear door. "You should get in the car, Boss."

"I'm talking to Savannah."

I looked behind me, then ahead. Coming the same speed, no hurry, no brights. No problem?

Then both cars stopped. Eighty feet ahead, eighty feet behind. They vanished in a blanket of moving fog, then appeared again. I couldn't tell makes or models, had no chance at all on the plates.

"Possible trouble, sir."

"Where?"

"Everywhere."

I kicked Will's dangling foot in and slammed the door, got the remote pad out of my pocket.

Car doors opening. The shuffle of feet on asphalt.

In the fog-dulled wash of the headlights in front of me I saw three figures moving, growing larger. One tall, two shorter. Long coats, collars up, faces hard to see.

I threw open my door and pulled on the headlights, slammed the door closed behind me and locked everything with the remote.

I put my right hand under my jacket and on the butt of one forty-five. I turned and looked behind: two more coats emerging through the smoky headlights of their car. I put my left hand on the other ACP, which left me crossing my chest with both hands, like I was cold.

Then a deep, resonant voice from ahead, bouncing off the alley wall and the garages, hard to locate but easy to hear.

"Will! Ah, Will Trona! Let's talk."

Will was out of the car before I could stop him.

"Watch Savannah," he said. "I'll get rid of this dingleberry."

I shut the door on her and stepped after him, but he reeled and hissed straight into my face.

"I said watch the girl, Joe! So watch the girl!"

I stayed back with her but I watched him walk away, blanched white in the cross fire of the headlight beams.

The Tall One stepped forward. I couldn't see much of his face: couldn't even guess an age. His hands were in his coat pockets.

The two guys behind me had shaded to their left, putting me between them and our car, automatic weapons held close up to their coats, barrels down.

They didn't move.

They had us and I knew it and there wasn't one thing I could do right then except stand there and watch.

Will stopped about six feet short of the guy, put his hands on his hips and spread his feet a little.

Words floated back with the engine noise and exhaust. I unlocked the car doors with the remote, reached in and killed the interior lights.

"What's going on, Joe?" asked the girl. "I can't see."

"Say nothing. Absolutely nothing."

"Okay."

"*. . . hard man to catch up with, Will Trona. . . .*"

There was a strange cadence to the voice, an almost cheerful lilt to the syllables. Just a little off, like a second language learned later in life.

Will: *Who the hell are you?*

. . . the girl in the car?

Will: *You with Alex?*

You're with Alex. Laughter. *Little shit too scared to show his face, ah?*

Then Will again: *We had a deal. Get the hell out of here. Now the deal is this.*

The Tall One leaned forward and a sharp explosion cracked through the alley. Will dropped to his knees and bent over.

I yanked open the rear door, jumped in, unbuckled Savannah and shoved her all the way across the seat.

Looking through the windshield I saw The Tall One step forward. I pushed open the far door, climbed around Savannah, dragged her out of the car by one arm.

"What's happening? Is Will okay?"

"*Shhh.*"

Pulling on the girl, I turned to see the shining end of the Tall One's hand pointed down at Will. Another hard crack, Will's head jerking once, smoke rising up against the fog and into the glare of the headlights.

"Savannah," I whispered. *"Get ready to run! Two honks is me. Two honks is me."*

I picked her up and dangled her over the cinder-block wall, then let go. I heard her land, then fast footsteps. The footsteps of the men behind me got louder.

I dropped to the pavement, drew one weapon and slid back into the rear seat of the dark car. The two behind me came fast, machine guns up. They were looking at the wall, where they'd last seen me.

When they got close enough I shot them both. The left one fell hard. The right one shuddered and stopped and unleashed a wild automatic burst that jerked the firing gun back into his own face. Then a clatter and a groan.

Staying low, I backed out and spilled again onto the pavement. On elbows and knees I wriggled to the front of the car, pressing in close to the body panel, gun out ahead of me.

Even in the headlights I only saw shapes: the Tall One, the two others walking slowly toward me. And Will on the ground. Distance off. Perspective off. Everything a pale haze.

Shit, what was that?

The deep voice again: *Go see.*

I pointed my .45 toward the voices, watched the fog beyond the sights.

I think there's two down, over by the car.

Go see!

I inched the sights to my left, tracking the voice.

Then footsteps came at me, two sets, close together. Shapes coalescing in the headlights.

I can't see a goddamned thing!

The footsteps stopped.

Shit . . . it's Nix and Luke. Wasted, man. I'm not going in there. . . .

The fog blew open, then closed again. Strange-looking men.

I heard the Tall One behind them, and his clear voice cutting through the fog.

Get back here. Now! Move!

The sound of men running, shapes illuminated in the wash of headlights.

Tall One: *Get over here.*

Nix and Luke are dead over there, man. . . .

I heard two sharp cracks, and two muffled thuds. Then two more shots, as twin orange comets flashed down from the Tall One's hand.

A moment later the car reversed with a chirp of rubber and jumped backwards, the bright slash of the headlights sweeping the asphalt. I saw the two men down beyond Will, one of them moving, one not. When the car backed out of the alley and roared down the street on the other side of the cinder blocks I ran.

Will was huddled on his knees, forehead to the ground, arms around his middle. Blood on his head and his clothes and the asphalt. I put my hand on his back.

"Oops," he whispered.

"Quiet, Boss. You're all right."

I ran back to the car and brought it forward. I got Will into the passenger seat. He sat up okay. Wet and heavy. Smell of metal. Blood on my face where his head had rested when I dragged him in.

One of the men that the Tall One had shot was still moving as I guided the big car around him. I tore out to Lincoln Boulevard running the late-night signals, my palm slick on the horn, clumps of fog tearing past the windows.

"You're okay, Will. You're going to be okay."

His head was back on the rest and his eyes were open to the headliner. A dull light in those eyes. Shoulder and shirt and lap full of blood.

"Hang on, Dad. Please hang on. We're almost there."

"Mary Ann."

I hit a hundred southbound. The cars seemed to rocket backwards at us. Will's head rattled when I shot across the lane dividers. Then he leaned forward like he always did, to watch the gauges and me.

"Everyone."

"Everyone *what*, Dad?"

He coughed a red mess onto the windshield and hung forward against his shoulder strap. Taillights rushed by.

I fishtailed down the Chapman off-ramp, ran three reds and skidded into the UC Irvine Medical Center Emergency lot, smoking to a stop on the ambulance ramp.

Will was slumped against the door. When I ran around and opened the door he fell into my arms and I carried him up the ramp, understanding that he didn't need a doctor.

I slipped to my knees but kept him balanced because it was the only thing I could do for him and I wanted to do it well. Two ER guys were running a gurney down toward us.

Hell is waiting.

I paced the emergency waiting room and the walkways outside, making the calls that needed to be made—first to my mother, Mary Ann, then to brothers Junior and Glenn.

Those were the hardest calls I'd made in my life, no contest. I couldn't tell them that Will was going to die. I couldn't tell them he was going to live. I blubbered only that he'd been shot, choking out the words.

I drove the car off the emergency ramp and parked it in the

lot. The interior was urgent with the smells of blood and leather and the ugly stink of human panic.

Twenty minutes later, an emergency room doctor told me that we had lost Will.

Lost.

That word was a bullet through my heart. It told me that Will was gone now, and gone forever. It told me that I'd let down the person I loved most on this earth, that I'd failed my primary mission. And on its spiraling, smoking way through my heart and into the night, it told me I would find the people who did this to Will and I would deal with them.

I managed to call my mother and brothers again. To give them the bullet.

Too late, of course. They were already on their way to the hospital.

Against the protests of a doctor and two sheriff deputies, I got into Will's car and drove back to the Lind Street apartment.

Red lights, yellow tape, neighbors everywhere and three blankets with bodies under them. Anaheim PD was on scene. A patrolman marched at my car with a flashlight, waving me away.

I backed out and drove the dark streets and wide empty boulevards looking for the girl. I crawled along at ten miles an hour, honking twice, lightly, over and over. Up and down, going slow, brights on and all four windows down. Come out, come out, wherever you are. The fog was still thick and sometimes I couldn't even see a block ahead. Every few minutes I'd pull over, stop, honk again and listen. Watch.

I finally got Mom on my cell phone and she sounded close to panic. She was at the hospital. They wouldn't let her see him. I did my best to keep her talking and settle her down, told her to call Reverend Alter, then turned my car around for UCI Medical Center just as an Anaheim PD cruiser pulled me over. Both officers were tight, fingering their sidearms as I badged them.

"What in hell are you doing here, Deputy?"

"Looking for a girl."

"Is that blood in the car?"

"Yes, it is."

"Step out, please, slowly. Hands away from your body, Mr. Trona."

Chapter Two

I spent the next three hours at the Anaheim PD with two homicide detectives—the tall pale one was Guy Alagna and the stocky dark one was Lucia Fuentes.

As soon as I told them about Savannah, Fuentes left the interview room and stayed away for half an hour. Alagna, whose nose hooked from his face like a sharp white beak, asked me for the third time if I could describe the tall gunman to him.

"Too dark," I said for the third time. "Too much fog. They were all wearing long coats."

I was getting weary. I was beginning to note all the things that had changed. Would change. The rest of my life without him alive. Ever. The world was brand-new to me, and I hated it.

"And those coats again, Joe. What did they look like?"

I described the long overcoats for the third time. I looked down at my hat, balanced on my knee.

"Color?"

"Night, Detective Alagna. Fog. No colors."

"Okay, all right."

Then he was silent for a long beat. I could feel his stare on my face. Sooner or later, most people have to gawk.

I drank bad coffee from a foam cup and looked at the two-way mirror, picturing the men in the June fog, Will approaching. June Gloom with the blade of murder hidden in it. I strained to catch a glimpse of the Tall One's face—just one feature, just one thing to go on. Nothing. Fog. Motion. Exhaust rising, voices. The insulting little pop of that handgun. And again.

Every few minutes a roar would start building in my ears, beginning low, like waves on a distant beach, then getting louder and louder until my head was two inches from a jet turbine. But it wasn't a jet, it was a voice, and the voice said only three words over and over, louder and louder: *you killed him you killed him you killed him you killed him you killed him you killed him you killed him . . .*

Please stop. Remember. Eyes open, mouth shut.

I'll get rid of this dingleberry.

How did Will know he was a dingleberry?

Will! Ah, Will Trona! Let's talk.

The deep and resonant voice replayed in my mind with a haunting clarity. I heard the odd lilt of the words, almost cheerful.

Did the shooter know him, or just pretend to?

. . . you with Alex?

"And you're sure they didn't take anything off him?" Alagna asked again.

"They took his life, sir."

In the corner of my eye I saw him studying me. Then I turned on him and he looked away. People are ashamed of themselves when I catch them staring, but not before I catch them.

"You know what I mean, Joe."

"Nothing that I saw, Detective."

"Back to the car again. They take anything from the car?"

"They never touched the car."

"Okay, all right. So, let me get this straight—the shooter

called Will by name. And Will asked if the shooter was with Alex. And Will said a deal's a deal, or something like that, and the guy shot him in the gut?"

"The shooter said, 'Now the deal is this.' "

And then he asked again about the two men I'd shot, both dead on scene when the cops got there. I told him again, exactly what had happened. He wouldn't give me their names or anything else about them.

"So, you couldn't see well enough to describe the man who shot your father, but you could see well enough to drop two guys, moving, with two shots."

"Like I said, sir, they were close—twenty feet maybe."

"I guess you're a good shot."

"I'm a good shot."

Everything I told Alagna and Fuentes was correct, though I forgot a few things.

For example, I forgot to mention Will's briefcase. He rarely went anywhere without it, so it contained the outlines of his life. More than the outlines. It held his calendar and appointment books, his notes and letters, his drafts and reports, his to-do list, his doodles. Everything he might use in a day—from a tiny tape recorder to a toothbrush and paste—Will carried with him in that old leather case. I carried it with me into the interview room and set it beside me as if it were my own. No one questioned it.

And I didn't consider the tennis bag we'd picked up from the HACF to be Alagna's business, either.

I wasn't about to offer too much to a cop I didn't know, some paleface who had to ask three times what an overcoat looked like.

I also forgot to mention Will's gift to Jennifer Avila that evening, the two thousand dollars I'd counted and rolled. Likewise, their private words.

I forgot that I heard anything but hello and good-bye between Will, Jaime Medina and the Reverend Daniel Alter.

I forgot to recount Will's quick conversations on his cell phone, just minutes before he died. And I wondered how I could get a phone company log of those calls. A homicide investigator sure could, but a fourth-year deputy? It would take a while.

And I forgot to mention that Mary Ann, my adoptive mother, had been blue lately, and that Will was trying hard to get home by ten.

All of that was Will's business; none of it was Alagna's.

Lucia Fuentes barreled back into the room. "One of the shooters is hanging on. No ID on him, but he's alive."

Alagna looked at me. "Maybe he can fill in some of Mr. Trona's sizable gaps."

I nodded but said nothing. Instead I stared down at Will's briefcase, noting the drop of dried blood near the handle. I hoped Alagna wouldn't notice it. I didn't think he would.

"But I struck out on the girl," Fuentes continued. "Nothing at all on a missing twelve-year-old named Savannah. The National Center, the FBI, Sacramento—not even Joe's sheriffs here—nobody's looking for her. Maybe it's an alias."

Alagna stared at me. "I doubt her daddy lets her run around with fifty-year-old guys after dark."

"Maybe that's exactly what her daddy does," snapped Fuentes.

"Joe, you know if the supervisor was bent that way?"

I stared back at Alagna then, and a flush came to his waxy skin.

"Detective Alagna, he was a good man," I said. "And I'll pretend you didn't ask that stupid question."

"Big words from a fourth-year jailer."

"We can settle differences any way you'd like, sir."

"I don't settle."

"Come on, you assholes," said Fuentes. "What's wrong with you, Guy?"

Alagna looked away, his ears turning red. It was quite a contrast with his white beak of a nose.

What was wrong with Guy was that he was afraid of me, and angry about it. Nothing in the world seems to make healthy, tough cops madder than a twenty-four-year-old monster who can't be intimidated.

I not only have a face that looks like something made in hell, but I'm tall and strong. I'm conversant with most weapons, and I've spent nearly my whole life learning how to defend myself—every method and school, every technique you can imagine—so that what happened when I was nine months old never happens again. I've promised myself that it will never happen again.

But my best weapon is that people sense I'm not afraid of anything. Maybe it's the scar tissue. My eyes. My voice. I really don't know.

In fact, there are two things I'm afraid of. One is my father, my real father, the one who did this to me when I was nine months old. His name is Thor Svendson and he's out there somewhere. If he ever appears again I'll be ready. I have five black belts, two regional Golden Gloves titles and a Sheriff Department Distinguished Marksman pin to prove I'm ready.

The other thing that terrified me—although I didn't know it until then—was living without Will. And of the two, life without Will was by far the worst.

So, with my ruined face and apparent fearlessness, most people are afraid of me. It's been true since I was very young. As I grew used to people fearing me, I tried to develop good manners, to strike some balance. I came to believe that they were mandatory for a man with a face like mine. I've worked almost as hard at having good manners as I have at mastering Ken-po, or the recoil nuances of the Colt .45 ACP.

"So Joe," said Lucia Fuentes. "Explain the girl to us. If your father wasn't that way, then what was he doing with her?"

"I'm not sure. He said he was trying to do a good deed."

They looked at each other.

Then the voice started building again inside me: *you killed him you killed him you killed him* . . .

I felt like I was in that fog again, the fog that rolled in the night before. Secret fog. Killer fog. I wished I could blow it all away, step from it into something clear and sunny and true. I couldn't do that, but I had a quiet spot I could go to. I can go there any time I want. So I went.

"I've told you what I know," I said, standing, hat in hand. "Call me anytime if I can help more. I'd like to know who the girl was, Detectives. I'd like to help her if I can. Pardon me, but I have to go to work now, or I'll be late."

Alagna looked at Fuentes like she should stop me. Fuentes looked at me like someone missing her bus. When I walked out the sun was just starting to come up.

The reporters converged and I was happy to see them. I just gave them the basics, but I made sure they knew that a girl named Savannah was loose in the night. I described her exactly, right down to her clothing and backpack and good manners and fine straight hair. I even sketched her face on my notepad as best I could. It came out slightly better than nothing.

The reporters liked this: here was a chance to help find her, maybe do something good. They're the second most cynical people, after cops.

Sunrise in the county, and me alone in Will's car, the freeways jammed already, everybody acting like Will was still alive. What was wrong with these fools? And what was wrong with

Alagna and Fuentes, letting me drive off in a car that was part of a homicide scene, instead of impounding it?

I got through to Mom on my cell phone again. Reverend Daniel Alter had met her at the hospital and she was now in the Chapel of Light sanctuary. She had taken a mild sedative. Her voice sounded light and insubstantial. One of the assistant ministers was going to take her home because she felt too woozy to drive. I told her I'd drive her home myself, but she insisted that I work, stay focused, stay useful. I told her I'd be over as soon as my shift was over.

In the sheriff's gym I showered, shaved and put on my uniform, then walked across the compound to my job.

Orange County Jail. Sixth largest in the nation. Three thousand inmates, three thousand orange jumpsuits. Seventy percent of them are felons. And a hundred jailers like me, mostly young guys, armed only with pepper spray, trying to keep order. Hundreds of new inmates come through the Intake-Release Center every day, a total of seventy thousand every year. Hundreds are released back into society, every day. In and out. In and out. We call it The Loop. The jail is an enormous rotating swirl, a storm system of defeat, fury, violence and boredom.

During the day, Men's Central is my world. It's a world of strict order and, usually, quiet compliance. Power and submission. Good guys green, bad guys orange. Hands in your pockets, eyes forward, shut-up. Pull your pockets, show your socks. Them and us. It's also a world of shanks whittled from bed frames, clubs made of knotted T-shirts filled with bars of soap, of rotgut liquor made from leftover bits of fruit and bread smuggled in from the mess hall, of drugs and black tattoos and kites—notes—smuggled down from the shot-callers in Tank 29 of Module F, or from protective custody in Module J, to the low-security guys who can pass them along to friends and allies on the outside. It's a world of silence. It's a world of dimly lit guard stations, so the inmates can't watch us watching them. A world of racial gangs, of respect and vengeance, of endless lies and infinite bullshit.

I like it. I like my friends and coworkers, and the delicate predatory balance between us and the inmates. I like some of the inmates at times. Their scams are clever and they manage to get away with things that surprise me. But what I like most is the orderliness of things: the buzzers and bells and schedules and rules, the heavy keys, the food we eat in the staff dining room. These are institutional things, and as an institutional boy I came to rely on them. My four years at Hillview Home for Children brought those things into my blood in a way I can't get rid of.

That morning I was scheduled to work in Module J, which is set up for the protective custody of the particularly dangerous, the notorious, the well-known, for child molesters and sexual deviants who would upset the general population, sometimes even for law enforcement personnel doing time on the wrong side of the bars.

Mod J is set up in four sectors, with a total of one hundred seventy inmates. It's one big circle, with our guard station in the center. Between the cells and the guard station are the day rooms, which have picnic-style benches and tables, and a TV. From the dimly lit confines of the station, we can look through the glass and see into every cell. In-cell cameras make every inmate visible on the station video console, and each cell is wired for sound.

It's very quiet in Module J, and the inmates are slightly more respectful of us than they are in the other mods. Maybe it's because of the seriousness of their crimes, or because many of them are on trial and facing very long, or perhaps capital, sentences. Whatever the reasons, the men in Mod J are a little less likely to amuse themselves with chatter about my face.

My first two years I rotated between the Men's Central modules and got my fill of "shitface," "acidhead," "Frankenstein," whatever. The names didn't get to me, though the repetition almost did. I never cracked, showed my anger or lost my manners. I just learned to withdraw into the quiet spot and view the inmates with the detached interest of a birdwatcher.

Happened to you?

Nothing, why?

'Cause you got shit all over your face, shitface!

You get the picture.

Of course, people behind bars are braver than most. You're protected from them, but they're protected from you, too. Even my most sincerely murderous stare often brings nothing but added volume: *OH, look at SHITface starin' at me NOW!* As a keeper, once you step through the heavy doors of the jail, you're not just working there, you're *in* it. Sometimes, you forget. Sometimes, it feels like you've been there forever and you're going to be there another forever. It's hard on a guy who tries to have good manners.

Then you take a deep breath and remember that you've got a shift and they've got a sentence. It's like coming out of a nightmare.

In the briefing room I signed in and sat down for roll call. After that, Sergeant Delano gave us the morning book: yesterday ten blacks and ten Latinos got into it in the mess hall. It was over quickly, didn't escalate, no time for us to get out the bats and hats—our batons and riot helmets. A few bruises, a few cuts. No weapons. As a result, we were 9–13—cleared and ready—to conduct a Module F cell search at 1300. We call a surprise search a shake. Deputy Smith had discovered a shank hidden in the sole of a shower sandal—sharpened and slid directly through the rubber. There were rumors of trouble upstate. They say that inmate violence trickles down from the max pens to the jails, and at first I thought it was myth. But after three years here, I can tell you that it's true, so rumors of trouble at Pelican Bay or Folsom or Cochran or San Quentin are always taken seriously. We took up a collection for a barbecue to celebrate our captain getting a promotion, then broke.

I checked out my radio and keys, then walked the tunnel down to Mod J. When I got to the guard station I glanced at the video monitors to check my prisoners. Everybody looked fine. Gary Sargola, the Ice-Box Killer, was asleep with one leg raised because he suffers phlebitis.

Dave Hauser, assistant district attorney turned drug dealer, was watching *Good Morning America*.

Dr. Chapin Fortnell, child psychiatrist awaiting trial on thirty-eight counts of molestation of six boys over the last ten years, sat upright and alert on his cot, writing something in crayon, the sharpest instrument we allow him since he tried to open a vein with a felt-tipped marker two months ago.

Serial rapist Frankie Dilsey, convicted of three forcibles and waiting sentencing for three more, was making faces in the steel mirror over his basin, drumming his long fingers on the rim, swaying his hips to a song playing only in his head.

Sammy Nguyen, a young Vietnamese gangster charged with killing a police officer during a traffic stop, lay on his bunk staring at a picture of his girlfriend that we had allowed him to tape to the ceiling. He glanced toward the video camera like he knew I was watching, smiled, turned back to his picture of Bernadette. He's a bright guy, Sammy. Quiet for the most part, fairly polite, has his code of honor and sticks with it. He's high up in the Vietnamese gang structure, probably has fifty guys under him.

Will and Sammy had a history. They'd only met once, about

two months before, in the Bamboo 33 nightclub. Will had gone there to help some of his Vietnamese friends. It was the club's grand opening, and the owners wanted Will there to certify their importance, maybe get their pictures in the papers. Will had taken Mary Ann, driven them himself, and that's why I wasn't there.

The grand opening went fine, Will said, but this handsome hood named Sammy Nguyen and his girlfriend, Bernadette, kept approaching him with some chatter about opening a savings and loan in Little Saigon. Will said he'd get back to them and tried to steer away, but Sammy and Bernadette kept hanging around until Will took Mary Ann to another table.

Next thing he knew, this Sammy cat was staring blankly at him. The gangsters call it a mad-dog, and you're supposed to show respect by looking away.

Will knew the score. He was a deputy for twenty-plus years. So he mad-dogged Sammy back, digging down deep for the thoughts that let you keep a stare. He told me he thought about 'Nam and some friends of his who died there so jerks like Sammy could live here. But a lot of good people came here, too, and he wondered what that whole war was worth. Will said he kind of got lost in the thought and time passed. And the next he knew, Sammy had looked away. That meant Sammy still hadn't gotten his respect, and according to the rules of gangland, he was entitled to murder Will Trona in order to finally get some.

Punk shit, was what Will had called it. He forgot about him until the next day, when Sammy Nguyen was arrested for allegedly gunning down a Westminster cop named Dennis Franklin. The shooting had taken place just a couple of hours after Will and Sammy talked at Bamboo 33.

Will took it hard. He didn't know Franklin but he wondered if he'd talked to Sammy better that night, heard him out about the savings and loan idea, didn't mad-dog him, maybe the hood would have left Bamboo 33 in a hopeful mood rather than a murderous one.

All Franklin had done to Sammy was pull him over for speeding on Bolsa Avenue. Will and Mary Ann contributed fifty thousand dollars to a trust for Franklin's widow and their two-year-old. The papers loved that, and wanted to know why the Tronas had singled out Dennis Franklin's family. Will said because he was a good cop, didn't mention what had happened between him and Sammy Nguyen.

I left the guard station and walked to Sammy's cell. Dim lights, near silence, the hushed setting of a dream. The he-shes—men in various stages of gender reassignment—stared at me. Clarkson, a mass murderer of children, ignored me. I walked up behind the runner—a trusty—as he pushed Sammy's breakfast tray through the slot.

"Hello, Deputy Joe. Sorry about your father."

Jailhouse gossip travels at the speed of light.

"Thank you."

Sammy sat down with the tray across his knees, but he didn't look at the food. "I met him once, you know."

I looked at him but said nothing. He'd shared this information before.

"And he was insulting to me and Bernadette. I could have had him killed for his behavior that night and been within my rights."

"Yes, you told me that before. It's baby-like, Sammy, that kind of thinking."

Sammy thought about this for a moment. He took off his glasses and set them on his pillow.

"But I didn't. I had nothing to do with this."

I believed him, because we'd been opening Sammy's incoming and outgoing mail since his arrest. I knew he was directing gang business through Bernadette. She was his lieutenant as well as his woman, and he told her everything in those letters. Sammy was inside on a murder rap, all right, but he was up to his elbows in gun trafficking, fraud, home invasion and stolen goods. He'd never once mentioned Will, or the insult, in any of his letters. If he let a contract on Will, he'd have done it through the mail with his woman.

It amazes me that a guy as bright and suspicious as Sammy wouldn't think that his mail was being read.

"Did you see it happen?"

"Yes. Five men."

"That's a contract, Joe."

"That's what it looked like."

"Were you close?"

"The fog was bad. They all wore long coats, collars up. The leader was tall."

Suspicion spread across Sammy's wide, guileful face. I routinely lie to Sammy and the other inmates—some lies too big to be believed, others too small to even sound untrue. If the inmates get only the truth, they'll strip it off you like piranha. You need some bluff to keep them back. You need a rap. That's what they use on us and that's what they get from us.

So even when you tell them the truth, like I was doing, they assume you're lying. In jail, not even the truth sounds true.

"The Cobra Kings," said Sammy. "They wear long coats, dress good. Not predictable, Joe, because their blood is mixed. Vietnamese and American. Vietnamese and black American. Vietnamese and Mexican American. GI's fucky-fucky and out comes—what do the newspapers call them, 'children of the war'? Mutts. Everybody hates them. They grow up, they find each other, make a gang in Saigon. Everybody still hates them. So they come here, land of the free. All that."

"Friends of yours?"

He shook his head no.

"The shooter knew Will by name," I said. "But I don't think Will knew him."

He smiled a flash of straight white teeth.

"Your father, maybe he had some friends that aren't so good for him. That happens in politics. People help you, but they're not good for you."

"That's not exactly news."

The smile again, wrinkles at the corners of his eyes. "You see the shooter's face, Joe?"

"Hard to see."

At this, Sammy's face was all cynicism and doubt. "You heard him say your father's name, but you didn't see his face?"

"Fog," I said.

He studied me, guessing my levels of treachery. I was happy to let him do that. Something like victory crossed his face and I wanted him to have it.

"I heard three guys got stepped on. One still alive. You do that?"

I nodded. "Two."

"How did it feel?"

"Not bad. Compared to watching my father die."

"You ever kill before?"

"No."

"This is sad, Joe. A very sad development. Who shot the other two?"

"The Tall One tried to thin the witness list."

Sammy considered. "Bad leadership. Very cold. Very Cobra King. I'd guess it was the money, though, Joe—less people to split it with."

"There was a girl," I said.

"What girl?"

"Savannah."

"Did they step on her, too?"

"No. Do you know her?"

"I do not."

"Something on a girl named Savannah would help me, Sammy. Maybe in connection with someone named Alex. No last name on either."

Sammy registers emotions convincingly and clearly, like an actor. I've watched him during interviews and visitations and he's a master of surprise, outrage, innocence, threat. He loves exaggeration.

But when he wants to give nothing away his cunning face becomes depthless and mute as a daisy. You can't see anything at all behind it, no matter how hard you look. That's what he gave me.

Then Sammy's blank look broke into a frankly optimistic expression.

"You get my rat trap yet?"

"You can't have a rat trap."

"I've got a huge rat in here. He comes and goes whenever he wants. Through the ducts."

We do have our share of rats, mice and cockroaches. But I thought he wanted the trap for something else, though I'm not sure what. Sammy likes gadgets, tools. In a cell search last week we found a pair of canine nail clippers, brand-new, still in the package. They're the kind with the small sharp blade that slides through the oval hole, and the heavy curved handles for power. He could make a good shank out of them, but I don't think he had anything that lowly in mind. Sammy isn't just a punk—Will was wrong about that. He's something more intelligent and more dangerous, and far less predictable.

Like I said, we've got stops on all of Sammy Nguyen's mail, incoming and outgoing, so the clippers didn't come through the post office. Sammy might have got them from Frankie Dilsey, in the adjacent cell, or in the day room. Maybe in the exercise pen, which is on the roof of the building. Or maybe from one of the guards. He also might have gotten them from a visitor, or his lawyer, which could get him disbarred.

I stared into Sammy Nguyen's dark eyes as he stared back into mine. His temper is well known. Not counting officer Dennis Franklin, our homicide detectives suspect Sammy Nguyen of personally carrying out eight murders. Seven are considered to be gangland business. The other was a young man they think was moving in on Bernadette Lee, shot three times in the face in a Garden Grove parking lot.

I thought of the shooter in the fog and wondered if Sammy could have let a contract on Will some other way than in a letter to Bernadette. Sammy got fifteen minutes a day on one of the Mod J pay phones—maybe he used that.

Then the voice inside my head again, just a taunting whisper: *you killed him you killed him you killed him . . .*

I could have stepped through the bars of the cell and forced the truth out of Sammy—if he had any truth in him. He was a clever man and a murderer, but he wouldn't stand a chance against me.

Whatever I got from him would be unconstitutional and not evidentiary, but a courtroom wouldn't be the point. I could arrange with the other deputies here so that no one would ever know what really happened in Sammy's cell, or why. Those things occur, though more rarely than you might think.

But inside my mind I climbed up and got to the quiet spot and I looked out of it and told myself that if I wasn't smart enough to figure out a guy like Sammy, then maybe I shouldn't be a deputy in the first place.

Like he'd been reading my thoughts, Sammy smiled and opened his hands, palms up. "I'm sorry your father got shot,

Joe. This girl, Savannah—maybe I can find something out. You get me that trap, I'll see what I can do."

In the briefing room I heated up one of the breakfast sandwiches I keep frozen in the refrigerator. While the microwave groaned I stared down at the floor. Tears fell from my eyes and I could feel them on my cheeks and on my big scar, where tears always feel cooler, and in my mind the fog started rolling in again, trying to choke off the noise.

I had had enough.

You killed him you killed him you . . .

Through the clamor, I tried to think. And this is what I came up with: I didn't think Sammy was behind what happened. I didn't think that Sammy knew this was going to go down. I think it surprised him as much as it did Will.

The real surprise was Savannah. I could tell by his empty look when I first asked about her that Sammy was hiding something. Something he didn't want to give me right away. Something that might be valuable to me.

I didn't get it. A sweet young girl sees terrible things, she runs away into the night, and a guy like Sammy Nguyen wants to parlay her into a new rat trap.

You tell me about human nature. I give up.

Chapter Three

Lunchtime in the Men's Central Jail mess hall, two hundred fifty inmates and three guards armed with nothing but pepper spray to keep the order. I stood with my back to one wall and watched the men walk in. The rules are: single file, hands in your pockets, seat yourself left to right at the next available table, no talking until you sit down with your tray. No talking with inmates at other tables.

It's quiet. Most of these guys can get along. Anyone who can't is put into protective custody in Module J, or given administrative segregation in Mod F, and they eat in their cells. Still, this is where the trouble happens if it's going to happen. The violence is usually quick. Nobody sees anything.

Last week one of the young Mexicans shanked a big black man—earning respect. The blacks will retaliate somehow, someday. If there's big violence in the air—the kind that trickles down from San Quentin or Pelican Bay—we guards can feel it. It gets even quieter than usual. Inmates do odd little things that are out of character for them: a glutton doesn't eat his food; an amiable guy goes froggy on you; nobody wants to use the shower or the day room. So we know something is going down, just by the feel of the place.

The inmates get fifteen minutes to eat and file out. Eyes usually down. Laceless jail-issue sneakers slapping quietly on the floor. They turn their pockets inside out when they pass the guard.

In the mess hall the inmates travel in self-segregated gangs known as cars. We're a "brown" jail—predominantly Latin. We've got two Latin cars—one for citizens, and one for illegals. Then there's the Asian car, the black car. The white car is called the "wood" car. Wood is short for peckerwood. The driver is the guy in the back of each car. He's the heavy, the leader. If we've got a problem with someone, we'll go to that heavy, let him establish some discipline. Otherwise we'll punish the whole car. In jail, peer pressure can be intense.

I made it through lunch before Sergeant Delano told me to go home and stay home.

"The shrinks will be in touch with you, Joe—the Deputy-Involved Shooting people. That's Sergeant Mehring and Norm Zussman. Don't worry about it, you did the right thing. They're not out to get you. Besides, you look like you could use some rest."

"Can't I come to work, sir?"

"You're on a paid leave, Joe. Take it. Go to the beach. Date a girl. Go fishing."

"I'd rather work."

The fact of the matter was that I didn't have anything better to do than work. The jail was my world, just as Hillview had been my world until Will Trona took me out of it.

"Go."

So I didn't fight it. I was so tired I could hardly get myself to the parking lot. The voice inside started to mock me, but even my conscience was too tired to keep it up.

I just put one foot in front of the other and told myself that

Will was dead, but life would go on, life would go on, life would go on.

When I finally got to Will's car one of the FBI guys from the Federal Building was standing there looking at the BMW. His name was Steve Marchant. Thirty-five, maybe, slender but strong.

"I wish I could work this homicide," he said.

"Anaheim PD's got it."

"Wrong—it's yours now. Birch and Ouderkirk have it. The sheriff prevailed because you're one of their own."

I didn't know what to say. I wondered how it would go, to have my fellow deputies investigating the murder of my father. Rick Birch in the homicide detail had a great reputation. I'd met him—he was old and weathered and smart. I didn't know Ouderkirk.

"Joe, this the girl you saw last night with Will?"

He palmed a wallet-sized school picture at me. Held it low and kind of secretively, like he was trying to sell me something he'd stolen.

Easy enough to answer, though.

"Yeah," I said. "That's Savannah."

"Bingo," he said, pocketing the photo. "Describe her clothing to me."

I did. "Is she okay, Steve?"

"She's missing."

"What can you tell me about her?"

"Absolutely nothing. Just watch any network news at five-thirty."

"But she's all right?"

"News at five-thirty. That's all I can do for you."

He stepped up closer to me, looked into my eyes. "Joe, did you see the shooter last night?"

"Not well."

"Don't let it get to you, Joe. You can't be everywhere, see everything. Hang tough. We'll get that puke and lay him down for a hotshot up in Quentin."

"Thanks, sir. I appreciate that."

"Be at my office, eight tomorrow morning, all right? You'll know why after the news. I'm going to ask for everything you remember about that girl, at least twice."

I called my mother from the car. Her voice sounded stronger but I could hear the thick catch of grief in it. "Will, Jr. and Glenn are coming into Orange County in an hour, Joe. Their families later."

"I'll pick them up, Mom."

"I'm already on my way."

"I'll meet you by the statue."

She gave me the airlines and arrival times, told me she loved me, and hung up.

I met her by the statue of John Wayne, a huge bronze likeness of the actor in his cowboy getup, full stride. I hugged her and she collapsed in my arms, sobbing. I'd heard her cry before, but never like that: big quivering heaves that seemed to come all the way up from her feet. I led her over to a bench, where some considerate people moved so we could sit down.

When she was in control of herself she looked me in the eyes, ran her hands over my face and asked me how I was. She's the only person in the world I allow to do that—touch both sides of my face. I told her I was fine and we both respected that lie enough to stand and find our way to Will, Jr.'s arrival gate.

An hour later the four of us, in two cars, drove past the news crews and cameras and then up the long shaded driveway of our old home in the Tustin hills. We stood on the front porch while Mom dug out her key. I smelled the eucalyptus and the roses that she had always tended with devotion. I looked at the old redwood door with the window in it and realized that it was the same door that had opened to me twenty years ago, welcoming me to the dreamiest, happiest days of my life. *A home.*

But when I walked in I felt like I was in a parody of happiness, a spoof on dreams coming true. Will's home, but no Will.

I shut the door behind me and looked at my brothers and my mother and I couldn't meet their eyes.

You killed him you killed him you killed him.

"I didn't kill him," I said.

"What's that supposed to mean, Joe?" asked Will, Jr. He put his arm on my shoulder and walked me into the living room.

I don't remember a lot about the next two hours, except that they were among the worst of my life.

Home. I moved my Mustang out of the garage and parked Will's BMW inside. Left the windows down. Sat there for a minute, wondering.

Then I got Will's briefcase and took it into the house. I have three big floor safes—one in the bedroom, one in the second bath, one in the den. The house was built in 1945 on a raised foundation, which made them easy to install. I opened the safe in the den.

To make room, I pulled out the Smith .357 magnum and one of my wooden treasure boxes. The boxes contain things I value from my life—rocks, shells, feathers, trinkets, notes, small gifts. The first thing Will gave me is in one of them: a book called *Shag: Last of the Plains Buffalo*. I'd been reading a library copy of that book when he first talked to me at Hillview. I was almost five. The next time he came, he gave me my own brand-new copy to keep.

I stared at the briefcase for a long moment, because it reminded me so much of Will. I touched a bloodstain and it left a dark crust on my finger. Good thing Alagna hadn't seen the blood, but if he was careless enough not to impound Will's BMW, he probably wouldn't have done anything useful with the briefcase either. I opened it and considered each mundane item as if it held some grand significance in Will's life: his last paper clip, his last Board agenda, his last aspirin. Then I closed it and put it on the bottom of the floor safe and set the treasure box on top.

I checked the handgun, wiped it with the oilcloth on which it sat, always loaded and always ready, then shut the safe door and spun the lock.

I walked into the living room and everything looked different. Exactly the same, but totally different. I studied the buffed maple floor, the black sofa and black chair and black ottoman, the magazines neatly in their rack, the chrome reading lamp. I looked at the white walls with the framed posters of race cars, the cheap print of Michaelangelo's "God Creating Adam" and my many framed photographs of Will, Mary Ann, Will, Jr., and Glenn.

In the kitchen I sat and looked down at the white and black checkerboard tile, the white walls and cupboards and counter and fixtures. The dinette was chrome with white padded chairs and a white vinyl tabletop. Faintly institutional. I'd painted and furnished the place myself. I kept it clean as an operating room. It all seemed so irrelevant now, so absolutely without meaning.

At five-thirty that afternoon, a news conference called by Savannah's father was carried on all four network news broadcasts.

Her name was Savannah Blazak, she was eleven years old, and she had been kidnapped three days ago, Monday afternoon.

The girl's father was Jack Blazak of Newport Beach. I knew him on sight because he was one of the county's richest and

most powerful men. And an acquaintance of Will's. His wife,
Lorna, stood at his side during the conference. Along with the
Jack Blazaks, FBI special agent Steve Marchant was on hand to
answer questions. They had three recent pictures of Savannah,
whom her father described as "very intelligent, very sensitive,
very imaginative."

She'd vanished from their home three days ago—sometime
Monday morning, Jack said—and he received a ransom demand
shortly thereafter. He stuttered briefly, sighed, then admitted
that he and his wife had at first agreed to pay the ransom demand out of fear for their daughter's life. Part of the demand
was that if they went to the authorities, Savannah's head would
be mailed to them in "an overnight freezer-pack, UPS."

Blazak's larynx bobbed in his throat as he confessed that
"after almost three days of living hell," his attempt to ransom
his daughter had "not been successful." But he had had reason
to believe that this evening, Thursday, he could make the payment to Savannah's kidnappers and secure her safe return.
When he heard this morning on the news that a girl named Savannah, matching his daughter's description, had fled a murder
scene the night before, he contacted the FBI immediately.

Blazak begged everyone watching to look out for his daughter. He offered a reward of five hundred thousand dollars for
information leading to Savannah's safe return. Absolutely no
questions asked.

Steve took over to explain where and when Savannah was
last seen and what she was wearing. He answered questions and
gave out a hotline number. He wanted everyone to know that
the Bureau was pursuing this case with every resource it had,
that the safe return of Savannah Blazak was a priority.

Steve looked eager, a little angry. Jack Blazak looked like
he'd been dragged behind a school bus for ten miles. Lorna

Blazak looked lovely and fragile and almost absent from the proceedings.

The next segment was all about Will. "Bloodbath in Anaheim. Orange County Runs Red." News footage of the Lind Street alley, UCI Medical Center, the closed door of his office in the County Building, clips of him in meetings of the Board of Supervisors. They'd gotten a few seconds of us coming down the street toward the home in the Tustin hills, and some footage from behind as we walked toward the front porch.

Even a picture of me, with "sources within the Sheriff Department confirming" that I'd fatally shot two of the killers while trying to protect my father. One other was reported dead, one critically wounded.

Dead suspects not yet identified.

No known motive at this time.

My phone rang every few minutes. Friends from the academy, the department, old friends, relatives. I talked to my family but let the strangers talk to the machine: Bruce, a newspaper reporter in New York; Seth, a television news-magazine producer in Los Angeles; June Dauer, a local radio host; Dr. Norman Zussman, the psychiatrist who would lead me through the Deputy-Involved Shooting Program.

I heated up three TV dinners and set them on the table with a carton of milk. I liked the institutional taste of TV dinners, and the compartmented trays—more leftovers from my days at Hillview.

I was just ready to eat when someone rang the doorbell. It was Rick Birch, looking tired and old. I invited him in, offered him one of the hot dinners. He declined.

"Go ahead," he said. "I just have a question or two."

I put the dinners back in the oven and sat down across from

him. He looked around the room like he was taking inventory.
He wore rimless glasses with thin, tinted lenses.

"How old are you, Joe?"

"Twenty-four, sir."

"How long have you lived here?"

"Three years."

"You keep it nice and neat."

"Thank you. I like things neat."

"The two guys you shot were Cobra Kings."

"I've heard of them."

"Ray Flatley in the gang unit can give you a rundown. But
basically, they're thieves who don't mind committing murder
when they feel like it." He slipped a small notebook from his
coat pocket, which was apparently already open to the right
place. "You got Luke Smith and Ming Nixon. Ages twenty-
seven and thirty-one, respectively. 'Luke' got changed from
Loc. Nixon was a name the other guy got stuck with growing
up a bastard in Saigon. The third deceased hasn't been identified
yet. The one still alive is Ike Cao—nineteen and a card-carrying
Cobra King."

He watched me over the top of his glasses, head tilted down.
I didn't know how to react. I felt bad for killing them, but not
that bad.

"I guess you've got some time off from work," he said.

"I didn't want it."

"Take your leave. You don't go through something like this
and not have it change you. Norm Zussman's a good shrink."

"I wish I could keep working."

"I understand the need."

Birch blinked his pale blue eyes. He looked like a farmer:
weathered face, big hands, an inner stillness that comes from
watching things grow.

"Joe, tell me about your father and Savannah Blazak."

"I don't know much."

"No?"

"No, sir. Will wasn't leveling with me about the girl. I'm his son. I was his driver and his guard. Sometimes he told me what he was up to, and sometimes not. I'd never heard of Savannah until last night around nine. When we went to Lind Street to pick her up. I didn't know anything about a kidnapping until five-thirty tonight when I watched the news."

Birch thought for a moment. "Let me get this straight: the girl's kidnapped Monday morning. The family can't seem to make the ransom payment, even though they've got the money and they're willing. By Wednesday night, Will Trona has found her. Explain that."

"I can't."

"You see the shooter?"

"Not well. The fog hid him."

"Could you ID him in a lineup?"

"If he spoke."

"Explain."

I did—the quality of the voice, the strange cadence.

"A voice ID does us no good at all. It's not enough to even hold someone on."

I knew that. So I said nothing.

"You know who did it, Joe?"

"No, sir. Of course not."

He rested his calm eyes on my face. "There's a whole bunch wrong with this."

"I think so, too."

"Can you give me a full statement tomorrow? I've got Alagna's tape, but I want to ask my own questions."

"Absolutely."

He nodded, looking around again, then back at me. "Have you talked to Marchant yet?"

"Tomorrow."

Birch drummed his fingertips on the table, fast. "Did he have this girl abducted?"

"Will?"

"I'm not the only one who's going to ask you that. She's kidnapped and she's last seen with him. You can draw a pretty straight line between those points."

"I'm sure he didn't, sir."

"You're not sure of much else."

I wondered how I could suggest that Birch get a phone company printout without also suggesting that I was holding out on him. I believed that there would be a time to come clean with Rick Birch. But I didn't believe it was then.

He waited for me to add something, but I didn't. He gave the impression of being able to wait forever.

"How were Will's finances?"

"Good, sir. Will's salary wasn't bad and my mother is wealthy. He never liked spending money."

He waited again, but I said nothing.

"Blazak didn't say what the ransom demand was."

My turn to wait. I can wait forever, too.

"Okay, Joe. We'll get to the fine print tomorrow. Do me a favor and write down what happened last night. Everything you can remember. It'll help both of us."

"Okay."

He stood. "I'm sorry. I really am sorry for you."

"Thank you."

We set a time and Rick Birch took one more look around my kitchen, shook my hand. I showed him to the door.

After dinner Jack Blazak called. He wanted me to be at his home in Newport the next morning, early. He didn't ask me anything about his daughter. He put on his wife, Lorna, to give me directions to "the Newport house."

She did. Then, "Don't hang up, Mr. Trona. I just have to ask you—how was she? Did she look okay? Was she upset or hurt or anything? I haven't seen my child in three days."

"She looked fine, Mrs. Blazak. She looked fine when I saw her."

Chapter Four

Six A.M. and the sun was just rising over the hills of south Newport Beach. My car idled beneath the towering marble archway that marked the entry to the Pelican Point development. A gate guard took my name, plates, badge and driver's license numbers. He stared at my face like he could handle it any time. The gate swung open and I drove in.

Ten days ago, Newport PD had shot a sixteen-year-old boy dead just outside this gate. Twelve shots, nine hits, dead-on-scene. The guy was armed with a machete and a sharpened screwdriver, screaming in Spanish. His name was Miguel Domingo. Jaime Medina's HACF was up in arms about the incident, demanding an investigation. He'd talked about it with Will that night, in fact. The shooting was the second violent death of an undocumented Guatemalan worker in a month. A week before the shooting, a young domestic worker, Luria Blas, was struck and killed by a car as she "wandered" onto a street close to her Fullerton apartment. It was ruled an accident. The woman in the Suburban that killed her got out and tried to help.

Driving into a place like Pelican Point, you saw the beauty and the wealth and had to admit the dizzying unfairness of things, the way some people lived in mansions by the beach and others got shot at the gates or run over by sport utility vehicles. Some guy trying to take his share, using a screwdriver and a machete. A lady trying to make it by cleaning other people's houses.

New asphalt on the old hills. Mansions, palaces, estates— some finished, some not. Georgian, Tudor, Tuscan, Roman, Frank Lloyd Wright–ish, postmodern glass and concrete. Gray sky with a seagull in it. Tan hillsides and a battalion of yellow Cat D-9s ready to scrape new pads off the horizon. Never too early to take out a hilltop.

The next gate had its own little gatehouse beside it, but no guard. A security camera followed my face to a stop. The intercom was easy to reach. I pushed the ringer and waited. Two gates per household, SOP in the Newport hills now.

"Yes."

"Joe Trona for the Blazaks."

"Come on in, Joe."

The Blazaks had gone Greco-Roman: a reflecting pool out front lined with olive trees, then an expanse of white marble steps leading to a columned portico and two immense, windowless front doors. The house was white marble, rectangular and flat-roofed. Bougainvillea and ocotillo spread upward along one side, casting shadows and bright purple bracts against the pale marble walls. Statuary, a nice little plot of grape vines with their arms out on wires and reaching for sun, a small stand of orange trees with dark waxy leaves and bright fruit.

I parked beside a polished red-and-white '63 split-window Corvette with plates that said "BoWar." The garage behind it was open, and stocked with a Silver Cloud, a Lexus SUV and a Jaguar with the dealer's ad still in the license-plate frame.

Jack Blazak came down the front steps to meet me. He shook my hand with conviction. Wavy dark hair, light brown eyes, thick and compact.

"Thanks for coming."

"My pleasure, sir."

"Lorna and Bo are inside."

His voice was gruff and he delivered his words in a fast bark, like he was saving time.

The entry room was spacious, with a high ceiling dome capped by a skylight. I took off my hat. White walls, the day's early sunlight rushing down, more white marble underfoot. Blazak's face looked pale as the walls.

He led me into a living room that was all glass on the western side, with a view of the hills and the ocean below.

Lorna Blazak sat at one end of a big leather couch, a guy I'd never seen before at the other end.

"Oh, Mr. Trona," she said. "I'm so glad you're here."

She offered her hand, which was bony and cold. Her eyes were dull and an air of exhaustion came off her.

"And meet Bo Warren—he's new head of security for the Chapel of Light."

Warren was already standing. He was a short, wiry man with a buzzed scalp and blue eyes under sharp, dubious brows. Camel blazer, black golf shirt buttoned up, duty boots polished into the fifth dimension. His handshake was brief and punishing and his eyes stayed right on mine.

BoWar, I thought.

"Nice to meet you, sir. I'm Joe Trona."

He didn't say anything, so Lorna took up the pause.

"Joe, anything to drink?"

"Nothing, thank you."

Jack sat down on the couch and motioned me into a chair across from them. There was a glass coffee table between us. It was shaped like a coastline, and the craftsman had etched waves along curved edges of the glass. I sat and put my hat on the waves.

"First things first, Joe," Blazak said. "We're grateful that you located our daughter. We thank you. We're beyond grateful that she's alive. We called you here to tell you a few things, get you straightened out and up to speed."

Again, his words were fast and his tone aggressive, a man used to being listened to.

I nodded. "I don't want to be crooked and slow, sir."

Warren snickered. Jack looked at me blankly, then turned to his wife.

"Jack's blunt these days, Mr. Trona," said Lorna. "He hasn't slept more than two hours a night since Savannah was taken. Neither have I. Forgive us both if we're kind of . . . short."

"I understand."

"Help," said Jack. "A little help is all we're after." Silence then, until Jack looked across at Warren. "You take it from here, Bo."

Warren moved to the edge of the sofa like he was ready to spring.

"Glad to," he said. "Joe, sometime between nine and eleven hundred hours on Monday, June eleven, Savannah Blazak was kidnapped."

Semper fi, I thought. 'Nam. His voice was much deeper and louder than you expected, like he had a speaker inside him.

"Jack was at work. Lorna was out. Marcie, that's the head maid here, was doing some light cleaning and keeping an eye on Savannah. Savannah was allegedly playing in her bedroom. When Marcie went to check on her at ten fifty-five, Savannah wasn't in her room. Marcie called and walked the house—no girl. Called and walked the grounds—no girl. She called the neighbors, who have a girl about Savannah's age, nobody home. At eleven ten she called Jack at work, then—on Jack's orders—nine one one. After that, she called Mrs. Blazak on her cell phone. Jack made it home in seventeen minutes. Newport PD was already on scene."

Warren stared at me, eyes blue and hard. "With me?"

I nodded.

"Then, in brief: the cops get here making a lot of noise, glance at the girl's room—"

"Call her Savannah, Bo. Not *the girl.*"

"I'm sorry, Mrs. Blazak. Savannah. They look in Savannah's room. Question Marcie. Question Jack. Take the report, say they think Savannah will show up unharmed. Ninety-nine times out of a hundred, they say, a missing juvenile shows up unharmed. They probably wanted to chew out Marcie for using nine one one for a non-emergency, but Jack Blazak's daughter was the subject of the call."

"Stick to the facts, Bo," said Blazak. "You're a gopher, not a prophet."

Warren's smile appeared and vanished, on then off, like a turn signal. He cleared his throat.

"Yes, sir. Okay. Now, Joe, about three hours after the maid called the cops, the Blazaks got a call here at home. The caller muffled his voice somehow—a cloth or towel or something. He said he had Savannah. He let her say 'Hello, Mom and Dad' to prove it. Affirmative, it was Savannah. Then he demanded half a million cash dollars for her safe release. He gave Jack and Lorna forty-six hours to pay the ransom. If they didn't pay it he'd kill Savannah. If they contacted the authorities about this, he'd kill Savannah. He said he would contact them before noon Wednesday. This was Monday, two o'clock, remember."

"Yes."

"Here's the first twist: Jack recognized the kidnapper's voice. Twist number two: the kidnapper is his son, Alex, known to his friends as Crazy Alex."

Are you with Alex?

"Damnit, Bo," pleaded Lorna. "Why do you have to be so crude?"

Warren's voice was resonant with apology. "Well, I'm sorry, but I was just trying to give Joe here a feel for what we're up against. I think the nickname is a good indicator of his character *at times,* Lorna. I'm not trying to drag your son's name through the mud, even though he is a convicted felon, a longtime mental patient and now, apparently, a kidnapper again."

"An accused felon. He wasn't convicted," Lorna said tiredly.

"A kidnapper again?" I asked.

"He took Savannah from the family home when she was three years old," said Warren.

"He was *thirteen*, Bo," hissed Lorna. "They ran away."

"Get on with it, Warren," snapped Blazak. He was leaning his head back against the couch, looking into the distant recesses of his living room ceiling. "You're wasting everybody's time again."

"All right, Jack, sure. So, Jack and Lorna didn't want to endanger Savannah any more than she was already. And, understandably, they didn't want to endanger their son, even though he's threatened to murder his own sister if he doesn't get a potload of money. Jack and Lorna confer. Jack and Lorna agonize. Really *agonize.* They decide to pray to God in heaven for guidance. They go to the Reverend Daniel Alter and they tell him what's happened. He leads them in a series of prayers and scriptural readings that lasts almost half an hour. When they've finished praying to the Lord for help, Jack and Lorna both believe that paying Alex for Savannah's safe return and getting help for Alex—rather than a prison term—is the Christian thing to do. The Reverend Alter agrees."

Warren leaned back and sighed. "I think you can fill in from there," he said.

"Reverend Alter volunteered your services for the ransom drop, because your line is security."

"Exactly."

"But something went wrong with the Wednesday exchange or none of us would be sitting here right now."

"Obviously. Enter Will Trona. The Reverend Daniel had asked him to help find Savannah and Alex, because of your father's connections throughout the county. Your father called Jack on Wednesday morning, saying that he'd talked to Alex and seen Savannah. He wouldn't say one word about where they were or how he found them. Will said that Alex now wanted one million dollars to let his sister go. Will said that he would collect that money, and when he'd collected it, he would gather up Savannah and bring her to us. This was all supposed to happen Wednesday night. Jack's money was given to Will, as planned. Not as planned, your father was murdered and Savannah vanished."

I tried to match Warren's story with what I had seen and heard. It seemed about right to me. But it surprised me in an empty way to learn that Will had known Savannah's whereabouts on Wednesday morning, but never bothered to tell me. Never even told me he was looking for a kidnapped girl. He'd left me in the dark before—for my own good, he always said later. But it hurt because Will's night business was supposed to be my business too.

"I understand," I said. "When Savannah's name hit the news yesterday, you figured it was time to call in the police and FBI, go public and try to get her back before Alex could find her again."

"Good," said Warren. "So you can see our troubles now."

"Yes, sir. The first trouble is, that was two nights ago and Savannah is still missing. The second is, Mr. and Mrs. Blazak still love their son. You convinced the FBI that a full-scale, highly publicized manhunt for Alex would lead him to either suicide or a breakdown. And may or may not get Savannah back. Steve Marchant indulged you for a few days, but they haven't found either of them, so they're about to plaster Alex's face and name all over the news, just like Savannah's were. That means an arrest on a federal kidnapping charge, not therapy for his disorders."

"That's it," said Warren. "Marchant says they'll hold off on launching a public manhunt for Alex until Monday. Three days. And that brings us to you. Because we're hoping that since you found her once, you can find her twice."

"I thought so."

"Well, you're a bright kid," said Warren with a smile. He chuckled.

"Joe," said Jack, leaning forward now, his voice soft. "We need a few other things from you."

"What things, sir?"

"We need to know everything that happened that night. Anything Will might have said. Anything you saw or heard about my daughter. Everything you told the Anaheim PD, the Orange County Sheriff's, the FBI, the media—I want to hear it again, from you. I'm going to tape record the whole story. Every *last* detail, Joe. Do you understand?"

"I understand."

Bo Warren stood and took a step toward me. Until then, he'd sounded like a colonel briefing the press, now he spoke like a general giving orders.

"Joe, we've got a crack hypnotherapist—works without drugs—who can put you in a state so deep you can remember details of your own birth. She's scheduled to be here in one hour and fifteen minutes. Before that, we want one hour with you, to hear your account, hear everything you remember. Then we need one hour from you, under hypnosis. We think you know how to find Savannah, because you and your father found her. Whether you *know* you know how, or not. We're asking you to help the girl. Help us. Help yourself. *One million dollars* if you can find her, Joe. Or if you can lead us to her. Either way. You might already hold the key in that good brain of yours. A million dollars is not a bad paycheck for lying on the couch in the Blazaks' den, just remembering that night."

I looked at them one at a time. Warren stood about eight feet away from me, to the side of the coffee table, eyes fixed on my face. Jack's hands were locked behind his head, elbows out, and he was staring at me.

Lorna stared at me too. Then she did something that astonished me.

She shook her head. It was slight and it was fast. But I saw it and it was clear. She was looking right at me.

She did it once more, and looked down.

"Agreed, then," Warren said.

"Terrific," said Blazak. "Let's get started."

"What's your answer, Mr. Trona?" Lorna asked. The glaze in her eyes was gone. I saw her jaw muscle move under the skin.

"No, for now. But I'll think about it."

In the silence I heard the *kyew, kyew, kyew* of a hawk outside. I heard the air conditioner sigh on.

"Uh, Joe?" said Warren. "You just listened to two parents telling you about the kidnapping of their daughter. *By their own son.* You saw that daughter briefly, on Wednesday, two nights ago. You know now that she was in the hands of a rather dangerous young psychopath, brother or not. May well be *back* in those hands, for all we know. And you're going to sit there after hearing all this, and tell us you won't help?"

"I'll look for her. I'll bring her to you if I find her. I won't tell you everything I know about that night."

"Why not, soldier?"

Warren took two steps toward me, which put me in range of his boots.

"Because," I said, "something else happened that night. Something I care about, even if none of you do."

"We care about Will," Warren snapped. "If that's what you mean."

"That's what I mean. And Will Trona is none of your business."

"Look, sonofabitch—whatever happened that involves this man's daughter is *definitely* his business. Help us, help yourself."

I gathered my hat and stood, watching Warren, then turned to the Blazaks. "Thank you for having me into your home. I'll do what I can to find Savannah. She seems like a wonderful girl."

Jack was staring at me. Lorna was staring at her husband. Warren was suddenly out of my field of vision, then directly in front of me. "Hey, *meatface,* hold it just one second—"

"Don't," I said.

But he grabbed my upper arm, hard. A strong man. I took his wrist in both hands, drop-spun and threw him over my shoulder like you would an ax. He landed flat on his back but very hard on the carpet and I heard the wind huff out of him. He turned over gasping, gnashing his mouth into the cream-colored wool.

"Oh, my God!" cried Lorna.

"Head of Security, my ass," said Jack.

"I'm sorry, and I'll pay for spot cleaning," I offered.

Lorna walked away. Jack stood and looked at Warren.

I picked up my hat and looked down at Warren, too. I shouldn't have been surprised by his shoulder rig but I was. Something about a five million dollar house and an automatic handgun don't go together, like finding a fly in your whipped cream.

He was still fighting for a good breath when I turned out of earshot and into the entry room on my way out.

Lorna Blazak held open the door for me with one hand, held out a business card to me with the other. I took it and read it.

Alex Jackson Blazak
Weapons Rare and Collectible
War Memorabilia
Appointment Only
(949) 555–2993

On the other side was an address, written in a woman's elegant longhand.

"Alex might have held her there. It's kind of a secret, because, well . . . Alex isn't a licensed dealer. Maybe something there can lead you to her. Jack doesn't know this place, neither do the police. I tried to get in, but it was locked."

For the second time that morning, she had astounded me. "Why are you protecting him?"

"Because if you find him first, he's got a chance, and so does my daughter."

"I'll arrest him."

"I hope so. Jack is so absolutely furious. I'm afraid for everyone."

"Anything else I should know, Mrs. Blazak?"

"I love my children. Go."

I thanked her and she shut the huge door behind me.

Driving out of the hills I thought this was a beautiful place. Tan hills and blue water and mansions.

I wondered why Savannah Blazak hadn't made it home. I

wondered if Alex had caught up with her before she could get
to the cops, or to some responsible adult. I wondered why Lorna
was protecting someone who had threatened to send her daughter's head home in a freezer-pack.

And I wondered for the hundredth time how Will had found
Savannah. How did he know where to look? Why had he kept
me out of it?

Savannah gets kidnapped on Monday morning. Her parents
tell no one but their spiritual advisor and his security man.

By Wednesday morning Will Trona has solved the mystery,
found the girl, arranged to get her back home safely. That night,
ten minutes after he tries to claim her, he's dead.

When I went through the marble archway there was a video
crew shooting some footage, maybe something about Miguel
Domingo, the sixteen-year-old Guatemalan with the machete.
But like Jaime Medina, I doubted if the media would pay that
much attention to the story. The camera crew was probably just
a promotional segment for Pelican Point development, where
one million dollars gets you nothing.

The guard was vibing them as hard as he could, but they
were on a public street.

Chapter Five

I walked up the stairs to the FBI Orange County Investigative Resident Agency. The public entrance door was heavily fortified with bulletproof glass and mesh and a video camera was trained on the entryway. In the lobby I walked past the Wall of Martyrs—photo-plaques of FBI personnel who'd lost their lives in the line of duty.

Steve Marchant led me into the FBI War Room, set up for Savannah. Impressive: ten agents, six computers, a phone bank with recording and listening equipment, a big radio console. There was a handwritten timeline on a twenty-foot sheet of butcher paper tacked to the wall, so you could see at a glance what had happened. Pictures of Savannah and Alex Blazak hung above it.

Some of the agents turned and looked at me, others stayed at their tasks.

"I wanted to give you a look at this before we talked," said Marchant. "Joe, we've got up to two hundred agents ready to roll when this thing breaks. We hate kidnappings, and we use every resource we've got to make them go our way."

He took me to a small conference room. There were a tape recorder and a video camera set up and ready to go.

"Make yourself comfortable, Joe. We're going to go through Wednesday night in detail. Coffee?"

"No thank you."

"How's your memory?"

"Very good."

Marchant sat down across from me and tested the tape recorder. He said the case number, date and time, my name, and asked me if I was here of my own free will, volunteering information. I said I was, and he Mirandized me anyway.

"Let's get started. Okay, Joe, tell me about Wednesday night."

Two hours and two tapes later I'd gone through a lot of what I remembered. Marchant was particularly interested in Will's conversations in the car, Will's relationship with Savannah, and my talk with Jack Blazak earlier in the morning. He made notes on a computer-generated sheet that may have been a phone company readout, or may not have been. He played his information very close to the chest—I learned nothing I didn't know already. The Feds are famous for being closed and tight when they want to.

For my part, I said nothing about Lorna Blazak's card, and Alex's "business" address. And nothing about Will's words to Jennifer Avila, or the money he'd passed to her, or about Mary Ann being blue that night. I'd been entrusted with those things and I didn't feel right about offering them to a man I barely knew.

After Marchant turned off the tape and video recorders, he sat back and looked at me. "What do you think of the father, Jack?"

"Intense. Distraught."

He nodded. "And Lorna?"

"Dazed."

"Yeah. If they contact you again, I want to know, immediately."

I agreed.

"At the tennis courts, when you dropped off the ransom cash—did you get a look at the players?"

"Doubles on one court—an older foursome. The other court were two teenagers, male, pretty good players, hitting hard."

"Those young men pay any attention to you?"

"None that I noticed."

"Joe—your mother and father have a good relationship?"

"I think it was strong. They loved each other and faced things together."

"You have any reason to think Will was sexually involved with Savannah?"

"None. He loved women, sir, not girls."

He made a note, then closed his book. "Joe, we'll be using sheriff's department personnel on this. Local PD's too, if we need them. I want you to know we're here to help, not to take the glory."

"I understand."

"But I'm going to get that girl back safely. Nothing is going to keep me from doing that. I'll do what it takes."

"It sounds like you're warning me, but I'm not sure what about."

Marchant stood and smiled. He's a tall man, but he stoops a little, like he's trying to hide it. "What I'm saying is, I appreciate your help. I'm on your side. All two hundred of us are on your side. Birch wants to run the homicide. That's fine by us. He's a little . . . protective sometimes. But I want you to know we'll help you out any way we can."

Half an hour later I was telling Rick Birch everything I'd told Marchant. But nothing more. Nothing about my mother, Will's lover, his anxious mood. Maybe I was trying to salvage some scrap of his privacy. Maybe I was trying to honor our pact of doing night business together, even though Will had flagrantly left me out of the darkest night business of his life.

By the time he finished asking me questions, I felt like I'd told my story to every person in Orange County law enforcement.

"Alex Blazak?" said Sammy Nguyen with an innocent look. "Why would I know Alex Blazak?"

"You're both in the gun business."

"I'm out of that now. But my business was legitimate. He'd sell machine guns to little kids if he could make money. He's got a sword that Hitler gave to Goering, first belonged to Napoleon, worth about a million three."

"How well do you know him?"

He eyed me, slipping on his glasses. "Joe, what are you doing here? You're off work for a while. Bereavement, deputy-involved shooting, all that."

"Tell me about Alex."

"Nice hat, Joe. Hides part of your face."

"Come on, Sammy. Help out."

It was early afternoon and Mod J was going through its daily drowsy time. About an hour after lunch the inmates run out of venom and energy, and they'll shut up for a while, take naps, maybe read. By three o'clock they'll be stirring again.

Sammy was lying on his cot, staring up at his picture of Bernadette.

"They call him Crazy Alex because he's crazy. Crazy people annoy me, Joe. Bad for business."

"If you wanted to find him, where would you look?"

He looked over at me, as if the idea interested him.

"I saw the news last night. His sister gets kidnapped, and you can't find *him*?"

"Correct."

"Then maybe he kidnapped her."

Some of the inmates put things together quickly. Takes one to know one.

"I doubt it. He skipped on a deal." I thought I could draw him out with talk of his competition.

"Who's the buyer?"

"None of your business."

"Probably some rich man who lives by the beach. Wants pink *nunchuks* to tickle his boyfriend. That's the kind of business Crazy Alex does best."

"It was small-caliber handguns, brand-new, numbers etched off."

Sammy considered this. Maybe he was in on something like it himself. Maybe he'd like to get in on this one.

"How can I find him, Sammy?"

"You ask me for information about a former business associate and I still don't have a rat trap."

"Try this."

I pulled a rat trap out of my coat pocket and held it out to Sammy through the bars. It was the kind that uses an adhesive to trap the animal, which then dies because it can't move. I got it from the supply desk, one of just a handful we've managed to keep on hand. He hopped off the cot and came over.

"This isn't the kind I need. I need the old-fashioned kind that breaks their necks."

"You didn't specify. These are the only kind allowed in a cell."

He cast his dark eyes on me. Measuring. Figuring.

"I talked to some people, you know, on the phone, but I

couldn't find out anything about that girl. You probably got what you needed from that press conference yesterday."

"I need to find her."

"I can't do that, from in here."

"I just wasted a good rat trap."

"I don't do things like that, Joe. When I say I'm going to produce, I produce. You know, within my capabilities. The girl got kidnapped, the FBI can't find her, and I'm supposed to? No. Not from in here. Now, her brother, maybe. Maybe I can do that. I know people who know Alex."

"I'd appreciate your help."

Sammy sat down with the trap, looked at me with pronounced sympathy.

"It's bad when a father dies. Mine was murdered in San Jose when I was eleven—did you know that?"

"Yes."

"They shot him while he locked up his nightclub."

"Robbery."

"They took the night's cash off him—eight hundred dollars, forty-eight cents. The forty-eight cents made me angry."

I'd read his sheet, and the report by a county psychologist, who included Sammy's account of his father's death.

Sammy's version of what happened after the murder interested me. I learned some of it by sneaking into the plumbing tunnel in Mod F of the old Men's Central and squatting behind the cell belonging to one of Sammy's lieutenants. You can hear through the vents. We deputies are encouraged to gather intel however we can, and lingering in the plumbing tunnels is one way. Another way is to use a mechanics' sled to roll quietly down the guard walk that separates the tanks in the older part of the jail. The walls of the guard walk are concrete up to waist height, then they're Plexiglas. If you stroll down the walkway, the inmate in the first cell yells out "Man walking!" and all the other inmates stop doing whatever they're doing. But if you slide along quietly on the mechanics' sled they can't see you, and you can stop and peek over the concrete and spy. We call it "sleighriding."

The rest of what I learned was put together by the court-ordered psychiatrist who had read letters that Sammy had written to a then-thirteen-year-old girl named Bernadette Lee, and never mailed.

According to Sammy, by fourteen he was immersed in the Asian underworld, which is pretty much where he'd spent his whole life. He eventually learned who killed his father, and was actually brushing shoulders with them by the time he was sixteen. They were traveling home-invaders, which was a good criminal living in the early Vietnamese refugee years, because the refugees didn't trust American banks. Thus, riches under beds, in safes, etc.

Anyway, Sammy got himself included in a job with these guys, did it well, and was invited along for another. Maybe they thought it was funny, using the son of a guy they'd killed. Maybe they were trying to help him—Sammy didn't know and obviously didn't ask. The next piece of work went well. Working off a tip, Sammy and his bosses had almost $65,000 in cash and jewelry and one terrified family duct-taped and gagged in the garage.

But just as they were ready to get out, young Sammy used his sawed-off twelve-gauge to force one of his bosses to tie and gag the other and sit him down with the family. Then Sammy tied up the other. He cut the first one's throat, made the other watch him bleed out, then cut the second one's. He used a Boker ceramic carried in a calf scabbard. He didn't harm the family, but he made sure they saw everything he did. And he told them to tell everybody they knew except cops that Sammy Nguyen was a good guy but if you crossed him, he'd damage you. In a compromised version of chivalry, he left the family about ten grand's worth of stuff—mostly jewelry.

That's what his letters to Bernadette said.

"You still have no arrests of who killed your father?"

"Not yet."

"Let me out and I'll deliver his killer within twenty-four hours. Talk to the DA, Phil Dent. He can get me out."

"You killed a cop, Sammy."

"I'm innocent. I'll prove I'm innocent."

"Until then, maybe you could find out about Alex."

"I need more phone time to do that."

"You've got half an hour coming up at four."

"I'm only supposed to get fifteen minutes."

"I'll get you a bonus, Sammy. Please produce."

"I've got some stuff on the Cobra Kings," said Sergeant Ray Flatley. Ray was in charge of the Gang Interdiction Unit. I sat in his sheriff's department office, looking out the narrow window at the city of Santa Ana below.

"I appreciate your time, sir."

Flatley's a slight man, graying hair that looks too neat to be real, but it is. He lost his wife to cancer two years ago, and it obviously haunts him. He's a piano player and his wife was a singer, and they used to moonlight as the Sharp Flats— restaurant lounges, private parties, that kind of thing. They played one of my Academy graduation parties. Ray imperson- ated popular singers, could sound like any one of them, really made good fun of them. But his wife was the one with a voice like an angel. I remember seeing his eyes get a little misty when he backed her on "When a Man Loves a Woman," though he'd heard her sing it a thousand times. Actors can mist on cue, but not Gang Interdiction cops.

"Sure," he said. "I always liked Will. We worked crimes against property when we were young."

"He always spoke highly of you too, Sergeant."

He studied me a moment. "Okay. The Cobra Kings are loose, spread across the country, nominal leadership in Houston. Locally, the Cobra Kings have something like forty men and women. They're equal opportunity that way. The older ones are mixed bloods—Vietnamese and American—and they started back in Vietnam after the war. Since then, they've picked up some of everything, mostly the kids who don't fit in racially. They're bad people, Joe. They're hard to figure, hard to penetrate. They've got the business sense of the Asians—they were stealing chips and other high tech hardware years ago, here and up in Silicon Valley. There's some talk of selling contraband to the Chinese for out-of-patent knockoffs, I can't confirm that. They've got the machismo of the American gangs. Their colors are overcoats, and sometimes caps of American baseball teams. The word is the soldiers take a scalp—a life—before they're in."

"Do we have any of them?"

"I wish. Rick Birch wishes. The nearest we have are two up in Pelican Bay—the contract killers who took out the Mexican mafia guy last year."

"With machine guns."

"Of course, we got the fourth guy from Will's murder in the ICU right now—Ike Cao. He's an eyewitness to all of it. If he pulls through, maybe we can get him to talk. The Kings are tough that way—nobody knows anything."

I remembered the four sharp pops as the Tall One silenced his men in the fog.

"Now, here in Southern California the top dog is John Gaylen. Twenty-six years old, born just after the fall of Saigon. Half black American GI and half Vietnamese prostitute, I've heard. Arrested three times for assault and battery—no charges filed. Once for selling stolen goods, no conviction. Once again for conspiracy to commit murder, but he beat us in court. Trouble is, people are scared to testify. We can't get close to him with undercover or even with snitches—he keeps smelling them out. We've tried a couple of times to turn his soldiers, but they won't play."

"Is English his first language?"

Flatley frowned and studied me. "Why?"

"I heard a voice that night. I'll never forget it and I know exactly how it sounded. Deep and very clear, with a funny . . . almost a lilt to it."

"Did it sound ah, maybe a little like this, Joe?"

"Exactly like that."

He smiled. "Vietnamese meets French meets English meets hip-hop and Southern Cal slang. I hear a lot of it."

He shook his head and sighed. For a minute I could tell that he wasn't thinking about John Gaylen at all. Maybe he was thinking what a sweet thing a woman's voice can be.

"Joe, I don't know what language he learned first. Vietnamese, I'd assume. Maybe French. Here, take a look at these. Surveillance pics."

He set a folder on the desk and I opened it. Gaylen looked humorless, a little wicked, too. I was surprised to see a shirt and tie on him, and said so.

"Yeah, the Cobra Kings are sharp dressers. They make a lot of money, like to show it off. Upscale gangsters. Check the toys. Check the girl."

Picture number three showed Gaylen opening the passenger door of a late-model black Mercedes four-door. His suit hung right, like only a good suit can. One hand on the car door, the other at his mouth with a big cigar.

The woman about to get into the car was a sullen black-haired beauty with pale skin and a necklace that sparked with light.

I knew her, because I'd seen her picture about one hour before. Bernadette Lee, the love of Sammy Nguyen's life. Of John Gaylen's, too?

I studied the pictures, eight in all.

Flatley leaned back in his chair. "The men who hit Will, caps and overcoats?"

"Overcoats with the collars pulled up."

"That's what the soldiers wear. We suspect Cobra Kings in a handful of unsolved homicides across the country. One of them here in Orange County. It's always been business, so far as we can tell. Doesn't seem like your father would be doing business with this kind of pond scum."

"I helped him with a lot of his business," I said. "He trusted me and we talked. Never a word about John Gaylen or the Cobra Kings. But that shooter knew who he was—called him by name. It was an execution, sir. No doubt what they were there for."

Flatley raised his eyebrows. "I'm surprised he didn't kill you, too. He left an eyewitness. Maybe two, depending on Cao. A shot in the chest and a shot in the head, though—doesn't look good."

"If he saw me as poorly as I saw him, I wouldn't have been a good target."

Flatley nodded. "What about the cars?"

"I couldn't make them in the headlight beams and the fog."

"The soldiers like the hot little Hondas, you know, the lowered Civics with the big stinger headers. The brass, guys like Gaylen, strictly Daimler-Benz."

"The headlights looked like Hondas. They were loud."

Flatley paused. He looked concerned, but very, very tired.

"Rick Birch has all this. He's one of our best. If there's some-one who can button this case, it's Rick."

"I know."

"He's trying. The Cobra Kings are tough to find because they don't have turf. They're mobile. They're like the damn fog that rolled in on you."

He looked at me again, a skeptical gleam in his eye. "Are you doing some extra work, maybe holding back a little from Rick?"

"Extra, yes, sir. Holding back, no."

He nodded and shrugged. "I understand. I wanted the doctors to let me in on my wife's surgeries. I thought I could do some good. Of course, they talked me out of that. Probably for the best."

"Now I know how you felt."

"You always wonder, though, if you could have done more."

"I do, sir."

"Five guns against one, Joe, and you took out two of them. I wouldn't wonder too much if I were you."

I put on my hat and stood.

"Did you hear about Savannah Blazak? Ten o'clock this morning, the FBI rolled on a sighting way down in San Diego County Rancho Santa Fe. Two eyewitnesses saw her. Both identified her from the press conference last night. By the time Marchant got there she was gone."

"Was she alone?"

"No word on that yet. Marchant didn't say."

I got some dinner at a drive-through and headed home. The food smelled good.

My old Mustang grumbled in the heavy traffic from light to light until I hit the freeway. It's a 1967 model, fairly rare, and I've got it pretty much restored. It's got the original tach and instruments. I put on some aftermarket stuff to up the horse-power. Sounds great when you punch it, and it'll throw your head back in every gear.

But cars on Orange County freeways at six o'clock move about as fast as cars on showroom floors. I only used the alleged freeway for a mile, got off and took my shortcut home, along with several thousand others.

I served the take-out food on one of the partitioned TV dinner trays that I keep for this purpose. I listened to the phone messages while I ate. A lot fewer calls now than the day before. I'd already talked to most of the people I wanted to talk to. I'd declined all of the press and media requests, except for June Dauer of KFOC. So she'd left her third message, asking me to be the subject of her afternoon show one day soon.

I called her back to say no and save her any more calls.

Her voice was pleasant enough and she thanked me for calling her back. I tried to explain why I couldn't do her show when she cut me off and said that her station was part of the Public Broadcasting System, and dedicated to public service. She explained her show, *Real Live*: interviews broadcast live, personal but not prying, informational but "definitely not bottom feeding." She tried to find "newsmakers who aren't necessarily celebrities, real people caught in an interesting moment in their lives."

She told me that she'd always been interested in my story, ever since she heard about the baby who got the acid thrown in his face by his father. She'd seen some pictures of me in the local paper when I was six and played Little League. She remembered the big spread on me when I turned twelve, and the full-color face shot on the front page of the *Journal* Living Section. She said she'd seen me interviewed several times, and still remembered quite clearly the ABC feature when I turned eighteen and was almost done with high school, bound for police science and history classes at Cal State Fullerton.

"I'm sorry but I can't, Ms.—"

"Dauer, June Dauer."

"I won't be able to do an interview, Ms. Dauer."

"Won't be able or aren't willing?"

"Am not willing."

Silence then. I was a little sorry to let her down. I don't like disappointing people.

"Joe?"

"Yes, ma'am, I mean, Ms., I mean— "

"Just say *June*, Joe. *June*. Okay?"

"All right, June."

"Joe, listen to me. I've been wanting to talk to you for just about my whole life. I wrote a report about you when we were both in the sixth grade. You're perfect for *Real Live*. Come *on*, Joe. Give me a chance! You let that lady on channel seven do it, the one who dabbed the tears off her surgically uplifted face while she blubbered her outro. I saw that, Joe, and she *used* you."

"She did? For what?"

"To incite pity in her viewers. I thought it was disgusting. And that was commercial network television—we're *public broadcasting*. We're *poor*!"

I considered this. "Well," I said. "Thanks for being interested."

She sighed. "Joe, you have to do this, and do you know why?"

"No."

"Because out there, there's some little boy or little girl who's going through something just like you did. Maybe something even *worse* than what you went through. And that little person is sitting in their own little, dark little . . . *hell* . . . and they're wondering what the use is, what's the damned use of going on, anyway? And Joe, you never know, but there's a chance that person could be listening when *Real Live* is broadcast. They could hear you and realize they have a chance."

I thought about this. She had a pleasant and honest and convincing voice. "Is inspiration better than pity?"

"I think it is, Joe! Inspiration gets listeners to go beyond themselves. Pity just makes them happy they're not you."

"Okay."

"You'll do it?"

"Yes."

"You might not be extremely happy about doing this, Joe. But I am. And somebody else might be, somebody you don't even know."

"I'm glad that you're pleased."

I was already regretting it while we agreed on a time and day and she gave me the KFOC address up in Huntington Beach.

Two hours later I parked down the street from Alex Blazak's secret place of business. It was a building in the light industrial zone of Costa Mesa—chain-link fence, no lights, dogs barking a few lots over.

I jumped the fence and walked to the door. Then I dialed Blazak's number on my cell phone. I picked the lock, went in, found the lights. Heard my voice on Blazak's answering machine. Saw the alarm pad on the wall. As soon as his machine got my message and clicked off I used his phone to call time, then put the handset beside the receiver. I could trip all the alarms I wanted then, but they couldn't call out.

A lobby. Old carpet, veneer wall panels, a countertop of peeling vinyl. The glass case under the counter was empty and dirty. There had been lights fixed inside the case, but there was nothing but wires now.

The room behind the lobby was large, with low ceilings and very good fluorescent lighting. No windows, pegboard walls, one door.

There were six circular stands arranged in a semicircle. The two on the left were long guns. The two in the middle were carbines and saddle rifles. The two on the right looked like military stuff. There were free-standing cases along three of the walls: pistols, automatics, machine pistols, derringers, knives, bayonets, swords, daggers, exotic martial arts weapons—*nunchuks,* throwing stars, throwing darts, throwing knives—blackjacks, metal knuckles, straight razors. Even an open case of antipersonnel bombs—the little finned ovals designed to penetrate helmets and skulls when dropped from above.

I toured. The place looked like something a TV-addled twelve-year-old would dream about. Or a deranged high schooler. Over two hundred guns, a hundred knives and exotic weapons. The ammunition was still in cases, stacked and organized along the far wall.

Beside the ammo cases was a stairway that led to a loft. In the loft I found a desk, two sofas with blankets and pillows on them, two chairs, a TV and computer, a bathroom and kitchenette. There was a coffee table between the sofas, complete with weapon-freak magazines, and an ashtray fashioned from the bottom inch of a large artillery shell.

In the ashtray were two half-smoked cigars. One was a Macanudo, the other didn't have a label. There was also a white stick with a small, flat purple circle on the end. Beside the tray was a book of matches from Bamboo 33.

The kitchenette had a small refrigerator that contained unspoiled milk and orange juice, bread, apples. The sell-by date on the milk was one week away. The apples were firm and the bread unopened. On the counter were almost-ripe bananas and a package of cookies that were not stale. I turned on the TV: a cartoon channel.

The bathroom had more magazines and a big can of room deodorant on the sink counter. Dirty mirror, clean toilet bowl, rattling fan.

I took some toilet paper and went back to the ashtray where I wrapped the cigar butts and put them in my pocket. Then the white stick. While I was picking out the stick I saw the Davidoff cigar label, neatly cut through the narrow part, still in its circular shape. I got another piece of toilet paper and took it, too.

I hoped Melissa, my friend in the crime lab, might be able to get DNA for me. Human saliva is rich in it.

Someone had been using the place to crash. Recently. The food and drink weren't a week old yet. The cartoon channel didn't seem like first pick for Crazy Alex Blazak. He'd probably graduated to Power Rangers. And it was hard to picture him working on a grape sucker.

Late that night Bo Warren knocked on my front door. When I opened it he smiled at me. His eyes looked merry in the porchlight.

"Joe, I just had to tell you, nobody on Earth can do what you did to me today and not pay a high price for it."

"I guess that's fair warning, sir."

"Could be any place, any time."

"I heard Marchant got pretty close to Savannah down in Rancho Santa Fe."

Warren shook his head. "Morons. So help us out, Joe. Do what your father did. Find her. The offer stands, the million if you do."

"You guys spend millions like I spend quarters."

"That's called *noblesse oblige,* you dumb ape. And don't forget trickle-down."

"What do you care if the Bureau finds her first?"

"Jack doesn't want her shot, for one thing. Alex either. Doesn't want a bunch of press in on it. Just a nice, quiet reunion is what that million is all about."

I thought about Crazy Alex and his calm, polite sister. "I'll try to find her, regardless of the money."

He looked at me hard, then. "Why bother?"

"I liked her."

He shook his head slightly, like I was crazy. "You're like that Guatemalan the Newport cops iced."

"In what way?"

"Trying to get inside. Trying to get where the big people are. Using crude tools and blunt instruments."

"I think you've got that wrong."

"We'll see."

He made a gun out of his finger and shot me in the gut, then in the head.

"Night, Joe. Don't let the bedbugs bite."

That night I dreamed poppies because I always dream poppies, a bright orange blanket of them that stretches up a mountain, but when I move closer I see they are not flowers but flames, and they are not on a mountain but on a human cheek magnified greatly, and that cheek is mine. Then I dream the pain.

I dreamed thick cables. Black pliant cables dangling all around me, covering me, smothering me. All I can do is try to climb them. I grab. I pull. I gather. Then I dream the pain. And when I wake up I'm clawing at the scars on my face, trying to pull them away.

I dreamed waves eating away beaches, revealing bone. Of rain washing rocks that bleed. Of a desert wind that melts the sand and leaves only gristle, gums, teeth. Of thick ivy consuming tree trunks made of skin.

I don't remember the agony, only that there was awareness of agony. I remember understanding that an overwhelming and decisive event was happening to me, that it involved one of the two great presences in my life. I remember sudden darkness and sudden light. I remember, later, the patient pulse of scars taking shape, the endless hours it took them to form. To me, that time was geologic. Surgeons. Grafts. Transplants. Patches. Gauze, mirrors, ointments. Half face, half horror.

And after all the time that's gone by, these hard scars are still wired to the past like an alarm, and when I brush them now they ignite a moment twenty-three years ago that was loud, crazy and murderous. It's still happening.

Oh, and I dreamed the faces of beautiful women.

I always do.

Chapter Six

On Monday the FBI launched its public manhunt for Alex Blazak. The story of Alex, the disturbed twenty-one-year-old, hit the papers that morning and TV that evening. Plenty of good photographs, accounts of his violence, many references to the fact that he was a "firearms dealer," which he wasn't, and a "suspected trafficker in illegal weapons," which he was.

Over the next two days there were two hot sightings of Alex, and the Bureau's Emergency Response Team rolled on both of them. But Marchant couldn't get his men out fast enough either time. It was like Alex had a sixth sense. One sighting was up in the mountain resort of Big Bear. Alex had rented a spacious two-bedroom chalet on the north shore. The second was a hotel up on the Sunset Strip in Hollywood.

According to the news, the witnesses said that Savannah was with him in both places. I thought of the fresh food in Alex's warehouse, the unopened loaf of bread, the not-quite-yellow bananas and the sell-by dates on the milk and juice. And I had to believe that somehow, Alex had done what I had failed to do that night. He'd found her in the fog and gotten her into his car. After what happened at Lind Street, she was probably glad to see him. A kidnapping brother must have been an improvement over five murderers in overcoats.

I tacked a map to my kitchen wall and drew red circles around the three sightings. Now he had her again and he was moving often and quickly, one step ahead of the snapping jaws of the Bureau. I wondered when, in all the running, he'd try to ransom her again. Why didn't he just use his tennis-bag million to clear out, dump his sister and head to Mexico?

I called Marchant twice a day but he didn't call back. I figured maybe he was catching his breath.

A friend of Will's at Anaheim Medical Center gave me twice-daily updates on the condition of murder suspect Ike Cao: unchanged, extremely critical condition, unconscious in the ICU, round-the-clock security by the sheriff department.

Dr. Norman Zussman called me twice more, and ordered me to return his call as soon as possible to set up a counseling appointment for the Deputy-Involved Shooting.

Reluctantly, I did.

June Dauer of KFOC called to confirm our interview. It fell on the day of Will's funeral, but I confirmed it anyway, because her voice was so hopeful and pleasant to listen to.

We buried Will on the first day of summer. It was Thursday, eight days after his death.

The Reverend Daniel Alter presided over a very crowded memorial service that was held in his enormous tinted-glass house of worship, the Chapel of Light. But the mourners numbered over two thousand, and when all the seats were filled the overflow crowd was herded into an auditorium with huge closed-circuit monitors on all four walls.

My brothers, true blood sons of Will and Mary Ann, sat on either side of me at the memorial service.

Will, Jr. wept. He's ten years older than me, married with

three children, a patent attorney, lives up in Seattle. Glenn, two years younger than Will, Jr., is married also, with young twins. They live in San Jose, where Glenn heads a company that runs fiber optic cable into new subdivisions. He stared straight ahead like he was seeing nothing, or maybe everything.

Mary Ann sat nearest the aisle, shrouded in black. I could hear her quiet sobs throughout the memorial service, and for most of it her eyes were focused on the floor.

The casket was mahogany and silver. It was donated by friends of Will's who owned the cemetery where he would be buried. Mary Ann decided to leave it open for viewing after talking to us three boys and the Reverend Alter. Glenn said to leave it closed because of the pain that Will's face would cause his loved ones. Ditto Daniel. Will, Jr. voted open, for the same reason. I voted open, too, because I wanted to see him again.

The dais was covered with white roses, thousands of them, draping from stand to floor, pouring like a liquid over the purple carpet and proscenium steps. They were donated by one of Will's friends, who owned a chain of flower stores.

Will's burial suit was given by a friend with his own line of Italian designed clothing. His fingers were manicured by Mary Ann's cosmetologist, no charge, of course.

With some fanfare, the Grove Club Foundation created a memorial fund that would benefit the new Hillview Home for Children. That morning the Orange County *Journal* reported that close to two million dollars had been donated in just three days—with a million of it coming from Jack and Lorna Blazak.

The Reverend Alter was very moving that day. He's one of the most emotional evangelists I've ever heard, but his performances are never loud or rhetorical or histrionic. They're solid and deeply felt. Or at least they seem that way. He may be a fine actor, but when his voice caught and his throat tightened and the tears ran off his face like rain, well, it got to me.

*. . . and God's merciful hands have received you back, Will
Trona, you, who offered helping hands to so many. . . .*

I stared at my own hands, fingers intertwined, the pulse in
my right wrist steady and blue. For whatever reasons, I kept an
eye on the thick yellow electrical cord trailed by the videocam
dedicated to stage left. Funny how your mind will focus on the
irrelevant when something important is taking place. But the yellow cord made me think of the two cars trapping us in the alley.
Almost everything I saw made me think of those cars and the
men inside them. I wondered if Rick Birch had requested a log
of calls made to and from Will's cell phone that night.

*. . . so as we mourn this death let us not forget to celebrate
this life. . . .*

Big jerks of Will, Jr.'s chest. He's always been an emotional
guy. Once he shot a sparrow with a BB gun, cried hard. I told
him not to shoot things for fun. He took it to heart. Because of
my face, people like to think I've got insight, moral weight. As
if the uglier you are on the outside the more beautiful you are
inside. Nice little formula, but not true. The only thing I had
over Junior was I knew what pain felt like, and I'd figured the
sparrow did, too.

I set my hand on my brother's knee. I gave him one of the
monogrammed handkerchiefs Will taught me to always carry
for the ladies. Before leaving home, I put four of them into
various pockets of my black funeral jacket. I'd already given
one to Mom. Two down.

*. . . and let rapture of God's glory be felt in the rapture of
our sadness. . . .*

I turned around just once to look at the crowd, a sea of grieving faces stretching all the way back to the blue glass walls that
rose in dizzying bevels into the pale June sky.

Just when I thought the service was over, the upper glass
walls of the Chapel of Light receded into the lower sections and

a great warm huff of air swept in. A collective murmur. Then thousands of white doves rose from behind the Reverend Alter. He spread his arms skyward and it looked like they were flying out his fingers. Their wings beat loud and they climbed in the hushed chapel and you could hear the panic beginning in them. But then they realized that the sky was all around them on four sides and they lifted away into the afternoon. They were pen-raised birds, had never flown before. White feathers dusted us as we made our way out of the chapel for the cemetery. I thought of Savannah Blazak, going over that wall and into the cool suburban night.

Maybe half the people wanted to see Will's body one last time. It took an hour. I was the second one, right after Glenn. I had seen cadavers in the lab and accident fatalities still bleeding. I'd seen Luke Smith and Ming Nixon. But this was my first *viewing*. Nothing had prepared me for the shock of seeing death on the face of someone I loved. I looked at him and I realized what a great power, what a great presence, what a great *life* had ended. I kissed my fingertips and ran them over his hard cheek and walked outside.

Tears swelled from my heart, and a cold passion for revenge rose up with them. I pulled my hat down low.

What I remember about the burial was the bright green expanse of grass on the hillsides and the long black motorcade inching to a stop around the hole in the ground. The hole was covered by a black tarp, betrayed only by the mounds of orange earth around the cover.

I stood there and watched the cars arrive, and I wondered how those shooters had known where Will and I would be.

Had they followed us, or had they been told where we were going? Did the people who sent us to that address also commit the murder? Was Will sent there to save Savannah Blazak, or only to die?

I hoped those killers had been waiting for us. Because, if they'd been waiting for us, I'd simply missed them. Maybe someday I could forgive myself for being surprised. But if they'd followed us, I'd failed Will in an even more flagrant way.

Mouth shut, eyes open.

My mind wandered, but it kept coming back to those cars, those men, that night. I knew I should feel pity for the men I'd shot. And guilt for taking their lives. I tried to allow myself to feel those things but I didn't. There's a cold place inside me where I put the bad things. It's like a freezer but the door is heavier. And once I put them in there, it's hard to get them out. I told myself that they were bad men who would have murdered me next, absolutely. This justified what I'd done, and the freezer door was closed now. But I couldn't close the door on all of the ifs: if I'd seen them earlier, if I'd thought faster, if I'd listened to my unsettled nerves, if the fog hadn't rolled in.

I watched from a distance as the mourners filed past my family. I'd said all I could say to anyone. So I faded back under a dense elm tree, alone, eyes open and mouth shut, hat brim down for privacy and shade.

I knew most of the people there. I saw Will's fellow supervisors; mayors and assemblypersons; judges; sheriff's department brass; the governor of California; two Congressional Representatives. Some were friends and some were enemies, but they all came.

The developers were all there. Land is still the most valuable commodity, the biggest money-maker in Orange County. Will had had disagreements with every one of them. And in his own strange way, friendships with many of them, too. I recognized the foot soldiers—the well-spoken guys and gals who make multimillions for their companies every year—The Irvine Company, Philip Morris, Rancho Santa Margarita Company. Their bosses were there, too, the CEOs and CFOs, chairmen of boards—the kinds of guys who come and go in their own jets and helicopters.

Then the entrepreneurs, the billionaires who did it on their own: technology whizzes, young darlings of the NASDAQ, inventors, marketers of all kinds. Jack Blazak, who'd made his first fortune with yellow lawn sprinklers that wouldn't clog, was there, of course. He looked even worse than the last time I'd seen him, as if every day his daughter was gone took another cubic foot of life out of him.

Next on the power scale were the bureaucrats. Will's cohorts, the pit bulls of government—humble and unassuming one minute, territorial and unmoving the next. They work for Districts, Agencies, Bureaus, Offices, Administrations, Commissions, Services, Sections, Departments, Boards, Authorities. They've got no money compared to developers or entrepreneurs, but they have power over them. That power can be friendly and helpful and profitable for everyone at times. It can make or break. The cost is negotiable.

Will was a bureaucrat, I may be one someday, too. I have probably the best training a bureaucrat can have: my first five institutional years.

Then there were his friends and family and neighbors and acquaintances; his doctor, his barber, his tennis pro. Even our old trash collector was there, a young father of three way back when I was a kid, now a middle-aged man with gray hair, a stiff body and lines of sadness around his eyes. Will used to yak it up with him on Wednesdays at 6:30 A.M., trash day on our street, before he dropped me off at the bus stop, then went on to the sheriff's department headquarters for work.

I watched them and wondered at how many lives a life is

made up of. I felt proud and empty at the same time. I felt invaded and defeated.

I felt betrayed when Jennifer Avila, chokingly beautiful in black, spoke to my mother.

Betrayed by Will, and somehow, by Jennifer, too.

My heart pounded hard, then hardly at all. The things I looked at were a little blurred—my eyes weren't working right. I felt a thick hot sweat on my back. How was I going to talk to a radio host in just a few short hours? I actually shuddered, hot as I was in my black suit.

Old Carl Rupaski, head of the Orange County Transportation Authority—and an admitted political enemy of my father's—lumbered over to my tree and shook my hand. His eyes were moist. I could smell tobacco and alcohol on him. "I want to talk to you sometime, Joe. Maybe when we're both not in shock. How about lunch next week, Monday, say?"

"Yes, sir. That would be fine."

He clamped a heavy hand onto my arm. "This is really the shits, kid. Really the shits."

Jaime Medina joined me in the shade after that. He looked more forlorn and wronged than usual, more stooped and hapless. We talked about Will for a while, and Jaime told me how much Will had done for the HACF, how things were going to be tough now, with their champion in government gone, and a criminal investigation pending.

"I never told those guys they could vote before they were citizens," he said. "It's a misunderstanding. That's all. What's a few dozen votes, anyway?"

I shrugged. I couldn't get worked up about HACF problems right then.

"You want to help us?"

"How, sir?"

"I got someone I want you to talk to. It's a big scandal. You can make some waves, become famous."

"I don't want to be famous."

"You already are. This would make you the new champion of justice. Look, talk to this boy. He's the brother of Miguel Domingo, the one the cops murdered. He's got a story to tell. You see, Miguel Domingo had a *reason* for trying to get into that gated place in Newport Beach. It's got to do with the woman."

"What woman?"

"Luria Blas, killed outside her apartment. Interested?"

"No, thank you, I have a lot to do right now."

"Such as what, Joe?"

"Look around you, sir."

Jaime did. He sighed. "I'm going to call you. We'll talk at a better time."

A few minutes later, Rick Birch ambled up. He stood beside me, rather than in front of me, which I thought was interesting. He looked out at the crowd with me. I liked the fact that he didn't say anything for a while. When he did talk, it wasn't about anything I could have anticipated.

"My brother was murdered when I was ten," he said. "He was eight years older than me—tough kid, tough neighborhood up in Oakland. Found him in a gutter behind a bar. No arrests. Made me want to become a cop, catch creeps, put them in jail."

"That's a good reason, sir."

"You holding up?"

"Yes, sir."

"Look, I've got John Gaylen coming in for a little informal talk tomorrow. I'd like you there, on the other side of the glass."

"Absolutely."

* * *

Later, at the wake, we three brothers found ourselves in a corner together. We were up sixteen stories in the Newport Marriott Hotel, in a restaurant provided for free by the manager, another friend of Will's. You could see the ocean from there, a smoke-gray plate under the June sky.

Will, Jr. and Glenn were drunk. I drank a lot too, for me anyway. I usually don't drink much, because it makes me feel less ready.

My brothers were both flying out the next day, back to their family lives and their jobs, and they felt bad about leaving Mary Ann and me.

Will, Jr. hugged me. "Anything I can do to help, Joe. All you have to do is call."

Then Glenn: "Take care of Mom. I wish I lived closer, to help with that. And take care of yourself, too."

Their children rushed past us, Will, Jr.'s waving cocktail swords and umbrellas, chasing the twins.

I felt abandoned by them. Why couldn't they just stop their lives, move back to Southern California for a while, help me find out who and why?

Because it wasn't practical. Life had to go on. What Will would have wanted, and all that.

We stood there a moment and watched the children play, and I understood one beautiful, heartbreaking truth: life was going on already.

I was the last person to leave the wake. I had a little time before my interview with June Dauer on KFOC, so I spent it with another martini and a window seat there on the sixteenth story. The restaurant workers took away the chafing dishes and the tables, rolling the circular ones, folding the rectangles. I listened to the clank of chairs and the grunts of labor but those sounds seemed to be happening a million miles away from me.

Everything did.

I was dreading the interview but I had another drink and went anyway.

I was drunk when I got there. More than I thought I was when I left the hotel. I regretted it. All I'd wanted to do was forget, and here I was, expected to remember. In front of a thousand bored listeners.

I remember sitting in a cool reception room with purple carpet and orange chairs with chrome legs. I chewed two pieces of cinnamon gum and drank black coffee. I watched the wadded-up gum foil roll around inside my hat.

Then the producer of *Real Live* came in, a smiling young man with long hair and a goatee. He introduced himself as Sean.

"June's about ready," he said. "Water, soft drink?"

"More coffee, please."

"Here's the green room. Have a seat and I'll get you some coffee. How 'bout a shot of Kahlua in that, take off the edge?"

"Better not."

I sat and looked out at the broadcast booths. Three dark, one dimly lit. In the lit one, a young woman with curly black hair was standing by one of the boom mikes, head down, apparently reading something on the table. The glass caught her reflection and reproduced her at an odd angle. I watched the reflection.

Sean came back with a foam cup and set it on the table in front of me. "Hot," he said. "We're on at the top of the hour. Just a few minutes. By the way, man, I'm sorry about what happened to your father."

"Thank you."

He hesitated, then walked out.

Five minutes later he escorted me into the lit booth. The sounds inside it were flat and the light was soft and silver. The curly haired woman came around the table and offered her hand.

"June Dauer."

"Nice to meet you, Ms. Dauer."

She smiled. Her eyes were dark and her face was very pretty. The lines of her jaw were straight and strong. Small nose, small mouth. She had on a sleeveless denim blouse tucked into wrinkled shorts, socks rolled down, blue canvas sneakers. Her legs were well shaped. She shook my hand.

"Joe, I'm so sorry this interview timed out with your father's funeral. I would never have scheduled it this way if I'd known."

"We didn't make the arrangements until after, Ms. Dauer. It's no trouble at all."

She shook her head, looking at me with her eyes narrowed just a little. "I asked you to leave those good manners at home, now, didn't I?"

"Sorry, I—"

"Relax, Joe. Have a seat here and put those headphones on. We'll do a voice check and then get it on."

I sat on the swivel chair, watched her round the table to the other side, then set my hat on the table in front of me. She sat down and rolled her chair forward. The studio was mostly dark, with a gentle overhead spotlight that set her off from the quiet shadows. I looked up and saw a light spotting me, too. My face felt hot and my collar felt tight and my heart was pounding like I was running a race. I put on the headphones and took three deep breaths and felt worse. I was about to go up to the Quiet Spot but June Dauer's clear, light voice suddenly entered my skull.

"Count to ten, Joe, normal voice. Get your mouth about three inches from the mike. Speak off to the side just a little, not straight on."

I did all that.

"Good, good. Had a little to drink, Joe?"

"More than usual."

"What's usual?"

"Hardly anything."

"You a good drunk?"

"Guess we'll find out."

She looked through the glass into the next room, where Sean nodded.

"And three, and two and one," he said. "And you are *on.*"

There was music, and a recorded voice announcing the show. Then she did an introduction. She told a little bit about my past and used the phrase "Acid Baby," which made my nerves bristle like it always did. When she spoke she kept her arms close to her sides and stared across the table at me like I was a zoo bear. Her voice was clear, with a little bit of a whisper in it, like she was only talking to one person. The earphones gave her head a funny shape and her curls stuck up behind the flat spot made by the band.

I'm a little hazy on how the first half of the interview went. I was nervous. I do remember that at first, my answers were just one or two words, and my voice was unusually thin and distant. I answered the same questions I'd answered a thousand times. I had stock responses all ready, from years of practice, and I gave them.

Thor. What happened. Pain. Memory. Surgery. Hillview. Other kids. Will and Mary Ann. School. Being known as "The Acid Baby." Baseball. College. Sheriff's Department. Working the jail.

But then June studied me from across the table and I focused on her eyes, which caught the overhead light in a way that made them very bright. And I began to feel relaxed and comfortable.

"I admire the way you've overcome all this, Joe. I've been following your story for years. You've made a good life out of a tragic beginning. People need to know that *they* can do it, too."

"It was mainly my parents. My adoptive parents, I mean."

She asked me what advice I could give to people with problems—especially young people. Where do you find genuine self-confidence? How do you keep away the anger and self-pity?

I gave her the stock answers I always give: believe in yourself, don't be afraid to be different, remember that there are always people worse off than you.

Then she asked something I'd never been asked before.

"Joe—what do you think when you look at a beautiful *face*?"

Maybe it was the newness of the question. Maybe it was the funeral or the alcohol or the heat inside my suit. Maybe it was just because beautiful faces are one of the few subjects I feel qualified to address. I'm not sure what caused it, but I suddenly wanted to talk.

"I think that person is lucky. I love beautiful faces, Ms. Dauer. There are so many kinds. I could stare at one for hours. But you know something? It's not that easy to do. Not many people will let you look at their face unless you know them."

"You must know a lot of people."

"Some. But you don't want to just stare."

"No. So what do you do?"

She leaned back a little and watched me closely. I saw the light hitting her hair, and the bright sparkle in her eyes again. I was aware of the dusky half-light of the sound booth, and of the muted acoustics. For a moment it seemed like June Dauer was the only other person in the whole building. Like we were alone and I was talking only to her.

"I watch movies or TV, June. Read magazines. I like romantic comedies with perfect faces in them. Sometimes I'll go to crowded places where I can get lost and just observe. But it all happens so fast. The movies and TV shows end, the people on the beach walk on or turn away, the shoppers in the mall pass by, so there's not enough time to really enjoy and appreciate a face."

"I know what you mean. It's like you're in a different world than theirs. Cut off, separate. I feel the same way sometimes, sitting here in this studio and talking to people out in the real world."

Suddenly I realized what a pleasure it was to be talking to June Dauer. She looked so alone in that beam of light, surrounded by the near-dark. I forgot where I was and why I was there, and that I had had too much to drink. And I just talked to her.

"Exactly, June. Like they're not *real.* I mean, none of those faces are real, in the sense that you could touch one, especially the faces in a crowd. You definitely can't touch those."

"No, you don't want to try that."

"Not that I want touch. I do not want to touch or be touched."

June Dauer leaned forward toward her mike. She was frowning slightly, like her earphones weren't working right or something.

"Don't want to touch or be touched? Do you think that's healthy?"

"I never think about it, Ms. Dauer."

"I've never heard anyone say that before. Everyone is always so hungry for contact. But you know, it seems to me that you could find plenty of beautiful faces to have a cup of coffee with you, talk, let you appreciate them."

"I paid a model once, to sit still and let me stare. Tracy. She was young and just starting off and needed the money. She came back one time and let me stare at her again, three hours for three hundred dollars. What a face she had. Unimaginable beauty. We had coffee after the second time, then talked. I liked her very much. I thought about her every day, then every hour, then every minute. I didn't call for a while because I wanted to get myself under control, didn't want to seem needy and scare her off. Later, when I did call, her roommate said she'd moved to Milan. I wrote her but didn't hear back."

A pause then in our conversation, while June Dauer looked at me. "I think that's sad. Well, now that we're kind of on the subject, what about dating, Joe? Do you date?"

"To be honest, my experience with dating is limited. I'm aware of my effect on women, and it doesn't seem right to frighten someone just so I can stare at her face."

I realized I was doing just that—staring at June Dauer's face. I looked away but bumped my cheek against the mike. It made a tremendous amplified thud. She laughed. She had a wonderful laugh, one of the nicest I'd heard.

"That was me, folks," she said. "Falling off my chair because Joe Trona stared at me!"

I felt my face get hot, but I smiled. I try to smile as little as possible because it's not something people enjoy seeing.

"Joe, I've noticed that you have very good manners. Why?"

"To put people at ease. And years ago, I thought women might find good manners attractive."

"In general, we do. So . . ."

"But you need more than good manners. You've got to . . . it's hard to explain. See . . . you don't want to be perceived as just a big scar under a hat saying yes, please. No, thank you. Or, it's a nice day today, isn't it, Ms. Dauer? You don't want to come off like a talking baboon, or an English butler morphed into Swamp Thing. You know what I mean?"

She paused just a beat, then. Like I'd caught her off guard.

"No, not really, Joe. But that's why I wanted you on the show. How *do* women react to you?"

"I had one date. She acted like being with me was completely normal. She fooled me until we were alone in her apartment and she asked to touch my face. I said she could touch it because I didn't want to disappoint her. I closed my eyes and set my jaws and waited. She took forever. I could hear her breathing. Then I felt her fingertip. I couldn't stand it. I held still as well as I could, but I started shaking. When I opened my eyes she was crying. I got up and apologized for making her cry, then left."

"Why did you leave?"

"Because she was crying. I don't want to be considered pathetic, Ms. Dauer. Repellent is acceptable. Repellent is appropriate. But pathetic is something I can't stand."

Again, that little pause before she spoke. And the same frown she'd had before.

"Let's change gears here. Joe Trona—what are you most proud of in your life?"

I thought about that. "That Will and Mary Ann Trona would take me."

The second I said that I remembered what I'd been doing just a few hours earlier. And then I remembered that night on Lind Street, and all the opportunities I'd had to make things come out better. And I realized I was talking to a whole county, not just to a woman who seemed sympathetic and easy to talk to.

"Are you proud of yourself at all, for the way you've handled adversity and overcome some pretty heavy roadblocks?"

"No."

"Okay, Joe—we've got two seconds left, so describe yourself in two words! Don't think—*two words!*"

I heard the music start up.

"Come on, Joe!"

"Needs improvement," I said.

June Dauer's voice came over the music.

"Don't we all! Joe Trona *is* Real Live. So are *you* and don't forget it. This is June Dauer saying have a nice evening, and if you can't be happy then be quiet! 'Til next time."

She pushed away the mike, lifted off her earphones and set them down in front of her. The overhead light was still catching her eyes and she was still frowning.

"Thank you."

"You're welcome." I felt a warm wave of relief break over me, took a deep breath, sagged. I wondered if there was such a thing as Stockholm Syndrome for media guests, because I felt half in love with June Dauer for getting me through the show.

"Let's walk it off," she said. "I had a public-speaking guru in here one day, she was so nervous when it was over she went into the restroom and vomited."

"I'm not going to do that."

"Come on."

We went back to the lobby, then outside. We walked. I get extremely self-conscious around an attractive woman, so I tried to keep half a step ahead and a good yard aside from her.

"I am not diseased," she said.

"Sorry. I get in a hurry."

"So slow down. You can't outwalk your own nerves."

I slowed down. It was almost six o'clock by then but still light. Just starting to cool. It seemed like the afternoon could last forever, like it was a record that skipped and kept playing the same phrase over and over. Walking in the sunlight, I wondered at all I'd said to her in the last half hour. It already seemed a long time ago.

The KFOC studios were on a junior college campus, so we strolled past the low buildings and the kiosks flapping with fliers. The rubber trees were deep green and shiny and the students had worn wide paths across the corners of the grass.

I took off my jacket and folded it over my arm. A cool evening breeze came through my shirt. While I pretended to arrange the jacket on my arm I watched June Dauer, who was turned slightly away, looking at the clouds. The same breeze that cooled my back lifted the curls off her forehead and showed her ears. Little red rubies in them. I imagined cupping two handfuls of those stones and gently pouring them over her head, watching them spill through her dark curls, run down her shoulders and legs, bounce and clatter around her feet—I don't know why. Too much to drink, I guess.

Or maybe it was TUT. Will had told me a few things about love and women. He told me to look for a sinner with a sense of humor. He told me to go into love with my eyes open and into marriage with my eyes shut. The other was *Look for TUT.*

TUT is The Unknown Thing. Some women have it, some don't. You might see it first in her eyes. It might be in her voice. It might be in her hands. You'll start to see it, then you'll realize it's all over her. But you'll never know what it is, because it's The Unknown Thing. TUT makes you come back. And back again and again. It's the glue, but you never know what it is. Mary Ann has gobs of it.

I kept looking at June Dauer but she looked at me so I turned away, face going warm.

It was obviously TUT. I saw it in her face, her eyes, the straight firm line of her chin. I'd seen it before but never in such blazing clarity. And so much of it.

"How were the services, Joe?"

"Very good. Reverend Daniel released a million white doves in the Chapel of Light. Then opened the ceiling and they flew out."

"Beautiful."

"It was the first time they'd flown."

"How could you tell?"

"They raise them in pens."

"Wow, first time you use your wings and you get organ music and two thousand people watching."

We walked around in a big square and ended up outside the studio. She offered her hand and I shook it and looked at her. In the outside light she was much more beautiful. Her skin was dark and a little bit moist. Her eyes, which had looked black in the studio, were actually a rich brown.

"Thanks for opening up," she said. "You were very generous with me. And who knows, Joe? Maybe some listener out there has had some problems, too. Maybe you inspired him to get on with his life. Her life. Whatever. I mean, you helped me fill a half hour of time—that's my job. But maybe you did something more than that."

"I hope so."

I drove home, then turned around and drove back to KFOC again. It's about a twenty-minute ride.

I felt foolish sitting in that parking lot, so I drove home for the second time in an hour. But I felt wrong there, somehow . . . stalled, so I drove *back* to the KFOC studios and parked again and took a deep breath and walked quickly to the lobby. *The Unknown Thing.* I took off my hat and asked the receptionist if I could possibly see Ms. Dauer.

The receptionist looked alarmed.

But June Dauer came down the studio hallway, smiling. "Come on back, Joe. We'll do a live-on-tape for a rainy day!"

"I can't," I said. "I can't stay. I just wanted to tell you that I'd appreciate having a date with you. We'll do whatever you want."

The receptionist smiled and looked busy.

June Dauer looked at me and laughed. "The only things I don't like are splatter movies and restaurants where they sing happy birthday. But maybe we should just have a cup of coffee, get acquainted."

"I'm extremely honored."

"Let's see what you think *after*."

We agreed on a time and place to meet and I drove home. It felt like the tires of my Mustang were floating a foot over the asphalt, though the car still handled quite well.

At first I thought it was the alcohol but I was stone sober by then. My heart was beating hard and fast so I rolled down both the front windows and let the wind blast in.

I didn't think about Will, or the men in those cars, for almost five straight minutes.

Chapter Seven

I used that endless summer evening to do something I'd been wanting to do for days but never had the chance to.

Back at my little house in Orange, I pulled Will's car out of the garage and into the driveway beside the house. There's a gate across that driveway, and when it's closed you get a nice privacy back there: the little house, the little yard, the big orange tree, the detached garage, the drive.

After changing from my funeral suit, I used that privacy and the long evening light to wash the car, by hand, every inch of it inside and out. The blood was impossible to get out of the tan leather, but I cleaned and conditioned it as best I could. The right front floormat was drenched in it, so I shampooed it twice, let it sit, then shampooed it again. There's no getting blood off of things like that.

So the dank and meaty smell of it mixed with the chipper aromas of shampoo and leather cleaner, and I guessed the car would smell that way forever.

I felt very close to him then. We spent so many hours in that car together. I could see him sitting there, leaning forward to check the tach, asking me how fast, bracing himself for one of those curves he liked so much. Or opening the black briefcase on his lap and peering in. Or leaning back and squinting out at the world with that disapproving but somehow hopeful gaze.

In the fading light I walked around his car, running my fingers along the smooth black paint. Nice animal. I'd washed it twice a week by hand, waxed it every month, steam cleaned the engine compartment and undercarriage every sixty days. I did Will's modifications myself, damn the lease: installed the Dinan chip; replaced the stock muffler for one that upped the horsepower a little and gave the sedan the rumble of a '70 Roadrunner; traded out the sixteen-inch alloys for stainless custom wheels. The only thing I didn't do was the scheduled maintenance, which fell to the County. I decided to keep the car until they demanded it back, even though it cost three times my yearly salary.

But I wasn't really thinking about these things as I ran my hand over the black flank of Will's car: I was wondering again if we'd been followed or ambushed.

Did they lead us there or follow us there?

I wanted to believe they had led us there. That they knew all along where we would finally land, on Lind Street in Anaheim. *And how could they have followed me?* It was night, but I was paying attention to the lights and the cars around us. I always did. And when Will said to flog it, I'd definitely flogged it. I remembered the needle hitting 114 mph. How had two cars kept up with me at speeds like that, without me seeing them?

Idea.

I jacked up the rear end of the car. That done, I got into a new pair of latex gloves, then lay down on my mechanics' sled and rolled under the car. Not enough light to see. So I pushed out, got the flashlight from the trunk and went under again.

The undercarriage was clean, just the way I had always kept it. I ran my left hand along the sides of the fuel tank, the muffler, the differential. Then along the axle and the rear struts. And last, under the plastic fender skirt and along the chassis. There, I found something I didn't recognize by touch.

It took some time to get it off—two trips to the workbench to find the shortest screwdriver I had. Just enough clearance.

Finally I lifted it off with two fingers and set in on the concrete beside my head. I turned my head and looked at it.

A short-wave transmitter, about the size of an electric razor. Designed to broadcast just one frequency.

A frequency broadcast for just one thing: to be followed.

I thought about that for a long moment. And about Will and Savannah, five men with guns, and a million dollars in a tennis bag. Even with the transmitter I still didn't want to admit they'd followed me there.

I took it inside the house and dusted it for fingerprints. I've been practicing fingerprint technique on my own, ever since I was twelve, when Will told me he'd like me to be a deputy someday. Good thing. Three nice latents—a thumb on the side and two fingers on the top. The lifts came out perfect: Dragon's Blood powder on white tape.

I took the transmitter outside and looked at it closely in the fading sunlight. I wondered. Since they knew I was dumb enough to fall for it once, maybe they figured I'd fall for it twice.

Maybe I already had.

So I slid under the car and screwed it back into place.

Then called my friend Melissa in the crime lab and asked her another favor.

I got Will's black leather briefcase from the floor safe.

The familiar smell came to me first. Then the familiar shape. I could hardly imagine him without it: on his lap in the car while I drove; in his hand as he marched into a room and made that room his own like only Will could do; dangling at his left side as he shook hands and looked somebody in the eye and won their vote with a firm grasp and a well-chosen word or two. Or sitting on the hot asphalt parking lot of the HACF as he listened to Jennifer Avila say she loved him.

Yes, I wanted to be close to him right then.

And it had also occurred to me that the reason for his death could be in there, somewhere among the people he knew. This, because of something Will had told me a thousand times: love a lot, trust a few.

I took the briefcase into the garage and got into Will's BMW. I sat in his place so the steering wheel wouldn't be in my way. I set the briefcase across my lap, just like Will used to do. I turned on the reading light and opened the case.

I surveyed the everyday tools of my father's life: date book and calendar; calculator; checkbook and wallet; a yellow legal pad with his handwriting on the top page; a small tape recorder; a multipurpose tool that folded out to provide everything from pliers to screwdrivers to a small saw; a disposable camera; four manila folders in bright colors containing papers on various subjects; the minutes of the last Board of Supervisors meeting; the agenda for the next one.

Down in a compartment for pens and pencils I found a key that I recognized because I had an identical one of my own. They both fit the same deposit box in a Santa Ana bank.

I remembered asking him about it three years ago, when he gave me the second key.

Since I have the key, sir, what's in the box?

Crap. Nothing.

I slid the key into my pocket. I'd have to clean out that box sooner or later.

There were two things in the briefcase that I didn't expect to be there: a picture of our family together, taken when I was six.

It was unframed, tattered and bent. I could see the smudges of fingerprints on it.

I thought about being six, one year into my new life, still wondering when I'd wake up from the wonderful dream of the house in the hills and the beautiful people who weren't afraid of me. Still feeling the first stir of love and having absolutely no idea what it was.

The other thing that surprised me was a little collection of articles clipped from the papers, held together by a paper clip. There were six. And they were all about Luria Blas and Miguel Domingo.

No annotations by Will. Just the articles. I scanned them and put them back.

I brought out the date book and opened it to that last week of my father's life.

I looked over his meetings and appearances, his lunches and committee meetings, his public engagements and his personal ones, all organized for me to see.

Two things stood out. Both were daytime dates that took place while I was working, neither of which he'd said anything about.

The first was a noon meeting with fellow supervisor Dana Millbrae and Transportation Authority director Carl Rupaski. This was held on Tuesday at the Grove, the day before Will's death. Will and Millbrae were antagonistic members of the same elected board. Millbrae represented the more moneyed south county; Will the poorer and more populous central county. They often argued, and often voted against each other.

Lately, however, Millbrae had joined Will on a few key votes relating to transportation issues.

One vote in particular came to my mind. It took place in late May. The issue was whether or not the county should buy one of the money-losing toll roads built with private dollars a few years back. The road was eight miles long. The toll at peak hours was $2.65. Nobody was using it. The consortium that built it was losing about a thousand dollars a day. They wanted Orange County to pay twenty-seven million dollars for it.

Will had argued hell no—let the private money take the loss, not the taxpayer. Rupaski had argued in favor of the buy-out, saying that his Transportation Authority could operate and maintain the toll road cheaper than the current owners and turn a profit by 2010. He said the toll road was a bargain at twice the price.

Will said the only bargain would be for Rupaski's friends— the private consortium that built the road—and that the county shouldn't be in the business of bailing out high rollers who face a loss.

Rupaski said it was do-gooders like Will who were clogging the county with traffic and making life miserable for everyone.

Will said Rupaski was a dummy sitting on the lap of developers.

I remembered that night very clearly.

The Board of Supervisors is a seven-member body. And Millbrae cast the surprising "nay" that kept the County from buying a money-pit toll road from friends of Carl Rupaski.

I clearly remembered Rupaski's face after that vote. Millbrae's, too. Rupaski looked like he'd just sat on a fish hook. Dana Millbrae—earnest, soft-spoken, bland as a cup of milk— looked upset, almost afraid.

Will had turned off his microphone, closed his briefcase, come down off the dais and nodded me toward an exit. On the way home he'd gloated about the vote. He called Millbrae "Millie" and said that Carl Rupaski was the ugliest thug he'd ever met.

Anybody who's got their own goons driving their own beat

cars enforcing their own laws has got too much power, Joe. Good for Millie, voting the sonofabitch down for once.

Those were his words, exactly. And I knew what cars he meant, because the Orange County Transportation Authority had a fleet of brand-new, gleaming white, dark-windowed Chevrolet Impalas that were purchased and maintained by the county for the take-home use of the OCTA management.

Joe, it frosts my balls to see low-level bureaucrats in giant gas-guzzling muscle cars, especially ones with dark windows so you can't see which suckass TA geek is behind the wheel.

This was one of the reasons he petitioned the county, and finally got, a car allowance adjustment that let him lease the giant gas-guzzling luxury muscle car in which I now sat. The hypocrisy wasn't lost on Will. He told me once that if the world was fair, supervisors would get GEOs and everybody in the OCTA—from Carl Rupaski on down—would have to walk.

So, a lunch date between the three of them at the Grove stood out as odd. Will hadn't mentioned it to me. He'd said nothing about it afterwards, though I do remember him being fretful and anxious those last few days of his life.

Are you carrying?

The other surprising entry in Will's calendar was an afternoon meeting with one Ellen E. on Wednesday, the day he died. The time was 2 P.M., the place a small Mexican restaurant out in Riverside, just over the county line.

I got out his address book and scanned through the E listings. An Ellen Erskine was listed, with two phone numbers and an address. I didn't know her, hadn't heard of her. A little late to call.

I lingered there in his car a while longer, running my hands over the things that he had touched, remembering, wondering.

Chapter Eight

I stood in an observation hall behind the big mirror in one of the sheriff's department interview rooms. Rick Birch opened the door for John Gaylen. I felt a flutter in my guts when Gaylen came into the room, turned, folded his hands and looked at me through the one-way mirror. More than a flutter: a buzz.

I looked away, took a deep breath and looked back.

Buzz.

I tried to put it out of my mind, to just watch and witness. *Mouth shut, eyes open.*

Behind them was Harmon Ouderkirk, Rick's partner. Ouderkirk was short, thick, around forty. He shut the door hard.

Gaylen stared in my direction, though he couldn't see me. He looked at the video camera in one corner. It's on a tripod, a decoy camera we leave turned off most of the time. The operational one is hidden behind the air conditioner vent on the opposite wall.

"You didn't say anything, about a taping."

Nerves rioted up my back. I felt my scalp get cold and tingle. The voice—deep and clear, with the funny, slightly skewed cadence.

It came through the video mike, amplified just enough for me to hear well.

Will! Ah, Will Trona! Let's talk.

The voice of the shooter? So close. So hard to remember the exact sound of a sound.

"We're not taping," said Birch.

"That's right, you're not."

"Turn the damned thing to the wall if you don't believe him," said Ouderkirk. "Unplug it."

Gaylen looked at the camera, then took off his suit coat, folded and hung it over the lens end and the microphone.

"Who's behind the mirror?"

"Nobody."

Gaylen looked at me through the mirror again. "He looks like a nobody."

I breathed deeply and observed him, trying to steady my nerves, trying to be sure about that voice. I was as sure as the memory of a voice could make me.

He was tall, with copper skin and a strangely handsome face. High cheeks, heavy epicanthic folds, full lips. His eyes were wary and quick. He wore a navy suit with a silver-blue silk shirt and a silver-blue silk tie. His watch was a Rolex or a knockoff.

There was a table in the interview room, bolted to the floor. Four chairs, two on each side, bolted also. They were originally painted tan but the paint has worn from the edges and corners to show the metal underneath. There are still cigarette scars from the days when people smoked while they talked. No smoking now. But the deputies decided years ago to leave the marks there, figuring someday they might make some creep feel even more desperate to know he couldn't smoke.

There's a push button hidden under the tabletop, in front of chair four, that lets you control the real camera, but Rick had already turned it on from outside.

"Have a seat, John," said Rick.

Gaylen picked the chair facing away from the decoy camera. The usual move. That left me a clear view of his face on the monitor, and a good angle through the mirror.

Ouderkirk leaned against the door and crossed his arms.

Birch sat across from Gaylen and brought out a pen and notepad.

"Wednesday night, John," Birch said. "We've got an eye-witness to the Trona shooting. Told us it was the Cobra Kings."

"Take it up with them."

"Which ones?"

"I wasn't there."

"Really. Where were you?"

"With a woman."

"I'd like a name and number."

Gaylen looked at me, then over at Ouderkirk, then back to Birch.

"Ah, I'll bet you would, wouldn't you?"

Ah, Will Trona!

Birch sat back, tapped his pen on the tabletop.

"We got a good description of the shooter that night. And it sounds a lot like you. Here, see what you think."

Birch flipped back in his notebook. "Tall, average build, overcoat or trenchcoat. Dark skin, maybe African American. Right-handed. Deep voice."

Gaylen stared at Birch while he read. He nodded twice, faintly. "That could be a lot of people."

"Not really. Five guys with long coats? What's the use of having your colors if you don't fly them? Five guys with long coats is five Cobra Kings."

"I wasn't there."

"Then who was? Help me out."

Gaylen sneered.

Ouderkirk walked out, slamming the door.

"Look, John, I'm going to bring your guys in. Every one of them. And I'm going to rattle their cages. Hard. If you know anything about that night you better tell it now. After today, you're looking at obstruction of justice, and that carries three-to-five. Think about three years without that woman you had two Wednesdays ago. Think about three years without any woman at all. If you're holding out on me, John, you're going to pay some pretty high rent."

Gaylen stared at him.

Ouderkirk joined me in the observation room. "That the guy?"

"Yes. The voice."

"We can't hold him on a voice, Joe. What about the face?"

I could hardly keep myself from going around the corner, into the interview room, and taking care of John Gaylen on my own.

"The fog blocked his face. But not his voice."

"Too bad. To me, he looks like the kind of guy who'd do two of his friends just to protect his own well-clad little ass."

"You might ask him if Sammy Nguyen knows about him and Bernadette Lee."

"The babe in the picture?"

"Yes. She's Sammy's girl. He's got a picture of her over his cell cot. He's a murderer, with plenty of friends on the outside."

"Got ya."

We watched as Birch continued. "John, maybe that wasn't you guys. Maybe it was five people trying to *look* like you guys. Not very likely, though, is it? We're on to you. We've got at least one witness—a good one. And one more, in the hospital. Cao's going to make it, you know. Tough young guy. And he'll be happy to talk, won't he? We know you shot him. Our wit, he saw everything."

"I don't shoot my friends. Maybe you do."

"Come on, John. Put yourself in Ike's shoes. Betrayed like that by his own guy? If he won't finger you, we'll crack one of your boys, maybe a young one, maybe somebody looking at his third strike. Maybe somebody who doesn't like you so much. And if your name comes up—wow. You're in the deepest possible shit. But right now you're in a position to help yourself, and help us."

"Help you? That's enough reason to walk out of here," said Gaylen.

"Any time. Door's open. How did you know Will Trona?"

Gaylen shook his head. "No. Didn't. Don't."

"That's not what Will Trona said."

"So you brought him back to life?"

"I read his appointment book."

It took Gaylen a second to think of something. "Don't tell me he had us down for lunch at Bamboo 33."

"No names, John. Just CK this and CK that."

Gaylen's face went hard. "Probably his boyfriend."

I knew Birch was making this up, because I'd photocopied every page of Will's calendar and his appointment book before handing them over to him.

"I don't see it that way. I see it as a link. That and the descriptions. Another reason to bring in Cobra Kings one at a time. Shake the chain until a link breaks. That's what I'm going to do."

Gaylen stood, walked to the dummy camera and pulled his coat off of it. He slipped it over his arm. "I guess we're done, then."

"Kings take scalps, don't you?"

"No."

"Sure you do—make the grunts kill to get full membership.

Your guys have told us that much, so there's no reason deny-
ing it."

"I've got no idea what you're talking about."

"Maybe you guys got a contract to take out the supervisor.
Be a nice opp for making bones. That would explain why you
called him by name that night. Might even explain why Trona
had you in his appointment book."

Gaylen smiled. "Make an appointment to get yourself
popped? You must be dreaming now, Detective."

Birch stood. "Every once in a while, one comes true."

"Then keep sleeping. You're good at it."

"How about the name and number for your date that night?"

"No. You'll have to arrest me for that."

"You could save us all a lot of trouble."

"I don't help cops."

"Then why'd you come in? A little worried maybe, wanted
to see what we had?"

"You've got nothing."

"When did you meet Alex Blazak?"

Gaylen stared at Birch. "Ah, another thing I haven't done."

"Then how'd you know where to find Savannah that night?"

Gaylen shook his head. "You've got no reason to hold me.
And the more you talk, the more you prove it."

I watched Ouderkirk blow back into the interview room. He
had something in his hand. "Leaving so soon?" he asked
Gaylen.

"Not so much to talk about."

"There might be, if Sammy Nguyen hears about you and
Bernadette."

Ouderkirk held up the surveillance photo of Gaylen and the
woman.

Gaylen took a step forward for a better look, and you could
tell that we'd caught him. He froze. Just briefly. He'd probably

heard the story of Nguyen and Bernadette Lee's admirer long before we did. But he'd never seen that picture before, guaranteed.

"That's not your business. You want me to help you do your jobs, then you turn around and fuck with me?"

"Saddening, isn't it?" said Ouderkirk. He glanced at the picture, shrugged and smiled.

"Asshole," said Gaylen. He started out of the room. Birch held the door for him while Ouderkirk waved the picture.

"Is she the alibi, Gaylen?" Birch asked. "Is that why you won't give us a name? You know, we can keep that picture real quiet. Or not."

"You can both go to hell or not."

Gaylen walked out, then Birch. Ouderkirk looked at me and nodded as he pulled the door behind him.

"I love this job," he said.

Birch came in and told me to wait at his desk. I waited a few minutes, then a few more. I looked at the picture of his family. Wife, children, grandchildren. Birch looked happy. There was a stack of case files on his desk, a clean blotter, a legal pad with Birch's handwriting on it. There was a standard Interview Contact form on the blotter, clean. But I couldn't help but see Gaylen's name, address and a phone number written down on a Post-It and stuck to the top sheet.

A few minutes later Birch called me into one of the empty conference rooms.

He looked at me cautiously but said nothing.

"It was him, sir. I could tell by the voice."

"Voice won't cut it for us, Joe."

"I understand that. I can't identify him visually."

"Then we can't arrest him."

"It was him, sir. *That's the man who shot my father.*"

"I believe you. But the DA can't make a homicide case with a voice ID. We'd never get past the preliminary. We need a lot more. What *else*, Joe?"

"I felt something wrong when he walked into the room, sir. Before he opened his mouth. I know that doesn't help you."

"No, it doesn't."

Birch sighed, sat back, considered. "If he pulled the trigger, why did he come in and let me question him?"

"Because he's bold and confident. He's got faith in the Cobra Kings not to break if you bend them. And he knows that you don't have enough to arrest him outright, or you would have."

Birch was quiet for a moment. "What if he's just a wiseguy who doesn't know anything about Will? Why come in and talk to a homicide cop?"

"He isn't."

"You didn't see him! What if he wasn't there? What if he's got a voice like the guy who *was* there?"

"It's not just the voice. It's the way he phrases things. Sir, I don't know why he'd come in and talk to you if he was innocent."

"I'll tell you why. What usually happens is, if they did it and they know you're on them, they'll haul ass while they have the chance. If they didn't, they'll come and talk, watch you run your circles, laugh you off. Gaylen didn't run for daylight. He came in. Talked tough. Wouldn't give us his alibi's name and number. He was even on time."

I wanted my words to be accurate, but it was hard to describe what I'd felt when Gaylen walked into the interview room. "He strikes me as unusual, sir. I still can't define my reaction to seeing him. Like a warning. A recognition. I can't describe it."

Birch looked at me, then shook his head. "I'm going to watch the video this evening at home—I always learn something. One thing, though, I think he's scared of what Sammy Nguyen would do to Bernadette Lee. If he knew about Gaylen and her."

I nodded. "Are you going to talk to her?"

"You can bet I am."

"I can give you her address, from Sammy's letters."

Another long slow look from Birch. "Why do that?"

"To help, sir."

His expression said that he wanted to believe me, but couldn't. "I think you know more about that night than you're saying. A lot more."

I felt my face grow warm, felt the scar tissue tingle. Yes, there were a few details I'd kept to myself. The last of Will's secrets, maybe, at least the last ones he entrusted to me.

"Joe, your father doesn't need your protection anymore. He's past that. He needs you to tell the truth. And let me tell you something else—a dog can keep a secret forever. But a man has to learn when he's doing more harm than good. Is this clear to you?"

"Yes, sir."

"It damned well should be if you want a career in law enforcement."

"Yes, I know."

He waited a long moment, then shook his head like I'd given the wrong answer.

From the privacy of my car and my cell phone, I called the home number for Ellen Erskine. No answer, no message recorder. I tried her work phone. A pleasant female voice said "Hillview Home for Children," and I asked for Ms. Erskine.

"She's in a meeting, may I take a message?"

"No message," I said, and hung up.

Hillview Home for Children, I thought: Why? A donation, a fund-raiser, a change in budget?

Lost in speculation that got me nothing, I went to Mod J to get what Sammy Nguyen had promised me.

Gary Sargola, the so-called Ice-Box Killer, demanded a doctor because his phlebitis-swollen leg was killing him. That wasn't my decision so I told Sergeant Delano.

"Let him suffer a while," he said. "That poor girl he put in the freezer did. By the way, nice hat."

Dave Hauser, the former assistant district attorney who went into the drug trade with a guy he prosecuted, showed me a picture of his newborn daughter. Dave had been in jail four months, and his daughter was now about two days old. Her name was Kristen. Dave said when he got out he was moving the whole family to Tahiti, had some land there, not far from Brando.

Dr. Chapin Fortnell lay on his cot sobbing. When I asked him what was wrong, he rolled over and looked at me with swollen red eyes. "It's all coming apart, Joe." Later, I learned that one of the six boys the good doctor was accused of molesting had hanged himself.

Serial rapist Frankie Dilsey was in the day room watching a soap opera. He turned to me when I passed by, pointing at the actress on the screen and smiling. *"Dat's what it's all about, Shitface. Dat's the ticket, right there, dat stuff."*

And so on.

My work.

I watched them take a new prisoner in that afternoon, to be given the cell next to Sammy. He was a meth biker named Giant Mike Staich who'd apparently taken a machete to a stoolie, severed his head and carried it around for a few weeks in a pillow-case tied to his hog. A motorcycle cop had driven behind him for a few miles, pulled up behind him at a red light, smelled the head and pulled him over. They'd shaved Staich at Intake. "Too many lice to kill with just soap, man." He had tattoos around his neck, all the way up to his chin. The middle finger of his left hand was missing. He stood six feet six, huge belly, short bowed legs like they were designed to straddle a gas tank ten hours a day.

He asked what they all do. "What the fuck happened to that face of yours?"

"Acid."

"Roadkill looks better than that. Why don't you get an operation?"

"I've had eight."

He considered, nodding. "Cover it up with a tat, man. Get a big-ass skull with a sword through it, or a lion with its mouth open, and nobody'll even know what's under. I gotta guy in Stanton's real good."

"Thanks for your advice."

In the next cell, Sammy Nguyen lay on his cot, as always, staring up at the picture of Bernadette. When I stopped to talk to him, he was sullen and hostile, complaining that we'd confiscated his dog nail clippers and wouldn't give them back.

"There's no dog in here," I said.

"Any idiot can see that, Joe. I use them for *my* nails. It's the only way to get the right angle, make them look right. You ask any beautician or cosmetologist. Maybe you can get them back for me."

"You still owe me for the rat trap."

He looked surprised. "Owe you what?"

"Alex Blazak."

Sammy suddenly looked lighter. He blew a kiss at Bernadette's picture, then came over to the bars. "I totally forgot."

"You're busy," I said.

He laughed at this and I smiled along with him.

"This is the deal," he said. He looked with conspiracy to his right, then his left. Then he leaned up close to the steel bars of his cage. "Do you know what a couturier is?"

I nodded.

"His girlfriend's one. She's got a shop on Laguna Canyon Road, by the big antique store. Christy or Christine or something like that. And her last name is Sands. Like sand at the beach."

"Good," I said.

"Then get me my clippers back."

"I'll be honest with you, Sammy—there's no way the captain is going to allow dog clippers."

He shrugged, made a face. "Screw the captain, Joe. I give you Christy Sands, you get my dog clippers back."

"I can't do that."

Back to the sullen pout then, a convincingly tragic expression. "Then get me a better trap to kill that rat with. I've seen him in here every night for two weeks. Look."

He pointed to the floor. I saw the plastic rat trap with the adhesive on the bottom. Apparently it was unmolested.

"I'll see about a better trap."

He gave me an injured look, then climbed back onto his cot. "Make sure it's a good one. One of the big ones, not the kind for mice. For *rats.*"

Giant Mike Staich, lodged right next to Sammy, had to get in on this.

"Just step on the damned thing," he growled. A wall separates the inmates. They could both see me, but not each other.

Sammy sighed, imploring me with an expression that said, why did you put a moron next to me?

"Hey rat-man," said Giant. "I'm Mike. I'm in for doing

some jerk-off and putting his head in a bag. Like I'm dumb enough to do that."

"Why'd you put it in a bag?" Sammy asked.

"It wasn't me."

Sammy looked disgusted. "I'm Sammy Nguyen," he said curtly. "I'm in for killing a cop I never saw in my life. When I'm released because of false imprisonment, I'm going to sue this place into another bankruptcy. Everybody except Joe, because he's a decent guy."

"Who's Joe?"

"He's standing right in front of you."

"Oh, you mean Shitface."

"It's scar tissue," said Sammy.

"Looks like cow shit that ain't dried yet. Get yourself the tattoo, boy. Fuck the hat."

"I'll consider it."

"A tattoo won't cover it," said Sammy. "He needs another surgery."

"He's had eight of them."

Even the cons talk about me like I'm not there.

My work.

But that was the good part of my job—meeting interesting people, making new and exotic friends.

The bad part was the boredom and the constant hustles, the constant lies. The constant bad jokes about my scars. I hadn't heard a good one in weeks.

I wanted out of there. Even though it reminded me on some primitive level of my early childhood, I still knew I had to get out.

The average jail time for a deputy in Orange County is five years. So I guess I didn't have it so bad. Almost four years down. But it still felt like a life sentence, eight hours at a time.

They don't reduce your time for good behavior. Only the inmates get that.

Chapter Nine

I don't know what I was expecting from a girlfriend of Crazy Alex Blazak, but Chrissa Sands was not it. Sammy Nguyen had her name wrong, but he'd gotten the location perfectly.

She was older than Alex by a few years—mid-twenties, I guessed. Tall and pretty, with high cheekbones and bangs and the rest of her thick blonde hair cut straight at the shoulders. I could feel the energy humming off her.

She took some time to study me. She considered the face, didn't look away.

"Nice hat."

"Thank you."

"Try this."

She shot across the little shop and came back with a rust-red felt fedora with a cream-colored band. In the two seconds it took her, I eyed the place. Four racks of dresses, some shelves along the walls with what appeared to be sweaters. In the back was a large table with three different sewing machines on it and three fitting mannequins wearing half-finished clothing. There were sketches and magazines and scissors everywhere.

We traded hats and I put it on. She reached up and tilted

back the brim a little. She wiggled a pin between her teeth, then stood back and considered.

"Excellent in every way," she said. "Here."

She pulled me by my arm to a full-length mirror. I heard her humming to herself. I thought the hat looked fine. She was nodding at it.

"I need to talk about Alex and Savannah," I said.

"I know who you are and I know you're a cop."

"I'm a jailer, actually."

"You don't look like a jailer."

"Well, thank you, I guess. The thing is, Ms. Sands—"

"Chrissa."

"Chrissa, I'm not here as a cop. I'm just trying to find Savannah Blazak."

"Yeah," she said quietly. "You and everybody else."

"Maybe we could sit down and talk a minute."

"We'll need longer than that. Let's go get lunch. I need a break from this place."

We exchanged hats and she put on the red one. I thought it looked fine with her jeans and white T-shirt and yellow blazer. She zoomed behind the sewing table and came back with a purse over her shoulder and a fat ring of keys in her hand. Her sunglasses had silver frames and tiny lenses.

"You drive," she said.

We went outside and she waved to two guys standing at a bus stop not far from the parking lot driveway. I'd always heard what a friendly town Laguna Beach was, but the guys didn't bother to wave back.

"Assholes," she said, clicking her seatbelt into place.

"Who are they?"

"Never mind."

We sat at a plastic table on a big patio overlooking the beach.

The waves were small and crisp and loud when they shattered on the sand. There was a light haze in the air that made the water shimmer like mercury in slow motion. There weren't a lot of people in the water, but the sand was crowded with sunbathers.

Chrissa Sands polished off a Bloody Mary and ordered another. She told me that Alex and Jack Blazak had "despised" each other for almost five years. Jack had expected perfection from his son; Alex had "felt the whip" and answered with rebellion. She said that Alex *was* a little crazy—nothing serious, in her opinion—just a willingness to take more risks than the average spoiled, rich young man. Sure, Alex liked to act tough. Liked his guns and knives and weapons, but once you got to know him, he was a really cool guy. Would never hurt anybody, not even an animal. Vegetarian, never ate anything with a face. The weapons were just something he liked to look at, the same way some people liked looking at art. They were a way to make money. Alex had a sword that was made for Napoleon and later given by Hitler to Himmler or maybe the other way around, worth something like five hundred grand. But Alex was "definitely non-violent and non-aggro."

"He's a sweet young guy," she said, with a tear welling up in her eye. "He walked into my store one day, looking for something for his mother, he says. He's got a gold-plated pistol in his briefcase—he tells me all about it, how it was owned by some admiral in Japan—but he's trying to buy mommy a birthday present. I wanted to hug him. So . . . cute. Acts like the toughest guy in the world, but he's not. He needs encouragement to do the right things. He needs protection from the wrong people. I've tried to do that for him. And when you've got his attention, it's the most wonderful feeling, because he's so intense, so completely *alive*. I mean, I'm like that too . . . we're both a little random, maybe, but in a good way. At least I hope it's good."

I handed her a monogrammed handkerchief. She dabbed and smiled.

"God, I love a man with decent manners. Handkerchiefs are so excellently cool. I really ought to do something with them. I'll clean this and return it to you."

"That's not necessary."

She smiled, waved the kerchief at me, then set it on the plastic table-top by my hand.

"Joe, you're such a complete square. But I like that. That's okay. Now watch you say thank you."

I didn't and smiled, because I was about to.

"When was the last time you saw Alex?"

"I want to get it right." Chrissa pulled over her purse and rummaged through it. A charge slip and a packet of tissues fell out. She chased around the bottom, elbow-deep in the bag, and came up with a small book from the bottom. The cover had van Gogh's sunflowers on it. She opened it and looked through.

"Sunday, June tenth."

"Where?"

"We met there, at the hotel lounge."

She nodded toward the darkened windows of the Laguna Hotel, just north of us. She stared at it for a while. I followed her line of sight to the boardwalk and the two guys she'd waved at when we left her store. One was watching the beach. The other was watching us.

Chrissa tilted back the rust red fedora, pulled off her sunglasses and used my hankie to dab her eyes again.

"Something's . . . really wrong."

"Start at the beginning and tell me."

"Can we walk? I can't talk about this while I eat."

I paid for the drinks and we walked down to the beach. When

we got to the boardwalk we went north, but Chrissa's unfriendly friends were gone.

"This is better," she said. "Okay, Alex stayed at my place Sunday, our usual thing. He went home late, like usual. Monday I didn't see him, even though Mondays are one of our usual lunch days. Alex comes to the shop, we go eat, have some drinks, and he brings me back to the studio. Well, that Monday he called, said he had some things to do, no time for lunch. He was vague but real excited, feeling good, I think. That night he called, really geared up, really high. Said he was working a deal, no details, but we'd be a half a million dollars richer. He likes saying he's going to score big, but he never has. I mean, he's said that before. He also likes being secretive. It makes him feel like he's in control. Anyway, Savannah was visiting him, so he put her on the phone and we talked a minute. She always wanted to know what I was working on—what kind of dresses and blouses and all. I told her about this sundress with gold lamé sand dollars on it. Then Alex told me he'd be real busy the next couple of days, not to worry. I didn't, until this guy showed up the next day at my studio. That would have been Tuesday morning."

"Bo Warren."

"Yes. He said he'd been sent by the Reverend Daniel Alter because the Reverend wanted to talk to my boyfriend. Mr. Warren seemed concerned about Alex. It's more than extremely important that his boss talks to my boyfriend. 'More than extremely important' were his exact words. He says they've been looking for him, can't find him anywhere. Can I help them?"

We walked along for a minute, Chrissa Sands watching the basketball games at Main Beach. She looked behind us, then back to me.

"Did you?"

"I called Reverend Alter's office on my cell phone and finally got through. I'd seen him on TV but never talked to him before. He was very calm and nice. He told me that Bo Warren was his head of security, and would appreciate it if I cooperated. He said they were trying to help Alex. That got me worried."

"So you talked to Warren?"

"Yes. I told him where Alex liked to hang out, what his haunts were. He asked me if I'd talked to him, and I told him what I told you about the phone call. He asked about Savannah. I told him I'd talked to her, too. And I kept asking what's wrong, what's happened, but he wouldn't tell me anything. Just that Alex might be in some trouble, and the Reverend Daniel Alter was trying to help him out of it. He wanted to look around my salon, like I was hiding something. I let him. I found out later that he'd gone to my house in town. At least a red-and-white Corvette was parked on my street for an hour, and that's the kind of car he was driving. We had some break-ins a few months ago, so the neighbors all look out for each other. He left me his card, with two more phone numbers written on the back. He asked me to call immediately if I knew where they could find Alex. 'Faster than immediately' is what he said. I was completely worried by the time he left. He's very intense, in a negative way."

"Do you have the card?"

She dug into her purse again and came up with it. The front had the Chapel of Light logo on it and Warren's information. On the back he'd handwritten two more numbers. I copied them into my notebook.

"Alex called that night, this would be Tuesday. He told me to meet him down at the beach in front of the Hotel Laguna. This was late, about midnight. Savannah was with him. And a new friend of Alex's, named Tony. Older guy. Anyway, Alex was very . . . well, jumpy. He's overly cautious sometimes,

thinks people are out to get him, but that night he was almost
paranoid. I tried to tell him about this Warren character, but he
seemed to know all about him already. We took a short walk
down by the water. Savannah and Tony walked along behind
us. We stopped by that beach wall with the painting on it and
Alex hugged and kissed me. I could feel the worry coming off
him. He told me he might be gone for a few days, maybe even
a few weeks. But when it was over, we'd be in the money.
Those were his words, 'in the money.' He was . . . saying good-
bye. He told me that if people were asking questions about him,
don't tell them anything true. Of course it was too late by then,
because I'd talked to this Warren guy."

We came to the steps and climbed them up to Heisler Park.
Some of the roses were in bloom and they made sharp dabs of
color against the blue Pacific. We walked past a restaurant and
a gazebo perched on the cliff. She looked behind us, sighed.
The friends were back, pretending to appreciate the roses.

She shook her head. "The next morning, Wednesday, a car
followed me to work. That afternoon, when I drove up to Santa
Ana to look at some fabrics, the same car was there in the mirror. After that, when I came home then walked downtown to get
some dinner, I saw it again, parked down my street. Two guys
followed me into Laguna, sat at the bar while I ate, trailed me
home."

"Describe the car."

"White, new and a Chevrolet. Had a logo on the trunk, like
a jumping deer. I walked right by it when I went home from
dinner. It had lights on top, but no emblems or anything. Like a
cop car without the information."

"The deer is an impala."

"Big ugly thing, either way. The car, I mean."

"And the men?"

"See for yourself. They're right back there, acting like rosarians."

They ignored us as soon as I looked over. One of the guys was older, maybe fifty. The other was half of that—twenties. The young guy was big, wore a suit and tie. The older one was bigger, with a gut under a white, short-sleeved shirt, a wide tie and trousers that shone funny in the sun.

My first thought was Steve Marchant's buds at the FBI. But these guys were onto Chrissa by Tuesday, the twelfth, two days before anybody told the Bureau about Savannah's disappearance from the Blazak home.

My second thought was because of their cars: Transportation Authority Enforcement. Carl Rupaski's men? That made no sense at all to me.

"Needless to say, Joe, by the time those creeps started following me around, I knew something bad was happening. Alex told me not to worry, but it isn't easy."

She said that Alex hadn't called Wednesday, didn't call Thursday.

"And then," she said. "I watched the news Thursday night and realized that Alex's friend Tony was Will Trona. I recognized him."

I hadn't seen that one coming. But I did remember that Tuesday night: Will hadn't needed me, because he wanted to stay home with Mary Ann. But he'd met with Savannah and Alex at the beach at midnight.

"And, of course, the other big TV news that night was Jack and Lorna, and I found out Savannah had been *kidnapped on Monday morning.* I was completely lost. She was fine when she talked to me on the phone. She was fine on Tuesday night at the beach with Alex and your father. So I called Jack and Lorna. I explained who I was. And I told them Savannah was fine as of Tuesday night—she was with their son. I thought that would be good news to them. Great news. But Jack didn't seem particularly interested. He was suspicious of me, like I was responsible somehow. He said he'd have the FBI call me in the morning. It was very strange. I knew Jack hated his son—and by extension he might hate me—but I was talking about his daughter. His allegedly kidnapped daughter. I couldn't figure it out. I still can't."

"I can help. The Blazaks' private story is that Alex kidnapped his sister and demanded a million dollars for her."

She stopped, looked at me, shook her head. "Bullshit."

"That's why Bo Warren showed up at your shop that morning, instead of the FBI. Because the Blazaks decided to pay the ransom quietly, without the cops, get Savannah back, get some help for Alex."

"Jack Blazak get help for Alex? Never. Keep his reputation buffed out, maybe. I *told* Jack that Savannah was fine. She sure didn't look kidnapped, walking along the beach with her brother and me and your father."

I thought about this and drew blanks. Why would Jack insist that his son had kidnapped his daughter, when he had evidence that she was all right? Why so eager to part with a million hard-earned dollars?

"Joe, it's impossible that Alex kidnapped his sister. He did not."

She brought a thumbnail to her teeth and turned toward the ocean. The sunlight made her hair bright but her face was still in the shadow of her hat brim. I saw the tight lines around her mouth as she worked on that nail.

"Don't chew it off, Chrissa. It won't change anything except your thumb."

She stopped. "Material people. Gross people. Greedy people. They make me sick. And angry. Then to blame Alex for it. Look, Alex is my boyfriend. Boyfriends are flakes, by definition. He didn't tell me much about his business, but he sure didn't kidnap his sister. They're tight, Alex and Savannah."

"Then what *was* he doing?"

Chrissa sighed and squinted at me. "Something for money. Something to hurt his dad. Other than that I have no idea at all."

I glanced back at Chrissa's guys, who stopped quickly and looked away.

"You told Bo Warren where Alex's hangouts are?"

Her eyes twinkled when she looked at me. "I didn't tell him where *all* of Alex's hangouts are. This Bo Warren, he really gives off bad energy—I don't care who he works for. His cheek muscles quiver when he inhales. He's kind of off-putting, so I . . . didn't really *lie* to him, I just forgot a few things."

"Can you unforget them for me?"

"There's the Rex in Newport, but I've been all over that place for a week and I haven't seen him. And the Surf and Sand lounge, but I know the piano player there and told him to call me if he saw Alex, and he hasn't. Alex also digs the Four Seasons. But he hasn't been there, either, because I know some of the waiters. He likes the Ritz-Carlton. He goes to those places a lot. He knows the people. They're his . . . hideouts. He'll go to one of them, do some kind of business, hang around."

She gave me a hard look then, and sighed. "He's also got a warehouse that hardly anybody knows about. Full of weird stuff."

"They were there. Lorna gave me the address."

She shook her head and looked away.

I asked her about the three places that Alex and Savannah had been spotted in the last four days—Rancho Santa Fe, Big Bear, Hollywood.

"No," she said.

New territory, I thought. "He's not trusting the old places."

She shook her head. "He's got an instinct for things. Sometimes it's paranoia, but he turns out to be right a lot. I've been to the old spots, asking about him. Nothing. I think he's got the brains to find somewhere new."

"What does he drive?"

"Black Porsche Carrera. Which he loves *almost* as much as me."

"I doubt it."

"See, you *can* be playful if you want to."

"No, I—"

"I know, you really meant it."

"I really did."

"You're hopeless."

I didn't understand that, but it seemed beside the point.

"What have you told the FBI?"

"What I told Warren. I knew from the start he didn't kidnap her. But as long as they think he did, I'm not helping them any more than I have to. But man, when they question, they *question*. I sat in some office up in Santa Ana for four hours that day with a guy named Steve. Then another hour the next day. Then, last Thursday, another hour. I had to let them put these big tape recorders next to my phones—both of them—home and work. Either that or I was obstructing justice. The second one of them rings, they start recording, and they got this thing that tells them the calling number. Then, those damned white cars are still following me every damned place I go. Those jerks. I've named them Suit and Gut. They won't even wave back. I told the Feebies about them, but there they are, hovering like flies. I'm about ready to close up shop and head for Fiji for a month. I can't sleep, I can't eat, all I can do is work and drink. I miss my guy. I miss my life. Man, it gets *tiring*."

"I think you should go to Fiji."

"I'm not ditching Alex. He's kind of weird, but he might

need me. But I'll tell you something. Another few weeks of this and I'm going to start getting pissed off at somebody."

"Does Alex know a man named John Gaylen?"

She thought, then shook her head. "Not that I ever heard. But Alex knows a lot of people."

I looked over at the men again. "I'll do what I can with these guys. If they're law enforcement, it won't be much."

"They're not exactly small."

"That doesn't matter."

I drove her back to her shop, waited while she collected a pile of mail from the box on Laguna Canyon Road, then walked her in. She pushed the play button on her answering machine.

"Chrissa, it's Heidi. How about a drink or four tonight after work? Call soon, let me know."

She shrugged. "My life now. Suit, Gut, girlfriends and drinks."

"It will get better."

"I've got no reason to complain. My father wasn't murdered."

"No."

"You holding up okay?"

"Fine."

"Tough guy, huh? Just like Alex, that way. Nothing hurts."

I didn't say anything to that.

"Know something, Joe? You're cute. If I didn't have a guy, I'd make you take me out again."

"That's very flattering. But I'm dating, now. I mean, a couple hours from now I'll be dating."

She smiled and sighed. "Good for you. You're what my dad would call a real boy scout. You're in the wrong century, or at least decade. I like that."

"Thank you for your help. Here."

I gave her my card, with my home and cell phone numbers on it.

"You can put it with Bo Warren's," I said. "But I hope you call me first."

"Don't worry about that, Joe. Here, wear this sometime."

She took off the rust-red fedora and handed it to me.

"Thank you."

"I'm just going to tell you this once: that thing on your face isn't as bad as you think it is. And the other half is perfect. You got nice thick blond hair and nice brown eyes and a really good jaw line. Try smiling someday—I'll bet you have a killer smile. And tall guys are sexy, *period.*"

I could feel the wave of red breaking over my skin, feel the tingle in the scar and this funny flutter in my chest.

"I don't know what to say."

"Nothing would be just fine."

I walked across the parking lot to the bus stop. Suit and Gut exchanged words and smiles. Suit had a lot of muscles under that fabric and Gut had forearms like a blacksmith.

I badged them. They badged me.

"We know who you are, Trona," said Gut. "I'm Hodge. He's Chapman. TA Enforcement, at your service."

"Why are you following her?"

"It's our job."

"Rupaski's idea?"

"Somebody's above us would be the answer to that."

"What for?"

"That's more of none of your business. But I can tell you it's boring. The gash is nice to look at, but I don't think she likes us too much. Chapman here, he's got a hard-on half the time."

Chapman smiled as if this revealed something good about himself.

"Keep it in your pants," I said to him. "And Mr. Hodge, don't call her a gash again. I hate that word to describe a woman."

"Those hats of yours should be white, not pink."

"It's rust red. And display only good manners toward her, Miss Sands, at all times."

They both laughed at that.

"Okay, Trona, sure. Is it good manners if I smile while I wag it at her?"

"No. And she'll tell me if you do."

"Then what?"

"You'll get extremely hurt."

Suit was big and young and full of himself, but I could tell he knew a little about me. He smiled, looked at his partner, then back at me.

"I'll be good. I promise."

"He'll be good," said Hodge. "I'll make sure he behaves, Trona. Don't you worry about a thing."

"Joe's got enough to worry about," said Chapman.

Hodge laughed. Chapman laughed.

"Have a nice afternoon."

I went back into Chrissa's fashion shop, found her sitting at her table with tears in her eyes.

The stack of mail was on the table in front of her. She held out a postcard. It was mailed from Mexico City six days earlier. The picture showed an Olmec head from the Anthropological Museum. The handwriting was sloppy but legible:

Baby—

   I'm fine don't worry. Miss you. Saw this picture, reminded me of Rosarito. I did the deal, gotta stay low. No matter what you hear, S. is fine.

                                        Cuddles,

                                          A.

Chrissa shook her head and inhaled. "Goddamned guy's in Mexico and I'm sitting here worrying like a widow. But at least I know he's okay. That Olmec head, it's like one we bought in a curio in Rosarito a few months ago. I mean the one in the picture is a real one. The one we bought cost about eighty cents, but it's made out of this beautiful light-green glass, like a Coke bottle."

"May I have this postcard?"

"Why?"

"I know people who need to see it. And people who don't."

She shook her head and stood. "Take it. *Take it.* Why did you come back in, anyway? Miss me?"

"I just wanted to tell you that if those guys outside get impolite, call me immediately. I mean, even a little tiny bit impolite."

"Okay. All right." She nodded slowly, studying me. "Do you wear a Panama when the weather gets hot?"

"I tried. I like the felt better."

"They're so hot. Why?"

"Better shadows."

She considered this but didn't speak.

Suit and Gut watched me from the bus stop as I came out and got into my car. Conferred, started laughing. They were still at it as I made my turn onto Laguna Canyon Road.

I cranked the car at them and stood on the gas. A sixty-seven Ford Mustang with 351 cubic inches, Edelbrock carbs, a Sig Ersen cam and Glaspaks puts out about two hundred twenty-five horses geared to smoke tire any time you want. The sound is like something from Revelation.

They jumped in different directions at the same time. Suit's face was a grimace of extreme disbelief as he cartwheeled past my side window.

I rolled it down and waved.

Chapter Ten

D r. Norman Zussman gave me a warm handshake and closed the door of his consultation room. He offered me a comfortable chair, and sat across from me on a small green couch. I set Will's briefcase on the floor beside me, and balanced my hat over one corner.

There was a coffee table between us, nothing on it. He was medium height and lightly built. He had short straight gray hair, blue eyes and a tanned face.

Dr. Zussman crossed his legs and set a yellow legal pad on his knee. "You succeeded in putting me off for nine days, Joe."

"I didn't want to talk to you, Doctor."

"I don't blame you for that. But it's better if you do. And it's required by your department. How are you doing?"

"Well."

He watched me. I get self-conscious when people stare and don't talk, but I knew he was just trying to get me to fill the silence. So I said nothing. I went to the quiet spot, got up in the tree and looked out. There is an eagle that sometimes shares my tree, but he wasn't there that day. I sat alone on the branch. The hillsides were tan and dry and I could smell them.

"Sleeping all right, Joe?"

"Yes, sir."

"Appetite good?"

"Yes."

"Drinking alcohol or using drugs of any kind?"

"I had some drinks a few nights back. I don't drink much, though."

"Why's that?"

"It makes me slow and stupid and feel bad in the morning."

He chuckled, wrote. "Tell me about the shooting, Joe. Take your time, start at the beginning."

I told him about it. I started with Will being shot and falling. Then heaving Savannah over the wall and sliding back into the backseat of the car. I explained that I was pretty sure the two men behind me would make for the wall and walk right past that open rear car door, and I'd have a good shot at them with the interior lights off. I told him the shots were easy and I could tell both men were hit hard.

He listened and wrote. When I was finished he sighed quietly. "Were you shooting to kill?"

"Yes."

"Did you feel forced by the circumstances to do what you did?"

I had to think about that. "No, sir. I could have jumped over the wall with Savannah."

"But you didn't, because your first loyalty was to your father."

I nodded.

"How did you feel when you pulled the trigger?"

"Alert but calm."

"How did you feel when you saw the men fall, and you knew they would probably die?"

"Relieved that they were not going to use their machine guns on me, or chase after Savannah."

Dr. Zussman was quiet for a long time. "Joe, how did you feel *after* the shooting? Say, an hour later?"

"I was looking for Savannah."

"But did you think about the men you'd just shot?"

"No."

"And the next day, how did you feel about what you'd done?"

"I didn't think about it very much. All I thought about was Will."

Zussman wrote and sighed again. "Joe, how do you feel right now, about what you did?"

"Just fine, doctor."

"Have you had any bad memories, regrets, bad dreams?"

"At my father's funeral, I tried to feel bad that two men were dead and that I had killed them. But I didn't feel anything about them. I thought it was self-defense, and that they'd gotten what they gambled for when they set out to kill a man."

Zussman watched me for a long while, then. He shifted on the couch, like he was uncomfortable. He recrossed his legs and set the legal pad on the other knee.

"When you think of the shooting, can you see it, or does it become unclear?"

"It's very clear. I can see the seams in the leather seat I was lying on, the moisture on the windows."

"Do you dwell on that scene?"

"I dwell on how I could have saved Will."

"So, it's more a tactical concern than a moral one?"

"Yes."

"Why do you think that is?"

I thought for a moment. "My job was to protect my father. It was the most important thing I could do. I was brought up to do that. I was trained to do it. I wanted, more than anything in the world, to do it well."

Zussman leaned forward and lay his pad on the table, wrote something on it. "How do you feel about failing to do your job?"

It took me a while to come up with a description. I knew how I felt, but I'd never thought to describe it to anyone, especially a stranger.

"Like sand."

"Sand? How is that?"

"Dry and loose and nothing holding it together."

He looked at me again. "Do you feel like you're going to fall apart, like sand?"

"No."

"But why not, if you're dry and loose and nothing is holding you together?"

"I wasn't accurate, sir. Something is holding me together. I need to find the man who shot Will. That has become very important to me."

"Ah. Of course."

Silence, then. Zussman gathered up his pad and sat back. "What do you anticipate happening, when you find that man, Joe?"

"I'll arrest him for murder, sir."

He looked at me for another long moment. He blinked, started to write something, then stopped.

"Joe, how did you feel about giving up your sidearm, as part of this counseling?"

"I didn't give it up."

"Why not?"

"No one asked me for it, so I have it."

"On your person? Here?"

I nodded and held out the left side of my sport coat.

"I'm going to ask you to leave it with me. I'll turn it over to Sergeant Mehring for safekeeping."

I unholstered the .45, ejected the clip and set it on the coffee table. Then I racked the action to make sure the chamber was empty, hit the safety. It was surprisingly loud in the quiet consultation room. I set the gun beside the clip.

I looked at Dr. Zussman and he looked at me.

"Does that worry you, Joe? Giving up your sidearm?"

"No, sir. I've got several more."

In fact, I had two more on me at that time. One was another .45 ACP that I keep high against my right rib cage, and that I can draw quickly with my left hand. The other is a small .32 on my ankle. No one expects three. Will told me once that nobody figures a cop will have three. One, certainly. Two, maybe. Three, never. Interestingly, Will never carried three sidearms during his days as a deputy. He carried one until the last few years on the department, when he didn't carry anything unless he was going into a situation. He didn't like guns, and was never a good shot. I think he overcompensated when he raised me to carry a small, but extremely accessible, arsenal. I practice with them, a lot.

He stared at the automatic. I hoped his hands weren't particularly oily, because even good bluing can rust from perspiration salts if you don't wipe a gun clean after you hold it. I took out one of my monogrammed handkerchiefs and set it next to the gun.

He looked up at me. "Do you feel remorse over the shootings?"

"Some."

"Can you describe how much?"

"That's a hard one, Doctor, to measure a feeling."

"Go ahead and try."

I thought about it. "About the amount you would put in a coffee cup. Not the whole cup, though. Say, about half."

"Half a coffee cup of remorse?"

"Yes, sir."

He nodded. Nodded again. "I'm concerned about you, Joe."

"Thank you."

"I mean, I'm not seeing a normal range of reaction out of you. I'm seeing something much less . . . expected."

"I'm not normal, sir."

After a long pause and some heavy note-taking, the doctor asked about women and love and relationships. He asked very direct questions. I told him the truth: that I'd never had any relationship that lasted more than a few "dates." I told him about some women I'd liked very much. He asked me if I'd ever had a meaningful relationship and I asked him what a meaningful relationship was. He looked flabbergasted, then suspicious that I was making fun of him. I told him about the professional models I'd paid to look at, and the sex that I had had with a prostitute. I told him about the faces I liked to look at in the movies and magazines. He wanted to know which movies and which magazines, so I told him: almost all romantic comedies, especially those of the fifties and seventies, and men's magazines such as *Esquire, Men's Journal* and *GQ*. I told him that I sometimes bought picture frames for the pictures of women that they came packaged with. I told him what scared me the most about women was that they'd feel sorry for me.

"How often do you masturbate?"

"I don't, sir."

"Why not?"

"My father told me not to."

"I see. What do you do about your sexual desires?"

"Nothing."

"What about nocturnal emissions, so-called wet dreams?"

"Yes, sir," I said. I looked down at my hat, wishing he wouldn't ask about things like that.

"How often?"

"Once a night, Doctor. Sometimes more."

"Every night?"

"I don't keep track. Since Will, a lot."

He swallowed, raised his eyebrows, and wrote something down. "Joe, we've got a lot to talk about. Next time, I would like to talk more about your mother and your father. Let's meet again next week."

We agreed on a day and time.

"Please treat that weapon with respect and care, Doctor."

"I shall."

I put on my hat and walked out.

My coffee date with June Dauer was for four o'clock, one hour before she did her show. I was supposed to meet her at a café near the studio. I got there early and sat at a corner table and thought about what Chrissa Sands had told me about Alex and Savannah Blazak.

When June walked into the café my heart started thumping like a washer with a bad leg. Black pants and sleeveless blouse, both tight with big shiny zippers on them, a silver belt looped around her waist, pointy black boots. Red lipstick. Rubies in her ears. Her skin is what got me most, though: brown and damp and extremely smooth looking.

The Unknown Thing seemed to just run off her, like rain off a roof.

I stood up and pulled out her stool.

"You look extremely nice today," I said.

She smiled. "Thank you very much."

The whole thing was a blur. A one-hour blur. She talked about growing up in Laguna Beach the same time I was growing up in Tustin. We graduated from different schools in the same years. She was twenty-four, like me. Her parents had told her about me when we were eight, and she had seen a picture of my face in a newspaper. She went to UC Irvine and got a double degree in history and English Lit, but spent a lot of her time at KUCI, learning radio. She won a broadcast award for a show she'd developed at KUCI called *Real Live*. She was pleasantly shocked to be offered a broadcast job at KFOC starting one week after her graduation from college. She did her show, plus dee-jaying four hours of music, plus news, traffic and weather. She'd been at the station for about six months.

"I love it," she said. "But I feel trapped. Twenty-four years old and I'm stuck in a dark studio six hours a day. I'm successful and some people are jealous of that. I picture myself in a cottage on the beach with two dogs, but I guess everybody pictures that."

I caught myself staring at her and made a point of looking away, looking at her coffee cup, her fingernails, the zipper down the middle of her blouse, anything to save her face from my eyes.

"Joe," she whispered. She curled a finger and I leaned in close. "You can look at my face."

"I'm sorry, I—"

"*I'm telling you not to be!*"

"Yes. All right."

She talked about herself some more and I appreciated it. It struck me that her talk was a gift for letting her question me on the air. I listened and asked questions and tried to look but not stare.

Look but not stare.

And then it was over. I walked her over to the studio and held open the door.

"I really enjoyed this time," I said. "I'd like there to be more of it. Can I take you out to dinner on Monday?"

She studied me for a moment. Mouth relaxed, no smile. Deep brown eyes shifting back and forth between mine, like they were examining them one at a time, really digging in. Her slender, rectangular face was expressionless. There was nothing in that face that I could read, except intensity, and I knew that some deep and close judgment was being made.

"All right," she said. "Call me and I'll tell you how to find me."

"I'm extremely happy about this."

"See you then."

She walked past the reception desk and the door buzzed open. She turned and waved, then disappeared.

The receptionist smiled at me.

At the sheriff's range I drew and shot fifty right-handed practice rounds, then drew and shot fifty with my left. Then I alternated another twenty-five from each side. I borrowed a .45 ACP from the firearms instructor, but it didn't have the butter-smooth action I'd tooled into the personal weapon that Dr. Zussman had confiscated. That lowered the group two inches on the silhouette. I drew and shot the little .32 twenty times. It's interesting how quickly you can drop to one knee, shuck up your cuff with your left hand, then pop the snap and draw with your right. The magic is that you're already kneeling, already stable for fire. But it's still tough to shoot a good group at fifty feet with a gun that small.

I cleaned the sidearms thoroughly when I was finished. Shot well, though the left hand got tired and shivered a little. Then I drove back to headquarters to lift some weights and collect the mail from my cubby.

There were three messages that Jaime Medina had called. Each one said IMPORTANT! PLEASE RETURN CALL SOON. There was also a letter from someone whose crowded handwriting I'd never seen, so I didn't bother to open it.

Last was a note from my friend Melissa in the crime lab.

It said, *Scored on your behalf, see me ASAP.*

Yes, she did score on my behalf: the sucker stick I'd bagged in Alex Blazak's weapons emporium held saliva with DNA almost certainly belonging to Savannah. Melissa was able to match it up with a water-glass saliva sample supplied by Jack and Lorna to Steve Marchant of the FBI. The FBI had turned the water glass over to our lab to get the DNA workup and Melissa had filched the results.

The Macanudo cigar was smoked by Alex, whose DNA patterns were on file with the California Department of Corrections. The Davidoff smoker, she said, was anybody's guess.

"I haven't run the fingerprints you lifted yet," she said. "Give me another day or two."

"I owe you, Melissa."

"How about a cup of coffee sometime?"

"Uh . . . it would be my pleasure."

I left headquarters with a strange feeling. I stopped for takeout and still had it. Driving home, I pictured them again, brother and sister sitting in the upstairs room in Alex's warehouse, watching cartoons. Savannah working on a grape sucker. Alex puffing a Macanudo. She wasn't tied up or knocked out or locked in a room. I remembered Savannah on the one night I'd seen her: calm and polite.

She didn't look kidnapped. She looked like a girl with a Pocahontas backpack, about to take a short trip.

Chapter Eleven

The letter with the cramped handwriting was from my father, Thor Svendson. It was the first one he'd ever written me.

I read his signature first. Just that glance was enough to make my heart beat faster and bring a choking thickness in my throat. My hands shook. A comet of pure white pain streaked across my face.

I set down the letter. I could smell the fear on myself—metal and ammonia. I took three deep breaths, got up and walked outside. The neighborhood looked like it always did, but everything was wavering and outlined in a faint haze of red. It was hard to get air, so I concentrated on my breathing.

All I could think to do was climb to the quiet spot, up into those trees where no one can see me but I can see everything. I found the tree. I climbed. I backed into the leafy branches, disappeared, stared out. My focus was back. The neighborhood was clear and specific.

I stayed there for a long time before going back into the house.

This is what the letter said:

Dear Joe,

Hi. I'm writing because I need you to forgive me. I
believe in God now and don't think I can get into
heaven unless you do it. That's what this book I got
says. You need to do it in person but that court thing
you got against me lasts my whole life unless you get
rid of it. I'm in Seattle. I'm coming into Santa Ana by
train on Saturday, the 23rd. Don't have me arrested.
Maybe we can have a drink and catch up a little. I'll
pay. Maybe it would be good for you to get to know
your old man, since your other one got shot. The least
you'd get is a free drink. And like I said I can't get
into heaven without you.

                                    Sincerely,
                                    Thor Svendson

I sat in the backyard patio and ate the take-out food. The
evening was cool and damp, like the night Will died. Not long
after sundown the fog rolled in and I could see the swirling
droplets of moisture, then the misty cloud of it around my patio
lights.

I got a jacket and went back outside. I pictured Thor Svendson from the newspaper and magazine photographs I'd seen of
him—plenty were published after he was arrested, more when
he was sentenced to thirteen years in Corcoran State Prison,
more when he was released after seven. I had quite a collection
of them at one time, and sometimes I'd read about him and
myself, just like any other subscriber would. I looked at the
pictures. In almost all of them he looked friendly enough, with
no obvious malice. But then, true malice isn't obvious.

No, Thor was somewhat large and potbellied, with longish
white hair and a white beard and large, very blue eyes. He
looked like Santa Claus. He would be sixty-four years old,

though even in those pictures taken just after his arrest, when he was forty, he looked old.

For reasons I've never understood he's smiling in many of his pictures. Not many men would smile after being convicted of mayhem and attempted murder, then sentenced to thirteen years in Corcoran. Thor did. It was a sorry smile, a smile that suggested hard-won wisdom. It's the ugliest smile I've ever seen.

When I dream of him and what he did, he's always smiling as he reaches out with the coffee cup and pours. His big blue eyes seem to be pitying. He's smiling a smile that looks genuine and caring. Very sincere. Like he doesn't truly endorse this but he has to do it anyway. In the dream I always wonder *why* he has to do it—but that's an important aspect of the dream—I can never know why. Because I deserve it? Because God told him to? Because it's the only way to teach me some hugely important lesson?

In my dreams, his expression terrifies me twice as much as the acid does. I don't actually remember his face at the time it happened. I don't remember him at all. I really only remember one thing: diving deep into myself to get away from something huge and evil, like diving under a monstrously large wave to get to that peaceful zone near the ocean floor, where you can dig your fingers into the sand and hang on for dear life.

According to the newspapers, Thor took me to a fire station after he did what he did. He told one magazine, months later, that God had told him to throw the acid, and God had told him to take me to the firehouse. The firemen took me to the hospital and called the cops on Thor. I don't know why he didn't just run for it and leave me screaming, and I don't want to know.

I don't dream about my real mother. Her name was Charlotte Wample and she was eighteen when I was born, so she'd be forty-two now. I don't know where she is, never have. She and

Thor were not married. According to the news accounts and court testimony—I've read every word of transcript several times, every *umm* and *hmm* and *uhh*—she wasn't home at the time Thor lost it. She was out getting family staples: diapers, bourbon and cigarettes.

I've only seen one picture of her. It was a newspaper shot taken as she left the Orange County Courthouse, though I didn't see that issue of the *Journal* until almost fourteen years later. She was a wiry, unhappy looking woman with long white hair and hard eyes. She's lighting a smoke as she comes out the door. Under cross, the prosecuting attorney got her to tell the court her nickname when she rode with the Hessians: Harlot. Charlotte the Harlot. Not hugely imaginative, but the Hessians are better at the meth racket than humor.

Six years ago, when I was eighteen, I looked up every Wample I could find in Orange County directories, and found two. I called them both. One was a man who said he'd never heard of a Charlotte Wample, but he'd been born in Charlotte, North Carolina, and talked for a while about that city. Nice guy.

But the other was a woman, Valeen, who said her daughter Charlotte was a whore, hopefully dead, definitely better off that way. I asked her if Charlotte's boyfriend hurt her baby and she hissed yes, that sonofabitchin' bastard Thor Svendson threw acid on him but what the hell is it to you, mister?

The short conversation made me feel much worse, rather than better. I don't know exactly why I called, what I expected to hear or say. If a Charlotte Wample had actually answered the phone, I probably would have hung up. What would I say? How come you never tried to see me? Don't you love me?

I'm sure Charlotte has moved away, married or at least changed her name by now. I have no interest in seeing her. But I did put the phone number for Valeen in my wallet, way down in one of the credit card slots. The last time I looked it was still there.

My grandmother was a scary lady. Even just on the phone. But blood is blood and you can't change it. I think about Valeen Wample occasionally. Grandmother. Grandma. Grams.

I called the Amtrak station in Santa Ana and got the recorded arrival schedule for the Coast Starlight. It was set to bring the devil himself, on a quest for forgiveness, into Santa Ana at 10:17 P.M. the next day.

Just after nine, Rick Birch called. "Meet me at Lind Street in one hour. Bring what you've been holding back, Joe. Do you understand?"

I said I did and Birch hung up.

Lind Street. I felt the hair on my neck rise, felt my scar throb when I stepped in behind Rick Birch and smelled the same bacon and cigarette smoke I'd smelled there before.

You killed him. You killed him. You killed him.

Same worn-out carpet, worn-out pad, same sheets on the windows. Same everything, except for the fresh smudges of fingerprint powder and the location tags left by the crime scene investigators.

"Nice place," said Birch. His eyes were clear and gray in his old, lined face. "Guess who paid the rent?"

"A guy with Alex Blazak's face and somebody else's name."

"Right. Paid first, last and a cleaning deposit on Monday, June the eleventh. His CDL said Mark Stoltz, useless address and phone number. Two days later, it all went down in the alley behind."

"What about the woman who was here?"

Birch brought out his pad. "Anaheim PD helped me out.

Rosa Descanso. Bonded, licensed baby-sitter. Hired by Stoltz through an agency down on Katella. I went to see her. She said the guy wanted a sitter with her own wheels. Descanso got here at seven o'clock that night. Alex and Savannah were here. Getting along real fine, she said—brother and sister. She liked Savannah right off, thought her brother was a 'not so good a person.' Alex left a few minutes later. You and Will got here at ten-fifteen, she said. When the shooting started a few minutes after that, she jumped into the bathtub. She figured it was some business with the Lincoln 18th gang."

I walked slowly across the small living room, down the hall, into the room where'd I'd first seen Savannah Blazak.

I'm Savannah. How do you do?

I'm not sure. Please come with me though.

I turned to Birch. "It's like having a bad dream twice."

He nodded but said nothing.

Being there stoked my memories, brought back images from that night: the headlights, the Tall One, the muzzle flash, Will slumped and bleeding.

Oops.

I heard a car zoom down the alley behind the apartment. The voice started up inside my head again: *you killed him you killed him you killed him.*

I could barely hear my own voice when I spoke. "I haven't lied to you, sir. But there are a few things I left out."

Birch shook his head and stared at me. "You ready to fill them in?"

"Yes, sir."

"Good. And cut this yes sir, no sir shit. I had enough of that in the Army."

I told him everything: Will's nerves that night, his conversations with Jaime and the Reverend Daniel, the roll of money he gave to Jennifer Avila. Their words. Mary Ann being blue. I told him about the transmitter on the BMW, the date in his appointment book with Carl Rupaski and Dana Millbrae. I told him what the Blazaks had said about Savannah's kidnapping, and about their psychopathic son. I told him about Bo Warren and the offer to hypnotize me so I could tell them what I'd seen and heard. I told him about Lorna Blazak giving me Alex's warehouse address, and what I'd found there. I told him about Will's meeting with Ellen Erskine of Hillview Home for Children. I told him about Chrissa Sands talking to Savannah, and to Jack. I told him that she'd seen Will with Alex and Savannah the night before he died. I gave him the postcard that Alex had written to Chrissa.

When I was finished I found myself standing at the window, looking at the floral pattern in the dirty sheet that served as a curtain. I couldn't shake the feeling that I'd somehow let down Will by telling everything I knew about that night. Or the feeling that I'd betrayed him as payment for keeping me in the dark about so much of it.

When I turned, Birch was looking at me over the tops of his rimless glasses.

"You did the right thing."

"Thank you."

"Do you think Alex kidnapped her, or do you think she ran away?"

"Ran away."

"Any idea why?"

"Absolutely none."

"Scamming the rich old man?"

"That occurred to me. She's awfully young to be doing something like that."

"Alex is about the right age, though, isn't he?"

"And Jack and Alex hate each other."

"I'll take the postcard into evidence," he said.

"I figured you would, sir."

"But I've got something for you," he said.

He slipped a folded sheet of paper from his notepad, handed it to me. It was the phone company readout, showing all cell calls to and from Will's phone on the night he died. The phone company security division had translated the numbers into names and billing addresses, which were neatly printed in the margins.

I eagerly looked for the last three calls of that terrible night.

Two were incoming, one outgoing.

Will had received the first at 9:38 P.M. I remembered it very clearly, when he'd said "Trona," then listened and asked, "You've got it, right?"

Then he'd given me the Lind Street address. According to Birch's annotated sheet, the number was for a phone belonging to Alex Blazak.

Alex, I thought, confirming that he'd gotten something, probably the tennis bag I'd left on the court bench. Ransom. Then, Lind Street.

Next, at 9:57 P.M., Will got another call. He said: *Things are lining up. I'll do what I can do, but I still can't turn coal into a diamond.*

And it had come from a telephone number belonging to Luz Escobar. Her address was on Raitt Street in Santa Ana. In the margin Rick had written, "Escobar's brother Felix popped for gang murder. Luz aka Pearlita. Shot caller."

I remembered Jennifer Avila's words on the phone that night, while I eavesdropped on Will and Jaime: *Get Pearlita.*

The last call of his life was placed at 10:01 P.M., placed by Will to a residential line in Newport Beach belonging to Ellen Erskine.

Looks like we'll be there on time.

Will, confirming the Lind Street pickup of Savannah Blazak, was how I read it.

"I talked to Erskine yesterday," he said. "After I got the call list. And guess what? Will wasn't going to return Savannah to her parents that night. He'd arranged to deliver the girl to Erskine at Hillview Home for Children."

"I don't understand that. Why?"

"Erskine had no idea. Will didn't give the girl's name. Didn't describe the girl's circumstances, except to say she needed to be safe. Will was due to meet Erskine at Child Protective Services between ten and ten-thirty. He obviously didn't show. When Erskine saw the news the next night, she went straight to Marchant."

I couldn't make sense of it, no matter how I tried.

"Joe, what kind of ugly stuff was your father mixed up in?"

"I can't answer that. I don't think there was anything ugly. I've told you everything I know."

"Yeah?" he said. "I almost believe you this time."

"It's the truth."

I stood on the stairway and waited for Rick to lock up the Lind Street apartment. When he was done we walked down the stairs and toward our cars.

"I've called Bernadette Lee. No answer. I've gone to that address you gave me. Not home. Maybe Sammy can shed some light."

"I'll see what I can do."

I left Lind Street with John Gaylen's strange lilting voice in my head. I replayed his conversation with Will as I drove to the address I'd seen gummed to Birch's Interview Contact form.

I found the number and parked across the street, two houses down. It was a sixties housing tract, well kept. Gaylen's house was yellow, with planters and window trim that looked faintly Swiss. The palm trees in the yard didn't.

It was a little after eleven. Houselights were on inside. The porchlight glowed dully and I could see moths fluttering against the fixture.

Will! Ah, Will Trona! Let's talk.

I sank down in the seat a little and leaned my head back. Just like Will used to do. I tried to imitate his drowsy look but alert, moving eyes. I tried to look judgmental but somehow possessive, too, like I was trying to figure a way to improve things.

While I watched the house I thought about Will. I remembered, very clearly, the first time I'd met him, at Hillview. It was a rainy Saturday. I was five years old, hidden in the corner of the Hillview library, almost reading *Shag: Last of the Plains Buffalo*. I could almost read it by that age because I had spent a lot of time with books in general, and with that book in particular. I loved it. I loved Shag. The pictures were fabulous.

I was a deeply suspicious and profoundly fearful five-year-old lost in a book. More than lost—*lost* isn't quite right. When I was in a book I was looking down, so no one could see the bad half of my face. No one could see the hideous, painful, red pulp of skin and muscle that was what I had to greet the world with.

But with my face hidden from sight I could forget about it, and my mind could travel wherever I wanted to go in space and time. I could travel thousands of miles from Hillview, to the American plains of two hundred years ago, and I could watch this magnificent animal Shag as he fought a grizzly, took an arrow, fled into Yellowstone with the last of his kind.

I was there with Shag in Yellowstone.

So I paid no attention to the person who had walked in and sat down across from me at the little table. Because I was with Shag. The man—I could tell he was a man by the sound of his walk and the cologne he wore—drummed his fingers. But I ran with Shag.

"Son," he finally said. "Look at me, because I'm looking at you."

So I did, and into the wisest, kindest, most handsome and sad and humorful face I'd ever seen in my life. I'd never thought about it before but when I saw that man I understood what a man should be. *Him.* It was as clear to me as it was clear to Shag that he had to get away into Yellowstone.

"It's only a scar," he said. "Everyone's got 'em. Yours is just on the outside."

I'd looked away by then, of course, but I found the courage to answer in a whisper: "Shag's got scars on his sides, from the bear."

"See? They're nothing to be ashamed of."

I really don't know what gave me the impossible courage to say what I said next. But I did. "Where are yours?"

"I'll answer when you look at me again."

I did.

He hit his chest lightly with his fist. "I'm Will Trona," he said.

Then he stood up and left.

I didn't see him again until the next Saturday. I was in the library again. He gave me a package wrapped in Sunday comics. Inside was a brand-new copy of *Shag: Last of the Plains Buffalo.*

"I thought you might like to have your own," he said.

"Thank you, sir."

"Mind if I sit?"

"No, sir."

"I've been talking with some of the people here about you. They tell me you're quite a boy."

I said nothing. I looked away and felt the hot scream beginning in my cheek.

"Joe, I was wondering if you'd like to blow this joint for a while, maybe go get ice cream or goof around on the pier down in Newport. It's a nice day. There's fishermen and skateboarders and pretty girls and all sorts of stuff to look at. I got these keepers of yours to cut you loose for two hours. What do you say?"

I knew what I wanted to say, but it was hard to say it. So few decisions had been mine to make, I wasn't sure how to answer for myself. The institutions had always answered for me: the courts, the hospitals, the state, the county, the homes.

At that moment I experienced the first flutter of liberty, and the first pain of freedom. I felt like I was standing on a high dive the width of a shoe box, wind blowing hard around me, trying to make my mind up whether to dive in, head back to the ladder, or just stand there and tremble.

Will Trona said nothing. He didn't prod me or hurry me or ask me again or drum his fingers or sigh.

Instead, he put his hands behind his head, leaned back and looked at me very calmly, almost sleepily. Like he was imagining a way to make me better.

"Okay, sir. Yes."

"Excellent, young man. Let's get out of this dive. I got a red 1980 TransAm with the big V-8 and a five-speed. *Guaranteed* to blow your hair back, Joe."

After an hour of sitting outside John Gaylen's house, nothing had happened, so I turned on the radio.

After another hour nothing had happened, so I turned it off.

I thought some more about Will.

After another hour it was pushing two-thirty and nothing at all had changed at Gaylen's house, except maybe the moths.

I sat up, started the car and drove home.

Chapter Twelve

Early the next morning I went to see Reverend Daniel Alter. I had questions for him, some things that weren't sitting right about Will and Savannah. And there was something else I wanted to ask him.

Daniel had been my pastor for almost ten years, though there was a year-long gap when I didn't see much of him. During that one year—beginning around my seventeenth birthday—I went through a craze that took me to almost twenty different baptisms. Most were mass baptisms, where an extra guy wouldn't be a burden. My face stirred the pity of more than one skeptical minister. Some Sundays I drove seventy miles each way.

The full immersions were best. There's something about being lowered and raised, something about the blessed water drenching my face and hard tissue, cooling, running off, cleansing away the heat, the sin, the hatred. Afterwards I'd be enormously hungry.

But that was years ago, when I was young. Now I'm content to listen to Daniel. He baptized me once and that will have to do. Sometimes I get the urge for more, but I control myself. I watch the others go forward and smile quietly as I imagine the holy water running down the violent furrows of my face. I'm also quite happy to have my face rained on. I like winter.

The Reverend Daniel's secretary buzzed me into the office elevator in the Chapel of Light. Seven stories up, a glass elevator, views across the county to the mountains. I walked across the royal blue carpet with the tiny oranges with green leaves on it as Daniel swiveled around to greet me.

He always dressed the same: chinos, black loafers, white polo shirt, his habitual Angels baseball cap. He told his congregation that the cap was to persuade the Father to get the Angels a division championship or at least some better hitting down the stretch.

"Oh, Joe. Joe *Trona.*"

"Good morning, Reverend. I'm sorry to barge in, but I wanted to talk to you."

"That door is never locked on you. You know that. Please, sit."

We sat. Orange leather sofas, blue cushions, the county spread out below in a blanket of summer haze and smog.

"I love it early on Saturdays here," he said. "No programs. No business. Nobody here, really, except me and the church mice. Joe, how can I help you?"

"Can I ask you a direct question?"

He smiled. "My favorite kind."

"Well, when you and Dad were talking in the Grove booth that night, the night he died, you two were talking about Savannah Blazak. One part of the conversation went exactly like this. Will said, *I know where she is. But I'm not so sure I trust those people with her.* And you said back, *What could you mean by that?*"

Daniel's eyes widened, magnified by his thick glasses.

"Joe, that's called eavesdropping!"

"I know, Reverend. It was always part of my job."

A big smile from Daniel, then, "What a memory you've got, Joe."

"It's a gift."

He watched me with his big eyes.

"Reverend, my father knew the Blazaks socially. Would he have any reason not to trust them?"

"Why, none that I know, Joe. I can tell you that Will and Jack Blazak crossed swords in the world. As you know, they had different views. Jack, very bullish on growth for the county. Will, believing that not all growth was good. They were not close friends. But I have no idea what Will didn't trust about Jack or Lorna. Or Bo."

Daniel looked pensively out the window.

"Sir, Will wouldn't find a kidnapped girl, then keep her away from her family unless he had a very good reason."

"Agreed."

"Reverend, what did you give him that night?"

"When?"

"In the booth at the Grove. When you said *here's this*."

Again the widened eyes—it was a trademark expression from his TV performances, indicating amazement at the mercy, wisdom and good humor of God. He laughed quietly.

"Joe, this memory of yours. I never knew it was so, uh . . ."

"They call it eidetic, Reverend."

"It could be a miracle, or a curse, couldn't it?"

"Not forgetting is both."

"So you *never* forget anything?"

"I don't know yet. I'm only twenty-four."

He smiled then, and sat back. Daniel's smile brought the lines of his face into their happy old alignment. And his eyes lit up like they always seemed to.

"Joe, you could count the cards in a blackjack game! Bet on a rich deck, beat the house."

Whenever Daniel's mind takes a sinful tack, it often comes to gambling. He mentions it in his performances, using it as an example of the kind of sin that's glittery and tempting. I've heard him talk about sports bets with Will. He knows a lot about sports, every kind. He surprises me sometimes, like that last night with Will when he walked past my table and called the shot and spin my ball needed. As if his seminary days were spent in casinos, pool halls and sports parks.

Maybe the idea of gambling thrills him, because Daniel is a tightwad. His Chapel of Light ministries take in untold millions of dollars every year—much of it never taxed—but Daniel himself lives in a modest home in Irvine. Drives a Taurus. His wife, Rosemary, is another story. Solomon in all his glory was not arrayed like her, and he did not keep apartments in Newport Beach, Majorca and Cabo San Lucas.

"Well, Joe, all I gave Will that night was payment for a small, friendly wager we made on the Freeway Series. The Angel relievers failed."

He shrugged and smiled, looking half ashamed of himself for wagering, half irritated with the Angel bullpen.

"We had a deal that all winning bets went to a charity—winner's choice. You know Will, always trying to help someone."

As a couple, my mother and father had donated $235,000 to charities the first six months of the year, not including the $50,000 memorial to the family of Sammy Nguyen's victim. This was reported in one of the articles that ran last week around the funeral. Over his lifetime the total was $2.75 million.

Most of it had to come from my mother, who had multiplied her share of the family fortune several times over, according to Will. That fortune had begun here in the county in the early nineteenth century, and evolved with the times—ranching to citrus to land to real estate.

"How much was the wager, Reverend?"

"One hundred dollars." Daniel looked down, then turned away from me to look out the window to the county that had made so many people rich.

"Do you pray regularly, Joe?"

"No, sir."

"You should. He listens."

I looked out again at the county spread before us. Almost three million souls. A lot for Him to listen to, but I believed Reverend Daniel anyway. If there's one thing in life I've learned, it's this: there's a lot I don't understand.

"Sir, do you believe that Alex Blazak kidnapped his sister and threatened to kill her?"

He looked confused. "Why, absolutely, Joe. Alex Blazak is certifiably insane, and a criminal. That's all a matter of record. He pulled a knife on me right here in this study one day, and threatened to throw me out the window. He was fourteen. It was just for fun—he laughed afterwards. Told his friends that I urinated through my robe, which I did not. I *absolutely* believe he would kidnap his sister. I believe he would kill her, too, if he didn't get what he wanted. The stories about him that I've heard from his parents are very frightening. He's a disturbed young man—just twenty-one years old. But very, very disturbed."

It wasn't hard to believe Daniel, even knowing that his business is making you believe him.

"My father wasn't going to take Savannah back to her parents. He was going to deliver her to Hillview."

The Reverend's eyes got large again. *"Why?"*

"He didn't tell me. I thought maybe he told you."

"Oh, no. No. I don't see any reason why he would do something like that."

"Dad used to say he could smell Blazak's soul rotting from ten feet away."

"That's graphic."

"It sounds like more than a disagreement about toll roads or airports."

"Well, yes, when you put it in those terms." Daniel nodded. "I can't see Will interfering with a good family simply to fuel political fires."

"I can't either. So it must have been something else."

I stood and thanked him. I thought again about the 10:17 Coast Starlight arriving in Santa Ana that night, and felt that chill in my fingers again. Daniel studied me, his expression patient and curious.

"Is there something else bothering you, Joe?"

"Yes. My father—you know, Thor, the real one—is coming into town tonight. He wants to see me. I don't know what to do."

I told Daniel about the letter, about Thor's plan for getting into heaven, about his need for my forgiveness.

"Oh, my," said Daniel. "This is a difficult situation."

"When I think of the Amtrak station at ten-seventeen tonight, my heart speeds up and my face hurts and I feel cold."

"As well you should, Joe." Daniel leaned back and studied me. "Is it fear?"

"Yes."

"But not of what he could do to you?"

"Do? No, he can't do anything to me now."

"Fear of what, then?"

"Of failing to hate him."

"You'll have to explain that, Joe."

"I always have hated him. It's been simple and safe and understandable. When Will died, it left me not as strong. I don't feel love or hate. I feel like everything's about the same as everything else and none of it matters. So, I wonder if I should see Thor. Talk to him. A month ago I wouldn't have considered."

"Did you wish to harm him?"

"I used to imagine that a lot, when I was learning a martial art or practicing with weapons. With pleasure. Now, there's no pleasure in it."

"What do you want to tell him, Joe? What does your heart want to say?"

I had to think about that. "Nothing, sir. I don't want to tell him one single thing."

"Oh?"

"Just the question: why?"

"Perhaps it would do you good to have an answer to that. You deserve one."

"I've always thought so. It's just that when I imagine standing there and watching him come off that train, my whole body gets wrong. Like my nerves are firing backwards."

"It's a huge thing, Joe. Will you pray with me? Let's ask God what you should do."

We prayed and Daniel ended it with the twenty-third Psalm, my favorite. I tried to listen in my heart for God but I didn't hear anything except a faint rushing in my ears. God is said to speak to people and I believe this, though he's never spoken to me. I felt like being baptized but didn't want to ask.

"Thank you, Reverend."

"Trust the Lord."

"Yes, sir."

"Honor your mother. She needs you now."

"I'll be seeing her in just a few minutes."

"Say hello to her from me."

My mother was the first woman I ever fell in love with.

The third time Will came to Hillview to see me, he brought Mary Ann. She was wearing a white dress. She looked like she'd just come from the beach, her face tanned and eyes clear, her blond hair a little windblown, her legs dark and smooth.

When they walked into the recreation room that Thursday evening I watched them come through the door with one of our supervisors, enter, look around. I was stunned by their beauty. Will so tall and capable; Mary Ann so radiant and composed. They looked to me like beings from a superior planet, on Earth for a look around. I wanted them to be looking for me. I *thought* they were looking for me. But a voice deep inside me said that they absolutely could not be looking for a meat-faced five-year-old who could barely stand to look another human in the eye.

I was stacking blocks to form a small house. I stepped away from the house, trying to stand out. I looked toward the couple but not directly at them. When I saw them start walking in my direction, my heart soared and my ears got red-hot and my vision got misty.

Will introduced me to his wife, Mary Ann. She stepped forward and held out a tanned hand with a thin gold bracelet around the wrist. Her fingers were cool and I could smell her very clearly: water, sun, something sweet and flowery and tropical. She let go of my hand and she straightened. I came up just barely past her waist. She smiled at me and I looked at her for just a second, like glancing at the sun, then turned the ruined side of my face away.

"I'm so pleased to meet you, Joe."

"I'm pleased to meet you, ma'am."

"Will's told me all about you."

There was nothing I could say to that.

We stood there for a moment and I felt something for the first time: belonging. It was such an easy, wonderful feeling. But one second later that sense of belonging turned into the glum assurance of abandonment. Orphans have a keen understanding of history. I knew that this thing with Will and Mary

Ann Trona—whatever it was—would be short-lived. In fact, I assumed as I stood there and struggled for something to say that it was already over.

"You can stay if you want," I said. I pointed to my project. "The house isn't finished."

"Let's have a look at it," said Will.

Unreasonably pleased, I led them over to the blocks. Pride of ownership.

"Too small," said Will. "You need somewhere you can spread out, play hard, learn something."

"It's a nicely designed space," said Mary Ann. "Isn't that the kitchen?"

I nodded.

One of my older institution mates wandered over, drawn like a moth to the light of the Tronas. He was a rough and confident boy, eight, maybe, who pinched my back or kicked my shins when the supers weren't looking. Called me Gargantua, after this gorilla who gets acid thrown on his face in a story. I angled to stand between him and my visitors, but he tried to squeeze past.

He tried to get close to Will and Mary Ann.

I attacked with a fury I always knew I had. By the time Will pulled me off, the boy was screaming and I could already feel the sharp pain in my hand where, later, x rays would show a cracked bone.

Save it, Joe, he'd said, holding me tight by the arms and settling me. *Save your anger. Save it. Save it.*

I spent the next three hours locked in the "Thinking Room," where you were supposed to reflect upon whatever deed it was that got you there. My hand was killing me, swelling up. There was a cut on the middle knuckle the size and shape of the cutting edge of a front tooth.

But I hardly thought about the pain. All I could think about was the fact that I'd never see the Tronas again. I wanted to put my face in cool water, but there was no sink in the Thinking Room. The next day I tried to draw Will and Mary Ann with Crayola and pencil, and the drawing came out pretty good. It decorated the wall beside my bed for nearly a week, until someone ripped it away, leaving only two jagged corners held to the plaster with strips of tape.

I wrote them several letters that I hid under my mattress. I thought about them every minute I was awake. I dreamed about them, that we were in a spaceship whistling through space to a planet where all you did was have fun and be together. But I didn't mention Will or Mary Ann to the supers or anyone else, because I'd learned by the age of five that dreams were not real and dreams you spoke about would almost always become a humiliation.

One week after the fight I was called to the director's office. I walked there slowly and with absolute dread. I glanced up at the motto on the wall outside the office, reading again the words I'd read so many times before: *Heal the Past, Save the Present, Create the Future.* My throat felt so thick it ached.

But there they were, waiting for me, Will and Mary Ann, from another planet, the future I had created in my mind. I sat and listened to the director and slowly came to understand— through a conflicting riot of excitement and pessimism—that these proceedings were to begin the process of my formal adoption into the family of Will and Mary Ann Trona. Her words were like words in a dream—pleasant but insubstantial and subject to change.

"Joe, what this means is that if you behave properly and everything works out, Will and Mary Ann could become your mother and father someday."

I sat very still and waited for the dream to end.

But it was just beginning.

* * *

I picked up Mary Ann and drove us out of the Tustin foothills and down Jamboree toward the County Art Museum.

She sat still beside me in a simple black dress, purse on her lap, hands on her purse, looking out the windows.

"These housing tracts were orange groves when I was a girl," she said. "Dad sold off these sections and made a potload. I look at it now and wish the groves were still here. Easy for me to say, though, with so much filthy lucre in my pockets."

"People need to live somewhere. And some people are better to have around than orange trees."

"Name three from any era in history."

"You, Dad and Lincoln."

She thought about that. "Dad and I. Will and I. I know you're trying to cheer me up, but you're not. We've got to change the subject."

"Summer's really here," I said.

"It makes me think of rafting those waves at Huntington."

"Let's do it again, when the water warms up."

"Sure, Joe."

My mother is a beautiful woman, full-bodied and shapely, with straight blonde hair, blue eyes and a lovely face. Her smile is easy and mischievous. When I fell in love with her at five, the second I met her, I really had no choice. My heart jumped into her, and there it stayed.

Back then, I didn't understand how I could go from the institutional halls of Hillview to a home in the fragrant foothills, taken in by those two magnificent people. I didn't truly believe it, kept waiting for the punchline, the laugh, the acid to fly.

It was only much later that Mary Ann told me that I was a miracle of sorts, for them. Because after the birth of Glenn, Mary Ann and Will had wanted another child. They'd tried and tried, consulted fertility specialists—everything. Nothing

worked. Six years of hope followed by frustration. And then
Will had a conversation with one of the Hillview staff and my
"case" had come up. Neither Will nor Mary Ann had considered adopting an older child. But the next weekend, Will Trona
had walked into the Hillview library to audition me. And my
"case" became a dream-come-true for all of us.

We ate our lunch outside at the museum, then sat in the mild
sun and drank lemonades. She wore her sunglasses and I
couldn't see what she was thinking.

"Mom, I've got to know what he was doing. You were closer
to him than anybody. He loved you and he trusted you. Anything he said about what he was doing that night. Anything he
said about Savannah Blazak. Anything he said to *anybody* about
anything."

She looked at me again and her chin trembled. She took a
deep breath. "Joe," she said quietly. "Will was world champion
at keeping me out of the loop."

"You must have heard something, you must have had a feeling something was going on."

"You're going to have to be more specific. I wouldn't know
where to start."

"Okay. Why didn't Dad trust Jack and Lorna Blazak?"

She studied me from behind the big dark glasses. "He hated
Jack—you know that. Hated his politics, his money, everything
about him. I suppose hatred makes distrust. So far as Lorna
goes, I couldn't say."

"That night, the night he died, he was all set to take Savannah to Child Protective Services, not back to her parents."

"Something to do with the money?"

"No. He'd already collected that."

"Then maybe he'd learned something."

"*What,* Mom? That's what I need to know."

She shook her head. "I can't give you what I don't have, Joe. Maybe he never *was* going to deliver her to them."

Interesting. I hadn't considered it. "Why not?"

"I don't know, Joe, I'm speculating."

If the life of an eleven-year-old child wasn't at stake, I'd admit that Will would have used just about anything to make things hard for Jack Blazak. He would have delighted in it. Because Jack Blazak was everything Will loathed.

Blazak was an immensely wealthy man, and his influence in the county was large. He'd put two politicians into the California Assembly recently, mostly with soft PAC contributions made through the Grove Club Research & Action Committee. Likewise, he backed both the north and south Orange County U.S. Congressional Representatives. He sat on the board of eleven companies, all of which rank in the Fortune 500. Estimated personal worth, something like $12 billion. He was four years younger than Will—fifty.

"What about the airport, Joe? Will would have . . . gone to some lengths to throw a monkey wrench into that."

The new airport was Jack Blazak's signature project. In the last year he'd spent hundreds of thousands of his own dollars, trying to convince voters to build a new international airport on the abandoned marine base at El Toro.

Although the airport we have now is new by airport standards, and one of the best organized and easiest to use in the whole country, Blazak and his business allies were contending that it was already too small, too outdated and too dangerous. He and his business allies also stood to make profane amounts of money by building it and—through their friends in government—running it. Blazak and his friends called themselves the Citizens' Committee for Airport Safety. Their bureaucratic dance partner was, of course, the Orange County Transportation Authority, led by Carl Rupaski.

To answer the question of cost, Blazak was proposing that the county spend eight hundred million dollars of its Federal tobacco settlement money to build that airport. The tobacco money was supposed to be spent on public health facilities and services, although technically each county is free to spend it however it wants.

The pro-airport people said Blazak's plan was a stroke of genius and had spent five million dollars to convince the voters of it. The anti-airport crowd said it was illegal and immoral, and spent two million to convince them otherwise.

It was a hot topic, gallons of ink and miles of videotape devoted to it. Easily, the most divisive issue in county history. A special election was set for November, and a huge voter turnout was already predicted.

And Will had been fighting that airport, tooth and nail, ever since Blazak had proposed it.

Yes, Will despised Blazak's greed, but I couldn't fit Savannah into it. Will wouldn't play with an eleven-year-old. He wasn't that kind of man.

What she said next surprised me.

"I'm so angry at him, Joe. For his scheming and his conniving and his philandering. I know you were privy to all that. I know *I* was supposed to be in the dark about it. Somehow, I think that's what got him killed. All that night business he did. All the intrigue he just couldn't live without."

I felt my face warming with shame.

"It's okay, Joe. I'm not blaming you in any way. Please believe that."

I couldn't speak. Even then I couldn't admit my father's secrets to her, even though she must have known many of them, even though my face betrayed my knowledge.

"You were his son for that," she said, matter-of-factly. "Junior got prosperity. Glenn got happiness. You got the truth."

I looked down, eyes stinging. Lowered my hat brim a little to cut the glare and keep Mom from seeing my face.

"And then, Joe, I hate myself for being angry at him. I think of what happened and I can't believe I could add anger to all that pain and loss. But I am."

"I feel some of that too, Mom."

She looked at me a long time. "I'll bet you feel more anger at yourself, and at those men. And I'll bet you torment yourself over how it happened, how you could have avoided it."

"Yes."

"Oh, my sweet, silent Joe."

Silent. Mom's term of endearment.

"Stop," I said.

"You want vengeance, don't you?"

"Very much."

"Now, see . . . I'm angry at Will again, for putting you through this."

"No. Dad didn't kill Dad. We have to keep things straight. If we don't, we'll do something stupid and make it all worse."

"I know. I know."

I felt the warm June breeze on my face, thick with the salt air of the ocean. I was aware of each second going by. They weren't happy seconds, but I wanted them anyway.

"Joe, you know what I do sometimes, late at night? I can't sleep so I get up and drive. Just drive, anywhere. Like Will used to do. Not many people are out and about then. Makes me feel like I'm getting a head start. Though a head start on *what* I couldn't say."

"I told you you'd enjoy it."

"You were right."

At the grave we stood and looked at the fresh rectangle of sod now covering the earth. On top of the rise, a crew with a Bobcat dug a new hole. The groan of the engine said that life and death go on. You could see Catalina Island far out in the west, peeking through the haze. Gulls wheeled and squealed over the manicured green lawn.

The tombstone said simply:

WILL TRONA
1947–2001
LOVING HUSBAND AND FATHER
SERVANT OF THE PEOPLE

I felt close to my mother, standing there and looking at the grave. I was sharply aware of how alone we were, of how far away Will, Jr. and Glenn had gone pursuing their lives. As a mother, Mary Ann had always championed independence and self-reliance. She was always willing to trust me, give me responsibilities and freedoms. She was an inward person, slow to reveal her feelings. Impeccable manners. But I wondered now if her elegant stoicism was more of a burden than a help.

I took Mary Ann's hand. "Mom? Will told me you were blue that night. Blue again, he said. Is there anything I should know about that?"

She looked down at the grave and shook her head. Then she sighed and looked back up at me. "Let's talk about it in the car."

Half an hour later we were winding down from the cemetery hills. A man in black waved to us at the gate.

"He was seeing someone. At the funeral I realized it was that pretty Mexican woman from Jaime's office. Not the first time he'd done that kind of thing. But you knew for years, didn't you?"

I was aware of four different "affairs" during the five years I was his driver, bodyguard, confidant, gopher, lackey and beard. Two were over within a month. Two went on longer. I suspected others.

"Yes."

"Did you ever look at me and think, Mom's just a big dumb blonde, too dumb to know when her own husband's unfaithful to her?"

"I thought you were the most beautiful woman in the world. I never understood why he'd spend time with anyone else. At first I thought you couldn't know. Then I knew you did."

"How?"

"The night you cried alone in your room. I'd seen a movie or read a book where the woman gets cheated on, cries alone in her room. It became clear to me. I think I was fourteen."

She laughed softly. "Well, that could have been any one of a number of cries."

I looked over at her. She smiled and I saw a tear roll out from under the rim of her glasses. Her voice was light and fragile, like it would break in a breeze. "I loved that man so much. But I hated him sometimes, too. It's my biggest regret, Joe, the biggest one I've ever had, that Will died with me hating him."

She put her hand on my arm and squeezed hard.

I went straight to jail. Didn't pass Go. I shot the breeze with Giant Mike Staich for a few minutes, hoping to get Sammy's attention. It worked. He called me over and waved me up closer to the bars. I got a little closer.

"Sands worked out," I said.

"Good-looking woman."

"Alex isn't calling in much."

"Maybe she's lonely. You can get a date with her."

"I wouldn't do that."

Sammy seemed to think about this. "They almost got Alex, twice."

"He's lucky."

"He's paranoid, too. It helps."

Giant Mike piped up: "It's 'cause the Feds are so dumb."

"Speaking of lonely, how's Bernadette?"

He eyed me with sudden distrust. "She's fine. Why wouldn't she be fine?"

"You brought up the lonely idea, not me."

Giant Mike: "She's lonely, Sammy. They all get lonely sooner or later. The prettier they are, the sooner."

"Shut up, Mike. You're annoying me again."

Sammy put both hands on the bars. The orange jail jumpsuit was a little big on him. He looked like an infant standing up in his crib. "You want a date with Bernadette?"

"No. I was thinking I could look in on her, if you wanted. Just make sure she was doing okay."

Sammy stared at me, confusion spreading across his face. "Why would you do that?"

"You helped me. I'll help you."

"I asked you for the good rat trap."

"I can't give you a good rat trap. Custodial's going to set some bait in the heater ducts."

Giant Mike Staich again: "The rats'll die and stink."

"The rat's in my cell, not the heater ducts," said Sammy.

"It's using the ducts to get in and out."

"If I had my own spring trap I could catch him."

"There's no way I can get you a spring trap. They're not permitted. You could sharpen up the parts, make a shank."

Sammy pouted.

"I made my own rat trap once," said Staich. "When I was in second grade."

Sammy rolled his eyes. "Age, what—sixteen?"

"I'd pinch your gook head if I had a chance."

"Thank God for Mod J. But it's amazing what I put up with around here. Rats and stupid people."

Giant Mike: "Hang yourself up, man."

"Mike, I have no shoelaces, no belt, and a camera watching everything I do."

Mike: "Swallow your tongue."

"The gag reflex prevents suicide. Shut up, Mike. Please. I can't even think when you talk. The IQ of the module drops when you open your mouth."

Mike: "Don't take a genius to know she's lonely. She's lonely."

Sammy watched me, pushed off from the bars and sat on his cot. He looked up at her picture.

"Well, you won't be here much longer, Sammy. You're going to trial soon, then you either walk or get a ticket to prison."

He shook his head. "I'll walk. I'm innocent. And I believe in America, I believe in this system."

"Good luck, then, Sammy."

He looked up again at his picture of Bernadette. He jumped off the cot and came to the bars again, waving me toward him. I stepped up close, but didn't take my eyes off him.

"Try Bamboo 33. Just see if she's there. See if anybody's giving her trouble."

I nodded.

Giant Mike Staich: "She's lonely, Sammy. They all get lonely."

The word lonely stuck in my head and I thought of Ray Flatley of the Gang Interdiction Unit. I went over to the HQ building and dropped in on him, just to say hello. He had a picture on his wall, of him fishing. In the picture he stood far out in the river, and he had a long rod in the air, bent behind him like a huge whip. I asked him about it and he said the river was the Green, in Utah. He'd been flyfishing it for years.

He looked at the picture. "There's something about standing

in a river. Things go through you. Things come out and drift away. Things come in. I don't know. It's hard to explain. It's not for everybody. The fish don't matter as much as the river."

"I think I'd enjoy that," I said.

We sat and talked a minute about the jail, the weather, the Angels. When we ran out of things to say, which didn't take long, I left.

I liked Ray. He reminded me of myself turned inside out. I'm not sure why I thought that talking to a fourth-year Sheriff Deputy-One would in any way cheer Ray or improve his life. It probably didn't. But it's human nature, I guess, to believe you can cheer a guy up just by going to see him.

Chapter Thirteen

Jennifer Avila agreed to meet me at the HACF center that evening. I drove through the barrio, always abuzz, even more animated now with the longer days and the summer heat. Walking across the HACF parking lot I could smell grilling food mixed with the narcotic of a trumpet vine that hung over a near fence. Barbecue smoke rose from behind the big pale blossoms. Music. Voices. Laughter.

Jennifer met me at the back door and came out. She locked up and started around the building, boots crunching on the gravel.

"Can we walk?"

"I'd be happy to."

"Oh—I didn't even say hello, did I? Hello, Joe."

"Hello, Ms. Avila."

It was hard for me to look at her. Black hair and deep brown eyes and smooth skin and the dark lipstick she'd worn before her thing with my father. A modest yellow summer dress that couldn't begin to hide her wonderful shape. It was the first time I'd seen her arms.

The tips of my fingers tingled. I felt ashamed of my attraction, ashamed to betray my mother and father, even secretly.

And angry with Jennifer too. For what she'd done with Will, and to Mary Ann.

Jennifer had The Unknown Thing. Will had seen it and I did, too.

We walked up the busy street in the shade of awnings and magnolias.

"What do you want, Joe?"

"I want to know how Will found Savannah Blazak."

"With help from us."

"Can you be more specific?"

"Alex Blazak did some business with the Raitt Street Boys and Lincoln 18th. We know people who used to be down for those gangs. So we just put the word out."

"What did you come up with?"

"A warehouse in Costa Mesa. A nightclub in Little Saigon—Bamboo 33. Some hotels. We told Will about them."

"Which one paid off?"

"The Ritz-Carlton. Will knew the GM. The GM told the bartenders to keep an eye out for Alex. Alex and Savannah ate there late one night and the bartender called him."

"What night?"

"I don't know. Early in the week."

"I've seen the warehouse. And I think they were both there—Alex and Savannah."

She said nothing.

"Did you know what was in the tennis bag?"

She nodded. "It was ransom. One million dollars in cash."

"Why didn't Daniel give it directly to Will?"

"Warren had it. Jack wanted it left in neutral territory, like an escrow account. Daniel vouched for Jaime, so they brought it here, until the last minute."

I thought about Jaime being the holder of one million dollars that his HACF could use. He was all but asking for some of it that night.

"Did Jaime know about the Lind Street apartment?"

She looked at me quickly. "I don't know."

"Did you?"

Again, just a flash of her dark eyes. She picked up her pace, like she could out-walk the question. "Why would I know?"

"Because lovers tell each other things."

"Stay out of my business."

"I can't."

"Look, I knew Will was making arrangements between Alex and the parents. He told me. I knew an apartment in Anaheim was some kind of pickup or drop-off. I didn't know more than that."

"How about the address?"

She shook her head.

Get Pearlita.

We crossed at a busy intersection, then headed back toward the HACF. We got a lot of stares—a beautiful woman in a yellow dress, and a scar under a hat.

"Did you know when he'd be at Lind Street?"

"Approximately. Why?"

"I need to know who knew where Will would be, and when."

She was nodding along but staring straight ahead. She seemed to be concentrating, trying to process the information while she walked.

Then she glanced quickly at me. "Yes. Okay. I knew where. I didn't know when."

"Why did you call Pearlita?"

She stopped and stared up at me, right into my eyes. "You're a professional listener, aren't you?"

"I hear and remember things."

"God."

She turned away, shaking her head, making time down the sidewalk now. I listened to the rhythm of her shoes on the cement. You can hear emotions in footsteps. Disgust. Anger. Shame.

We walked past a *joyeria* and the *discoteca* blaring music onto the street.

"She's an old friend. She came up with the Ritz and the Ritz came up with Savannah, so she thought Will owed her a favor. I called her when you got to Jaime's."

. . . *Okay, okay. Yeah, right now.*

"But she didn't show."

"Some things came up, she said."

"What things?"

"She didn't say."

"Why did she want to meet him?"

"Luz . . . Pearlita wanted to talk about her brother. Her brother is Felix Escobar."

And then it made sense to me. Will's good friend, DA Philip Dent, was arguing the penalty phase of Felix Escobar's double-murder trial. Escobar was a Mexican mafia soldier who'd shot-gunned two men at close range during a convenience-store holdup. Dent had gotten the conviction just two weeks ago, from a jury that deliberated forty-five minutes. He was trying for a death sentence.

"Pearlita wanted to plead his case to Will," I said, "hoping Will could talk to Dent."

"She wanted leniency for him."

"Felix didn't show much leniency."

She stopped in front of a café window and turned to me. "Go away, Joe. You're ignorant and dangerous."

"Just leave you right here on the street?"

"Get away from me."

My ears got hot. A car went down Fourth Street with music so loud it rattled the window glass. I looked down at the rage in Jennifer Avila's beautiful face. I waited for the loud car to go by.

"Miss Avila, Pearlita knew some of the *when*. She knew that he was in the HACF office because you called her when we got there. And later that night she knew that Will was on his way because she called him. Maybe she shared that information. Did you tell her about the money, the arrangement? The *where*?"

"I don't remember every word I said. I help friends."

"Did you give Pearlita Will's number?"

"Maybe. I don't remember. What's a phone number? Anyone can get anyone else's."

"You must have known how dangerous that could be, with everything that was going on."

"I help friends."

"Maybe they took your help and burned Will with it."

She slapped me, hard, but not on the scar.

"What were you doing with the cash that Will gave you? I counted and rolled it, so I know how much and how often—it was two grand per week for the last—"

"I know how much it was!"

She opened her arms to encompass the street. I noticed the faint tattoo scar just below the shoulder, reaching all the way around the soft flesh of her underarm.

"It was for us. For them. The poor and the sick. That money was to keep the HACF open during the DA's probe. Our county money stopped when the press said we were flooding the polls with alien voters. That was a lie. So Will helped us."

She stepped toward me and hissed into my face: "You want to do something useful, Joe? You want to be like Will? Then return Jaime's calls. He's trying to help the family of Miguel Domingo. Jaime needs you just like he needed Will. You're supposed to be his son. So do what your father would do, talk to Jaime."

"Miss Avila, who were you down for? The tattoo is why I ask."

"Raitt Street."

"Pearlita's gang."

"That was a long time ago. Get away from me. I would never have hurt him. How can you even say that giving his number to a friend is the same as killing him? You don't know anything about friendship and loyalty and respect. You don't know anything but how to take orders from a man who used you to do the things he didn't have the *cojones* for. He's gone and you still take his orders. So be useful, and call Jaime."

I felt the heat come into my face. I thought about Jaime and Miguel Domingo and Luria Blas. Maybe I could honor Will by continuing something he believed in. Certainly, I could help a woman that he loved, even if she detested me.

She turned with a flash of black hair and yellow dress and pulled open the screen door of Café Los Ponchos.

At 10:17 P.M. I parked at the Santa Ana Amtrak depot. I walked into the station, then out to the platform and looked at the tracks narrowing back into the darkness. It was cool and cloudy again and there wasn't a star in the sky.

Then the speaker announced the arrival of the Coast Starlight. I walked to the far side of the arrivals room and stood behind a potted palm. Sleepers rose from the wooden benches. A family with lots of children pressed up close to the door. A minute later I felt the vibration, then the deep rhythmic rumble of the Starlight. It plowed through the dark and stopped alongside the station.

I saw him once, through the window, when he got off. Then again as he walked into the station. Same as the pictures, same as the dreams: downy white hair and beard, potbelly; big head low on his shoulders like he'd been assembled without a neck.

He came into the waiting area with a duffel slung over his shoulder. I stepped away from the tree.

Thor stopped and looked at me. His blue eyes caught the light. He shifted the duffel. He nodded.

"Joe."

"Thor."

"You didn't call the cops on me."

"I am the cops."

"Yup. Don't bust me. I can't do lockup again. It'd kill me."

His voice was high and clear. His teeth showed when he talked, but you couldn't say it was a smile.

A family came up behind him and split into two parts as they went past. The dad had a kid on his shoulders and the boy towered over Thor. I'd never realized how short he was, though I remembered his height from the intake records I'd gotten from Corcoran: 5'6".

"You going to let me stay at your place?"

"No."

"I already know where it is."

"Don't show up without an invite."

He sighed like he was disappointed. "You sure?"

"Extremely."

"Yeah, well, I really don't blame you. I'd be pressed out of shape, too."

Some of the people were watching us now. Thor looked at them and seemed to be smiling. A girl in a pink dress and shiny shoes stopped and looked up at me, then made a face and backed away. Her mother gathered her up and I heard the muffled words, but I hardly paid attention to them.

I watched Thor. I had no memory of seeing him. I was ready to feel like I was in the presence of something evil and eternal.

But with all his stage time in my nightmares, in the flesh he seemed mortal and matter-of-fact.

"You've been on the TV and papers a lot, Joe. All the way up in Seattle, even. They find that girl and her brother yet?"

"No."

"Crazy world."

"You'd know."

"Yeah." He took two steps toward me and lowered his duffel to the ground. "Shake my hand."

I shook it. My scar flared hot and my bones felt frozen. I could barely grip his hard, rough hand. It seemed like every bad emotion was roaring inside of me, every single bad feeling a person could have, all at once. No order or logic to them at all.

I saw his blue eyes studying me in the light from the station. "It don't really look that bad, Joe. Hurt?"

"Sometimes."

"You look good in the hat and suit. Expensive, I can tell."

"I shop the sales."

He eyed me. "Well, look now. I'm sorry for what I did and I need you to forgive me. I've checked out a bunch of religions. And any one that's got any kind of hell, a guy like me goes right to it."

"You should have picked a religion without one."

"No. I wanted a God with some teeth in Him. These touchy-feely ones don't get through to me. The Bible says I ought to square things with you, and I believe it. Eye for an eye, and all that. I got some acid in a peanut butter jar, right there in my duffel. You can pour it on me if that will get you to forgive. It's more than got poured on you. Then you could tell me it's okay, what happened. You could see there's more to your old man than the worst thing that happened in his life."

"I forgive you," I said. It surprised me. "But if I ever see you again I'm going to empty my gun in your heart. From this second on, you don't exist."

With shaking hands I got out my wallet and found three hundreds. I handed them to him.

"Good luck, old man. That ought to be enough to get you home."

"Thank you, son. Great to see you. Good luck to you, too."

I drove the 241 Toll Road fast, up over a hundred and thirty as I whizzed past the Windy Ridge toll plaza, windows down and sunroof open and the wind slamming into my face.

Then a high-velocity merge onto the 91 and a tire-screeching exit at Green River, where I turned around and roared back the way I came.

Sometimes you just can't go fast enough to get away. Because it's inside you and the speed doesn't matter.

I needed a baptism but couldn't get one this late, close to midnight. So I drove down to Diver's Cove in Laguna, where I'd gone snorkeling with Mom when I was little, and I walked out into the water with all my clothes on except shoes, guns and wallet, and went under and held my breath. I drove my fingers into the hard bottom sand and felt the surge try to draw me in and out. Like a piece of driftwood or a big snarl of kelp. I came up and got another big breath and went down again. I wished I could hit one-thirty under water because I thought that would rub it all off—the scar, the past, the fear—everything, polish me clean and shiny like a shell. Then I got so cold it was worse than shaking hands with Thor so I pushed off for the surface and dove into a breaking wave that carried me to shore.

Back home I broke down both my .45s—one of them a replacement for the weapon that Dr. Zussman had taken—then cleaned and oiled them. Then the .32. Nervous activity is all it was, because the guns were already clean and oiled and perfect.

I thought about Thor and cleaned them all again. Then I cleaned and oiled the shells before loading them into the clips.

I called Jaime Medina. He'd been sleeping, but his mood cheered when I told him I was ready to help him. I made a date to talk to him and Enrique Domingo, brother to the slain Miguel.

"You're doing the right thing, Joe," he said. "Just like your father always tried to do. You'll see, Miguel Domingo was a hero, not an insane criminal, like the cops made him out to be."

"The media said that, sir. Not the cops."

"You will see."

"I hope so, sir."

Melissa had called so I called her back. She said the finger-prints on the transmitter belonged to Del Pritchard, a pay-grade three automobile and bus mechanic employed by the Orange County Transportation Authority. She'd done a check on him as a favor to me, and Del had come back clean.

I took a long hot shower, then got into bed. I stared up at the ceiling. I'd tacked a picture from a magazine up there, just like Sammy had taped his picture of Bernadette. It showed a huge oak tree on a gentle, summer-tan central California hillside. The tree cast a dark blue shadow on the dry grass. High up in the oak tree the leaves were so dark and dense you couldn't see anything behind them, not even sky. And there in that dark canopy was my quiet spot, the place I could go and see but not be seen, hear and not be heard. I went there. My eagle friend was there, too. He moved over and made room for me. I looked down at the tawny hills and the golden grass and the smooth dirt road leading around a bend. The big bird pushed off from the branch and sailed away. I could feel the branch jiggle, lighten. So I pushed off too, unfurled my arms and followed.

Chapter Fourteen

"Del Pritchard? My name is Joe Trona."

"I know who you are."

"Can we talk a minute?"

"I got to punch in. Then I got a job to do."

He walked past me and into the Transportation Authority maintenance yard headquarters. It was Monday morning. It had taken me an hour to get from my house in Orange to the TA yard in Irvine—a distance of about fifteen miles. My ankle was stiff from working the Mustang's clutch.

I followed Pritchard, stood behind him while he slipped a timecard into an electronic clock, then into a slotted holder on the wall.

"It might be better if we found a quiet place," I said.

"Let me get some coffee."

Pritchard fished out some change and fed it into a machine in the corner. The coffee steamed up in front of his face as he took a sip. He was thick, baby-faced, blue-eyed. My age, maybe younger. His fingers were stained black from his work. His OCTA shirt was clean and his boots looked new.

"What's this about? You're a deputy, right?"

"Yes. Maybe we could go outside."

He looked at me hard, then led the way into the maintenance yard. The big OCTA buses were grouped along one side. The white TA Enforcement Impalas that Will detested so much were parked on another. There were shuttle vans the county used for short bus routes; emergency SUVs; a fleet of sheriff's department cruisers; another fleet of unmarked county sedans; a dozen new Kawasaki 1200s motorcycles.

There were three big, high bays. I watched an electric door roll up. More vehicles in there. The mechanics were already throwing open engine compartments and raising hoods.

"You do it all," I said.

"Yep. All the county stuff—sheriff's, TA, all the buses and emergency vehicles. Anything that rolls. We don't do the fire trucks or the Jeeps the lifeguards use. Separate garage and mechanics for those. Sanitation does its own thing, too."

"How about the supervisors' lease cars?"

"Sure. There's only, what, seven of them?"

"That's right. My dad drove a black BMW. One of the big seven series."

"I remember it. Sorry, what happened and all."

"Thank you."

Del Pritchard sipped his coffee again, looked out toward the OCTA buses. "So, what do you want?"

"I want to know who told you to put the homing transmitter on my father's car. Undercarriage, right side, down between the chassis and the body molding. It has your fingerprints on it."

His face went red. "You need to talk to my supervisor. I just do what they tell me, you know?"

"We can leave him out of this if you tell me who gave the order."

He glanced out to the yard, then back at me. "I don't know anything about a transmitter. Nothing at all. Everything here is by the rules."

"Then take me to your boss."

"Come on."

The maintenance yard supervisor was Frank Beals. Pritchard said they had a problem and Beals excused him, then took me into his office and shut the door. Beals hadn't heard anything about a transmitter. He called the TA maintenance department manager, Soessner, who lumbered into the office about thirty seconds later. He didn't know what I was talking about, either, said they fix cars, not bug them. He told me to come with him.

Soessner took me to the office of the Transportation Authority technical director, Adamson.

Adamson, a suit-and-tie man, heard me out.

"Is this part of an official investigation?"

"Yes," I said.

"I thought homicide detail would do that."

"I'm working with Birch."

"Rick's a good guy."

I waited.

Adamson made a call on his cell phone. "Carl, we got a deputy here, Joe Trona, asking about a transmitter on a supervisor's car. He says the transmitter had one of our guys' prints on it. Pritchard."

Adamson listened and nodded, then punched off.

"Rupaski says you're having lunch today at the Grove. He told me to tell you he'd clear it all up then."

I got to the Grove a few minutes early. The guard at the first gate took my name and plate numbers, the name of the member I was going to meet, slipped a card under the left windshield wiper, then let me in.

The road wound back into the hills. They were tan by now, wouldn't green up until the first rain—probably November, maybe later. The air was warm and still. Through the dense trees I could see purple bougainvillea shivering against the stucco of the hacienda-style buildings. I parked in the shade.

An off-duty deputy working the entrance recognized me, made the call inside, then opened the door. I took off my hat and stepped inside to the smell of food, the hushed clink of dishes, soft music and low voices.

The maitre d' smiled and crossed my name off a list. "Mr. Rupaski's booth is this way, Mr. Trona."

We passed through the main dining room and took the stairs up to the lounge. I looked at the burnished redwood floor, the rough-hewn wooden chandeliers hung by chain from the high ceiling, the billiards table where I'd listened in on Will and the Reverend Daniel. I recognized Rupaski's driver—Travis— sitting alone at the bar, chewing something. He nodded at me.

Rupaski's booth was in a far corner. He stood and shook my hand, motioned me to sit. The maitre d' started to draw the privacy curtain but Rupaski stopped him.

"No need for that, Erik. We've got nothing to hide in this booth. For once."

He laughed and Erik laughed. "But bring me a Partagas Churchill and a Glenfiddich in a water glass. Joe, smokes or drinks?"

"Lemonade, please."

Rupaski was a big man, seventy maybe, with a high fore-head, bald on top with long gray hair combed back on the sides. The hair made a little ducktail flip in the back. His eyes were dark brown and set deep in his face. Thick brows. Black suit and a white shirt, no tie. The jacket was too small for his barrel chest and he looked uncomfortable in it. His hands were thick and rough, his fingers blunt. He was a Chicagoan hired away from that city ten years ago. He grew up poor there, was known to be street tough and able to get his way in a backroom deal. A good boss and a crafty bureaucrat.

"Don't sweat the bug in the Beemer," he said. "Will asked me to put one on so I put one on. Simple as that."

"Sir, it doesn't sound that simple to me."

He raised a bushy eyebrow, smiled. His teeth were big and crowded. "I'll tell you exactly what he told me. He said Mary Ann was keeping some strange dates, late at night. Usually she drove her own car. Sometimes she drove his. He wanted to follow her at a discreet distance. 'Discreet distance.' Those were his words. So I had Pritchard do Will's car one morning out in the maintenance yard. And I gave Will a transmitter to put on Mary Ann's. Something with adhesive he could just stick right on."

It almost played. I knew Mary Ann liked to drive the sleek new lease car. A couple of times, out on our night business, we'd use Mary Ann's Jeep because she wanted the sedan. And she'd told me she liked to drive sometimes, late, going nowhere fast. But Will had never said anything about her going out. If he was worried, why didn't he tell me? And I'd never seen a radio receiver in Will's possession—not in the car, not in his briefcase, nowhere. Most of all, Will and Rupaski were enemies. Why trust an enemy with something like that? Why not have your son, driver, bodyguard and gopher do the job?

"I understand now," I said.

"Good. Hey, smokes and spirits."

A waiter in a tuxedo set down a big glass ashtray with a cutter, wooden matches and a thick cigar in it. Then a simple water glass with golden liquid in the bottom fourth. And my lemonade.

"The special today is poached Chilean sea bass in a cilantro sauce, served with endive salad and garlic-mushroom couscous."

"Steak, mashed potatoes and a salad with Thousand Island

for me," said Rupaski. "That would be a T-bone, rare. Get the same for Joe, here. He's a growing boy."

"May I cut and light your cigar, sir?"

"Yeah."

"Slot cut or straight, sir?"

"Goddamned straight cut, Kenny. We go through this every time."

"Yes, sir. Of course."

When Kenny was done cutting the cigar, Rupaski stuck it in his mouth and aimed it up while the waiter torched it with a surprisingly powerful butane lighter. The smoke came out thick and powerful, rising in a lazy cloud toward the ceiling. Kenny bowed and turned away. Rupaski held out the cigar.

"Some guys say they draw better without the band." His voice was thick, like there was a blanket over him. "I say that's bullshit."

He inhaled again, blew another cloud. "Best thing about a private club is you can do what you want. Here in California, Joe, we've got teenagers carrying guns to school, but you can't smoke a cigar in a bar. Something's wrong when individual rights get smaller and the crimes get bigger."

We watched an elegantly dressed young woman descend the staircase from the third-level conference rooms. Alone, walking briskly, a small purse in one hand, which she held slightly out, for balance, as she came down the steps. Red hair past her shoulders, green satiny dress. I heard her shoes on the wood.

"Yes, sir, individual rights. You met Will and Dana Millbrae for lunch here the day before he died. Can you tell me what you talked about?"

He took his gaze off the woman and put it on me. He chuckled. He sipped his Scotch and took another puff of his cigar. "You're direct. I like that. Sure, we talked about the county buying the toll roads and building the new airport. Will was against both of them, as I'm sure you know. We were just trying to make him see the light."

"What light was that, sir?"

"Just logic and good common sense. You see, the toll roads can turn a profit if the TA can run them. A big profit, over the years. It's a sound investment for the county, if you take the long view. But your father didn't want to see that. He wanted the private consortium to keep taking a shellacking on the things. I'll tell you something—private roads won't work in the West. Too much land to cover. The sooner the county can get control of them, the better. I think Will knew that. But it pissed him off to spend public money to bail out private enterprise. Same thing with the new airport. We'll need one someday, and that day is coming. We were trying to get Will to come over, throw his vote and his influence behind us. It's a free election in November, but we needed Will to get his first district going our way."

Rupaski coughed, looked at the cigar, set it in the ashtray. "I'm sorry, Joe. I'm goddamned sorry about what happened. Will and I agreed on nothing. But I loved him. He was a good man and a good enemy and I respected him. How's Mary Ann holding up?"

"Holding up well, sir, considering."

He nodded. "Where was she going, so late at night, not telling her own husband?"

"She liked to drive."

Rupaski shook his head and grunted. Then he took another drink, swirled the liquid, set down the glass. "I didn't invite you here to talk about politics. Or your family. I invited you here to offer you a job."

"I've got one, sir."

"Hear me out. Double your salary, which will bring you in at about sixty-five a year to start. Mostly nights, so your days can be free to finish up college, sleep late, bang some women, whatever you want. You give up your Sheriff's badge and get a Transportation Authority shield. That puts you with me and I'm a good man to work for. It gets you a new county drive-home car—those big Impalas with the V-8s, side spotlights and short-wave radios. Gets you a concealed carry permit for your weapon. It gives you power within TA jurisdiction, which is big and getting bigger—the Transit Department, the Highway and Roads Administration, the Airport Authority. Lots to do. It puts you in line for some fantastic benefits, better than sheriff's by far."

"What would I do?"

"You'd be doing for me what you did for Will. Joe, I worry. People are crazy these days. Look what happened to Will. A man of his quality and his standing. You took out two of those bastards before they got to him. I want somebody who can do that. I want somebody just a little bit scary. Son, that's you."

I looked at him but said nothing. Everyone wants someone scary. To do what they are afraid of, go to the dark places, get their hands dirty. Will trained me to do that. I understood it while he was making me and I understand it now.

"My scariness didn't save Will's life, sir."

He stopped his glass in front of his mouth. "You don't blame yourself for that, do you?"

"I just look at the facts as they are."

"You're valuable, Joe. Everybody wishes they had someone like you. You've got manners and brains and guts. You've got style—like what you did with those guys shadowing Chrissa Sands. I really liked that. You got some celebrity. You got a face that everybody knows. You've got the respect of people for handling your problems in a good way, for going on with your life when some people would just stay home in the dark all day. You learned a lot from Will, and he was great. I know you know things. But let me show you what I know. Joe, with your years as a deputy, and a few more with the TA, you can go anywhere you want in the county. You'd have depth and contacts and an inside view of how things work. I can see you as a supervisor someday. Or head of the TA, if you liked it. Or even the State Assembly or the House. You've got star quality, Joe. I can use you and I can help you."

"What about Travis?"

"He'd be happy about it if I told him to be."

"Well, thank you, sir. But no. I like being a deputy."

"You like jail?"

"I'm on the right side of the bars."

Rupaski smiled and drank again. The waiter brought the lunches. "Think about it, Joe. Just tell me you'll think about it."

"All right. I will. Sir, why do you have Hodge and Chapman shadowing Chrissa Sands?"

"On the off chance that she'll lead us to Savannah Blazak."

"But they were following her way back on Wednesday morning, the day Will died. Blazak didn't go public with news of the kidnapping until Thursday evening."

Rupaski nodded. "Right, but he went private with it. Straight to me. We're friends, Joe. We talk. I knew his son was crazy—last year the dumb kid ran one of Jack's Jaguars into the Windy Ridge toll plaza, took out a wall and trashed the Jag. He was drunk and high, and when my men dragged him out he tried to pull a gun on them. Luckily, they had the presence of mind to kick the shit out of him. Anyway, I offered to help find Savannah. I think Savannah Blazak is one of the sweetest kids I've ever met. Love her. So we shadowed the girlfriend. We're still shadowing the girlfriend. A few years ago, Jack Blazak helped persuade the county to establish the Transportation Authority. He helped me get the top spot. He's a friend and friends help each other. Same way I'd use the power of the TA to help you, if you were one of us."

"You ought to tell your men to be more polite to her."

"Thanks for bringing that to my attention, Joe. And to theirs." Under the thick brows, Rupaski's eyes glittered merrily. "Joe, I'm going to *make* you work for me, whether you want to or not."

"How?"

"I don't know yet. I guess I'll have to come up with a better offer. How about that car of Will's? Two-year lease, isn't it? I can arrange for you to keep it, then buy it dirt cheap when the lease runs out. Consider it a signing bonus. Yours for the asking. And I'll still throw in the hot Impala, for work-related stuff."

I had to smile to myself at the idea. "I'll think about that."

The lunch was excellent. The only way it could have been better was if the food wasn't touching on the plate.

Halfway through lunch, a young guy in a tuxedo ambled down the stairs from the conference level. His hair glistened from a shower, or maybe hair gel. Tall glass of orange juice in one hand, a silver Halliburton case in the other. Lifted his glass to Rupaski when he spotted us.

I drove back down to the toll road, thinking about something Will had said to me a hundred times: *Save your friends, spend your enemies.*

Enrique Domingo was short and thin, with large clear eyes and black hair. His English was poor, so we spoke Spanish. Will had insisted that I learn Spanish, and I'd done okay with it at school.

The three of us met in Jaime's HACF office. Jennifer Avila nodded at me in greeting, but said nothing.

Jaime asked Enrique to tell me his story. In a quiet voice, he did.

He explained that he was fourteen years old. Miguel, his brother, had been sixteen when the police shot him. His older sister, Luria Blas, had been eighteen when the Suburban hit her on Pacific Coast Highway.

His sister.

I saw him differently then, knowing that he'd lost not only a brother, but a sister, in just a few short weeks. He seemed to me so completely alone, even sitting there with Jaime and me. Solitude surrounded him, like rings around a planet.

I told him I had no idea that Luria was his sister. Why did she have a different name?

He said that Blas was the name she used to enter and work as a domestic in the *Estados Unidos*. She'd used it to qualify for a green card, claiming to be the sister of a family friend who was now a citizen.

Enrique's face colored as he told me this.

"Very common," said Jaime. "They do what is necessary to get *papeles*."

"Why haven't the police and the newspapers made that connection?" I asked.

Jaime stretched out his arms, hands up. "They know, but they don't *care*. The police say an accident is an accident. A coincidence is a coincidence. The English newspapers ran very small items—so small that you yourself did not see them, correct? Our Spanish newspaper has run the story much larger, but who listens? This is why we were hoping for your help."

I told him I was sorry for what had happened to his brother and sister. He looked away.

Then he told me that for a while things were good for him and Luria and Miguel. They were able to send money home to Guatemala to their parents and young siblings. Enrique and his brother both worked as gardeners, had gotten on with a regular crew that did lawn cleanup and light tree trimming. Eight dollars an hour. Luria worked as a domestic and had twelve regular households she cleaned, two each, six days a week. Sixty-five dollars per house. She was popular because she worked hard, was pleasant and beautiful, but not expensive.

But over the months, Luria had become sullen and with-drawn, not herself. Usually, she was a very happy person. And she began going out at night with girlfriends who had cars, who dressed in expensive American clothes. She wouldn't come home until late. She drank liquor often and cut back her domes-tic work, then stopped doing it altogether. But it seemed that the less she worked, the more money she had to spend. She sent less of it home, said Enrique.

He blushed again as he told me that.

One night she had come home with one eye purple and swol-len shut. She was very frightened. Miguel was furious.

Two weeks later, she was killed just a block from their apart-ment in Fullerton.

Enrique looked out the window in Jaime's office as he told me this. His eyes were set high in his face and shaped like al-monds. It looked like he was going somewhere else in his mind, back to a time when his brother and sister were alive, maybe, back to a time when what little he had seemed enough. I won-dered if he had a quiet spot to go to, an eagle to perch beside, some view of a better world when he needed it.

He said that Miguel was distraught over Luria's death. En-rique had seen him, the night after Luria died, trying to disguise a machete in a couple of old jackets. Miguel told Enrique that he was investigating her death. Miguel, he said, was a very hot-blooded man.

He looked at me, and in a quiet voice said that five days after Luria was killed, Miguel was shot by the police.

Enrique told me that Luria was more *sympatico* with Miguel

than with him, because Enrique was much younger and wouldn't understand adult problems.

I thought about it, but couldn't see what Miguel had to investigate. Luria's death was an accident. The woman who hit her stopped and tried to help.

"I thought the same thing you're thinking, Joe," said Jaime. "So I called a friend in the coroner's office. They did an autopsy on Luria, as they do with any violent or questionable death. But they will answer no questions from me. Because I'm not family. I'm not law enforcement. It makes me believe what any sane man would believe—that they are hiding something."

I weighed the possibilities, but said nothing.

"I suspect foul play, Joe. This is more evidence of foul play against Latinos in America, and nobody is interested. The DA will not return my calls. The police in Newport say that Miguel Domingo brandished weapons and failed to surrender them to officers of the law. The police in Fullerton say that Luria died strictly of an accident. How can I believe this? What if these people were not the Latino poor? What if it had happened to you, Joe? Your father would never have let this be ignored. This is why Will was a great man. Now, what can you do to help us?"

"Let me think about this."

"Your father would do more than think."

"He'd think first, Señor Medina. And please don't tell me what Will would have done. With all respect, señor, I knew him a lot better than you did, no matter what he did for the HACF."

Jaime stood and exhaled loudly. "I'm sorry, Joe. You're right. I'm like Miguel. I have hot blood sometimes, when I see injustice. Please, I apologize very sincerely to you."

"I'll find out more."

I told Enrique that I needed the names and addresses of Luria's twelve employers. He told me he would try, but didn't think he could do that. Luria didn't tell him everything, like she told the older Miguel.

Jaime walked me to the door. "I was wrong. You are just like your father, Joe."

"Thank you, sir. But I know I'm not."

I drove to the coroner's facility near headquarters, went in and asked for the director. Brian McCallum had been close to Will—they played tennis together as a doubles team, and liked to hit the club bar after their matches. McCallum was a heavyset man who moved surprisingly well on a tennis court. I remember noticing how strong his wrists were because he moved the racquet so easily. He told me he'd played baseball through college, which explained it.

He took me into his office and nodded along as I told him part of what Enrique Domingo and Jaime Medina had told me.

"Well, yeah," he said. "I was the one who talked to Medina. He's prying, pushy, acting like he owns the place because tax dollars pay our salaries. He told us that Blas and Domingo were brother and sister, and I passed that along to Newport and Fullerton. He wanted information on Blas, but the policy here is if you're not family or law enforcement, we're not going to give you information about autopsies. We just don't do it."

"Can you tell me?"

"Are you doing them a favor?"

"Yes, sir."

He looked at me for a moment, then sat back. "Luria Blas was hit from behind by a Chevy Suburban. The time was about three P.M., a Thursday. The impact point was her shoulder blade, and the collision threw her away from the vehicle instead of under it. Death occurred within twenty minutes. Her lungs and heart were heavily contused, her neck was broken in two places. Twelve breaks in eight different bones. The X ray of her left shoulder blade looked like . . . well, multiple fractures. The internal hemorrhaging was severe, considering her heart only had a few minutes of life left in it. Cause of death was cardio-pulmonary collapse due to impact. If by some miracle she'd lived, she'd have been paralyzed from the neck down."

I imagined the scene, though I didn't want to. "How fast was the vehicle going?"

"Accident investigators put it between fifty and sixty. Skid marks *after* impact. The driver said she never saw the woman. Like she jumped out into the boulevard."

It was hard to reconcile the newspaper pictures of Luria Blas's lovely smile with a Suburban going sixty.

"There was more, Joe. First, the woman had been severely beaten before she died. Abdomen, ribs, sternum all bruised. Two ribs cracked. Some bleeding from the liver and pancreas, *not* associated with the blow from the car."

"Beaten with what?"

"Hard to say. Fists, probably. Nothing that left any trace evidence on her skin. No chips or shards, nothing."

"How long before she died?"

"Frank Yee said within twenty-four hours. He's good at the times. She was pregnant, too. Six weeks. The beating didn't kill the fetus. The Suburban did."

Again I imagined Luria Blas meeting her end against a Chevy Suburban doing sixty. "She staggered into the boule-vard," I said. "Not in control of herself, because of the beating?"

McCallum nodded. "Sure. She could easily have been dis-oriented. She was certainly in some pain. No drugs in her sys-tem. No alcohol. She could have thrown herself in front of the car, that's a possibility. There's one small point of light we came up with—flesh under the nails. Maybe she got a piece of the beater. She got a piece of somebody. We checked her very closely for marks, thinking reflexive or self-inflicted. It wasn't herself she clawed. But tell Jaime Medina not to worry— Fullerton PD is up to speed on all this."

I sat for a moment, remembering Enrique's tale of his sister's withdrawal and unhappiness. Young, poor, unmarried, in a foreign country and pregnant.

What would you do?

It made me think of Will, because all sadness made me think of Will. I shook my head, trying to separate the two, trying to give Luria Blas the respect she deserved.

"What are you thinking, Joe?"

"What a waste it all is."

"Sometimes it seems that way."

"Thank you. Medina wanted information because he's tight with Luria's brother."

"I figured. I know Jaime does good deeds."

"They think it's tied in with the brother getting shot."

McCallum raised his eyebrows and shook his head. "I don't see how."

"Can I look at Miguel Domingo's personal items, the things he had on him when he died?"

"We've got everything but the weapons."

He led me back to the property room, talked to the sergeant on duty. He made a call. A few minutes later a deputy brought a plastic box to the counter and set it down. McCallum signed for it and we took it back to the lab.

There wasn't much: a plastic bag with $6.85; a pack of matches from a convenience store; a black plastic comb; an OCTA ticket stub; a wallet and a ballpoint pen. A bloody shirt in white butcher paper. Bloody pants. Another bag with socks and underwear. Two worn athletic shoes with the laces tied loosely together.

"The wallet, may I?"

"Go."

I opened the bag and took out the wallet. It was old and worn and lopsided the way a wallet can get. One picture of five children and two adults, all standing in front of a wall with climbing roses on it. I recognized a face that looked like Enrique's, one that looked like Luria's. No ID. In the billfold was a small, folded piece of newsprint. I unfolded it and saw the *Journal* article that told of Luria Blas's accidental death. I folded it and put it back.

"Pants?" I asked.

"They're a mess."

I worked the butcher paper loose. Black jeans, bloodstains a deep rust color on the fabric. Nothing in the front pockets. Nothing in the back. I slipped a finger into the watch pocket and felt something slick. I worked my finger around and tried to get it out but it was stuck. I used the tweezers on a pocketknife I carry. The tweezers slipped off twice before the dried blood gave way and a square of paper came out. I unfolded it and flattened it against the table. It looked like part of an envelope—you could see the diagonal seam in the paper. It had been torn into an approximate square, about five inches on each side. One edge was dark and wilted with blood.

The handwriting was cramped and difficult to read.

Señora Catrin—Puerto Nuevo
Señor Mark—Punta Dana
Señora Julia—Laguna
Señora Marcie—Puerto Nuevo

The first three names had lines through them. Señora Marcie of Newport Beach did not. I read them twice.

I remembered Bo Warren's words from that first time we'd

talked in the Blazak living room: *Marcie, that's the head maid here.*

"Jesus," said McCallum. "We missed this. What, just names and cities?"

"Miguel was distraught. He was investigating Luria's death. Maybe these are contacts, or suspects."

"Well, the Suburban driver was Gershon—Barbara Gershon. Her name was published. It wasn't withheld."

I tried to come up with a logical explanation but I couldn't. Although I knew there was one phone call I'd have to make, soon.

"Joe, I'll have to log this in, make sure Newport PD knows about it."

"Yes, sir."

"You okay?" McCallum asked.

"Yes. I'm just tired of bullets and blood and broken bones."

"Job security," he said.

I stopped off at the bank to retrieve the contents of the safe-deposit box. *Crap. Nothing.* Even if that was true, it was time to deal with it. I emptied the box into Will's briefcase, signed myself out and headed back over to the sheriff's department shooting facility.

I drew and fired one hundred rounds through my .45s, half right-handed and half left. Fifty with the .32 on my ankle. I shot the Tall One and Whoever Beat Luria and Whoever Kidnapped Savannah, if someone even had. I shot Thor, but took less pleasure in it than usual. Then I shot some monsters and some ghosts and some demons. I shot Satan himself, right in the heart.

I'm good with the left hand but there's less endurance. The last ten rounds went all over the torso at fifty feet, but at least they hit black. I don't use wad-cutters for targets. I use the full-grain loads, copper-jacketed bullets, factory brass. I don't want anything behaving differently if I have to hit something other than paper. The devil, for example.

When I was done I broke down the guns and cleaned them. Light oil. Wonderful smell, Hoppe's gun oil. My left hand was buzzing and sore, and both of them smelled like gunpowder.

"Luz Escobar," said Ray Flatley. "Aka Pearlita. That's her name with the Raitt Street Boys. She carried a pearl-handled derringer in her pocket when she was thirteen. Still does, for all I know."

"May I see the file?"

He handed it across to me. I looked at her mugs. She was five feet six, 170 pounds. Hair cropped short.

"She dresses like a man," said Flatley. "We had her for a drive-by in Santa Ana. But our witness was shot dead one night in his living room. Good-bye case against Pearlita. She's a shot-caller, Joe. Runs the hits and the retaliations. We've got our witness against Felix under protective arrest in another state. We keep waiting for Pearlita's punks to make a move, but so far, he's still alive."

I looked at the picture again. Even with the killers and rapists I'd guarded in jail, I'd rarely seen such malice in a person's face. She didn't look like a woman. She didn't look like a man. She looked like something neutral and mean.

"What's up?" Flatley asked. "What's your interest in Luz Escobar?"

"Will talked to her on the phone the night he died. I think she wanted to get him to influence Phil Dent."

Flatley stared at me. "Rick know?"

"I came clean, sir. Everything."

"Good, Joe. Because Pearlita is bad company. And if Will wasn't willing to talk to Phil Dent on the behalf of a cold-blooded killer, maybe Pearlita's famous temper was tripped."

"Do the Raitt Street Boys and the Cobra Kings mix?"

"They hate each other."

I spent a few minutes over in Mod F, locked in the plumbing tunnel. I sat behind a cell occupied by a low-level Asian hood named Hai Phan. I leaned back against the dusty wall and looked at the pipes and the ducts. Phan was talking to the guy next to him—another Asian gangster—but they were speaking Vietnamese. I remained still, trying to overhear anything that might relate to Will or Savannah or Alex.

Nothing. I may as well have been listening to cats fighting or trees hissing in the wind.

Then I went to the guard station in the mess hall and watched the inmates filing in for dinner. Dinner starts at four. It looked like it always looked: an institutional dining room, guards with their backs to the walls, a seemingly endless river of orange jumpsuits filing in and out. As usual, the Mexican car was the biggest, then the wood car, the black car, the Asians. Sullen. Quiet. Orderly. Another peaceful day, so far.

I went to my cubby and picked up my mail.

One item only: a postcard from Las Vegas. It showed a big hotel made to resemble an Italian city. The handwriting was neat and large.

> *Dear Joe,*
>   *You saved my life and I'm okay for now. I'm very*
> *afraid of what might happen.*
>
>   *S.B.*

It was postmarked three days earlier. I called Steve Marchant.

"I want you to do two things," he said. "One, put it in a

paper bag, touching only the edges. Use tweezers or tongs. Two, bring that bag over here immediately or sooner."

Marchant took me into the small FBI workroom on the third floor and shut the door. He took the bag and slid out the postcard, using his pen to right it on the light table in front of him. He swung an infrared lamp over the light table and clicked it on.

"IR will illuminate the salts in body oil," he said. Then, "Look at this."

He stepped aside and let me look. I could see the nice thumbprint. It looked like it had been rolled in a booking room.

"Wait here."

He slammed the door behind him on his way out, slammed it when he came back in. He set two fingerprint cards and a folder on the table next to the postcard, then swung out a magnifier that was clamped to the table.

"Yeah, cute. Real cute."

He whispered something I couldn't hear, then stepped away. I looked down through the magnifier at the print, then at the thumb cards, then at the print again.

"To the naked eye, that's Savannah Blazak's," said Marchant. "I'll get Washington to run the points and make it official."

He clicked off the IR light and pushed the magnifier back against the wall. He turned and looked at me, and I could see the anger in his face.

From the folder he removed a handmade Mother's Day card and slipped one of the clear plastic holders over the top. It said "Mom, I love you more than all the stars put together. Your Girl, Savannah." Marchant pushed the postcard up next to the card, then used a pair of tweezers to turn it over.

I looked over his shoulder. The writing was identical.

From the other folder he brought out a sheet of stationery

with "Alex Jackson Blazak" embossed at the top, and his home address at the bottom. I read the salutation and first two lines.

Dear Chrissa,

    I can't tell you how long ago it seems since I saw you. That Valentine's Day dinner was dyno.

"Savannah wrote the postcard," said Marchant.

"And she's afraid of what might happen."

He stood back and looked at me. "I'm going to get this guy, and I'm going to spring his hostage. You can quote me on that."

I nodded.

"Thanks, Joe. Thanks for the quick heads-up. Excuse me now, I've got to get on the line to Las Vegas. Interstate flight with a juvenile, for immoral purposes. We've got so much mileage out of the Mann Act you wouldn't believe it."

"Do you believe the immoral purposes part?"

Marchant thought a moment. "I'm going to tell you something I probably shouldn't. Don't let it leave this room. We polygraphed the mom and dad as soon as they came to us about their daughter. They both passed, but I didn't like some of what I saw with Jack. That's all I'm going to say right now."

"I found out yesterday about the arrangement with Ellen Erskine."

"Your father kept her in the dark, didn't even give her Savannah's name. Erskine wasn't sure if he was on the level about it or not."

I waited for more, but Marchant said nothing. Then: "What about you? You still think he was on the level?"

"Yes. I'd bet my life on it."

On my way home I called Lorna Blazak on my cell phone.

"Mr. Trona, have you heard from her?"

"She sent me a postcard from Las Vegas. I got it just an hour ago. She's fine, Mrs. Blazak, but she's afraid."

"Dear God . . . and my son?"

"I can only assume he's there with her."

"I don't know what to do. Tell me what I can do."

"Wait, Mrs. Blazak. Help the Bureau help you."

Silence.

"Mrs. Blazak, did you employ a woman named Luria Blas as a housecleaner?"

"No. Why?"

"I have some evidence that she was in contact with Marcie."

"That may well be, but no one named Luria Blas has worked here in this home. She was the one killed in Fullerton, right?"

"That's correct."

"My heart goes out to her and her family, Mr. Trona. But please don't add her to our list of woes here."

"I won't do that, Mrs. Blazak. I was just checking on a lead. It's important to follow through."

"I understand."

"Marcie is your main domestic help, correct?"

"Yes."

"May I have her last name?"

Silence again. "Diaz. Mr. Trona, bear in mind there must be more than one Marcie doing domestic work in this county."

"I will. And thank you. Ma'am, we're doing everything we can to find your daughter and son."

"It's absolutely frustrating, Mr. Trona. They're seen, they disappear. They're seen again, they disappear again."

"Please be patient."

"I need *something* I can hold on to."

"Hold on to the knowledge that Savannah is alive. Hold on hard, Mrs. Blazak."

"Thank you. And thank you for calling."

Chapter Fifteen

I wasn't sure what kind of gift to bring June Dauer on our first real date but I knew she liked rubies. I bought a bracelet with rubies all around it and had it wrapped up very nicely. Then I realized that flowers were customary, so I got some of those too, and some chocolates to go with them, and a big basket of gourmet coffees and liqueurs because the gift store had a sale on them.

It all cost almost a month's salary, but I hardly spent my work money because my house is paid for. Will and Mary Ann bought it for me when I started working full-time. Mary Ann wanted me in on the dizzying Orange County real estate market as early as possible. It's worth about $50,000 more than they paid for it, and all I've really done is run the vacuum and water the trees.

June's home was an upstairs apartment overlooking Newport Harbor. I stood on her porch and listened to the yacht lanyards ringing against the masts and the echoing cries of seagulls. My knees felt weak. I'd worn my best suit and hat. I rang the bell and waited.

She opened the door and stepped aside to let me in. Her

smile went funny when she looked at the gift basket and jewel box in one of my hands, the flowers and chocolates in the other.

"It's great to see you again," I said.

"Joe, nice to see you too, but you shouldn't have brought me all that."

"You don't have to take it."

The darkness that crossed her face was genuine. I felt like my heart was about to stop beating.

"Well, come in."

"Thank you."

The apartment was drenched in sunlight. The walls and carpet were white. Through the big picture window the harbor water twinkled and the bright clean boats rocked. A big yacht motored across the channel.

"This is beautiful here," I said. "It's like being in a postcard."

"They actually shot one from the roof of this building. Here, let me take these things, I guess."

She took my gifts and set them on a glass dining table. She was wearing a silk, coffee-colored dress and brown shoes with heels. Her legs shone. I could smell the seawater through the open windows but I could smell her perfume too. She looked down at the basket and chocolates, the jewelry box and flowers.

"Overkill?" I asked.

"Uh-huh. We'll figure out an appropriate response later. But I will put these roses in some water. They're beautiful, Joe. I've always loved the lavender-colored ones. They symbolize something but I forgot what."

I watched her take a big crystal vase from a cupboard, put in some water, cut the stems and arrange the flowers. She carried it to the fireplace mantel. The tops of her arms were dark and the undersides were pale. I helped her move some pictures and get the vase arranged in the middle.

She stood back and considered. The lavender roses stood out against the white paint of the mantel and the wall behind it. So did June Dauer. I'd never realized what a beautiful color brown was. Or how harmoniously two browns could go together: the flat dark brown of the silk and brighter glow of her skin. She looked like something fresh and graceful being born out of something dry.

The Unknown Thing again. It had me.

"Nice," she said. She looked at me and really smiled for the first time. The sunlight coming through the window behind her caught her curls. Her eyes were dark and bright. "Thank you, Joe."

"The pleasure is mine."

She shook her head but she was still smiling. "You know what effect you have on me, the way you're so polite and always saying please and thank you and my pleasure and all that?"

"No."

"You make me want to scream profanities at the top of my lungs."

I smiled and looked away. "I feel like that sometimes, too."

"Really?"

"The thought track that runs through my head while I'm speaking, it doesn't always match the words. I'll call a man 'sir' and feel like breaking his arm."

"You ever do it?"

"Once."

"Really?"

I shrugged. "I pretty much had to. Academy stuff, competition and hazing and all that. It worked out okay. They were going to wash this guy out anyhow."

"Well, on that happy note, let's go eat."

* * *

I'd picked a restaurant that was one of Will's favorites, a quiet Italian place on Balboa Island. The table was quite small, and it forced us face-to-face in a way that I would have found unbearable with anyone but June Dauer.

She got prettier by the minute. We drank a bottle of Chianti that lasted all the way through dinner, then we had dessert and cognac. My ears hummed pleasantly and my body felt warm and light. Like I was filled with helium and I could float up and rest against the ceiling if I didn't clamp my fingers to the side of the chair.

After dinner we walked around the island and June showed me the different places she'd lived in when she was a student at UCI. We watched the sunset from the west side, where the bay-front windows threw orange reflections and the ferry chugged back and forth loaded with cars. Her skin went gold and her chocolate eyes turned to a light tan as she squinted out. Like the flank of a lion. More browns I'd never noticed—subtle and glorious.

When the sun went down the sea breeze came up cool and she moved up against my side. I put my arm around her shoulder. I'd never done anything that dramatic with a woman before, but she didn't flinch or recoil. I started to take it away and apologize, but caught myself.

Her skin was cool, with tiny bumps on it. I had never touched anything that exciting in my entire life.

When she let us back into her place, it was dark. But you could see the silver water of the harbor and a pale bank of fog moving in from the west.

She opened the French doors to the deck, then turned on a lamp by the couch, just one click. The room filled with soft light and shadow, and a cool damp breeze. Then she took the jewel box off the table.

"Come sit on the couch with me," she said.

I sat at a respectful distance and looked out the window. The tops of the tall masts swayed in the moonlight.

June set the gift box on her right knee. "I'm afraid to open this."

"It was just to show how pleased I am."

"You can overdo things, Joe."

"I'm capable of that, June."

She looked down at the box. It was wrapped in silver paper that caught the light. Her leg nearest the lamp was shot with the same light but the one closest to me was rounded with shadow. I looked at the place where her legs met her dress and felt a deep, rising ache.

She unwrapped the gift as women will: slid off the bow, worked up the tape with her fingernail, peeled back the wrapping paper, folded it, set it aside. The box was black velvet. She opened it. Even in the soft light I could see the red glimmer of the rubies stretched against the dark liner. Like a hundred tiny brake lights caught on a miniature freeway.

"Ah, Joe."

No way to read her inflection.

"They're rubies," I said.

"I see that. This is much too . . . much. Really."

"Really?"

She looked at me. "Yes."

"Okay. Here."

I stood and held out my hand. She put the box in it. I walked out to the patio.

"Joe, *no*."

I dropped it ten feet down into the bay.

She was suddenly standing beside me at the railing, looking down.

"Shit, Joe—my bracelet!"

"It's floating."

"Not forever, it won't! I'd rather have it on me than at the bottom of the harbor."

"You could have said that before I threw it in."

I pulled off my shoes and coat and handed her my wallet. I'd left my guns in the trunk of the Mustang.

"Oh, man," she said.

I dove in to make as little splash as possible. Then I surfaced and breast-stroked over to the bobbing box. The water was cold but it felt good on my face. Like ice. I put the box in my mouth and turned to swim back.

Then I heard a splash behind me and the surface broke and June Dauer's shiny wet head appeared.

"Cold," she said.

I tried to say yes, ma'am, but got only, "Yeah-meah."

"What's that in your mouth, Fido, a box of rubies?"

I nodded. She paddled up closer. Breathing in and out fast like you do when it's cold. I could feel her legs churning next to mine and smell the warm human breath on the surface of the water. Our feet knocked, then our knees. She locked one hand on the collar of my shirt and pulled the box out of my mouth. In place of it came her mouth, and a warm tongue. I pulled her close with one arm, felt the pumping of her legs echoed in the smooth muscles of her side. Started to sink. Had to let go and scull with my hands to keep our heads up. That made my body drift away a little. She laughed and grabbed my shirt and pulled herself closer, putting the box back in my mouth. She laughed low and kind of wicked, then confidently pressed a hand to my personal area.

"You're a cold hard man, Joe Trona."

"Yeah-meah."

"Can't say yes ma'am, no ma'am, pleased to meet you, how do you do, my pleasure now, can you?"

"Ah caw saw maw pwashure."

"You can say my pleasure? Mean this?"

The water felt like ice down there. She reached down with both hands and I felt a tug. Then I could feel her hand *directly on me* through all that ice and it was a sensation I'd never imagined.

"Wow," she whispered.

I pulled the box from my mouth and kept treading water with it clenched in my hand.

She let go and locked both her hands on my cheeks and kissed me hard. I tried to get things back where they belonged, but the zipper stuck and I started sinking. Then she spun off with a splash of silver water and swam to a ladder built into the bottom of her patio deck.

She climbed up ahead of me with her silk dress stuck to her body and her legs straightening up the rungs and the patio lights catching the water streaming off her.

She helped me climb onto the deck, took the box from my mouth and set it on the patio table. I turned away, still trying to get myself presentable, but she put a hand on my shoulder and turned me to her and locked her mouth on mine again. She aimed me through the French doors and guided me inside. I backpedaled. I bumped into some things but nothing fell or crashed. Through the living room with the lavender roses on the mantel. Past the kitchen, past the dining room with the chocolates and the on-sale gourmet coffee basket, down the hallway with the framed pictures receding along both sides of my vision, but really all I could see was her forehead angled below mine and one cheek and the glimmering blur of one eye as she pushed me into the bedroom, marched me through a ninety-degree left turn and into a bathroom. Her mouth never left mine. I felt her reach for something and heard the hiss of the shower. She reached for something else and I heard a hum overhead and felt the warm exhale of a heat lamp on the back of my neck. The door shut and it went dark. Almost dark. Looking past June's tilted-up cheek I saw the top half of us in a mirror over the sinks.

It took a while to get off our clothes. We held each other and kissed deeply and shivered while we waited for the warmth from the heat lamp to melt down over us and the steam from the shower to build up. It didn't take long. Or maybe it did. That kiss could have altered my perception of time and I couldn't get a look at my watch.

Then the click of the shower door and the step up and in, and hot water streaming down. Soap suds and shampoo lather and this smooth, supple, strong rubbery body against mine, hands spreading and exploring and stroking and exploring again. Unbearable pleasure. She got down on her knees and washed me. I told her to take it easy on the personal area but it seemed to me she deliberately didn't. I stood there, hard as a statue, arms braced against the tiles, shaking as she stroked me into the dark. When she was done I got down and washed her the same way. She was wetter than water. Then she cried out quietly and dug her fingernails into the back of my scalp and pulled my face into her. Another small cry. A growl, actually. Then amperage. Fingers strong on my skull. While her shudders got faster the hot water finally got through my skin and into my muscles and bones. And I felt so light again, like in the restaurant. I thought I could float to the shower ceiling and grab the nozzle like a balloon caught in a tree and watch June from above.

Not that I wanted to. We got out and tried to dry off in the steam. Damp with sweat, she led me to her bed. When my skin hit the cool night air the bumps came up under the sweat and it felt like invisible flowers blooming. She threw back the blanket and pulled the sheet over us.

We began making love at 10:13. I know because June had a digital clock on the bedstand with big green numbers on it. We began again at 12:25, 3:19, 5:58 and 8:44. At 11:40, 2:05 and 8:20 we were eating in bed—ice cream with chocolate syrup; leftovers from the restaurant; microwave sausage and pancake breakfasts served in small partitioned plates with the syrup bubbling hot from a divot in the plastic. We made love again later that morning, then I left. Walking down the stairs from her apartment, my legs were sore and my personal area was sore and so were my jaws. And I was happier than I'd been in my life, with the possible exception of the first time I stepped into Will and Mary Ann's home in the Tustin hills. The two experiences were very much alike. My heart pounded and my ears rang. And I greedily saw and smelled and felt everything I could see and smell and feel, because I was pretty sure that my new home—and June Dauer—would be taken away very soon.

Chapter Sixteen

Bamboo 33 nightclub was on Bolsa, in the heart of Little Saigon. I parked far back in the lot, shut off the engine of Will's car. It was eleven o'clock the next night and the lot was half full. The night was clear: no fog, no clouds. Just a warm breeze from the desert to the east, and a sky of scattered stars.

Birch and Ouderkirk arrived a few minutes later and I signaled them with a flash of the headlights.

We leaned against Birch's Crown Victoria. I could smell the food from the noodle shops mixed with the faint scent of the desert on the breeze. The lights of Little Saigon were bright along Bolsa and the traffic was light but fast.

"I don't think you'll get a welcome mat," said Rick. "If you find Bernadette, show her the picture of her and Gaylen. Tell her it's pretty easy to drop that picture into Sammy's cell. See if she'll come outside where we can all have a little talk."

I'd wondered about getting her outside. "That might look bad—her leaving with me. Sammy's going to hear about it."

Birch handed me a copy of the photo, which I folded and slid into my coat pocket. "If she'll give you what we need, take it and leave. If you're not back here in one hour, we're coming in for a look around."

I stood in a short line at the entrance, showed my badge. Twenty dollars admission. The woman in the ticket booth didn't look me in the face, but she waved away the money and pointed to the door.

The security man was huge and looked Hawaiian. His uniform was pressed and his baton had dents in it. He looked at the badge and frowned at me. "No trouble. We don't have trouble here."

"That's an excellent record," I said.

"Who you looking for?"

"Bernadette."

"Upstairs table."

"I appreciate it."

He eyed me again and swung the door. The room was large and open. The dance floor was a crowded swirl of bodies and light. A glitter ball hung over the dancers and strobes chopped them into herky-jerky motion. There were café tables around the floor. Lots of people at the tables. All Vietnamese that I could see—some young, some old. Mostly suits and dresses, cigarette smoke heavy in the air.

The band was on the stage, playing the Stones' "Beast of Burden." The singer was a woman, slender and very pretty, dressed in black pants and vest that were either leather or vinyl. The bar was to my right. There were stairs on either side of the room, leading to tables that had a view of the dance floor.

A lot of eyes on me. I moved to the stairway and climbed up. Eyes still on me. A waiter in a black suit clattered down and past me, balancing his drink tray and watching his feet.

At the landing I stopped and looked down the row of tables along the balcony. Bernadette Lee sat alone where the balcony made its turn. She looked at me, then back down to the dance floor.

When the song ended I walked over.

"I'm Joe Trona."

"I know. Sammy's friend."

"I just guard him. Can I sit down?"

She nodded and I sat. Bernadette Lee was tremendously beautiful. Her eyes were dark and they sparkled. High, arched brows. Strong cheekbones, small nose, graceful lines tapering to full, red lips. Her skin was very pale and she was dressed in a black dress with lace across the top of her chest and down her arms. Her hair was black and cut at her shoulders, with long bangs. Slender white fingers, long red nails. She tapped one of them on a cell phone on the table in front of her.

"Did Sammy send you?" Her voice was soft and a little hoarse.

"He's worried about you."

"Why?"

"Because this new guy next to him keeps telling him you're lonely."

"Giant Mike?"

"Giant Mike. Look, Miss Lee, I want to talk to you about somebody. It isn't Sammy."

"Then who?"

I leaned toward her, but not real close. Her perfume was soft, with the smell of cinnamon in it.

"John Gaylen."

She looked at me and all the beauty seemed to drain from her face. "I've never heard of him."

"Miss Lee, I have a picture in my pocket of you getting into his car."

She looked away, down at the dancers, dialing her cell phone without looking at it. I couldn't hear what she said. She punched off, stood and took a purse off the chair beside her.

"Come with me."

Two young Vietnamese men appeared at the table. Slender,

dark suits. One led and one followed as we walked single file down the stairs. We snaked behind the dance floor to the other side of the room. Another young man waited by a door and let us in. The door closed behind us. The hallway was dimly lit and I could hear the band through the walls. Bernadette's shoes clicked on the old linoleum floor as she led us down the hall and through another door, into a small room. There was a conference table in the middle, six chairs, a refrigerator. Overhead fluorescent lighting that flickered and hummed. Posters of Vietnamese singers on the walls. A small window, blinds closed.

Bernadette slung her purse onto the beat-up conference table. "Let me see it," she said. She lit a cigarette and sat.

I unfolded the photocopy and set it in front of her. She barely glanced at it, then looked up at me.

"So Giant Mike was right. I was lonely."

"What about Wednesday night, June the thirteenth? Were you with him?"

She tapped her fingernails on the table, quick and light. She sighed, got into her purse and came out with a small date book. A metal fastener separated the past from the present. She undid it and flipped back a few pages. Then she locked the fastener back on and dropped the book back into her purse.

"No."

"Where was he, Miss Lee?"

"I have no idea. I only saw him a few times."

"Enough times to check your date book, though."

Her beautiful eyes looked cold and a very small sneer came to her red lips. "Enough for that. What could you possibly care?"

"He killed my father."

She shrugged, eyes wandering the room. "I think people get what they deserve."

"Did Dennis Franklin?"

"Sammy didn't kill him. The cops manufactured evidence and the DA is happy to use it."

"There were two eyewitnesses, Miss Lee. And a bullet in Franklin's head that came from Sammy's gun."

"Evidence can be planted. You know that." She took a dainty puff on the cigarette then broke the ash off in an ashtray and rolled the edges out. The smoke rose toward the buzzing lights. "So, are you going to rat me to Sammy?"

"I don't know. Would you deserve that, Miss Lee?"

She looked at me again. "You're one of the ugliest men I've ever seen in my life. You think your manners are good but they're false."

"I've worked hard on them," I said.

"Go ahead and show Sammy the picture. And live with your conscience after that. But I wasn't with John Gaylen that night. I was here at the club, alone. The usual."

"Where was Gaylen?"

She glared at me.

"If you knew where Gaylen was, it could help, Miss Lee."

"Fuck!" She swept the ashtray and her purse to the floor, standing up so quick her chair flipped over. *"Fuck you. You know what Sammy calls you in his letters? He calls you Godzilla!"*

I actually did know that, from reading his mail, and from eavesdropping on his friends in the plumbing tunnel of Mod F.

"It's really just scar tissue," I said. "Where *was* John Gaylen that night, Miss Lee?"

"Fuck you."

"That has happened."

"What, is that a come-on? You offering me a deal now?"

"No, not at all."

"Then I'll offer you one. First you promise that picture

doesn't get to Sammy. Then I tell what Gaylen said about that night."

"I promise the picture doesn't get to Sammy."

"Give it to me."

"It's just a copy. It wouldn't do you any good at all."

She flipped the chair upright with her foot and caught the back with one hand, then collected her purse off the floor.

I set the picture on the table.

"John said he had a job to do that night. Probably wouldn't be around for a few days after that. The night before, he was in here, drinking hard. Not saying much. The three guys who got killed and the one still in the hospital—they were with him."

"When did you see him next?"

"A few days later. In here. He tried to get me to go out with him but I said no. I shouldn't have gone out with him in the first place. The Cobra Kings don't play by the rules."

"Sammy's rules?"

"Any rules I've ever known."

"What did Gaylen say about how the job went?"

"He said it went fine. He was ready to party, have some fun."

I heard the band start into another song. The fluorescent lights flickered and trembled.

"Miss Lee, Gaylen wasted two of his own men to keep them quiet. Is that what you mean about the rules?"

She looked at me, then up at the lights. "Maybe."

"Miss Lee, was John Gaylen in contact with Alex Blazak?"

Another casual glare. "Not that I know. I don't know anyone who liked to be in contact with that boy. Crazy and dangerous. Not businesslike."

I said nothing for a long moment.

"I've got something for you," she said. "I can give it to you.

But you've got to get a rat trap for Sammy. He hates rats. They're the only thing in the world that he's scared of."

"They won't let him have a spring trap. Custodial is going to put some bait in the heater vents. I told him that."

"Then how about more phone time?"

"I just got him more phone time."

"It isn't enough."

I thought about it for a moment. Getting more phone time wasn't a problem "I can get him another five minutes a day."

She huffed quietly, blew some more smoke. "Five minutes? I thought you were an important man."

I waited.

"The night before the murders I saw John meet some people in the parking lot here. Two people. One driving, one in the other seat. The passenger rolled the window down and they talked. Five minutes, maybe more. He told me later it was about the job."

"Can you ID them?"

"No."

"Describe the car."

"A red-and-white Corvette. Old. Good paint, very shiny."

BoWar.

Bernadette watched me like a poker player. "Then the Corvette laid down some rubber and smoked out of here."

Warren, I thought, but who was with him?

"I'm going to educate you, Mr. Trona," said Bernadette Lee. "You don't even have to give Sammy anything for this. You listen to me and you'll learn something. It's just like in ancient Rome, or China or anywhere. If a man like your father gets killed, his friends do it."

"His friends didn't kill him, Miss Lee. His enemies did."

"Friends? Enemies? Call them what you want. They're the same. People who knew him. People who worked with him.

That's who did it. Not John Gaylen. You Americans are naive. You always look at everything but the obvious."

I thought about that for a moment. "Here's another obvious thing I should probably be thinking about. My father disrespected you and Sammy one night, at the grand opening of this nightclub. He mad-dogged Sammy and Sammy lost face. That's a license to kill, if you're a gangster."

She shook her head. "Sammy outgrew that kind of thinking years ago."

"Did you?"

"The disrespect wasn't worth our energy. Our code applies to the people we take seriously. Your father wasn't that. He was only a politician."

What I said next surprised me. It came out faster than I could analyze it. It just seemed like the right thing to do.

"Cao woke up this afternoon," I said. "Only for a few minutes, but the doctor told me that usually means they're going to make it."

Bernadette Lee studied me. Her eyes were placid and unblinking.

"What did he say?"

"I haven't been told. But two homicide investigators will be there the next time he comes to. They'll have their tape recorders on and their pencils ready."

She lit another cigarette. "Liar."

I smiled. I never smile because it's an ugly thing, but I thought it would communicate all the satisfaction I would feel if Ike Cao really had come out of his coma.

She pouted at the ceiling; out came the smoke. Her eyes never left my face. I saw mostly the whites, like a shark's.

Back out in the parking lot I told Birch and Ouderkirk what she'd said.

"Gaylen had something going on Wednesday, the thirteenth," I said. "And he wasn't with Bernadette Lee."

Birch scribbled something into his notepad, then looked at me over the tops of his glasses. "All four of those men were with him the night before?"

"That's what she said."

I told them about Gaylen's furtive meeting with two men in an old, shiny red-and-white Corvette. I even told them who it probably belonged to.

Birch looked at me. His expression reminded me of Bernadette's—controlled but hungry. "Blazak asked Reverend Daniel to help find his daughter, right?"

I nodded. "And Reverend Daniel used his security man, Warren, to handle the ransom money and the exchange. Until Will came on stage."

Birch said nothing for a moment. He scribbled something else into his notepad. "Then was Gaylen passing information to Warren, or the other way around?"

"I've been thinking about that ever since she told me about the Corvette."

We stood for a minute, leaning against the Crown Vic, not speaking. The cars sped in and out of the Bamboo 33 lot, many of them the low-slung Hondas with the noisy headers.

I watched them but didn't really see them. I was haunted by the image of Warren's red-and-white Corvette parked right here in this lot, and John Gaylen leaning toward the passenger's window.

Who was the Mystery Passenger in that seat?

Why were Warren and Mystery Passenger talking to Gaylen?

One of the little Hondas screamed across the asphalt, fishtailing, raising acrid white smoke from its tires, music pounding from the trunk woofers.

It brought me back to the present.

"Sir, I told Ms. Lee that Ike Cao came out of his coma this afternoon, briefly, and talked. I said I hadn't been told what he said. That a doctor told me that kind of thing usually means a patient is going to pull out of it. That two homicide investigators would be there the next time Cao said anything. I said it all before I had time to think about going to prison for falsifying evidence."

Birch and Ouderkirk both stared at me. Then they started laughing. I wasn't sure how to take it. But they didn't stop. I turned away, not sure what to do.

"Joe's a cop," said Birch. "Look at that, a twenty-four-year-old newjack and already a cop."

Ouderkirk was shaking his head. "I'll get a twenty-four-seven on Gaylen, Rick."

"Well done, Harmon. Well done, Trona."

"What did Lee look like when you told her that?" Ouderkirk asked.

"Like a white shark, sir."

Laughter again.

"Man, I love this job," said Ouderkirk. "Joe, when you're old enough to work homicide, I'll take you as a partner."

"I'd be honored."

Bernadette Lee strode quickly across the lot, a remote pad in her hand. I heard an alarm chirp and saw a light go on.

"Sirs?" I nodded at her.

"Let her get in," said Birch.

As soon as she did, we slipped into the Ford. I sat in the back and looked between Birch and Ouderkirk as Lee's black Jaguar slid onto Bolsa. Rick followed without the lights until he hit the boulevard.

"I predict seven-forty-one Washington Street in Garden Grove," said Ouderkirk. "That's Gaylen's place."

* * *

But she didn't stop in Garden Grove. She sped out Bolsa until it changed into First Street in Santa Ana. Then a left on Raitt Street, and into the barrio. She made a quick right turn and I knew she'd see us if Rick followed, but he played it cool, passing straight through the intersection, then looping back fast, but not fast enough to screech the tires. We saw the Jag pulling into a driveway, through a wrought-iron gate opened by two Latinos in baggy clothes. Two pit bulls sniffed the car tires as it came to a stop inside.

Birch turned the other way, took another turn before coming back around. He parked on the opposite side of the house, four doors down.

"Let's magnify this situation," said Ouderkirk, pulling a small pair of binoculars from the glove box. "Ah. Two unidentified males and the Dragon Lady, going through the front door. Dogs are Staffordshire terriers, aka pit bulls. One brindle, one white. There's no street number on the house. Looks like two rooms lit inside. Iron gate, iron windows, iron door. Fancy filigrees on it, like it's trying to be decorative. Flowerpots on the porch, no flowers. Trees and hedges trimmed back—nowhere for a shooter to lie in wait. Floodlights in the side yard and over the driveway, hence my detailed reporting. Uh, floodlights out now—they're in lockdown mode."

"Come on," said Birch. "Can't you read the names on the dog tags?"

"One says 'Gang,' the other says 'Banger.' "

"Descriptive," said Birch.

We sat and waited. We had to roll down the windows to keep the car from fogging up. Even with that, Birch kept wiping the windshield with his hand.

The house to the right had an address stenciled on the curb. Using that, I knew the two possibilities for this house, and I recognized one of them from the phone company call list for Will's cell phone.

"It's Pearlita's house," I said quietly.

Birch turned to me and I saw the uncertainty register, then resolve. "The call sheet," he whispered. "You've got a good memory, Joe."

"It's eidetic."

"That's a nice gift," he said. "So, now we've got a woman with a Cobra King boyfriend, and urgent business with the Raitt Street Boys. This is interesting. Makes you wonder what would bring two gangs like that together."

"Money, money and money," said Ouderkirk.

Half an hour later the outside lights came on and Bernadette stepped onto the porch. The two baggy-clothed males were with her, and another, much wider guy. Maybe two hundred pounds, I guessed. He wore loose chinos and what looked like a Pendleton shirt, untucked, shiny black boots. His hair was cut short, no cap. Sunglasses, even in the dark. He walked Bernadette Lee to her car. His walk was loose, ambling. I could see that they were talking, but all I could hear on the damp summer air was the distant murmur. The pit bulls came to the gate and sniffed the air.

"No Pearlita," whispered Ouderkirk. "She's not home, or she stayed inside."

"That's her," I whispered back. "The guy is Pearlita. She dresses like a man. I've seen pictures of her face and that's her face."

"No *way.*"

"Way, sir."

"If I was that ugly I'd shoot people, too."

"The others might be brothers," said Birch. "She's got two more. Twenty-one and twenty-five, something like that. Allegedly, no gang affiliation."

"Obviously not," said Ouderkirk.

Ahead of us, headlights swung onto the street and came our way. We melted into the vinyl, below the window line.

"I feel like a five-year-old when I do this," Ouderkirk whispered. "It's fun."

"You should try sleighriding in the jail, sir."

"What's that?"

"I'll tell you later."

I listened to the car approach, saw the headlights wash through the Ford and continue down Raitt Street.

A moment later we all sat back up. Lee's Jaguar was backing out, the gate almost open. The fat gangster stood with her hands on her hips, watching. The two others turned and went inside.

Bernadette swung her car onto the street in a tight reverse turn, then put it into forward gear and sped off. Pearlita watched her. She shook a smoke from a pack in her flannel shirt, used a lighter on it. A moment later the floodlights went off but I could still see her standing in front of the porch, with the cherry of the cigarette slowly growing larger and smaller, larger and smaller. Then the cherry dropped in a little shower of sparks. The door opened and Pearlita went in, the dogs barging ahead of her.

Five minutes later we pulled away from the curb and U-turned, heading out the opposite direction of Lee.

Gaylen and Pearlita, I thought. The Cobra Kings and the Raitt Street Boys. "Since when do street gangs care who runs the county government?"

"They don't," said Birch. "The question isn't who was helping Gaylen, but who hired him."

On the way back to Bamboo 33, all I could think about was Bo Warren and his Mystery Passenger, huddling with John Gaylen in the parking lot.

I told Ouderkirk about sleighriding—rolling down the guard walk in Mod F of Men's Central, lying on the mechanics' sled,

then sneaking a look at what the inmates were doing. He said
he wanted to try it and I told him to talk to Sergeant Delano.

Half an hour later I parked three houses down from Gaylen's
home. Same faux Swiss window trim, same non-Swiss palms.
Same lights inside and on the porch. I half expected to see Bernadette Lee's Jaguar there, but it wasn't. I half believed that Lee
would have already called him to say that Cao was getting
strong enough to wake up and point a finger at him, that Gaylen
would be packing up his Mercedes for a long trip.

Neither seemed to be true.

So I leaned my head back and watched.

Forty minutes later the front door opened. Gaylen came out,
walked halfway across the yard and stood under one of the palm
trees. He was wearing jeans, no shirt, no shoes. He looked like
a guy who ran a lot and lifted weights—ropey muscles but not
big ones.

He got something from his pocket and looked down. Both
elbows came up but I couldn't see what he had in his hands.
Something small and white fluttered to the ground.

Then he looked up at the sky and lit a cigar, rotating the end
in the flame of a lighter. He blew a cloud of smoke against the
tree trunk.

A girl walked out of the house. Fourteen, sixteen, eighteen—
hard to tell. Short, very slender, straight black hair. Black robe
cinched tight, bare feet. She came up behind him and slipped
her arms around his back. Her black hair fell down across her
face. She reached around Gaylen with one hand, took the cigar,
drew on it, and reached around him again to put it back.

She took his free hand and pulled him toward the door but
he swatted her away. I could hear her quiet laughter.

A few minutes later they went inside. I waited another hour,
then turned off the interior lights so they'd stay off when the

door was opened. I got out and nudged the door shut with my hip.

I kept to the sidewalk on the opposite side of the street, then jogged a straight line across to Gaylen's yard. I found the white thing on the grass under the palm tree and cupped it up like you would a butterfly. I hustled back to the sidewalk with long light steps.

Once I got on the freeway I hit the reading light and pulled the white object from my coat pocket.

Pay dirt, just what I'd expected: a Davidoff cigar band cut neatly in two, curved into its original shape.

I wondered what Gaylen had talked to Alex Blazak about in the gun warehouse that night. Wondered what took a half a cigar apiece for them to decide.

You with Alex?

You're with Alex. Laughter. *Little shit too scared to show his face, ah?*

Chapter Seventeen

In the morning I sat in my kitchen and arranged the contents of Will's safe-deposit box on the dinette table. Then I re-arranged them. Then I arranged them again.

The day was warm and I opened the windows to let the breeze come through. The orange tree in my backyard was heavy with fruit and I knew that the sharp sweet smell of citrus was around me as I sat at the table.

But I couldn't smell it. All I could smell was my own human breath, my own human body, and the faint metallic odor of blood. And all I could think about was Alex and Savannah Blazak, Luria Blas and Miguel Domingo. And Will. Always Will. First and foremost, Will, ground zero for everything in my life.

I moved the items around again, trying to put them in some kind of order. Order. Reason. Logic. The rational. The understandable. Order—at least a small bit of it—spread on the table before me like some kind of talisman against everything else that had happened in the last two weeks.

There were seven items. Four of them were personal, and somehow surprising to me, given how commonplace they really were.

The first was a packet of love letters written to him almost four decades ago by a girl named Teresa. She was his high school sweetheart. He'd hardly told me anything about her. But I did remember him telling me once that young love is the purest. The letters were faded and frayed, very well read.

I fingered them lightly, set them aside, to my right, the side of goodness and love and light.

Next was a black-and-white photograph of Will, age eight or so, kneeling beside a dog. The dog was a mix of some kind, black, with a tongue lolling out of what appeared to be a large smile. Sparky, Will's first dog. I didn't know the dog had meant that much to him.

I propped it up against the bundle of love letters. Love and loyalty go together, I thought.

Then, an envelope containing color photographs of the war. One picture showed the inside of a bar or restaurant, four GI's around a table, four petite Vietnamese women with their arms around the men. Will looked very drunk, and too young to be in a uniform. He was so slender, then, with none of the weight he'd put on as a middle-aged man. I remembered him telling me about his unsuccessful days as a high school athlete, the way he played three sports every year and mostly sat out. Loved the games, but never made varsity.

Another was a picture of Will alone, in a hotel, maybe, with yellow sunlight coming in through the blinds. He was sitting on a bed, leaning forward slightly, naked to the waist. His dog tags had swung out from his chest. A cigarette burned in an ashtray beside him. The expression on his face was the most forlorn I'd ever seen. I'd never seen him look that alone. He hated to be alone. And a few other shots: a buddy smoking a giant joint; a couple of prostitutes hugging each other; an American soldier lying in a tree with his face and one arm blown off. The other arm was wrapped around a branch as if to keep him from falling out.

The last was a snapshot of Will sitting in a Jeep, his M16 on his lap. He was looking away from the camera. I noticed how he held the gun, tightly and away from his body, with the muzzle pointed down. Like it was going to strike at him. And I thought of how uncertain Will had always been around firearms, how they always looked wrong in his hands, even when he was a sheriff's deputy. I thought of Will introducing me to the department arms instructor when I was ten, so I could begin learning the basics of safety and marksmanship—things that a thousand other fathers taught their sons on every weekend of the year. Guns, I thought: one of the few things that scared him.

I put the pictures back in the envelope and closed the flap, then slid it under the bundle of letters because love is stronger than war.

Next was a small empty turtle shell, painted white with red letters across the carapace. The letters said DEKEY! I looked through the front leg holes, then the rear ones, holding it up to the sunlight coming through the window. Inside, the shell was smooth as the curve of a tablespoon. Will had never told me about the turtle.

I set the small shell behind the love letters, out of my sight. I'd had enough of things that used to be alive and now were not.

Sparky smiled.

The love letters lay intact, safe, well-read.

Item five was a folded sheet of white paper with a mini audiotape inside, and the following notes made in Will's handwriting:

Rup to Millie per B. convers. of 5/02/01:
1/22/01—25
3/14/01—25
4/07/01—35
Windy Ridge see att. tape made 5/12/01

I played the attached tape. There were ten seconds of hiss, then some pleasantries that didn't sound real pleasant. When those were over, this:

GRUFF VOICE, MALE: *Okay, Milky, to business. It's the usual spot.*

CAUTIOUS VOICE, MALE: *Got it.*

GRUFF: *It's better you don't send her.*

CAUTIOUS: *Let me handle it my way.*

GRUFF: *Can't tell you how important Thursday is.*

CAUTIOUS: *Might be some problems with this whole thing.*

GRUFF: *What in hell would those be?*

CAUTIOUS: *Basic security. I don't know. Just a feeling.*

GRUFF: *The biggest problem would be a red light Thursday.*

CAUTIOUS: *Don't worry.*

GRUFF: *I hate it when people tell me that. Always means trouble. Just do your job, Milky. You want to blubber and whine, do it to your wife.*

CAUTIOUS: *Yeah, yeah. We'll talk.*

I listened to it again. I recognized Rupaski's rough old voice. Milky/Millie was Dana Millbrae—Will's sometime friend and sometime foe on the Board of Supervisors. The B of line one was Bridget Andersen, Millbrae's secretary, and one of my father's very secret friends.

The conversation itself had almost certainly been caught by an intercept and recorder installed on Millbrae's office telephone line. I knew about that intercept and recorder because I'd installed them one Saturday while Will lounged in Millbrae's empty reception area, his feet up on Bridget's desk, reading a magazine. Will supplied the intercept device. I didn't know where he got it, though I had an idea. All it took was an electric drill, a couple of brackets and four screws. I mounted a micro-recorder to the back of Millbrae's center desk drawer. I hid the mike in the mass of cables running up through the cable hole on the desktop. Then ran a line to the intercept. Any voice would start the recorder running, and the intercept relayed both parties of the call onto tape. Took about twenty minutes and Will said *slick. That's for Bridget, son. You just did a good thing for the Bridge.*

That was the last I'd heard about it, until now.

I thought about Bridget, a forty-ish, handsome woman who had been Millbrae's secretary for all of his six years as a supervisor. She was extremely shy. Widowed. When I installed that tape recorder back in February of this year, I assumed that Bridget would be the operator, but I had no illusion that the tap was for her benefit and not Will's.

The next item was a letter-sized envelope, unsealed. Inside were two receipts for $10,000 cash donations from Will Trona to the Hillview Home for Children. Will and Ellen Erskine had scratched their signatures on the bottoms.

The last thing on the dinette table was another envelope. This one wasn't sealed either, and I couldn't feel or see anything inside.

I opened it and shook out two strips of eight-millimeter-film, each containing twenty frames in sequence. They looked like identical photographs of the same thing: Reverend Daniel and a woman. He had both hands loosely around her neck, thumbs supporting her jaws. He was looking down at her slightly, his face up close. His expression was dreamy. It looked like he was getting ready to kiss her, although he may not have been. She looked up at him with her eyes open in an expression of conditional surrender. She was young, black-haired and dark-skinned.

The room they were in looked like one of the hospitality suites above the lounge at the Grub.

I recognized the woman from the newspaper and TV stills:

Luria Blas. She had the same big clear eyes as her little brother, Enrique.

I got up from the table and went into the backyard. The sun was getting high and there was a breeze that almost cleaned away the smog.

I sat on a bench by the orange tree and looked at the sky. A squirrel ran along the power line above me and I watched her shadow cross the grass. Then another, smaller one.

I wanted my mommy, too. So I called her and we talked and made a date.

Bridget Andersen told me it wouldn't be good to be seen with me. We set up a noon meeting at a park up in the Orange hills. I was early so I found a picnic bench in the shade and sat. I smelled the sagebrush and listened to the cars hissing on the avenue far below.

Bridget, brightly blond with big dark glasses, parked and walked toward me. Blue skirt and heels, white blouse, a purse over one shoulder. She smoothed her skirt with her left hand as she sat down across from me. She looked uncomfortable with herself, like she often did. Like she didn't know what to do with the fact that she was attractive. When she took off her glasses I saw that her stunning, ice-blue eyes were shot with pink.

"What? Didn't the eyedrops get the red out?"

"Not all of it, Ms. Andersen."

"Bridget. What took you so long to call?"

"I'm slow sometimes. But I finally heard the tape of Millbrae and Rupaski."

"Ah, of course. Your father's bounty."

"I wasn't sure what to make of it."

"Will was."

"Can you explain it?"

She put her glasses back on. "I trusted your father. Can I trust you?"

"I'm here for him, not for myself."

Her gaze was calm and discerning, in spite of the bloodshot eyes. "He trained you well."

Even a dog can keep secrets.

"Look, Joe," she said. "Everybody knew that Rupaski's unofficial bosses wanted to unload the 91 Toll Road on the county because they're losing their shirts on it. You know the cast—Blazak and his developer friends, that ilk. Price? Call it twenty-seven million, round figures. But they needed the Board of Supervisors to approve a county purchase. Three against. Three for it, with Millbrae undecided as of February. Well, the Grove Club Research and Action Committee came up with some funds to influence the right people. Most of it went to the PR flaks, to get the public to see it their way and pressure the pols. Some was soft money for PACs, the usual unregulated bribery. Some of it was not-so-soft. Will smelled weakness in Millie. He was ready."

"He had me put in the tape recorder."

She smiled without any happiness at all. "That was nice work, Joe. You even cleaned up the drill shavings."

"Thank you."

"Rupaski was in charge of the hard money disbursements. Millie's part was put into brown bags and set in a gully, by a bush exactly one hundred feet northeast of the Windy Ridge toll plaza. The bush is a wild buckwheat, to be precise. That was what Rupaski called 'the usual spot.' I know because Millbrae sent me to pick up those bags."

Will's handwritten notes, I thought: dates and amounts. "That's what the taped conversation is about."

"Exactly—another slop bucket, filled up and ready for Millie's pale little fingers. It was the big bucket, too, because the vote was the following Thursday. This was about a month before your father was killed."

"But Millie voted against the sale. He sided with Will."

"That he did."

I remembered the night very clearly. The look on Rupaski's face. The way Millbrae hustled out of the meeting. Will's gloating in the car later, about Millie *voting the sonofabith down for once.*

It took me just a second to figure out what had really happened.

"Oh," I said. "I see."

"Like father, like son."

"Will played the tape for Millbrae before the vote."

"They call it blackmail, Joe."

I thought for a moment. Millbrae getting payola from the Grove Trust Research and Action Committee. Rupaski the bagman. Will with the incriminating evidence. And Bridget making the actual pickups.

"Did Millbrae know you were helping Will?"

"No. Millie thinks everyone loves him as much as he loves himself."

"Did Millbrae tell Rupaski why he had to vote no?"

"Sure he did. The first thing any politician learns is to pass the blame. Millie's a natural."

"So both of them realized that Will had them over a barrel."

She nodded, studying me. "They were terrified he'd go to the grand jury or to his friends on the Sheriff's. He never would, of course, because that would sink me, and maybe even himself."

"They didn't know that."

"No, they didn't. Will had them good and tight. They even argued about whose phone had the bug on it. I'd pulled out the tape recorder before Millie started looking."

Bridget took a deep breath and sighed. She looked past me with one of those gazes that see nothing but the backside of thoughts.

Then she laughed quietly. "Will drove us out to Windy Ridge the night of the last payoff, before he'd played that tape for Millie. He took the money out of the bag, put in some sand and rocks, handed the bag to me. I delivered it to Millie, per usual. Innocent, loyal Bridget, doing her mule work. I didn't see Millie's face when he opened it, but I wish I could have. Will told me Jaime over at the HACF needed a shot of help. Ninety grand must have gotten them something."

Didn't the ninety help?

Will, I thought. Robin Hood of Orange County. Fine, until it gets you killed.

"Joe, I'd have shot Millie with poison darts if that's what Will wanted me to do. I loved your father."

"I know."

"What did he say about me?"

"He said you had the biggest, meanest heart in Orange County."

She thought about that, and finally smiled. "He liked to cast me against type. I almost got an ulcer, knowing that telephone was bugged."

I could have said that Will told me The Unknown Thing *ran amok* in Bridget Andersen, but I didn't.

She stood up and walked back to her car.

Driving back out of the hills I realized that Rupaski and Millbrae had good reasons to hate my father. Good enough reasons to kill him, too?

I kept my appointment with Dr. Zussman, though I had nothing I wanted to tell him. My heart warmed with even so much as a thought about June Dauer, but she wasn't for Dr. Zussman, or

for anybody else. She was for me. So I told him about my years
at Hillview and my relationships with Will and Mary Ann and
my brothers. Then we talked about the shooting again, and I
told him I felt the same as before. He brought up what I'd said
about half a coffee cup's worth of remorse and I said that was
still a good comparison. He seemed disappointed. He kept asking me about remorse and denial and anger and sublimation. I
could tell I wasn't telling him what he wanted to hear. He said
he thought I could go back to work in a week. Then it was my
turn to be disappointed, and I told him so. He smiled and nodded and we made another appointment.

I spent part of the afternoon alone in the plumbing tunnel of
Mod F, just listening randomly, hoping to pick up something
useful. I learned about some dope being smuggled in through
the staff dining kitchen, and that some of the inmates were passing kites in the chapel on Sunday mornings. Nothing new.
Somehow, being locked in that narrow little tunnel made me
feel secure. I took the mechanics' sled for a sleighride, and got
a good look at a couple of Aryan Brotherhood thugs in the day
room, tormenting the Mexican gangster in the cell next door.
The Aryans sang one of their racist songs loud, together, salut-
ing with their arms straight out, laughing in between the verses.

Later, when I told Sergeant Delano what I'd learned, he
chewed me out for being stupid enough to come back here when
I didn't have to. But he let me hang around in the bubble for a
while—that's the main guard station in the intake-release center—not working, just being.

I talked briefly with the Mod J guards and inmates. Sammy
Nguyen had seen the rat again, was agitating for the trap I told
him he'd never get. He asked me for a small flashlight, one of
the good MagLite brands, so he could see the damned rat in the
dark and throw something at it. Flashlights were forbidden in
the jail, and I told him so. I told him that Bernadette was doing

well and missing him very much. He gave me a suspicious stare, then flopped onto his bunk and stared up at her picture.

Giant Mike Staich was in a holding tank while they searched his cell: someone had ratted him out for having a weapon. I watched the search detail work through the small cell. They found nothing, left Giant Mike's few possessions in the middle of the floor and walked out.

Dr. Chapin Fortnell was in trial.

Dave Hauser, assistant DA turned drug supplier, showed me a picture of the property he and his family would purchase as soon as he got this "stupid misunderstanding cleared up." The property had palms and a white sand beach and a lagoon of water the same color blue as the sky above it.

Serial rapist Frankie Dilsey lay on his cot with his back to the bars, humming. His feet were moving, like a dog running in a dream.

Ice-Box Killer Gary Sargola looked at me mournfully as I walked by, but said nothing. His penalty phase was due to start next week, and the DA was asking for death. He was a pasty, bespectacled man and it was hard to imagine him doing what he'd done. But when you thought about it, none of the guys in there looked any worse than anybody else. In fact, they looked a lot better than me.

I sat with some of the other deputies for a while in the staff dining room. We gossiped about the inmates and the bosses and drank coffee. Some were brand-new, and had almost an entire five-year stretch to go. Others were down to their last few months, even weeks. I was getting close to the end of my jail days—four years down and one to go.

When Sergeant Delano came in, we sat up a little straighter and quit talking.

"Trona," he said, "you've got a hot call on four."

I went to the guard station, punched the code for the outside line and said hello.

It was Rick Birch. He said the surveillance team had followed John Gaylen to a public park in Irvine. Gaylen had sat on a bench by a lake for two hours. He had made three calls on his cell phone and received two others.

"That was between noon and two this afternoon," he said. "At one-thirty, someone put a silenced bullet through Ike Cao's forehead in the ICU. We're still working it, but there was a new nurse in the unit just before it happened. Nobody's seen her since."

"What did she look like?"

"Fresh out of surgery—scrubs, hair net, mask, maybe a stethoscope and a clipboard. Short, wide, overweight. Dark hair and eyes. They got her on security video. The picture's terrible. Like the fog that night—hard to make out."

"Pearlita," I said.

"We've got six teams down on Raitt Street right now. If she shows, she's ours."

My little trick had worked. It had worked well enough to get Ike Cao killed. My heart sank then, just a little, even though I told myself that Ike was an attempted murderer, that his own gang boss had killed him.

Birch read my mind.

"Don't let your heart bleed out, Trona. Ike Cao helped murder your father. He'd have murdered you, too, if he had a chance."

"Thank you, sir," I said.

"The bullet was still inside Cao's head. We'll recover it, run it through DrugFire and the Bureau."

The Reverend Daniel Alter's face went bright red when I showed him the film strips from the safe deposit box. Out of respect, I looked away from him and stared out the windows of the Chapel of Light. The long summer evening was just beginning to fall. The sky was pale blue and the moon was an upended curl of white over Saddleback Mountain.

"I'm humiliated," he said. "And absolutely outraged."

"Yes, sir."

"What am I supposed to say to this?"

"I don't know."

"In Will's *safe-deposit box*?"

I nodded. "But you knew that, Reverend. He didn't keep those in the bank because he liked them. He kept them there because they were valuable. How much was he getting out of you?"

His eyes got big, magnified by the thick lenses of his glasses. Disbelief. But even I—a great fan of Reverend Daniel's performances—could see how forced it was. He sighed and dropped the astonishment. He looked up at me.

"We agreed on ten thousand a month for one year. I paid twice, so I owed ten more installments."

"That's not much money, is it, Reverend? For a very wealthy man like yourself?"

"Will said if I'd have gone any further he would have pauperized me. I laughed at that, because we both knew he wouldn't. You see, Will was illegally taking advantage of me, I know. But I wasn't really paying him, because he was donating that ten thousand to the Hillview Home for Children every month. He had no interest in the money as *money*. He was interested in it for what it could *do*. So, he caught me in a sin, and I'm paying for it. I didn't hate Will for what he was doing. I actually thought it was . . . fair."

I thought of the ten-thousand-dollar receipts I'd found in the safe-deposit box.

"When was that film shot?"

He gazed out the window. "Two months ago. At the Grove. Luria was lovely and lonely and when I went upstairs to rest, she and a lady friend followed me into the room. We talked and talked. They drank a little. Actually, they drank like Packers fans. Will came in at some point, as did several others—to talk and freshen up their drinks. The bar in the hospitality suite was open. People coming and going. Everyone was a little crazy, actually. Some rather provocative things on the television. And that moment caught on the film, well, yes, I kissed her. I confess to that. I couldn't help myself, Joe. In fact, it was supposed to be a professional kiss—a peck on the cheek. But she turned her lips to mine at the very last moment, and I was . . . well, Joe, I *fell*. And as soon as I'd done it, I knew it was very, very wrong. So I apologized and I went back down to the lounge. I had a strong drink, I must say. Then I had someone drive me home. To my Rosemary. The wife I love. Well, I mean she wasn't actually *at* home, at that specific point. She was on Majorca, ministering to the ah . . . ministering to herself, I think. Believe me, when I saw the film later, I cursed Will and his little brief-case camera. What trickery he was capable of."

Daniel looked suddenly smaller to me, as if he'd shrunk a size in the last five minutes. He wouldn't look at me.

"Two weeks later, Luria was killed on Coast Highway."

"I was crushed. I recognized her picture in the papers. I prayed for her. And I prayed for me, that your father would never show people what I'd done to her."

"Did you know that the kid who was killed outside the Pelican Point guardhouse was her brother? Luria was pregnant. She was severely beaten before that truck hit her. Miguel Domingo knew all that. His answer was a machete and a screwdriver."

"Jaime told me."

He bowed his head.

"Who brought her to the Grub, Reverend?"

"I have no idea, Joe."

"You don't get in without a sponsor, party girl or not."

"Yes, yes."

He pursed his lips and frowned. He closed his eyes. "I believe, Joe, that the party was thrown by the Committee to Reelect Dana Millbrae. In conjunction with the Research and Action Committee of the Grove Foundation."

It figured. I remembered the night. It was back in April and I'd been there, down in the bar, drinking sodas while the party went on upstairs. The players came out for that event. I remembered Daniel, in fact, a little tipsy. Will was all over the place—downstairs in the restaurant, then in the bar, then upstairs into the hospitality suite and back down again. Lots of attractive, single women, though I didn't see Luria Blas.

"Reverend, your security man, Bo Warren, met with the man who killed Will. This was the night before it happened. Why?"

This time, Daniel's astonishment was real. "I . . . I can't imagine that, Joe, let alone explain it. I can't believe that."

"I've got a witness. Somebody was in the car with Warren. I need to know who it was."

"I'll talk to him. I will absolutely talk to him."

"Tell me, please, sir, as soon as you know."

I stood and gathered up my hat and briefcase. I went to the window and looked out at the old day and the young night.

"Joe, I'm . . . willing to pay *you* the remaining hundred thousand dollars. The Hillview Children's Home would be glad to have the money. If you take away that incriminating film strip on my desk here, all you're left with is a legitimate charitable donation to a very worthy cause."

"Will could fake ten grand a month from the family fortune. I can't do that, sir."

"Then I'll make the donation myself and save you both the headache."

I wondered why Daniel hadn't been making his payments to Hillview directly, all along. It took me just a second to see it from Will's angle, and I had my answer: Will didn't trust him enough.

I turned and looked at Daniel. I wanted him to be holy but he wasn't. I wanted him to be strong, but he seemed to me to be weak when it mattered and strong when it didn't. I wanted him to be honest and forthright, but he wasn't really those things, either.

"You look so disappointed, Joe."

"I spilled a lot of blood, sir. But Will died anyway. I thought you were close to God, but with all respect, Reverend, you strike me as kind of dishonest. You know what it seems like to me? It seems to me that if just one man would have stood up and done the right thing, this whole chain of things wouldn't have happened. Lies on lies, then more lies. Greed on greed on more greed. Nobody stopped. Nobody tried to stop."

"That's where you're wrong. We all try. We try every day. But we're imperfect and we're flawed. So we fail. Don't let perfection become the enemy of right."

"Those words are true. But they leave an awfully big hole, sir."

"Yes. I know. Please sit down another minute, Joe. Sit down, please."

I went back over to the chair, put down the briefcase and hat, and sat again.

"Joe, Will was not a saint. I see you're learning that about him. During the course of a man's life, Joe, he'll be faced with many difficult decisions. Men in power, like your father, they have to make more of them than others. It's difficult. That's why we need God to guide us. We cannot captain our own vessels alone."

"Reverend, I always thought Will was right. Even when I

saw him doing something that wasn't right, I figured he was working toward a larger good. I thought when I got older and wiser, I'd see behind the actions to the larger things behind them. I thought his wrongs were . . . necessary detours."

"As well they may have been."

I collected my things and stood. "What if they weren't?"

"Here," he said. He handed me back the envelope with the film strips in them. "These are yours."

"Do what you want with them, sir."

"Thank you very much. Do what you think is proper with this."

He gave me another envelope, sealed. It was thick and heavy and I knew what it was. I weighed it on the palm of my hand and looked at Reverend Daniel.

"For Hillview Home," he said. "For Luria's family, if you can find any of them. For the memory of Will and all that he did that was good."

"Put it back in the offering plate, Reverend," I said.

I set it on his desk and left.

I caught Carl Rupaski in his office. His secretary was gone and Rupaski was sitting at his desk, big brown wingtips on the mahogany, gazing out one window. Orange sunlight filtered down through the smog and onto Santa Ana.

He smiled when I walked in, but he didn't get up. "So, you're coming to work for the Transportation Authority?"

"No, sir. It was a flattering offer, though."

"What's that you got?"

"A tape player. I want to play something for you."

"If I said it, it can't be good."

"It's interesting. And I've got a few questions, sir."

At this, Rupaski pulled his feet off the desk and leaned forward. "This an official sheriff's department visit, Joe?"

"No, sir. I found this tape recording and some notes, and I wondered if you could clear some things up."

"Will's tape?"

"Yes, sir."

He sat back heavily and locked his fingers behind his head. I played it.

His face went hard when he heard his voice, then Millbrae's. He stared at me. Brown eyes under bushy eyebrows. Small eyes, and keen, like a vulture's. "So?"

"The *usual spot* was the wild buckwheat bush northeast of the Windy Ridge toll plaza. *Her* is Bridget. *Thursday night* was May tenth, which was the supervisors' vote on the toll road purchase. The reason for the conversation was money—ninety grand—that you paid Millbrae to vote your way. Millbrae ended up with nothing, because Will took the money. And Mr. Millbrae voted against you that night, because Will had played him this same tape."

The eyebrows raised, then lowered. "Try this. The *usual spot* was the Grove, for drinks and a strategy session. *Her* is Bridget, all right, who loves sticking her nose into Millie's business, and, quite frankly, influences his decisions in ways I don't like. *Thursday night* was the supervisors' vote, and it was important, just like I said in the tape. The reason for the conversation was how to get Millbrae into our camp with time running out. Now, Joe, just how in the hell do you get ninety grand and blackmail out of it?"

I couldn't answer that without exposing Bridget, so I took a chance.

"Will told me. I made the pickup that night at Windy Ridge. I filled the sack with rocks."

Rupaski's face went red. He shrugged. He looked out the window. "So what the fuck do you want?"

"I want to know who paid John Gaylen to kill my father."

"And I'm supposed to know?"

"When I heard the tape, sir, I realized he was blackmailing Millbrae. You put a transmitter on Will's car. You said he asked you to, but I don't believe you. I think that story is like the one you just told—convincing and quick and a lie. I think you bugged his car so you could get him on something like he had on you and Millbrae. Some kind of leverage. Anything—an affair, a pay-off, anything that you could use against him. Your men followed him on the Tuesday before he died. They followed him to a beach in Laguna and saw him with Alex and Savannah Blazak. You told Jack. He told you that Alex was using Will to deliver Savannah and collect the money. So you knew Will would go to the girl, as soon as Alex told him where she was. You had a motive to silence Will, and the means of locating him. One of your men could follow at a distance, use the transmitter and get word back to Gaylen as fast as a voice travels through a telephone cell."

"So *I* set him up for Gaylen?"

"That's a possibility I'm considering, sir."

He shook his head and kept staring at me. "That tape isn't evidence, you know. It's illegal—you can't tape a conversation when there's an expectation of privacy. And there's no chain of custody on it. I've already talked to the DA about it—a hypothetical case, of course. It's useless."

"The grand jury might not think so, after I tell them about the ninety thousand for Millbrae's vote. You see, sir, Will's dead. So if it comes out that he was blackmailing you, well, that really isn't going to hurt him any more than Gaylen's bullets already did."

"You'd do that? Crap on his name that way?"

"To get to who hired John Gaylen? Yes, sir."

Rupaski stood and looked down at me. Then he went to the big map of the county on his wall, the one with all the roads that the county was planning to build. The roads were shown in different colors: black for now; blue for the next decade; red for the one after that.

"It's going to be a great county, Joe. And Will, you, me—we all did our part."

"Will didn't like most of those blues and reds. He fought you on them."

"His part was to fight them. That's what I said."

I looked at the dizzying blue and red future. The lines looked like veins and arteries wrapped around a funny shaped heart.

"I'll come clean with you, Joe. This alleged ninety-grand payola! I don't know anything about that, or a bag full of rocks. You want to make your father out to be a blackmailer, go ahead. But I do admit that my guys were following Will. Why? Because Jack came to me when Savannah was taken, just like I told you. And Jack confided in me when Will got himself into the middle of it. So I bugged up his BMW in the service yard, hoping he'd lead us to the girl. *I did it for Savannah.* It worked, because we found all three of them down at the beach in Laguna that night. Yep, my boys followed that radio signal all the way, right to them. I told Jack what we found. So we decided to stay with you, so as not to lose Savannah. Honestly, my best guys were on you the night Will died. But you lost them somewhere between the Grove and Lind Street, Joe. You're too damned good a driver. That damned BMW is too fast. You outran us. That transmitter's only good for about two miles. And I'll tell you this, too, young man—I never heard of John Gaylen until you told me about him."

Rupaski was as convincing a man as I'd ever met. He'd half-way fooled me with the original transmitter story. Now this. I gathered up the tape recorder and slid it back into my pocket.

"And remember this, too, Joe. Bridget is a good woman and a good employee and you don't want her hurt. I get the feeling

Bridget was behind that recording. I can't prove it. But a court
can make her testify and ask her some hard questions. Perjury
is a felony. You might not be concerned about her well-being,
but Will was. And I am."

"Bridget has nothing to do with this."

He smiled. "Let me ask you something again. Are you *really*
willing to drag Will's name through the mud? An illegal wire-
tap, blackmail of a fellow supervisor, stealing *ninety thousand*
dollars that weren't his?"

I stood. "I'm going to solve his murder."

"At any cost?"

"Absolutely, sir."

He shook his head. "What if he wouldn't have wanted you
to?"

"I would anyway."

"Maybe you didn't learn as much from him as I thought you
did. You're looking for blame in the wrong places. You're
pissed off. I understand that. But be careful, Joe. Don't go making enemies out of your father's friends."

"A lot of people, sir, say they were his friend. But they never
said that when he was alive."

"It's a system, Joe. It's a process. Preserve and utilize. Build
and condemn. Tax and spend. Conservative and liberal. All
parts of the same system. Think *forest*, Joe. Don't think trees.
Millions of trees, but just one forest. And that's where all of us
live."

Chapter Eighteen

Later that evening I walked into the house in the Tustin hills just as I had a hundred thousand times. And I felt exactly what I'd felt every one of those hundred thousand times except maybe the first few hundred: safe and part of.

Not much had changed. Same worn Mexican paving tiles, same white walls in the entryway, same black wrought-iron table with a big cobalt-blue vase for flowers, same mirror that threw your reflection back at you as soon as you opened the door. I was eleven before I was tall enough to see my whole face in that mirror, and I remember believing that when I was tall enough to see it, I'd be a man and not a boy. I also remember believing that by the time I was tall enough to see my whole face, they would have found some cure for it. Neither was true, but the belief was.

I hugged my mother, then followed her down the hallway, past the TV room on our left, then around the corner and into the big living room. Same good leather furniture, same smell of fresh-cut flowers and sautéed garlic and the faint, high-pitched scent of the ammonia that Mary Ann used to clean the windows every week. *Can't have a clear view through dirty glass, can you, Joe?* I used to help her with that chore, her on the inside and me outside, worrying away the streaks with our squeegees and newspaper. It was one job she didn't leave to the maid. Between us, we never left a streak.

"Sit, Joe. I'll make drinks."

"I'll help."

"Get a lemon, will you?"

I went out the slider to the backyard and picked a good lemon. The Tustin hills are lovely in the evening, with the light softening and the trees drooping in the heat and the precise lines and angles of the homes showing through the foliage. I wanted to be ten again, living there with Will and Mary Ann and Junior and Glenn.

Mom made lemonade and vodka, sliced two wheels off the lemon and floated them on top. We took the drinks back outside and sat by the pool. The pool furniture was new, bright blue canvas on white enamel frames. A big umbrella, tilted west. Made you feel like you were in a resort. I took off my hat and set it on the table, hung my coat over the back of the chair.

"What's wrong, Joe?"

I told her about Luria and Miguel, Ike Cao. I told her about Savannah and Alex. "Sometimes I wish I could just wash it all off."

"It doesn't help, working in the jail."

"No."

Mom cleared her throat, took a sip of her drink. "Have you ever thought about dropping that line of work? I know you wanted to be a deputy. I know Will pushed you into it, because that's how he started out. But really, you've got a four-year degree and a good head on your shoulders. You've got friends in the community, people who know you. You can choose something different if you want."

"I like it."

"But what about it do you like?"

It took me a minute. Answers are hard for someone brought up not to question. "The usefulness."

"Of being a cop?"

I nodded. I looked at the breezy glimmer of the pool and thought about a baptism I had in Los Angeles one hot May morning, a full-immersion one with a band playing Christian rock in the background. One of the best I ever had, even though I think Christian rock is bad for both God and rock and roll. I don't know why, but that baptism just seemed to wash everything away, and the feeling lasted a full week.

"Well, there's a million other ways to be useful, Joe. And they don't leave your heart stained at the end of the day. Will got out just in time. Almost twenty years for him, with the sheriff's. When he got elected supervisor, it was like a new world for him."

"He planned it that way."

"Maybe you should have a plan, too."

"Carl Rupaski tried to get me over to the Transportation Authority. Big pay raise, different kind of work. He said I could go anywhere from there. It would be more of a white-collar kind of job. I think he changed his mind, though."

She was quiet for a while. "Rupaski's unprincipled."

"He put a homing device on Dad's car."

"Why?"

"He says he hoped Will would lead him to Savannah. But I think Rupaski was looking for something to shut Dad up. Something to use against him. Dad had proof of some pretty big money going from the Grove Action Committee to Rupaski to Millbrae. For Millbrae's vote on the toll road sale to the county. Will was using that proof to buy Millbrae's vote back to his side."

"Will was blackmailing them."

"Yes."

I told her about the tape I'd just listened to, and the notes Will had written. I even told her how the mini recorder got attached to Dana Millbrae's desk.

She sighed and set her drink down on the table. "Always collecting on the sly. Always finding things out without anyone knowing. It seemed harmless enough when we were young, because Will was a cop working vice and that's what vice cops do. And he was always kind. So, I adjusted to it. But the older he got the more . . . surreptitious he became. I mean, a week before he died he spent three hundred dollars on some gadget you put on the phone, encrypts your voice or something. He . . . he actually filmed us in the dining room once, without my knowing. I was furious when he showed it to me. He'd hidden the camera in a special briefcase with a hole for the lens. Another stupid toy he bought, I suppose. It disgusts me that he'd put you up to breaking the law, to advance his career. *Bugging a supervisor's office!* I'm getting furious at him again, Joe. I don't like it. But I can't help myself."

"I was always eager."

"Because he made you that way. And you know something, Joe? I *asked* him about that. I asked him if he was drawing you into all that night business, all his games. He said he wasn't. He said you were just driving and watching out for him. What an idiot I was. What a naive fool."

I was culpable, and I knew it. Over the years I could have told her any time what Will had asked me to do. The bug in the desk was only one of scores of furtive deeds I did for him. There was the summer job he got me with the County Risk Management Department so I could report which deputies and firemen were suspected of scamming the county with phony bad backs. I was eighteen, then. There was the famous defense lawyer's Cadillac I disabled late one night outside a yacht club in Newport Beach; the college professor accused of statutory rape that I roughed up in a university parking lot, my face hidden inside one of Mary Ann's cutoff panty hose. There was the house I'd burgled while Will was attending a fund-raiser hosted by the owner of that house. I'd found what Will suspected was there—counterfeit stocks and bonds—and weeks later, they busted the guy. There were the envelopes I'd shuttled from various drops to various destinations. For that matter, there was the standard cheap briefcase that Will had purchased and given me to make "movie-friendly." I'd managed that with an Xacto knife, jigsaw, some padding, glue and black window screen. For that matter, just keeping my mouth shut about his affairs was furtive ten times over.

But I never told her. I didn't because I loved Will and I loved her and I loved doing what he needed me to do. Because I loved being useful.

A dog can keep a secret, but a man has to learn when he's doing more harm than good with it.

"I've been a fool, too," I said.

"Get out from under it, Joe," she said. "Drop it, lose it, start over. Get a job with the forest service in Utah, do anything but work in that filthy jail with the ghost of your father everywhere you look. You deserve better than that."

She tipped back her glass and emptied her drink down to the ice. She set the glass on the table with a smack. Then she shook her head.

"Don't try to be him," she said.

"I need to finish a couple of things."

"Don't risk your life for revenge, Joe. Will won't profit from that. I won't. You won't."

"It's not revenge. It's justice."

"Don't let justice be an excuse."

I stared out at the hills and houses, heard a car winding down the road. I looked at the darkening water of the swimming pool, watched a moth struggle his way out of it and labor through the air. I'd never seen a moth accomplish that before.

"I'll make dinner," I said.

Chapter Nineteen

It was still early when I got home so I put in one of my
favorite romantic comedies. It was the first time since Will
had died that I'd done anything so unproductive as watch a
movie. I was ashamed of myself at first, but by the time boy
met girl I was thinking of June and I'd forgotten my shame.

Then the phone rang.

I answered it and heard the sound of a television announcer
and voices. I hit the mute on my movie.

"Hello?"

"I need Joe Trona." A young man's voice, clear and agi-
tated.

"This is Joe."

"This is Alex Blazak. I want you to tell my father I'll sell it
to him for two million dollars. And Savannah finally gets to go
home."

"Sell what?"

"He'll know. You won't. If we have a deal, be standing
alone on the southwest corner of Balboa Boulevard and Pavilion on the peninsula at five o'clock tomorrow afternoon. If I
like what I see, I'll be in touch."

"I can tell you right now you don't have a deal."

"I'll kill her. Everything you believe is wrong. I will kill her."

With the remote, I turned off the VCR and hit the cable button, then the mute again.

"I want Savannah," I said.

"Everyone does. For what?"

"Child Protective Services."

There was a long pause, then. The background voices were loud and echoed, like in a big bar. I could hear the excited voice of the TV announcer, but couldn't make out his words. A big cheer went up. I started switching channels.

"Mr. Blazak," I said. "Tonight I'll pitch the deal like you want it. If your father agrees, I'll be standing on the southwest corner of Balboa and Pavilion at five tomorrow. But when it's time to do the deal, Savannah comes with me."

"Then to CPS?"

"Correct."

"Savannah says I can trust you."

"I do what I say I'll do."

Another big cheer, then a big chorus of *wooahhh*, like somebody had missed a shot or hit one out. I punched in Channel 5 just in time to see the Angels' first baseman running around the bases, enjoying his home-run jog.

"Perfect," said Alex Blazak.

He slammed the phone in my ear.

My car idled in the darkness as I waited for Jack Blazak to buzz me through the second gate. I checked my watch: almost eleven. When the gate rolled open I followed the circular drive toward the huge Greco-Roman house. I saw him coming down the broad stairway from the front door, then along the reflecting pool. I pulled up by the pool and Blazak got in.

"Head back out," he said. "I think Marchant has this entire property wired for sound."

Blazak said nothing as we drove through the dark hills. We passed the first gate, wound down toward Coast Highway and went through the second. The guard stared at us.

"What do you know about Miguel Domingo?" I asked.

"The cops killed him right there. Machete, screwdriver."

"His sister was the one who got run over the week before."

Blazak looked at me, then back out the window. He said nothing as I waited to turn north on PCH.

"I didn't read that."

"The papers covered it, back page."

"We did *not* employ her, either. Lorna told me about your call."

We rode for a minute.

"I wish it wasn't that way," said Blazak.

"What way, sir?"

"People coming two thousand miles to work for seven bucks an hour. But you know, every once in a while, they get ahead, make it. Odds are better than the lottery. Better than the goddamned jungles where they came from. If I were one of them, I'd come here, too."

I made the turn and headed north. Off to the left the black ocean and black sky disappeared into a bank of pale fog. The fog just stopped a few hundred yards offshore, like smoke trapped behind a pane of glass.

"Your son called me about an hour ago. He'll sell it to you, and hand over Savannah. Two million."

Blazak was looking at me. "Sell me what?"

"You'll know, I won't—Alex."

He looked out the window as I headed up the hill toward Corona del Mar.

"And he's using you now instead of your father."

"Apparently, sir."

"And you'll get Marchant into it."

"I don't know, yet. It depends what you do."

"That thing with Will—it didn't have to happen. Alex is insane, Trona. And he's playing with lives."

"What's Alex selling you, along with your daughter?"

"A videotape."

I waited.

"Me, Lorna, another party. Female. I'll tell you something, Trona—I'm not ashamed of what I do. It's just kicks to me and nobody gets hurt. Consenting adults. But I've got Lorna to protect. I don't want that thing out in the general population, if you know what I mean."

"I wouldn't either, sir. Did you make it?"

"Yeah. I disguised it in the cover of one of Savannah's old cartoon videos. Something she'd outgrown. Stashed way in the back of my movie collection, which is substantial and somewhat cluttered. But Savannah is into everything. Plays this game called Savannah the Spy—always digging around in my stuff, Lorna's stuff, anybody's. Apparently, it was in her backpack when she was taken. They must have tried to watch it. Alex realized he could add that to the ransom demand. A two-for-one offer. He can keep the damned tape, for all I care. My daughter, he cannot keep."

"How long will it take you to get up the money?"

"I'll have it at ten tomorrow morning. Trona, I got ripped off once doing this. I love my girl, so I'm willing to risk getting ripped off again. I'm not willing to expose her to gunplay and the kind of bullshit my son thinks is so amusing. If I don't want to risk the FBI shooting them both dead, I've got no choice but to trust you. So I'm going to trust you. But you should know not to fuck with me. I'm just a businessman, but when I need to have ass kicked, I find a way to kick it."

I looked out at the juice stand and the thick trees bunched in a gully between the highway and the ocean.

"Sir, you're not hugely impressive to me. Your threats are really just bad manners."

He chuckled. "You're a weird guy, Trona. Not hugely impressive to you. I like that. And I like what you did to Bo in my living room."

I made a U-turn at Poppy and headed back toward Blazak's home.

"I'm demanding that you leave Marchant out of this," he said. "That's *my* condition."

I thought about that. "They're good at this kind of thing."

"I remember how good they were at Waco and Ruby Ridge."

"They got Elian back to his father."

"Elian wasn't being held by someone who set a homeless guy on fire then pissed on him to put it out. Or dropped his own cat into a bucket of acid. Shit, maybe I shouldn't have said that to you."

"I'm over it, Mr. Blazak. Even if my face isn't."

His wave got us through the first gate.

"No Marchant. I'll have the money at ten," he said. "When we need to talk, call Lorna at the house. She'll get me and I'll call you back. Marchant's got tape recorders on the phones."

We wound up into the dark hills toward the second gate.

"My father was shot by a gangster named John Gaylen. We're closing in on him."

"Congratulations."

"The night before he killed Will, he met with Bo Warren."

In the periphery of my sight I saw Blazak studying me. He said nothing for a long minute. I listened to the grumble of the Mustang's V-8 as we cantered up the road.

"I've got no idea what that sonofabitch Bo would be talking to this gangster for. He's Dan Alter's man, not mine."

"He looked like he was yours in your house that day."

"On loan. He's all bluff and no results. He failed to secure my daughter. He succeeded in costing me one million dollars in cash."

"We think Gaylen was hired to hit Will."

"And you think Warren had something to do with it?"

"I think Warren is a gopher, sir. That's what you called him. But he wasn't alone with Gaylen. He had someone in the car with him. I want to know who."

Blazak shook his head. "How would I know that? You guys. You cops. You FBI men. You head-of-security types. People like you and Will and Rick Birch and Steve Marchant. You see plots inside plots. You have the nerve to polygraph me and my wife, then act secretive about the results. All this conjecture you come up with, all the coincidence and speculation. And all I want is my daughter back. One small eleven-year-old girl is all I want. *You* figure out Bo Warren and the killer. I can't. I don't even care. I'm a businessman. I get things done. You guys are a totally different breed."

"Yes, sir. We clean up messes for people like you."

He shook his head and flicked his hand, like he was waving a bee off a picnic plate. "Maybe you can ask Alex when you drop off two million more of my dollars and pick up Savannah. I've never even heard of this Gaylen character until now."

"Everything's going to go right with Savannah."

"Stop at the gate, Joe. Look, I'll do anything to get my daughter back safely. If you're the one I need to work with, then I'll work with you. I'll consider you a business partner until you show me I should consider you something else."

He slammed the door of my Mustang and went to the gate pad to punch in his code.

When I was back on Coast Highway I called Steve Marchant's pager, hung up and waited.

He called back in less than one minute. I told him that Alex Blazak had asked me to broker a deal for his sister and a dirty movie. Cost to Jack, two million in cash. Jack had agreed.

"Finally," he said. "Now we've got some room to move. You and I are going to kick some ass and get that girl back. I'll call Sheriff Vale, see how he wants to work this."

Chapter Twenty

The next morning I was parked outside the Chapel of Light entrance a little after sunrise, waiting for Bo Warren's red Corvette. The huge parking lot was locked at night, opened by security in the morning. Vandals had broken glass and spray-painted obscenities on the sidewalks a few years back, so Daniel had decided to take preventive measures.

Warren's car grumbled around the corner and paused at the gate. The gate was iron, with slats running down, big cloudlike curls at the top, and angels playing trumpets above the curls. It was painted white. Warren punched in a code and drove through and I followed him before the gate could roll back.

When he saw me behind him he slammed on his brakes and got out. I met him about halfway between the two cars.

"Get the hell out of here," he said. "This isn't just sacred ground, it's private, too."

He looked freshly showered: hair damp and neat, clothes crisp, boots almost unbelievably shiny. His sunglasses threw a small rising sun back at me. I thought of another shower I'd taken recently, and had to wrestle my mind off of that memory.

"I want to talk about John Gaylen."

"Then talk about him, soldier."

"You met with him in the parking lot of Bamboo 33 the night before he shot Will."

"Sounds like you should be talking to him, not me."

"We are."

"I'll tell you what I told His Holiness—I didn't meet with John Anybody. Got no idea where the Bamboo 33 even is. What is it, some gook joint?"

"It's a Vietnamese nightclub. And we've got an eyewitness who puts you there. Car, plates, good description of the driver. You, Mr. Warren."

He stared at me without moving, face hard, sun bright on his glasses.

"Here's how it could work, Mr. Warren. Rick Birch is lead on Will's case. If I tell him what I know, he'll bring you in for questioning. If he brings you in, it's easy to make sure a reporter or two knows about it. That's news in this county—Reverend Daniel's head of security brought in for questioning in the Trona murder case. You being new to the Chapel of Light, it might not be so good for your performance review."

I could see his jaws moving, the pronounced throb of his carotid. That artery is the first thing a police interrogator looks for when his subject starts talking.

"I thought Daniel was your friend."

"He is, Mr. Warren, but you're not."

"What a pissy way to do business, Joe. Don't you understand the meaning of loyalty?"

I said nothing.

"Look Joe. Jennifer Avila put me onto a hood named Luz Escobar. Aka Pearlita. Escobar said her friend Gaylen had mentioned Alex Blazak. I thought he might know something about where Alex had gone with Savannah. So I talked to him. He didn't. Or at least he didn't tell me. Routine investigation work, Joe. That's all it was."

"Who was with you?"

"Pearlita, who do you think?"

"Jack Blazak came to mind."

Warren smiled and shook his head. Like a boxer who's been tagged and doesn't want to show it.

"No. Jack left all the footwork to me. Delegation. That's what makes him a smart man."

"Not smart enough to get his daughter back."

"He'll get her. Guys like that always get what they want. Everything's for sale, and they can afford it all."

"What happened when you tried to pay the ransom to Alex and pick up Savannah? Before Will got involved. What went wrong?"

He shook his head. "Alex didn't show. So I didn't leave the money. No Savannah, no money. That was the original deal. That's where Will blew it. First rule of a kidnapping for ransom—you never pay out before you pick up. I'm surprised an ex-sheriff deputy would have tried something so dumb. Of course, maybe that's why Alex wanted to use him. The way it played out, Alex got the money and kept the girl."

"What about the video?"

"Incidental. A bored businessman in a three-way with his own wife and some bimbo. Christ, these rich people are revolting."

Warren looked over at the chapel. "I'm late for work. And I'm glad to help out, Joe. Now get the fuck off this sacred ground. Your judo might work on me, but you can't throw God."

"It surprises me you say that, Mr. Warren. You don't brim with amazing grace."

"I brim when the paychecks clear."

I went back to the car. The exit side of the gate has a sensor so the angels with their trumpets slid open and let me out.

* * *

I met June for lunch in a park near her work. I hadn't seen her since our date, though I'd called her twice and thought about her every few minutes.

I didn't think she would be as beautiful to me in person again as she was in my memory of that outstanding night. I was wrong about that: when I walked over the grassy rise and saw her standing in the shade of a magnolia tree my heart swelled into my throat and I wondered if I'd be able to say hello.

I managed, barely.

We sat in the shade of the tree and ate cold chicken sandwiches she'd made. She was wearing the bracelet and the ruby earrings. We spread a blanket and lay down and kissed once. It lasted approximately forty-five minutes. My left arm went numb and I finally rolled over onto my back. From there the magnolia tree looked like the quiet spot. I thought how nice it was to be in a quiet spot instead of just imagining one.

"Can I touch your face?"

"Okay."

She reached across my face and set her hand on my cheek. I could smell her body and her perfume and I tried to concentrate on those things. Her fingers were soft. When a scar like that gets touched it feels like the whole thing is trying to move. Like a plate. She pressed gently on the bottom, down at the jawline, and the top of it—up above my eye—moved against the good flesh around it.

"Does it hurt?"

"Hot and cold, yes. Touch, no."

"How do you shave?"

"Very extremely carefully."

She laughed. I smiled.

"You should do that more."

"I've seen it in the mirror. Tough sledding."

"I disagree. Joe Trona doesn't feel sorry for himself, does he?"

Her fingers moved up my cheek. Flowers on rock.

"I try not to. I try very hard to realize that Will was right. The first time I met him he said everyone has scars but most people have them on the inside."

"That's beautiful and true."

"He said good things. He did good things."

"Why did they do that to him?"

"I don't know."

We were quiet for a while. The breeze hissed and rattled the big magnolia leaves and the grass was cool on my back through the blanket.

Her fingers came up around my eye. Petals on steel.

"Would you walk through Hillview with me and my mike sometime? Remember for me and talk about it? If Joe Trona going back to visit Hillview isn't *Real Live* material, nothing is."

"I'll think about it."

"Am I taking advantage?"

"It's not that. But the wrong people will notice. Your show, when we talked? I was saying things I've never said before to anyone. If we do it again, people might know."

"Are you making your father's enemies?"

"I think I am."

"And you think they'd hear us and try to hurt me to hurt you?"

"Yes."

"Fuck 'em, Joe. Let's do the interview right now."

I rolled over and looked at her. "You don't understand."

"I understand that it doesn't scare me."

"It scares *me,* June. I love you and if anything happened to you I'd lose it."

Silence, then.

"You're right. And I was being flip."

"I am right this time. You've got courage to burn. Burn it at the right times."

One more kiss, ten minutes, more or less. June broke it off.

"It's showtime," she whispered. "Time to go yap."

When I got home I removed the radio transmitter from Will's car and locked it in one of my floor safes. I was getting that feeling again, of things lining up in bad ways. The same feeling I'd had that night with Will. This time, I tried to listen to it a little more closely.

The feeling got even stronger when I picked up the mail at my cubby later that afternoon. Another postcard—this time from Monterey, California:

Dear Joe,

I hope I can trust you. Don't let anything go crazy like before. I'm getting very tired.

With Love,
S.B.

I was standing on the corner of Balboa Boulevard and Pavilion at 4:58 P.M.

Alex had picked a good place to lose himself and observe me. The boulevard was crowded with cars going both directions, but the traffic was moving along well. Pavilion was a smaller street that emptied into parking lots on either side of Balboa. There were pedestrians all over—tourists and beachgoers, boogie-boarders and fishermen, students and families and retired couples. There were two bars and two restaurants with easy views of my corner. Even a hotel. Alex Blazak could have been in almost any car or behind almost any window and I couldn't have seen him. He could have been one of the tourists or the students. He could have glassed me from the foot of the pier or from the beach.

Marchant had planted agents in the area, but he didn't tell me how many and he didn't tell me where.

I headed for my car, feeling seen.

I drove back up Balboa Boulevard and called Marchant, told him Alex was a no-show.

"Of course he's a no-show," said Steve. "He's just getting you used to taking orders, seeing if you can keep your word. We won't get a look at him until he's coming for the money. He might have you run a few more senseless errands for him. Always agree, always do what he says. And always tell me."

I had just driven off the peninsula when Rick Birch called. "Good news," he said.

"I would like some."

"McCallum ran the slug that killed Ike Cao through the Federal DrugFire registry. We got lucky. The same gun that fired that bullet also fired bullets into two Lincoln 18th gangsters— Felix Escobar's victims."

"Pearlita's brother," I said.

"Maybe he gave it to her for safekeeping. Maybe she wanted to keep it in good working order, so she used it on Cao. Anyway, we picked her up half an hour ago on suspicion of first-degree murder. She had a twenty-two auto in her glove compartment."

"Maybe she'll roll over on Gaylen."

"Let's hope so. She did him a big favor, with Ike Cao. Now we'll see if she's stand-up or not."

"If she could ID the guy in Bo Warren's car that night, I'd be pleased."

"So would I. We'll let her get used to lockup tonight, then see if she wants to deal."

* * *

I drove to the Grove, waiting for my cell phone to ring again, but it didn't. I listened to June's show. Her guest was the general curator of the Los Angeles Zoo, who had grown up in Orange County. As a boy, he'd kept a crocodile in his backyard, an anteater in his bedroom and a collection of snakes in his garage. Driven his mom crazy. Sounded like a nice guy. At the sound of June Dauer's pleasant whisper of a voice I could feel my skin warm and my heart beat harder. I wanted to pull her out of the radio and kiss her for a few hours.

The head of security at the Grove Club is Bob Spahn, a retired sheriff department lieutenant. Tall, slender, pale gray eyes and short black hair. He was still the Department martial arts instructor, in spite of giving up his job. Rumor had it that he had tripled his salary going private for the Grub.

Spahn had agreed to talk "a quick five minutes" before he left work at six. His office was on the second floor, down the hallway from the bar kitchen. An off-duty Santa Ana PD patrolman walked me through the dining room, up the stairs, past the private booths and the pool tables.

Spahn rose from his desk and shook my hand. His hand felt thick and padded, something I recognized from my own competition days in the martial arts. We used to spend hours a week stabbing our fingers and fists into buckets of bird seed. Later, we graduated to beach sand. It strengthens the joints and builds calluses on the fingertips and knuckles.

"Still training, I guess," he said.

"Just twice a week now, sir."

"Miss the competition?"

"Yes. The sparring isn't fast enough."

"Yeah. What can I do for you, Joe?"

"I want to know who brought Luria Blas into the Grove. It was a fund-raiser for Millbrae, April of this year."

"I remember it. You think the businessmen know how to party, until you see the politicians. Get them *together* and watch out."

"I've seen that too, sir."

"Blas . . . killed by the Suburban, right?"

I nodded.

"She an outcall girl?"

"I think it's possible she was prostituting herself."

"You sure she was here?"

"Yes."

"Grove policy is no prostitutes of any kind, any time. Strictly enforced."

"Of course. But sometimes it's hard to make the call, isn't it?"

He looked at me. "Well, yeah—a billionaire with a well-dressed woman—you can't do much with that. No singles, though, unless we know them. They've got to have class and manners. You need those women around just for atmosphere. Like good furnishings."

"Yes, sir, furnishings."

"Anything else, Joe?"

"So there's no real policy on who the members bring in, so far as female company goes?"

He studied me again, then shook his head. "Not really. I'm not paid for that. The Grove is for the members. They rule. I'm a glorified baby-sitter. My main job? Make sure the staff leaves the silverware here. Make sure the bartenders don't raid the till. Really, it's pretty sandbox."

"Can you help with Luria Blas, that night?"

"Why should I?"

"She was poor. She was pregnant when she died. She was beaten before she died. Her brother got killed, looking into who did it."

He shrugged. I waited.

"You sound like your father," he said. "But I liked that about him—always a friend of the underdog."

"I like underdogs, too, sir."

"But Will, you know, always careful to look out for himself, too. No martyr in that man. What's in this for you?"

"Just this. I met Luria's other brother. He struck me as a nice boy."

He was nodding again. "I'll see what I can find out. Give me your number and the date again, would you?"

I thought of something. "Sir, if a party is held here at the Grove, does the host need to reserve a suite, or the restaurant, or whatever he needs?"

"Yeah, sure. Chaos, otherwise."

"Who signed for the Millbrae hospitality suite that night?"

"That's confidential, Joe. We're a club."

"I understand that."

"Then understand why I can't tell you. I'll look into the Blas thing. But I won't lose my job over it."

"No, sir. And thanks again."

Once I got off the 241 Toll Road and back into cell phone territory I called the general manager of the Grove. His name was Rex Sauers and he was an old friend of Will's. He ran some places on the Lower East Side for twenty years, then a resort in Palm Springs, then a five-star restaurant in Newport Beach until the Grove hired him away. His secretary put me through when I told her I was Will's son.

"Joe, how are you?"

"Things are okay, Mr. Sauers. I miss him."

"We all do. What do you need?"

"I'm going through my father's bills. He's got a payable here for his part of the Millbrae fund-raiser back in April. It says three thousand plus change, but there's nothing on the note about who to pay."

"Lemme check."

I waited a moment, listened to the static.

"Jack Blazak."

"Thank you, sir. Most of the creditors have called me. But Mr. Blazak probably just felt uncomfortable, trying to collect from a dead man's family."

"Jack's a good guy. Hey, come by sometime and let my buy you dinner. I'd like to keep in touch."

"I'd be honored, sir."

"You guys close to an arrest?"

"We've got a suspect. We're building a case. It's been hard because I heard the shooter talk to Will that night, but I couldn't see him. What I think is, my father got in the middle of something he didn't understand."

"I think it stinks—Will trying to help out with Jack's daughter, and this happens. My opinion of Will Trona went way up when I heard what he was doing. He and Blazak didn't get along. They were opposites on everything. But Will put that aside to help Jack. That says a lot to me about what kind of man he was."

"He was a great man."

"Amen. Keep in touch, Joe. Lemme know if I can help again. You want a table for you and a lady friend, you're my guest. If Will's got any more payables here at the Grove, forget them. They're covered."

The idea struck me that I was inheriting my father's friends, as well as his enemies. I just wasn't positive which was which. I wondered if Will was. You only had to be wrong once.

Love a lot. Trust a few.

Chapter Twenty-One

I cooked three expensive TV dinners and waited for the phone to ring. Maybe Alex hadn't liked what he'd seen. Maybe he'd changed his mind. Maybe he'd just take his sweet time, like he'd done all along. Eighteen days he'd had her. I thought about how much can happen so quickly, and of the lifetimes you can live in eighteen long summer days.

At eight-thirty I got a call.

"Hello, Joe, this is Thor."

"How did you get the number?"

"Private investigator."

I said nothing. As quickly as I'd forgotten him—tried to forget him—he was back. I felt my scar grow hot and my fingers grow cold and weak. I heard the hollow thunk of liquid falling back down to the bottom of a bottle.

"Look," he said. "There's some stuff we should talk about."

"I forgave you."

"Not that. This is other stuff. About what happened."

"I'll listen."

"I . . . uh . . . well, you know how the police are. They can get you to say things that aren't true. And maybe, if the lies help you out, too, then you just tell them."

"What's the lie, Thor? Get there fast."

"You aren't my son, Joe. I thought you were, for almost a
year. I named you and fed you the bottle and changed your
diapers, spent a lot of my money on you. I treated you like you
were part of me. But you weren't."

I felt like I was in an elevator plunging—a fast, claustropho-
bic plummet into darkness. I heard a human voice roaring in the
descent. Mine, but not mine.

I heard him drink again, burp. When he spoke again I could
barely hear the words because I was falling so fast.

"There," he said. "I said it. I thought you should know. I'm
done."

He hung up. I pressed star 69 but his line wouldn't accept it.

Speed. All the windows open and the Mustang's 351 revving
high as I shot down the freeway into Santa Ana.

You aren't my son, Joe.

I got off and sanely rode Edinger into Santa Ana, heading
for the Amtrak station. My heart slowed. I tried to get myself to
the quiet spot. I could see the tree and the eagle and the hills
beyond, but I just couldn't will myself up into the branches.

When I got to the station I parked and looked around for
lodging. Nothing. In a five-block drive I found an Econo Lodge
and a rundown place called the Paloma. Neither nervous desk
clerk had seen anyone matching Thor's description. I drove an
ever-widening maze outward from the station.

Fernandez Motel, Superior Hotel, Fourth Street Apartments—weekly/monthly, even the YMCA. Nothing.

So I widened the circle: Oak Tree Motel, Saddleback Inn, La
Siesta.

The desk clerk at the Rancho Lodge was a young Indian
woman whose eyes widened when I walked in. Then she turned

her gaze away from my face and looked at the chain-mounted pen on the counter. I described Thor Svendson.

"Twelve," she said to the pen. "Perhaps you can use the phone behind you."

"I'll just knock. Thank you."

Room twelve was the last one on the ground floor, right of the lobby. Moths buzzed the lights of the walkway. A loud TV in room nine. I stood outside the turquoise-colored door and knocked.

Silence. No movement. No sounds. I knocked again.

"Who's there?"

"Joe."

"Second."

I heard the chain slide out, the door lock being turned. Then the door opened and Thor stood before me. His face was pale and his eyes were blue and he had the same unsmiling smile he always had. White beard, white hair. Baggy jeans, a smudged T-shirt that was taut against his belly. Bare, white feet.

"How'd you find me?"

"I drove. I'm coming in."

He stepped aside and I walked into the faintly lit room. The TV was on with no sound. It smelled like cigarettes and booze and french fries. Just a room with a kitchenette in one corner. The bathroom door was closed. Thor slumped into a chair in the corner, across from the TV. There was a half-gone bottle of supermarket-brand vodka on the nightstand, and a carton of orange juice.

"I was gonna tell you when I saw you the first time," he said. "But that forgiveness thing was important. Didn't want to overdose you."

"How do you know I'm not yours?"

"First I suspected. Then I checked the calendar. Then I beat her up. She admitted it."

"Whose am I?"

"She wasn't sure. A woman like that can't know. When I was in jail, waiting for trial, she offered me money not to say any of that. To just let everybody believe you were mine and I did it because I was crazy. I took the money. I was gonna do some time, so I figured I might as well get paid for it. I ended up not testifying at all, never took the stand. But letting people think it was my own kid I poured the acid on, it made me stand out. I noticed it real early, like as soon as they booked me. It kept me in protective block, which is a good thing. It got me some interviews. Fuck, I was famous. So I made up the angle about doing it because I heard the Lord telling me to do it. My own son. Like Abraham. He had a white beard like mine in this picture I saw."

I looked into his merry, childlike eyes. "Why did you?"

He looked at me. A bit of surprise on his face. "To hurt her! I was drunk and high and pissed off. It wasn't anything personal against you. I want you to know that. It was just to hurt something of hers. To get back at her for what she did to me. I'm not saying it was the right thing to do, and I'm not saying it wasn't. But there are some things, Joe, a man can't forgive."

We let those words hang in the air. And hang some more. Thor looked down, took another drag on the bottle, another sip of the juice.

"And you expect me to forgive you?"

He looked up. Blue innocence. An attempted smile. Santa Claus beard. "You already did. Remember? Now we can move on. Forget about it. Start over. Hey, have a drink. This isn't bad vodka, for Food King."

"Where is she?"

"Charlotte? I haven't seen her in twenty-three years. Haven't talked, nothin'. Except for the money. She'd always send it on time. I bet she cleaned up, changed her name and married a banker."

"How much? When?"

He looked past me then, like he was remembering. If you just took a picture of him and showed it to someone, they'd think he was jolly. Except for the big dark bags under his eyes, and the pale, sweaty skin.

"Thousand a month for twenty-three years. I've made two hundred seventy-six grand. She gave me five grand to sign on. Like a bonus. It's all spent."

"But you've never talked to her, not even on the phone?"

"Once or twice she called, maybe. Didn't say nothin'. There wasn't ever a return address on the money, so don't bother asking."

"How did she know where to send it?"

"Always to my P.O. box in Seattle."

"Where is the last place you know she lived?"

"Where it all happened—in Lake Elsinore, out in Riverside County. Years ago a guy in prison told me she'd gone to L.A. Don't know how true it was."

"What was the postmark on the envelopes?"

"San Diego."

"The whole time? Twenty-three years?"

"Yeah. So?"

"You have one of the envelopes the money came in?"

"I just kept the bills."

Thor picked up the bottle and took a long drink. Then one from the orange juice carton.

"Drink, Joe?"

"When did you get the last payment?"

"Three weeks ago. It always comes on the first."

"What kind of bills?"

"Ten hundreds. Used ones. Not new ones."

"What did you do with it?"

"Rent. Vodka. A girlfriend or two, over the years. Gotta live, you know."

I looked at him, at the room, at the bottle and the mute TV and the terrible look of innocence in his eyes.

"Yes. You have to live."

"I thought maybe you were going to say I didn't, then kill me like you said you'd do."

"Things change."

"How they do."

He seemed to be considering something. He drank and set the bottle down with a clunk. "You want to see her?"

"That's correct."

"I guess if you were going to kill me, you'd just take that gun out from behind your coat and blast away."

"I'd break your neck."

He looked away, the half smile still in place, his white hair awry, his blue eyes so open and clear and empty.

I stepped forward and took his head in both my hands. It might have looked like one man steadying the face of another, to look into his eyes, maybe, to tell him something heartfelt. But I was positioning my hands for a head twist, getting the balance and weight right, estimating the potential of his resistance. A head twist is deadly because the guy doesn't know which direction you're going to go, or when. Thor seemed to understand all this. I got my face up close to his. I could smell the fumes of vodka, the sour tang of orange juice.

"Has this been the truth?" I asked him.

"Oh, everything. I got no reason to lie."

"I'm glad I'm not yours. I'd rather be human."

"See?" he whispered. "I'm not so bad."

* * *

Back home I sat in the darkness and wondered. There was just enough moonlight to make pale stripes through the blinds. I'd been made fatherless twice in two weeks, and my emotions couldn't catch up with the facts. The emotions were there, all right—I could sense them just below the surface. But the surface was frozen numb and in need of a good baptism. And all I had was a bathtub.

June called and I told her I couldn't talk because I was expecting a very important call. I tried to be polite but maybe I could have said it better. She wasn't happy when she hung up and my heart felt much heavier than it should have. I wondered if love was always irrational, or only in my own retarded history.

I felt cut loose. Adrift. I had needed Thor more than I'd known. He was my Lucifer, and always my blame for the darkness inside me. I'd needed Will, too—my light. Now, with both of them gone in his own way, I felt like the past life I'd lived had become false. It's a terrible emptiness to see your own history dissolve. To feel the foundations that you labored so hard to construct slipping, sliding, turning to liquid.

With my heart thumping fast, I called June back and explained what I could explain. Thor and Charlotte. Drunk and high. To hurt Charlotte. Nothing personal. A thousand a month for twenty-plus years to keep the world thinking that I was his son. Postmark: San Diego.

A lot of time passed before June spoke.

"You're new now," she said very quietly. "You're free. And by the way, I love you. I knew it the minute our interview was over."

"I love you, too. I knew it the minute you jumped into the bay with me."

*   *   *

An hour later the phone rang. My cell, not the house line.

"Get the money. Keep this phone ready. If one tiny thing doesn't smell right from a thousand miles out, I'll kill her. If I get a whiff of the FBI I'll kill her. If I don't like your tone of voice I'll kill her."

"Don't kill her. Get rich instead."

He hung up.

I punched off, set the cell phone back on the table and called his father on the hard line.

Chapter Twenty-Two

I waited for Jack Blazak at the entrance to Diver's Cove in Laguna Beach. It was half past midnight. The sky was clear and I could see stars twinkling beyond the trees. The night smelled of ocean spray and eucalyptus and jasmine.

Blazak got there five minutes late. He showed me the suitcase in the trunk of his new Jaguar. The bills were bundled in stacks of what looked like a hundred each. I hefted the suitcase into the trunk of my Mustang.

"That's a lot of money, Joe."

"Two million dollars, I hope."

"A man could buy himself a nice house near the beach with half of it. Live pretty well for a while on the other half."

"Maybe that's what Alex is going to do."

"He'll piss it away. Like everything else."

"Why do you hate each other?"

He looked at me and shook his head. "I don't hate him. I'm disappointed in him. Every advantage, no performance. He's undermined everything we've ever done for him. Run off with your own sister and demand a ransom for her? What the hell kind of young man does that?"

I didn't have an answer. All I knew was what I'd seen of

Savannah—a sweet young girl in very bad trouble. That was enough. It meant more than Jack and Alex put together.

Blazak stepped up close to me. "Don't bring Savannah to the house. Bring her here. Call Lorna, like you did before. Ask her if she's heard from Savannah. *If she's heard from Savannah.* Lorna will be able to get me without Marchant or anybody else knowing. I'll pick her up right here."

I agreed.

"And the tape we talked about—I'm trusting you to return it to me along with my daughter."

"That's the deal, sir."

"You *think* that's the deal, Trona. But you don't know Alex. It's almost guaranteed, he'll try to rob us somehow."

"I'll make sure he doesn't."

He looked at me doubtfully. "You're alone on this—no Bureau or sheriffs?"

"That's right."

"No friends along to help?"

"I'll handle it."

Blazak stared at me, then stepped back. "What do you want? Why are you doing this?"

"For Will. And your daughter."

"There's a hundred grand in it for you, if everything goes like it's supposed to."

"Thank you, sir."

"That doesn't impress you?"

"No."

"Do you even want it?"

I had to think about that, even though I had no intention of returning his daughter to him. "I'd like a hundred thousand dollars."

He smiled. Like I'd seen the light, or agreed with him on

some crucial point. The thing about people who love money is they think everybody loves money. It makes a big blind spot.

"No tape, no deal," he said. "Savannah *and* the tape. Remember that."

Driving out Laguna Canyon with two million dollars in my trunk, I did remember it. I kept the cell phone on the seat beside me, waiting for the call that would let me finish what Will had failed to.

The War Room was buzzing: Marchant and twelve other agents, Birch and Ouderkirk and Sheriff Dwight Vale, and the captain of the sheriff's SWAT team.

Marchant put the two million into a beat-up black duffel bag that was fitted with an electronic tracking system in the handles. He put another small transmitter between the bills in one stack.

"You can't even see our ace," he said. "It's hidden in the lining. An infrared emitter. It makes a heat signature we can see from the air—either fixed wing or helo. Wherever this duffel goes, we can track it. It'll show up like a firefly."

Sheriff Vale is a tall, heavy man, and his nickname in the department is the Bull. He made the calls for our end, but everybody in the room knew that the Bureau's word was going to be final.

Marchant and Vale had already arranged for two "CPS social workers" to accompany me. They would be sheriff's homicide detective Irene Collier, and a Santa Ana PD detective named Cheryl Redd. Collier was fortyish and stout; Redd was slightly built, mid-fifties with long gray-black hair. When she put on her reading glasses and held her hair back behind her head, she looked harmless enough.

"Call me Church Lady," she said with a wicked little smile. "But watch out for the Sig."

Marchant nodded. "Joe, when Alex calls to set the drop, tell him you want to bring along two female social workers. Tell him you need them there to get Savannah into protective custody—otherwise, she goes back to her father and mother."

They fixed me up with a second cell phone to communicate with the War Room, and a van that would hold anything you wanted it to, just in case Alex Blazak was trusting enough to let me drive the vehicle of my choice. I even got a new set of body armor, the expensive SpectraFlex Point Blank model designed for heavy hits and lots of them.

"Not bad for a Deputy-One," said Birch. "I didn't get this kind of opportunity until I was thirty."

"All right," said Marchant. "Nervous time. Start waiting and stay ready."

He walked me to the secure lot, where we locked the duffel bag in the trunk of my Mustang.

We ate lunch as a group in the courthouse cafeteria—Marchant, Birch and Ouderkirk, Irene Collier and Cheryl Redd. The special agent and the four detectives seemed loose and comfortable with each other and nobody asked me anything about my life or my face or Will or Thor. It was just us, doing a job. It was similar to sitting in the staff dining room, eating lunch with the other deputies in Men's Central. A team. People on your side. Family. But it meant more to me now. It was like sitting in my future. I thought of Will and the terrible beauty of the world he'd guided me into.

Twenty years of that, then get yourself into politics or business, Joe. You already got more name recognition than I ever had. Acid Baby. Jesus—play the cards they give you. Acid Baby for President. That's got a nice ring, doesn't it?

When lunch was over, Birch took me aside. "I hit Pearlita pretty hard this morning. The tape, the DrugFire match with the twenty-two she had. I threw in some witnesses who were sure it was her behind that nurse's mask. Anyway, she's willing to deal. She says she can finger Gaylen for Will's murder if we can let her walk. I told her we didn't do things like that in the real world. I told her we could start with a little light trading— like who was with Bo Warren the night he talked to Gaylen at Bamboo 33. She says she knows, and she'll trade the name for a reduced charge. I talked to Phil Dent, who's usually willing to play ball. We'll see."

It was 1:35 P.M. No call from Alex.

I loitered in the homicide pen. I loitered at Men's Central. I fell asleep, briefly, with my head leaning against the table in the call room.

I worked out in the jail gym, which is "green only," no civilians, and nicely air conditioned. The gym is partially a memorial to one of our fallen deputies—Brad Riches—a young guy who was gunned down by a robber with an automatic weapon when he parked at a convenience store. One wall is a painting of Brad's prowl car, with some brass littered on the floor in front of it. On the opposite wall is another painting of four deputies drawing down. The barrels of their arms open big at you. You can see the bad guys reflected in their glasses. A banner painted over the entry door says:

The power of the wolf is in the pack; the power of the pack is in the wolf.

I worked out extra hard, thinking of Riches and the pack and John Gaylen. What were the chances that he'd appear again at the drop? What were the chances that whoever wanted Will dead would like to have me dead, too, and try again what had worked so well once? Little chance, I knew, but I couldn't help but be afraid of the symmetry, the repetition, the opportunity.

Already 3:43 P.M. No call.

I walked over to the courthouse and watched some of Dr.

Chapin Fortnell's trial. When I went into the courtroom he was
staring down, apparently at the defense table. He turned around
and looked at me sleepily as I sat. An assistant DA was examining one of Fortnell's victims—a man of twenty-one now, but a
boy of twelve when Fortnell had first fondled him.

> *And where were you, specifically, when this first fondling*
>   *took place?*
> *In his office. In Newport Beach.*
> *His consultation room? Where he practiced his family*
>   *psychotherapy on young boys and girls?*
> *Objection, Your Honor! Compound, for one thing. And*
>   *this witness isn't versed in the specifics of the ages of*
>   *Dr. Fortnell's—*
> *Sustained. Proceed, Mr. Evans.*

It made me think of an incident that happened when I was
eleven. I joined the Boy's Club in Tustin and used to ride to the
beach with two of the Boy's Club employees and a bunch of
other kids. One day in the public restrooms at 15th Street, I had
just completed my business when a short, stocky older man with
sunglasses and long red hair blocked my way from the stainless
steel toilet and asked me if I knew what sex was. I said, no, sir,
I don't. I looked away and tried to get past him. I can still remember the damp stink of that restroom, the wet grit underfoot,
the filthy latrine and puddles of who-knew-what on the concrete
floor. Trying to walk past that man, with my face down, I saw
his bare feet moving into my path and felt his big hard hand on
my arm. I was five years into my martial arts training by then,
a green belt in three different styles. I chopped his outstretched
arm with my free hand, then raked his eye. That made him let
go, so I raked his other eye. As he stood there covering his eyes
in the gritty stink of the restroom I caught his left kneecap with

a snap kick and he collapsed with a scream. I ran to the lifeguard stand, but when I got there I couldn't bring myself to tell him what happened. I just couldn't get the words to come. There was shame even in that, even in just being touched and propositioned. The lifeguard was talking to some girls, so he wasn't hugely interested in me anyhow. I remember getting my Duck Feet on and swimming out into the cold, powerful waves. I was learning to bodysurf and I caught wave after wave until I was exhausted and purified. I never went into that bathroom again without my skin tightening across my back, and my face burning hot with fear.

When I left, Dr. Fortnell was still looking down at the table.

At five o'clock I went to my car and listened to June's show. Her guests were a construction worker and an eighty-two-year-old woman. The worker had pulled the woman from a car that was underwater. The woman had pushed the accelerator rather than the brake, rammed her car through a carport and a wrought-iron fence and landed in the community swimming pool. Nobody hurt, not even the woman. She said she felt the hand of God on her arm just as she was about to drown.

Talk about a baptism.

I went home at seven. Still no call. I ate my TV dinners with the two million dollars under the table. I talked to June on my house line, briefly. I told her that things were fine and that something would happen soon. Her sweet whisper of a voice was so beautiful to me I wanted to reach into the mouthpiece with two fingers and draw it out. Wave it through the air. Listen to it laugh. Drop it into my mouth and swallow it. I could taste it and her: salt, flowers, milk.

Alex Blazak called at 9:37. "Take the package to the Newport Pavilion. Drive the Mustang. There's a pay phone north of the entrance. Occupy it at ten-ten sharp. If I like what I see, we'll talk again."

"I'm bringing two women from Child Protective Services. It's the only way they'll intake Savannah tonight."

"You can bring the Pope if you want. You won't see me."

He hung up. I realized that Alex Blazak was a fool, and that he was in way over his head.

I dialed the dedicated line for the War Room and got Marchant. I told him what had just happened.

"We're rolling by helo. Collier and Redd will be near that phone booth before ten. Over and out."

I made it to the phone booth at 10:05. Taken. A husky young man in white shorts and a red muscle T-shirt was talking loudly. I set the duffel bag on the ground, tapped on his shoulder and badged him. He frowned and put his hand over the phone. I explained what I needed. He raised the phone back to his mouth and kept talking to me.

"All yours, Joe," he said. "I'm Larson. Collier and Redd are sitting in the window of that bar, watching. I'll be around."

He nodded, nodded again, then slammed the phone and walked off. It rang at 10:10.

"Where are your friends?"

"In the bar."

"The waterfront must be crawling with them."

"Two social workers. That was the deal."

"Get on the next ferry across to Balboa Island. Stand at the starboard bow. When you get off, wait at the phone booth on the right. Go now. It's *leaving*."

I hung up, waved to Collier and Redd and made for the landing. The last of three cars was being waved into place. The bow attendants were chocking the tires on the front car. I stepped on with the bag over my shoulder. Collier and Redd followed me onboard. Collier had on jeans and an old cardigan, carried a big purse. Redd wore a long dowdy skirt and shapeless sweater and tennis shoes; her hair was pulled back into a bun. I could see the amplifier in her ear and the tiny speaker angled up her chin. Marchant's dedicated line, I thought: Redd is calling in our plays. Pedestrians lined the sides of the ferry boat around us— tourists in bright colors, couples snuggled close against the cool night breeze, kids with skateboards and bikes.

I led the way through them, excusing myself as I worked to the front right corner of the vessel. I looked back on the Fun Zone Ferris wheel and the merry-go-round and set the duffel at my feet. Collier and Redd stood on either side of me.

The ferry engine groaned. I could feel the deep vibration in my legs as we moved away from the landing and made for open water. A ketch moved along under power toward the channel. A couple of teenagers in a rental skiff buzzed past in front of us, fishing rods wobbling in the lights of the Pavilion. Across the harbor I could see Balboa Island. A young attendant in khaki shorts and a floral print shirt took my dollar for the three of us and gave me back a quarter.

The ferry pilot pulled the boat to port, working against the current. I could see the other landing and it looked like we'd miss it on this course. The ketch disappeared into the darkness, its shield-shaped stern slowly vanishing. A Zodiac puttered alongside us, thirty yards out.

My cell phone rang.

"Get it ready."

I lifted the bag with one arm and balanced it on the railing. I sensed Collier and Redd steadying themselves while I looked out at the black water. The Zodiac fell back but moved in closer to the ferry.

"I'm behind you. I'm coming alongside and you're throwing it in. Don't move yet."

"Where is she?"

"You'll know when I get my money. If you or those cops with you want to take me out, just remember this: Savannah's got enough oxygen for about two hours. You kill me, you kill her. Absolutely a done deal. Get it ready, scarface. When I say drop it, drop it. Keep the phone up. Up!"

I looked at Redd and shook my head. "He's got her stashed without much air. Hold your fire."

The Zodiac came up swiftly then, outboard buzzing. I could see the man in it, dark clothing, a baseball cap on backwards, half-turned to work the rudder. Ten yards. Twenty feet. Then he was just six feet off the side, inching along toward me. I muscled up the bag in one hand and waited for the Zodiac to get under it. I couldn't see Alex Blazak very well, but the first thing I thought of when his face came under the running lights was his father: compact, tense, explosive.

He smiled up at me. "Drop it!"

I dropped it. The duffel landed on the water with a smack. The Zodiac lurched forward and I saw Alex Blazak sweep a long gaff through one handle and bring it up close. He leaned over, dunked it twice, then hauled it in with two hands. Looking up at me, he nodded and smiled again.

The Zodiac turned like a spooked deer and glided into the darkness with a scream of engine and a cloud of exhaust.

I watched it blend into the night, heading down the channel toward the harbor entrance.

The wake wobbled and widened on the bay. The engine whine grew fainter and the wake lines settled into the black water. I wondered if he got the electronic transmitters too wet to work, and if the IR emitters could survive that dunking.

I still had the phone to my ear.

"Trona, I'll call you again when I'm where I want to be. Call off the dogs and Savannah will be okay. So long, dipshit."

I signaled Redd to cut out and speed-dialed Marchant on my second phone. I told him that Blazak had the money and was heading west in the harbor, toward the channel that led to the sea. "He's got Savannah without much air, sir. He's going to call us when he feels safe."

"Larson's still getting signal from the duffel. So far, so good. We've got three unmarked units heading down the peninsula now. Two more on Balboa Island. They're running parallel to the harbor. The Harbor Patrol is moving in. I'm calling in the helos, too. We're going to take him down. Hold for me, Joe."

I could hear him talking to someone else, but couldn't make out the words. Then he was back.

"Yeah, yeah, okay, Joe—Harbor Patrol's working the south half, between the ferry landings and the channel. No visual on the Zodiac yet. Take the next ferry back the way you came. Wait by your car, all three of you."

"Copy, sir. Take him alive. You've got to take him alive."

The helicopters roared in from the dark and I could see the searchlights of the Harbor Patrol boat to the south. My heart was beating fast and steady and every light on the water seemed to hold some promise before it broke up in the chop of the bay.

"You did your part, Joe," said Collier. She steadied my arm. "Now Alex has to do his."

We stood against my car. I felt foolish, doing nothing, standing there like a tourist.

Five minutes. Ten.

Marchant called at 11:05. "Joe, go ahead and proceed south on the peninsula, down Balboa Boulevard. Harbor Patrol's got a visual now and the signal is loud and clear. Subject has pulled up at a private dock, looks like he's tied off on a pier at K Street. If something breaks, we might need you there."

"Don't kill him."

"We're staying cool. You stay cool. Over and out."

I drove slowly down the peninsula, past the big homes and the bungalows and the palms and the bougainvillea. The traffic was thick. We passed K Street and I tried to see everything without looking eager. I leaned my head back a little, like Will used to do, with my eyelids relaxed while my eyes did their work.

Three NBPD cruisers were parked to our left. Two sheriff's department radio cars lurked on L Street. I made out three more unmarked sheriff cars and two that were probably Marchant's.

I could see both helicopters hovering out over the water, their searchlights crossing in the sky. Tourists started pulling over to watch.

The boulevard ended down by the channel, so I looped around and started back. One of the unmarked cars was parked near the jetty. Another one passed us going back toward K Street.

I wondered. Twenty minutes and still on the water?

Past K Street again. Nothing. I called Marchant.

"Is he still docked?"

"Harbor Patrol's making the approach right now. Joe, get your social workers and get over to the beach there at K Street. Stay on the line. Over."

"We're there."

I shot down K Street and parked right in front of the sand.

"Sir, what about Blazak?"

"No visual on Blazak yet."

"He ditched the boat and the duffel," I said. "I'd bet on it, sir."

"Joe, hold for me."

I could hear him talking on another line. Then he was back.

"Joe, I'm on with the patrol skipper. They've closed but they can't see Blazak. They've got the night-vision stuff and the visibility is pretty good. They can see the Zodiac. They can even see what might be a duffel bag thrown across one of the benches. But no Blazak. Joe, SWAT's still three minutes out, so I'm sending you three in for a look at that boat. Let Redd lead it. She's experienced. Watch it. Over and out."

Collier took one side of the little street and Redd and I the other. When we came to the last house before the water, Redd went first. I fell in behind, and then Collier. It was my first real patrol action, and I was proud and calm. It was like my night business with Will, but better, somehow. Redd had drawn her sidearm and was carrying it close, against her leg. I did the same.

The Harbor Patrol boat stood offshore thirty yards, but the big searchlights threw their bright clean beams onto the K Street dock. I could just make out the outlines of the prow and the deputies. The choppers roared lower and the water pocked and rippled and sprayed.

Ahead of me, Redd stepped onto the brightly lit dock. I followed. Her hair blew loose in the wind from the rotors and she glanced back at me.

Then she crouched into a ready stance, her sidearm out and aimed at the Zodiac. I did, too. She crab-walked closer and so did I.

She said something and lowered her gun, but I couldn't hear what with the helicopters so close.

When I caught up with her I looked down at the wilted duffel bag tossed on the bow bench.

Collier's footsteps thumped behind me.

"You called it," she said.

"He's good at this," I said.

Then the boom of an amplified voice coming from the patrol vessel.

SONOFABITCH GONE?

"Sonofabitch is way gone," called Redd. "Sonofa*bitch.*"

I holstered my weapon and said a secret prayer of thanks that he was way gone. It meant he could lead us to his sister, if he could find it in his heart to let his biggest profit-maker finally go free.

"We're alive," I said. "She's alive."

Redd turned to me. "Don't count on it, Joe."

My cell phone rang. Redd turned and tried to wave off the helos as I punched the answer button and brought the phone to my ear.

Chapter Twenty-Three

"W here is she?"

Alex Blazak laughed. It sounded to me like he was in a vehicle. The reception was full of static and background noise.

"You didn't really think I'd hurt her, did you?"

"You never know what crazy people will do."

"That's me. Certifiable. She's waiting for you at the Bay Breeze Motel. If you're still on K Street, fucking around with my boat, the motel's about two miles away. Room fourteen, Trona. Hey, nice doing business with you. Chrissa says you're a real cool guy."

He gave me the motel address and hung up. I told Redd, and she told Marchant, and we rolled.

Five minutes later we approached the Bay Breeze Motel. It was on the beach side of Coast Highway. Two sheriff's cruisers were already parked in the motel lot. Two NBPD radio cars were double parked along PCH. I could see two helos descending from opposite ends of the sky.

"I'll go first, Joe. If I need help with the door, you're the man. We'll get the uniforms to cover the rear and sides."

Room fourteen was up a flight of cement stairs, then left. I

could see that a light was on. Collier and I took one side of the
door and Redd the other.

She knocked twice.

"Yes?"

"Savannah Blazak?"

"Yes."

"I'm Sergeant Cheryl Redd, Orange County Sheriff's. Are
you alone?"

"Yes."

"Open the door, please."

I heard the lock being turned, then the chain sliding back.
The door swung inward and Savannah Blazak stood in the weak
light. Her hair was cropped short. Jeans and a halter top. Bare-
foot. She looked pale and dirty.

"Hello, Joe. Hello, Deputies. I'm all right. And I'm very
sorry for all the trouble I've caused you."

"You're going to be okay," I said. "It's good to see you
again."

"Is Alex all right?"

"So far as we know."

"It was my fault. It was all my fault."

"Let's get you out of here. We can talk later."

"I will not go home. I will not."

"We're taking you into protective custody at Hillview Home
for Children," I said. "It's a safe place. I was there a while."

She sighed and looked down. "Okay. May I please get my
things?"

"We've got Savannah," said Redd, into her phone mike.
"She's all right by the looks of her."

Savannah rode in the back of my car, with Collier beside her.
Redd sat up front with me.

Redd told Savannah her rights under Miranda, and asked if she'd like to talk to us without a lawyer.

"Sure."

"Tell us what happened, Savannah."

"I was playing Savannah the Spy, where I take my video camera and spy on people. It's a game. And I took this tape that showed my dad doing something bad. I was scared. When he loses his temper he goes psycho. He hit me once and broke my eardrum but made me tell the doctor it was Alex. So I didn't know what to do with my spy tape. So I ran away to my brother's and told him everything. And he said not to worry about any of it. He said we could live together and be safe and forget about what Dad had done. But we needed lots of money. And the tape was worth money to my dad. So Alex called him and said he had it and that he wanted money for it. Dad said he'd kill Alex if he showed anybody the tape. Then Will found us at the Ritz and said he'd help. Then he got killed. Then Dad went on TV and called Alex a kidnapper and the FBI started chasing us all over the place. Then we thought maybe Joe could help us without getting Alex killed and it worked. Here's the tape. You can have it."

I turned to see her digging into her Pocahontas backpack.

"Thank you," said Collier.

Savannah sighed and started sobbing.

"Hey," said Collier, gently. "Hey, you're okay, young lady. You've done the right thing. You're safe. You're sitting in a car with three cops. Cheer up."

But Savannah kept sobbing. "Joe—I never got to say it, but thanks for throwing me over that wall."

"You're welcome. Where did you go?"

"To the corner of Lincoln and Beach. That was our place to meet, if anything went wrong."

"Alex picked you up."

"Yes."

I listened to her sobs. "Savannah, I never got to thank you for what you did that night we met at Lind Street."

"What did I do?"

"You looked me in the face and said how do you do."

"I like your face. It's unconventional."

"I like you. Hang in there. We'll be at Hillview in just a few minutes."

Strange, to walk back into Hillview. I'd been back before, dozens of times, working as a peer counselor, attending some of the social functions, helping out as best I could. I believed in Hillview.

But to go through those doors again always took me back to the years I'd spent there, to the changing faces, the routine, the loneliness, the anxiety, the sadness and the doubt. As we sat in the intake room, I looked out at the library, where I'd first seen Will and Mary Ann; to the gym where I'd played endless half-court games with kids bigger and stronger than me; to the cottages for the teenaged mothers and their tiny infants; to the barbecue patio and the playground. I looked out at the neat walkways that I always secretly told myself would lead me out of this place and away to something else, something better and more real and more permanent, a home that I couldn't be taken away from, ever, and could never be taken away from me.

Savannah caught me looking out the window, so she looked out it, too.

A doctor examined Savannah and pronounced her unharmed and healthy. Trauma counseling would follow, but for now, Savannah was fit for admission.

The intake procedure at Hillview took less than an hour. The Hillview director and an intake counselor filled out the forms and officially accepted Savannah Blazak into protective custody. Within seventy-two hours, the state would have to convince a judge that Savannah needed to be kept there for her own protection, or her parents would get her back.

That was going to be difficult, given the status of Jack and Lorna. But the reason for it was safe in Collier's purse, and I was burning to leave Hillview and slide that videotape into a player back at headquarters.

I shook Savannah's hand, then went to one knee and hugged her lightly. My heart raced like a stick in a fast river, because I'd never even imagined saying good-bye to someone and leaving them at Hillview, my old Palace of Good-byes. For one of the few times in my life I believed I knew how another person felt. Really *knew*.

"I'll be back, Savannah. And you won't be here forever." I looked at the director and the intake counselor. "These are good people."

"Joe ought to know," said the director, "he's one of our most famous graduates!"

I was just opening the doors of my car when my department-issue cell phone rang. It was Marchant.

"We took Alex Blazak into custody about five minutes ago. No shots fired."

On our way over to department headquarters I called Lorna Blazak. I had just started to tell her where her daughter was when I heard Jack tell her to beat it and give him the phone.

"You got her?"

"She's in protective custody."

"Where?"

"I can't tell you right now. You'll be informed of visitation rights in a timely fashion."

"I'm her father! What the fuck are you doing with her?"

"She's being protected. Your two million dollars made her safe, sir. I'd be happy about that if I were you."

"I'm happy," he said. His voice was so tight it sounded like he was swallowing glass. "I'm very pleased. And the other?"

"I've got it."

"Then meet me at Diver's Cove immediately. I'll take what's mine and give you what we agreed on."

"No, sir. I'm going to look at it first."

"That is private property and you do not have my permission to handle it."

"It's evidence collected in a police investigation, sir. Your permission isn't necessary or relevant."

"I own the best lawyers in the country."

"Congratulations."

"I'll pay a million for it back. Before you or anyone sees it. And I've *told* you what's on it. You've got to understand what an embarrassment it would be to my wife and myself."

"I understand embarrassment, sir."

"Then give me the tape! Two million, Joe. Last offer. That's *private property.*"

"By the way, Savannah is doing very well. A little tired, but otherwise well. Be sure to tell your wife."

"I'm going to sue you out of that department if I don't get my tape back."

"And your son—that would be Alex—has been arrested."

"I'll go three million for the tape. All yours. Three *million* dollars, Joe."

"Go fish, sir."

I hung up.

Twenty minutes later, just before one A.M., we were sitting in one of the Bureau conference rooms: Marchant, Birch and Ouderkirk, Redd and Collier. Marchant hit the play button on the VCR, then sat down next to Birch.

First was black and white snow, but a date and time at the top. May 12, 2:35 P.M.

Then the sound of a girl, giggling. The beach. Crystal Cove, between Newport and Laguna. Lorna Blazak walking along, in shorts and a pink sweatshirt. A Jack Russell terrier racing back and forth in front of her, chasing the water out, retreating when it came back in.

"This is Savannah the Spy, getting Mom. This is Crystal Cove. Mom can get a ticket because Abner is not on a leash. Spies notice these kinds of things. I'll see the cop first and warn them. Mom. Mom! Mom . . . smile!"

Lorna smiled and her hair blew across her face. The camera zoomed in close. Barking, the dog retreated from a rush of whitewater.

"I'll be taking Abner on our next dangerous mission, somewhere in either Africa or New York. He's getting in shape for it. Abner! Abner! Smile at the camera, Abs!"

Then the picture cut to a room like something from a decorating magazine: ocean through the windows, a big golden vase on the floor, Egyptian style, handles sculpted to look like cobras with their hoods flared. The date was now May 18, the time was 11:58 A.M.

Jack Blazak stood by the window, wearing a singlet and a pair of loose satin trunks. He was on the phone, but breathing hard, arm muscles taut, a white towel over his shoulders.

"Savannah the Spy gets Dad doing business after his boxing workout. Did you hit hard, Dad?"

Blazak looked blankly at the camera, then pushed one of the phone buttons. He made a muscle. He smiled. *"I'm no Muhammad, but it feels good!"*

"Who's going to win the next big one?"

"Me! It's gotta be me!"

"Spies don't like blood, Dad."

"I'll knock him out in the first—not a drop spilled!"

"You're the champ."

"I'm pretty! I'm scientific! I'll beat the gorilla in the thrilla in Manila!"

"Dad, that's racist."

"So? Hey, I can make about four MILLION dollars in thirty seconds, if you'll let me finish this call!"

Blazak smiled again, took a deep breath, and punched another button on the phone.

"Sorry, Carl. Savannah's spying on me again. Savannah, Carl says hello."

"Hi, Carl. I drove the Volkswagen go-cart you gave me this morning. It was my favorite present."

"Carl says you're welcome. Now beat it, honey—Dad's back on the chain gang."

"All you do is work and—"

"NOW! GO! I'm working, goddamnit!"

The image jiggled and jumped into nonsense as Savannah ran from the room. A moment later, a long hallway came into focus, and a high ceiling with recessed skylights, and French doors open to a small vineyard. I recognized them from my visit to the Blazak home.

"All Dad does is work and box. He bought us another home last week, in Florence. I'll be spying there this summer!"

"How many homes do they have?" asked Redd.

"Four," said Birch. "Newport Beach, Aspen, Key West and Florence. Blazak hit number forty-one on the richest men list last year."

"Kind of a short temper with his daughter," said Ouderkirk. "But I'd go three rounds with him any day."

Collier asked about the room with the cobra vase.

"It's their Newport place," I said. "I was there three weeks ago."

The next scene was the living room where I'd sat with the Blazaks and Bo Warren. It was May 21, 10:20 A.M. Savannah was apparently hidden behind one of the sofas that faced the windows. A short, dark-haired woman was dusting the fireplace mantel, lifting pictures to wipe underneath. Abner, the terrier, sat looking up at her with intent interest. The day was bright and clear and beyond her you could see Catalina Island crisp against the blue sky and blue Pacific. The woman finished the mantel, then turned toward the camera. Savannah must have shrunk behind the couch, because all you saw for a moment was carpet and wall. The camera jiggled and refocused on the cleaning woman, who was now in a corner of the room, working the high ceiling with a long pole that had a bright pink dust attachment at the end. She was humming quietly.

Marcie, I thought: the Blazak domestic.

Suddenly she turned. Savannah giggled.

"I thought I felt eyes on me! I catch you!"

"Savannah the Spy, caught by Marcie! Caught red-handed."

Laughter, and a fade-out.

Then the image cut to a night scene. The date was May 29, the time was 10:40 P.M. It was hard to make out at first, but I finally realized that the camera was up close on the ocotillo that grew along the south wall of the house. The ground lights threw shadows against the wall and when the camera pulled back, the thin, twisted stalks of the plant came into focus.

Savannah's voice was a whisper:

"Savannah the Spy on the family estate of international financier Simon Carny, whose wealth can be measured in the billions of trillions. A handsome man, a man of mystery and tons of secrets."

She panned the camera to take in the dark vineyard, the huge swimming pool surrounded by stout Canary Island palms, the guest house beyond the pool. The guest house was a smaller version of the main house, a cross between a Grecian temple and a Roman estate—pillars and columns, a large portico that looked like marble, the same heavy rectangular shape, the same flat roof.

"Due to extraordinary viewing conditions at the present time, Savannah is on an especially dangerous mission. Her mother is away for the week. Her nanny is watching TV, and Savannah was put to bed almost two hours ago. But she has . . . slipped silently out of her window and . . . stealthily detected that the trillionaire strongman Simon Carny is holed up in his Roman office which sits between his lavish pool and his vineyard of the finest Bordeaux grapes in all of Tuscany."

Savannah entered the vineyard. The vines were leafy and you could see the small clusters of grapes. Slowly, the guest house came into focus. Savannah got down on her stomach and inched along.

"Savannah the Spy takes no chances that the recluse Carny will spot her. Even the great spy dog Abner has been locked away so as not to blow Savannah's cover. The greatest virtue of the spy is silence. Boy, this is hard crawling on your stomach over dirt. Better watch out for anacondas."

The vines slowly passed by the camera and the guest house got closer. There were lights on inside.

"Three more rows, then Savannah the Spy will have to sneak very quietly to the window, hoping for just a peek of the trillionaire power broker Simon Carny."

The guest house grew larger as Savannah carried the camera close. There was a recessed window with vertical wrought iron bars over it. The window was half open and a gauzy white fabric lilted in and out. There were sconces brimming with red geraniums on either side. On the ground was a curved concrete bench.

You could hear a man's voice as she got closer. And another sound, too, high-pitched and intermittent: someone crying or laughing. Savannah approached the bench, then got up onto it.

Through the bars and the swaying curtain you could see the living area, the kitchen, and a doorway that led to the back part of the guest house.

The Man's Voice: *"Here, this'll fix it."*

Then a flat *whump,* like a feather pillow being smacked.

The high-pitched sound wasn't laughter at all, but a woman gagging, fighting for breath.

Whump!

"You think you can pull that shit on a man like me?"

The woman gagging, but no words.

Whump!

"So you're going to take care of it, right, bitch?"

Gagging, then: *"Yes. Yes!"*

"Goddamnit right the answer is yes. You'll take what I give you and get the rest of those stupid ideas out of your rotten little brain. Right?"

Whump!

"Yes. Yes."

Then a big intake of breath as the woman was allowed to breathe. Giant gulps choked by sobs and unintelligible syllables. Like somebody who's been held under by waves.

"Get your fuckin' clothes on. You're outta here forever, bitch. Hey, here's a reminder of what you're going to do."

Whump!

"Shuttup. Shuttup. There, breathe all you want. I'm a nice guy once you get to know me."

Jack Blazak stormed into the living room wearing nothing but shorts. He pulled a polo shirt over his head and jammed his arms through. Then he stormed back out of the picture.

"No! No!"

Whump.

"Get your clothes on, you scrawny bitch. I can't stand the sight of you."

Blazak came back out, balancing on one foot, the other raised as he worked it into a boat shoe.

Sobbing from the back of the house.

"Stupidest goddamned woman on earth, and that's saying something."

He put on the other shoe.

He sat at the small kitchen bar and looked at a *Forbes* magazine. He touched the back of his neck and looked at his fingers. He glanced toward the woman, then went back to the magazine.

A few minutes later she staggered out. Short black dress, black heels, a small cashmere sweater with mother-of-pearl and sequins woven into it. She was hunched over, wobbling on the shoes. In one hand she clutched a thick wad of money. She pulled the sweater against her shoulders like she was freezing. Her arms were thin and brown. Her long black hair was tangled and covered her face. She reached up and took a handful of her hair and threw it back, revealing her terrified and beautiful face.

Birch froze the frame.

"Luria Blas," I said. "Eighteen years old and pregnant by then. Severely beaten a few hours before she died. It looks to me like she just gave Blazak the news."

"The woman who got run over?" asked Collier.

"It sounds like she was shaking him down for money," said Ouderkirk.

"Shit, Harmon," said Redd. "If she's eighteen, unmarried and pregnant by number forty-one on the richest assholes in America list, maybe she was just asking for some *help.*"

"Sorry, that's what I meant."

"Jesus, Harmon, he was beating the fetus."

"I know! I give! I was trying to establish motive for the

beating. Blazak was trying to get her to have an abortion. She was threatening to keep the baby and file a paternity suit."

A moment of silence then, while the ugliness of what we'd just watched settled in.

Birch hit play again. Luria wobbled over to the bar and collected a small black purse. She stuffed the money inside and tried to work a zipper but the bills were in the way. Black hair falling around her face. The smudge of an old bruise still showing under one eye. Dark legs trembling.

Blazak watched her like she was a waitress doing a lousy job. He fingered the back of his neck again.

"You scratched me."

"Sorry."

"Get out."

"I'm go."

"That'll cover everything. And more. Use it to go back where you came from."

"I'm go home."

Luria moved toward the door and the camera. The picture jostled wildly, then went black.

"The lab has a skin sample taken from under Luria's fingernail," I said. "Maybe that scratch is what we'll use to convict him."

"And this tape," Birch said. "And Savannah Blazak's testimony."

Again, a moment of silence, as the pieces continued to fall into place. Marchant stood. "Rick, do what you need to do. We're here to help."

"Look, Blazak paid three million dollars to get his daughter and this tape," said Birch. "He needs Savannah silent. He needs this tape destroyed. Now he's got neither. Cheryl, get two more uniforms over to Hillview."

"Will do."

"Harmon, dupe this tape, then dupe it again."

"Got it."

"Collier, get to McCallum when he opens the lab. Explain our situation and tell him I'll have a comparison sample by noon. We'll see if Blazak left his skin under Luria Blas's fingernail."

"I'll be waiting for him," said Collier.

"Joe, it's two in the morning. Go home and get some rest. And congratulations. You just saved a girl from a crazy brother and a father who beats women with his fists. Hillview is where she belongs right now. And be careful. That mutt Jack might want a piece of you."

Birch offered his hand and I shook it. Then the rest of them offered theirs. Even Marchant. Ouderkirk slapped my back.

It was the third proudest moment of my life, after the day that Will and Mary Ann walked into Hillview to see *me* and the first time June Dauer and I made love. I smiled and turned the bad side of my face away and walked out.

When I got to my car I called June. She answered on the third ring, in a voice that sounded unsurprised and lucid.

"It's over," I said. "She's okay. She's safe. Nobody got shot. I was wondering if I could come over."

"You *better* come over."

A little before three A.M. I was standing on June Dauer's patio overlooking Newport Harbor. The lights twinkled on the water and the air smelled of salt and barnacles and nightshade. I knocked and waited. She answered the door in the dark and whispered for me to come in.

We started making love at 3:08, 5:22 and 7:12. We ate cereal with whole milk and honey on it at 4:15, and I fried up some eggs, bacon, sausage, and potatoes at 6:30, which I served with waffles, melon and orange juice.

June left for work around nine and told me to sleep as long as I wanted.

I woke up at noon. I walked around her apartment with a cup of coffee. The morning haze was burning off and the water of the bay was glassy gray. It felt like another world to me, another universe entirely. No bars. No uniforms. No guns. No creeps.

June Dauer was everywhere I looked: sitting on the sofa, standing in the kitchen, looking out the window, sitting on the patio. I could see her dark curls, the beautiful straight lines of her face, her strong tan legs. I could hear the clear, soft whisper of her voice.

I wondered what it would be like to inhabit this place. If it could accommodate a big man, a scar, a gun. It was funny, though, because when I imagined myself here I didn't feel like I was those things. I felt different. I felt smaller, lighter, softer. No scar. No gun. I felt like a smile with legs, and a body in between that only wanted to be close to hers. To be home. As if her flesh was a house and I could move in.

Chapter Twenty-Four

I stood outside cell eight in Module J, set the dinner tray in the slot and looked into the bright eyes of Alex Blazak. It was four in the afternoon and Sergeant Delano had agreed to let me serve Alex his in-cell dinner. Tonight was meat loaf, mashed potatoes, vegetables and milk.

"Acid Baby."

"My name is Joe Trona."

"Yeah, yeah. I know. Will's son. Too bad what happened. He shouldn't have gotten himself mixed up with the heavy-weights."

"Who set him up for Gaylen?"

"Get me out of here and I'll tell you."

"Only the DA can do that."

"He'll spring me, when he talks to Savannah and finds out there was no kidnapping. That was Dad's story."

"There's the blackmail."

Alex smiled, jumped off his bed and walked up to the bars. He looked down at the steaming tray and took it.

"Hey, I didn't beat that lady half to death. He did."

"Who hired Gaylen?"

He sat on the bed with the tray on his knees. "Don't ask me. Ask Dad. That was all at his end."

"But you knew something was going to happen. You'd talked with Gaylen. That's why you left Savannah on her own at Lind Street. Sacrificed her, after you'd gotten your money. That's why you had a fallback plan to meet her at Beach and Lincoln."

"Pure instinct. If you grew up with Jack as a father, you'd have it, too. How do you shave that thing?"

"What I wonder is, since you got an extra half million, maybe it was for you to help set up Will. You were dealing through him, but around him, too. With someone who wanted him dead."

Blazak colored slightly, looked down at his food. "These vegetables fresh?"

"Frozen. Your face just went pink."

He looked up at me. More color. "Don't talk to me about faces."

I stared at him and said nothing.

"You give me the creeps," he said.

I kept staring. Blazak turned away from me and sat cross-legged on the bed, facing the rear wall.

I let myself in with the cell key Sergeant Delano had given me. Alex was just turning around to look when I asked him for his tray. He handed it to me and I set it on the floor. Then I picked him up by his neck, cranked him to face me, and pinned him to the far wall by his throat. He kicked, then stood on his tiptoes. I could feel his life pulsing urgently beneath my hands.

"Who set him up?"

I lowered him, keeping my grip on his neck.

He sucked some air, eyes wide.

"Want to dangle some more?" I asked.

He coughed and sputtered and coughed again.

"It was just Gaylen," he rasped. "I'd done business with some friends of his. Months ago. So he knew how to find me. He told me what he needed for the exchange—a place without lots of witnesses, after dark, somewhere they could get in and out of by car. He said there was another three grand in it for me. I figured I'd make some beer money. I didn't know about any setup. Something just told me to get the hell out of there. He still owes me the money. God, my *neck*."

"Friends of Gaylen? Who?"

"Pearlita and Felix Escobar."

"And you agreed to do what he said?"

"Well, yeah. Money's money, right? But I didn't know anything about why. I didn't know he was going to take out your father. Or try to get Savannah. If I'd have been there, he'd have probably stepped on me, too. But it was Gaylen. He came to me, man. I don't know how the hell he found out what was going on. He just showed up at my warehouse."

"You were supposed to be at Lind Street for the pickup, weren't you?"

"That's what they all assumed. My dad and yours."

Hands still on his neck, I guided him back to his bed and sat him down. I picked up the dinner tray and handed it to him.

"Eat your vegetables."

"All right."

"You're almost twenty-two years old. You should have known better than to risk your sister like that. Just turn her out there on her own? She came close to getting shot. What's wrong with you?"

"She's a survivor."

"You're a coward. All your guns and weapons, but you're a coward."

"Hey, I just needed the money. My dad's the forty-first richest man in America. I got used to certain things."

He looked at me sullenly, rubbing his neck.

Rick Birch and I interviewed Savannah late that afternoon. The doctor told us she'd slept most of the day, and awakened disoriented and depressed.

The three of us sat at a small table in the Hillview Library. I suggested that place, thinking that Savannah would feel comfortable there. I told her the story about Will and *Shag: Last of the Plains Buffalo*. She was very interested in it. Wanted to know if I remembered what page I was on when he sat down. I did: page thirty, where Shag is fighting for control of the herd. The table was the same one I'd been sitting at on that fateful day. I knew because there was a faint X carved into the top by some creative Hillview student. Will had fingered it while he talked to me. The X was still there, dulled by the years but visible.

We tape-recorded the whole story. It went on for almost an hour. Savannah spoke quickly and covered large amounts of time and action with just a few words. We let her tell the whole thing before we went back and started asking questions.

"When did you decide to take the tape and run away to Alex?"

"When I saw the woman's face in the paper. And that she had been run over and died."

"Did she ever work for your family?"

"Yes. She cleaned our house a few times. I remembered her because she was very pretty and very quiet, with a smile like a big light. I asked her how she got her hair so shiny and she said she would rinse it in beer."

"Who thought of charging your father money in order to get the tape?"

"Alex. He always wants money."

"Did you think that was a good idea?"

"No. But I was afraid to take the tape to the police, because of what Dad would do to me. Alex said if we got lots of money from Dad, we could give some to the maid's family."

"When Alex first asked for the money, who was he calling on the phone about how much, and when, and where?"

"First Dad. Then someone named Bo. Then Will."

"Where and when, exactly, did you meet Will Trona?"

"At Laguna Beach. I can't remember exactly, but I think it was one or two nights before he got murdered."

"After that, did Alex call Will about making the arrangements?"

"He called Will. But he talked to a lot of other people, too. About money, and places, and who would be there and where we would be."

"What other people?"

"One called Daniel, which I think is Reverend Alter. One called John. One called Pearl. And a woman named . . . Donna? Renee? Something like that."

I made a note of that name: Donna or Renee—a new face in the game.

"Did you know that Alex was telling your father that he would return you to him?"

"Yes. But Alex was lying. We were going to take the money and buy a little house by the beach to live in."

"Did you know how much money Alex asked for, at first?"

"Five hundred thousand dollars."

"Did you know he raised the price?"

"That was Will's idea."

"Did Will know about the tape?"

"Alex played it for him. And Will said to double the amount

of money. And Will said Alex should collect the money, and turn me and the tape over to him."

"What did you think of going with Will?"

"I liked Will. I could trust him. He said he'd take me to Child Protective Services and I wouldn't have to worry about what my father might do. He said there was no reason to give the tape to either Dad or the police. He said he'd work things out so that everyone would be happy again."

I thought what a perfect opportunity Will had had to blackmail Blazak. What fat concessions he could get from Blazak, simply with the threat of taking that tape to the authorities.

"Can you tell us where you went, you and Alex, after the night when Will was killed?"

"I can't remember the order. But we went to Big Bear, Lake Arrowhead, La Jolla, Imperial Beach, Julian, Hollywood, Santa Monica, Santa Barbara, San Francisco. And Mendocino, Reno, Las Vegas, Bullthorn City, Yuma, Palm Springs and Mexico City. And Zihautanejo and Tucson and some other places."

"A new place every night?"

"We stayed two in Las Vegas so Alex could gamble and see a fight. And four in Mexico City because we were tired. The rest were one night."

"You drove to all these places?"

"All except Mexico City and Zihautanejo. We flew out of Tijuana for those. Alex's Porsche is very fast."

"Did Alex ever hurt you?"

Savannah looked at me with an expression of surprise. *"Hurt me? He did everything he could to protect me and make me happy. I got sick in Mexico City and he stayed up with me all night, putting washcloths on my forehead. He had room service bring me tortilla soup and bottled water. He's the best big brother a girl could ever have."*

I made a note of that. I thought about innocence and trust and fear and being eleven years old.

I also thought of Savannah the Spy.

"Savannah, did you play Savannah the Spy when you and Alex were running?"

"Yes, of course. I used up two whole tapes. I shot us everywhere, doing our secret things. Alex thought it was funny."

"Where are those tapes now?"

"In my backpack with my camcorder. Want to watch them?"

"Yes. We'd like that very much."

One of the Hillview staff was kind enough to roll a TV/VCR into the library. For the next two hours we watched Alex and Savannah Blazak zooming across the west in his shiny black Porsche, splashing in the blue bay of Zihuatanejo, checking into their suites, having food fights with room service hamburgers, watching out windows for anyone coming after them, hastily packing and hitting the road while Alex muttered paranoid conspiracy theories and Savannah narrated. There was tape of Alex throwing his million in cash around a suite at the Venetian in Las Vegas. Tape of the grim border at Tijuana, the vendors selling purple Buddha coin banks, *Star Wars* figurines wearing sombreros, shellacked sand sharks on strings, boxes painted bright pinks and yellows and blues. Tape of the beautifully violent Mendocino coast; of the Golden Gate Bridge; the hills of Santa Barbara; the cotton fields in Yuma; the bighorn sheep outside the Ritz-Carlton in Palm Desert; the dreamy mountains around Tucson.

"Why did Alex call me?" I asked. "What made you want to try another deal with your father?"

"Alex wanted more money. And to be honest, Joe, I was tired of running. It was nice, but I do have to start sixth grade in a few months. I'll be in accelerated math *and* English."

"Why did you choose me? Why not call your father directly?"

"Oh, no, Joe. I trust you. That's why I sent you those postcards. I needed to say something to somebody, but I couldn't worry my mother with things like that. She's very fragile. So I picked you. And Alex trusted your father. You can never deal with Dad directly, because he's such a good businessman. He'll always get a better deal than you, even if it sounds like he's not."

I thought about Jack Blazak and his temper, his duplicity and his power.

"What about your mother, Savannah? Do you trust her?"

She looked at me, then at Rick Birch. Then away. She sighed. "She always agrees with him. Even when she knows he's wrong. It's one of his laws, that she always has to agree with him."

I wondered if Jack had ever done to Lorna what he'd done to Luria Blas.

"Did your father ever hit your mother?"

Savannah was still looking out one of the Library windows.

"I never saw him do that. Mom spends lots of days in bed. I'm not sure why, but it usually happens after they fight. They fight very loud, with bad language. Usually that happens when Mom drinks a lot."

"Did you ever see bruises on her, or cuts?"

"No."

I followed her line of sight out the window. The playground was filled with young children. Two of the Hillview counselors were playing, too.

"Savannah, can you remember if it was Donna or Renee that Alex was talking to?"

She closed her eyes and thought. She breathed deeply and let it out slowly. "No. A woman's name, like those but maybe not those."

"So it wasn't Donna or Renee, but close?"

"Yes. I don't like it when I can't remember. I'm sorry. Do you think I could have some lunch now? And a few minutes to myself? I don't know why, but I'm so extremely weary today."

That evening Birch, Ouderkirk and I drove up to the Pelican Point entrance. We had a sheriff's black-and-white behind us. Birch badged the guard.

"Who are you here to see?"

"None of your business. Open the gate."

With a smirk, he did.

At the second gate, Jack Blazak's voice came through the speaker. "What the hell do you want?"

Birch identified himself, said he'd like to talk to Mr. Blazak.

"About what?"

"Luria Blas."

A moment of static. "All right."

The second gate opened and Birch steered the Crown Vic along the winding drive. The Greco-Roman house finally came into view.

"Look at this," said Ouderkirk. "A palace. A pool and tennis court and reflecting pond and helipad. A five-car garage and what's that—a vineyard? I'm in the wrong business. I knew it. I *knew* it. I can't even afford a maid, and this guy beats them up because they get pregnant when he screws them. Makes me want to be reincarnated as an asshole."

"You can still accomplish that in this life," said Birch.

"I'll just follow your example."

"Look at those statues. The one on the right's a Rodin copy."

"Maybe it's real," said Ouderkirk. "If you can afford a place like this, you can afford the knickknacks."

There was a Bentley the size of an oil tanker parked in the

shade behind Blazak's garage. The driver was dozing when we pulled up. He got out a cell phone and dialed.

"I think Blazak's got his lawyer," I said.

"This will be interesting," said Birch. Then he spoke over his shoulder to me. "Joe, don't say anything unless you're asked."

"I won't."

The black-and-white pulled away from us and parked in the shade, facing the Bentley. Birch nodded at the deputies, then led the way past the reflecting pool.

Blazak met us at the front door, wearing jeans and a white shirt, boat shoes. He was freshly shaved and his eyes were clear and unrepentant. He shook hands with Birch and Ouderkirk and looked at me with disgust.

We went into the same bright living room where the Blazaks and Bo Warren had first spun their elaborate lie for me. Sitting where Bo Warren had sat was an older gentleman in a trim blue suit. His hair was white. His eyes were blue and had the open twinkle of a two-year-old's.

He rose lithely, introduced himself as Adam Duessler and shook hands all around, then sat back down and crossed his legs. "Jack's hired me to guide him through this situation," he said. "I've advised him to remain silent for the time being. I'm not up to speed on everything yet, and that's part of the reason. I'm also not sure what you three are doing here, exactly. So, gentlemen, proceed."

Birch and Ouderkirk sat on one of the cream-colored couches. I took a chair off to the side, placed my hat on my thigh and folded my hands in front of me.

Birch leaned forward. "Mr. Blazak isn't charged with any crime. Funny he'd have a lawyer here."

"It's his right," said Duessler.

"Well, sure," said Birch. "I can take my lawyer to the car wash if I want. But the right to counsel is only for the accused."

Birch let that hang in the air.

"We're impressed by your grasp of procedure," said Duessler. "So, again, proceed."

"We've got evidence that Mr. Blazak assaulted a young domestic worker named Luria Blas on June eighth of this year. We've got an eyewitness. Before we jump to any conclusions we wanted to hear Mr. Blazak's explanation. Maybe we're not seeing what we think we're seeing."

"It's kind of you to run it past us," said Duessler.

"It's out of respect for Mr. Blazak's standing in the community, and because of the ugly nature of what happened."

There was a moment of silence.

"Mr. Blazak," said Birch. "We've got a videotape of you and Ms. Blas out in the guest house. It was taken by your daughter, Savannah, as part of a game she liked to play. Have you seen it?"

"Mr. Blazak won't answer that question at this time, on my counsel," said Duessler.

"We're just asking if he's seen a tape," said Ouderkirk.

"Jack?" Duessler asked.

Blazak shook his head.

Birch took out his notepad and pen. Blazak watched him. Birch wrote something, then looked out at Blazak. "Did you employ Luria Blas?"

"Mr. Blazak won't answer that question at this time, on my counsel," said Duessler.

"Did you have intercourse with Luria Blas?"

"Mr. Blazak won't answer that question at this time, on my counsel," said Duessler.

"He's paying you too much to say the same thing over and over," said Ouderkirk.

"Isn't that the truth!" said Duessler. "Look, gentlemen, my client is willing to answer these and any other questions you come up with, but not at this time. The two of us have barely had time to speak about these matters. Give us a week to get up to speed on these things, and we can meet again. There's absolutely no reason we can't all get what we want from this."

Birch nodded and stood. "What do you think about that, Mr. Blazak? You going to take orders from a lawyer, or maybe straighten things out for yourself?"

"I'll take orders for now."

"It helps when we hear things from your mouth. You want us getting our information from everybody but you?"

"Get it where you want."

"Have it your way," said Birch.

"Get out of my house, you losers."

Birch and Ouderkirk exchanged looks. Something was asked and answered right then.

Birch shook his head. "Mr. Blazak, you are under arrest for the assault and battery of Luria Blas. You have the right to an attorney and you have the right to remain silent. Anything you say can and will be used against you in a court of law. Put your hands behind your head and turn around."

Blazak's face went red.

"Gentlemen, gentlemen," said Duessler. "There's no need to cuff my client, or even to transport him at this time. Give Mr. Blazak the courtesy of a voluntary surrender at noon tomorrow. You surely can't consider him a flight risk."

"I consider him a flight risk," said Ouderkirk.

"You fucking bastards," said Blazak.

"Be reasonable," said Duessler.

"This guy screwed the maid," said Ouderkirk. "Then he beat her half to death when she got pregnant. That's how reasonable your client is, Mr. Duessler."

Birch cuffed him and led him outside.

"See you in court," said Ouderkirk. "Our DA's gonna swallow your client whole."

As we made our way down to Pacific Coast Highway I looked at the airborne hawks and the darkening sky and the mansions with their lights coming on. Saturday evening in Newport Beach, a little corner of paradise for a few of the people on Earth.

I wondered how a man could have everything in the world except common decency and common sense. His marriage, his family, his reputation, his business would all suffer and possibly collapse. He'd do time in prison, maybe a lot of it. All of that, because he thought his penis was more important than the rights of another human being, poor as she was.

He'd have a lot of money left over. That was about all you could say for him.

I turned and watched the black-and-white coming down behind us. Twelve billion dollars behind the security screen of a prowl car, and two deputies who make maybe a hundred grand a year between them, if they work all the overtime they can. What an odd glory, I thought, when the mighty fall. Somehow, I always try to pull for them. They should be better than us, shine a brighter light, show us the way.

We passed the guard gate, where Miguel Domingo had died trying to defend the honor of his sister. A woman who had traded that honor for a little bit of money. All she'd left the man who beat her was a scratch. A machete, a sharpened screwdriver and a fingernail against the richest man in Orange County.

Miguel and Luria were about to win, I thought. It had cost them their lives, in a battle they had never wanted to fight in the first place.

Good for them.

Chapter Twenty-Five

I called Valeen Wample that night from home. Grandma. The limp scrap of paper that had held her number in my wallet for all those years came apart as I unfolded it. The ink had faded to the color of a vein. The area code was down in the Southern California desert. She answered on the fifth ring.

"Yeah?"

"This is Joe Trona."

A pause. I heard TV in the background, and something blowing—an air conditioner or a fan.

"So?"

"Your daughter's son, ma'am."

"I know that. What do you want?"

"Charlotte's address and phone number."

"I assume she's dead."

"The last ones you have, then."

"Why?"

"It's important that I talk to her."

Silence again. "You don't want to call Charlotte."

"Why?"

"Exactly. *Why?*"

"To get some things straight."

"She's worthless, gutless and heartless. For starters."

"Thor isn't my father."

"Says who?"

"Thor. Charlotte paid him not to tell why he threw the acid."

"Oh, horseshit."

"Maybe, ma'am. But Charlotte can clear it up."

Another pause. I heard her set the phone down. TV. Fan. Then she was back, ice clinking on glass.

"This number worked five years ago. I called her to get some money. She didn't give me any. I haven't called it since then."

She gave me the phone number and an address in a small town called Fallbrook, not far from San Diego.

"Where do you live, ma'am?"

"Bombay Beach. It's the worst place in the world. We're so bad, we made the TV. Dead fish on the sand. Birds fall dead out of the sky from botulism. Filthy Salton Sea. A hundred and ten degrees all summer. Scorpions and snakes. A real hellhole, but I can't afford nothin' better."

"I can send you some money."

"How much?"

"Would ten thousand help?"

"Fifteen would help more. Zoom it right over, grandson Joe. I need every penny."

She gave me her address. I heard the ice clinking. "I wish you weren't going to talk to her. She's rotten. Ruins everything she touches."

"I'll give her your regards."

"Don't."

"Thank you for your help."

"You call it help. I call it stupid."

"Thanks, anyway."

"How'd your face heal up?"

"Some scarring."

"Tough break. Take my advice. Don't call her. Whatever you got, she'll make it worse. Oh, she changed her name to Julie. And her last name is Falbo."

I wrote out a check for fifteen grand. My account was almost empty because the rubies had cost so much. Then I looked through my collection of complimentary Paralyzed Veterans of America greeting cards. I donate once a year and they send me the cards as a thank-you. I found a blank one with a kitten and a ball of yarn on it, but couldn't think of what to write.

So I drove to the drugstore and looked in the card rack. I wasn't sure what a grandson was supposed to feel for a grandmother, especially one he'd only talked to twice in his life. She didn't seem to be a very likable woman, but you can't judge a person by two calls. I settled on one with a front that looked like a knitted sweater. It said *FOR GRANDMA* on the label. Inside, it said: *Just thinking of you, someone special in my life.*

Back home I signed the card "With Respect and Affection," put the check inside and addressed the envelope. I went ahead and put the return address on it, wondering if she'd write.

I poured a large glass of vodka over ice and took it out to my back-yard. In the dark I could hear the squirrels running along the power lines. If they fall the cats get them. The orange tree was losing the last of its blossoms but the yard still smelled sweet and good and it reminded me of those first months in the Tustin foothills with Will and Mary Ann because the citrus was in bloom the first day I walked into that home of dreams.

Rick Birch called me about two minutes later. "Pearlita's dealing," he said. "Dent told her he'd withdraw his death penalty demand for Felix. The truth is, he didn't think he'd get it with that jury, so he's throwing her a bone she'd probably get anyway. Here's Pearlita's ID on the passenger in Bo Warren's car that night—Orange County Supervisor, Second District, Dana Millbrae."

A woman's name. Kind of like Donna or Renee but maybe not either.

Dana.

I called Ray Flatley at home and apologized sincerely for doing so.

"No problem, Joe. I was working through some of that new Warren Zevon on the piano. I guess he's sort of a bad boy, but he's awfully funny. And those ballads of his actually make my scalp crawl they're so beautiful."

"I want you to help me make a recording."

"I didn't know you sang."

"Not music, sir," I said. "Just a few words."

"Whose words?"

"Mine. I'm going to play me. You're going to play John Gaylen."

A long pause. "And who gets to hear this piece of illegal police trickery?"

"You won't ever know."

"When does it get destroyed?"

"By ten o'clock tomorrow night. I'll hand you a melted glob of tape and plastic if you want, sir."

Another moment of silence before Flatley's deep, resonant reply: "Ah, Joe Trona, I can do what you want. When do you need John Gaylen to speak?"

"Right now."

He gave me his address and hung up.

I was back home by ten. I got Dana Millbrae's home number from Will's address book.

Millbrae answered the phone himself. I told him we needed to talk and he didn't even ask about what.

"Call my secretary for an appointment," he said.

"It needs to be soon, sir."

"Police business, Joe?"

I heard the fear in his voice. It was impossible for me not to use it against him. "Yes."

"Not here."

"How about the Grove, in one hour?"

"I'm not a member and neither are you."

"I'll take care of that, sir. You'll be my guest."

I hung up and called Rex Sauers. He said he'd have a booth ready for us.

Dana Millbrae shuffled self-consciously across the Grove lounge toward our booth, hands in his pants pockets and his eyes aimed downward. A sharp suit. He sat down and looked at me. He had a boyish face, earnest eyes and pale hair falling over his forehead. USC, Stanford MBA. This was his first term as a supervisor and he was thirty-four years old. Married, four children. He had told me at Will's funeral that losing Will was like losing a father: Will had taught him everything he knew about being one of the seven most powerful elected officers in the county.

We shook hands. He sat and glanced at me, then over at a waiter.

"Mind if I smoke?" he asked.

I told him I didn't. The waiter came and Millbrae ordered a double Stolichnaya martini, up with a twist. He held a lighter to a cigar, puffed it to life and drew deeply on it.

"Okay, what?" he asked.

"You and Bo Warren met John Gaylen in the parking lot of Bamboo 33 the night before Will died. I want to know what you talked about."

He stood and drew the privacy curtain, looking at me uncertainly as he sat back down.

"We talked about getting Savannah Blazak back."

"What did Gaylen know about Savannah Blazak?"

"He was in touch with Alex. They'd done business."

"What did Gaylen say, exactly?"

Millbrae puffed and finally met my eyes. "I don't remember, exactly."

"Give me the generalities, then."

The waiter parted the curtain, set Millbrae's drink on the table, drew the curtain closed behind him.

Millbrae sipped deeply, then sipped again. "He told us that she was all right. That everything was going to work out."

"You and Bo Warren drove all the way to Bamboo 33 after midnight, just to hear that?"

He nodded.

"I don't believe you."

"Ask Bo. That was the truth."

"Bo said he was there with Pearlita."

Millbrae cleared his throat, fist in front of his mouth. "No. I was the passenger."

"I appreciate your honesty. Mr. Millbrae, I'm going to speak frankly to you now. Will knew you were taking money from Rupaski, for your vote on the toll road buyout. Will had you two on tape, talking about a cash pickup at Windy Ridge. I'm sure Carl told you all of this already, right?"

He nodded. He looked like a schoolboy who'd been caught with a cigarette.

"Well, Will also had some unpleasant evidence against Jack Blazak. And some more unpleasant evidence against the Reverend Daniel Alter. He blackmailed you into a no vote on the toll road buyout. He blackmailed Daniel into some cash payments. He was getting ready to blackmail Blazak. And he could have had Carl Rupaski arrested on bribery and conspiracy charges anytime he wanted. I've got all this documented in a way that would stand up in court. Does most of this ring true to you?"

Millbrae nodded again. A light sheen of sweat showed at his temples. He took a big gulp of the vodka and washed it down with some more smoke. "That . . ."

"That what?"

"That fucker had something on everybody."

"Yes. He did. And that's why you arranged to have John Gaylen take him out."

"Absolutely untrue."

Even in the dim light of the booth I could see that Millbrae's face had flushed. He kept looking around for something to settle his eyes on, but there wasn't much to choose from in a booth sealed off by a privacy curtain. So he looked at his cigar.

"Want to hear Gaylen tell his version?"

Millbrae colored more deeply. He took another long drink. "No."

"Listen anyway."

I got out my micro-tape recorder and played the tape that Ray Flatley had helped me make.

ME: *So who spoke to you first about taking a contract on Will Trona?*

FLATLEY: *First was Bo Warren. Pearlita put me with him. Then Millbrae, the supervisor, he got into it. There was an asshole named Carl. And the girl's father, Jack. I thought they'd want the girl back, bad. But what they wanted most was for someone to step on Will Trona. Millbrae was just the gopher. They called him Millie, dissed him when he wasn't there.*

I turned it off, rewound it a bit, then looked at Millbrae.

"We questioned him this morning," I lied. "He's dealing

you guys away as fast as he can. That tape is about six hours old."

His face had gone from red to white. He ran a hand over the sweat on his forehead, took another big drag on the cigar. He looked into his empty glass.

"That voice could be faked."

"Your lawyer can hire an examiner at your expense."

I put the tape player back in Will's briefcase, threw open the curtain to let out the smoke, and pointed out Millbrae's empty glass to the waiter.

A minute later another double martini landed in front of him. He drank some, looked at me with a kind of disheveled malice, then muttered something.

"What was that, Mr. Millbrae?"

"I said your father was a complete asshole."

I reached out and pulled the curtain shut again. I stared at him.

"Don't," he said. "I know you could tear me apart."

"That would be bad manners."

"Yeah. A place like this." He drank again, looked down at the dead cigar. "You going to arrest me?"

"That depends on what you do in the next hour."

"We could work something out."

"I'll listen."

"I'm not taking a fall for all those guys. I'm the junior man, and I'm not going to do it."

"Instead, you're looking for a way to let them take the fall. To let Dana Millbrae float a little closer to the top. Where he wants so badly to be."

He glared at me again, fumbled with the cigar. "I can trade. Me for them. Can you keep me out of it if I do that?"

"I can keep you partway out of it. Not all the way."

"I'm basically fucked."

"I'll tell you what I can do, Mr. Millbrae. You tell me the truth right now, into that little machine, and I'll take it as far as I can without you. Gaylen said you were the gopher. I believe that. And if you give me enough to button down Blazak, Rupaski and Bo Warren, then I'll have what I want. They used you. I understand. I need to know exactly how. And let me tell you one more thing. If I play this tape to those men, they'll all point straight at you, and you will go to prison for a long time."

"This is awful. This is terrible."

"It's a parlor game, compared to what you did to Will."

Millbrae tried to bring some hardness to his eyes, but all I could see was a cowardly man and a failed politician. His chin quivered.

"I went into public life to serve the public. Really, that's true. All I managed to do was fuck them, and myself."

"You didn't let the county buy the toll road and make Rupaski's friends richer."

He smiled bitterly and drank again.

"Thanks to Will. Whose office was the tape recorder in, anyway—Rupaski's or mine?"

"Yours. You'll live to fight another day, Mr. Millbrae. Who knows? If you can help me nail this case shut, maybe it won't cost you as much as it should. But you were thinking that. You're already whiffing the sweet scent of opportunity in the stink you've made of your life."

He huffed something like a laugh. Then he actually looked down his nose at me. I wondered which fancy school he learned that at.

"You can change your mind, though, Trona. You could come back and get me anytime you want. You can keep me in your pocket, like your father did to everybody he ever met in his life. This thing I did won't ever die."

"That's correct. Will did the dying."

Sometimes you'll see something pass behind the eyes of a man, and you can't know what it is. And you understand that you could live a hundred more years and see it a thousand more times, and still not know what it was. I saw such a thing in Millbrae's right then.

"I watched you drive up in his car," he said. "I see you carry that old briefcase of his. Here you sit, making shady deals with Orange County supervisors at the Grove. You're getting to be just like him. You must love it. I would. Twenty-four years old, and you got all the same shit your father worked a lifetime for."

"I enjoy the car."

"I got a green one, same model, but seventeen-inch rims."

"The big wheels are cosmetic. They detract from the handling and the fuel economy."

He looked at me, and took another drink. "Get out that shitty little machine of yours, Trona. Man . . . I can't believe this is happening. I'm about to see how good I am at covering my own ass."

"You'll do just fine, Mr. Millbrae."

"It was a combination of things, Trona. It was like that perfect storm, when three meteorological events happened at the same time. Except there were more than three, maybe twenty or a hundred. It was like history made it happen, circumstances just came into alignment against Will. First, there was the tape that Will had against Carl and me. I shouldn't have been taking money to influence my votes, but I did. I got the kids' college to pay for and a big mortgage, and supervisors' salaries aren't exactly huge. But it was wrong. And Will caught me at it— caught *us* at it. You know, when he played me that tape on the same machine you're using right now, it was like he had my entire life at his disposal. I was dead. Everything I'd worked for could be taken away, if that tape got into the wrong hands."

Millbrae sighed and looked down at the table.

"How about another drink, Mr. Millbrae?"

"Why not?"

I signaled the waiter for another round of drinks. We sat silently until he brought them and I slid the curtain shut again. He ran his lemon twist around the edge of the glass then dropped it in and took a swig.

"Carl was furious. Of course it was my fault that one of our conversations got recorded. Carl needed that yes vote on the toll road buyout, but I couldn't defy Will. He had us and we knew it. Carl got some of his guys to follow Will around at night, trying to get him at something. We all knew that Will had a soft spot for the ladies, so we were hoping we could get something to cancel out what he had on us. Carl even had one of his guys put a radio homer on Will's BMW when it came through the Transportation Authority yard for service. That's how Carl found out that Will was in contact with Savannah Blazak. Carl and I talked to Jack.

"All of us got together on Monday night, two nights before Will was killed. Right here at the Grove. We shot some pool and had some drinks and talked up some of the women. But mostly we just stewed about Will Trona, and the way he could play so damned dirty and get away with it. Jack introduced me to Bo Warren, and Warren implied that even the Reverend Daniel Alter was having some trouble with Will. It was like a love fest in reverse—a bunch of people admitting to each other how much they hate somebody. No, not hate, but . . . fear. I mean, Will was *always* doing something like this. He spent his life collecting dirt and confessions and favors and money and using all of them to build his own power. He was the Prince, man, right out of Machiavelli. Then things started getting kind of . . . serious. It came out that night that Jack had found this hood named John Gaylen, and hired him to scare the piss out of his son. Jack was making arrangements through Will to pay a fat ransom and get his girl back. But when it came time to get Savannah, Jack wanted to make sure that Alex got the scare of his life. Gaylen and his guys were supposed to claim the girl, beat the piss out of Alex and take the money from Will back to Jack. Teach the kid a lesson, right? For a price, of course."

"What price?"

"Blazak never said. So, we're here shooting pool and Bo Warren says, why don't we pay Gaylen to rough up Will, instead? Maybe get him to back off, think twice about the shit he's pulling on everyone. And that would mean Gaylen wouldn't even have to beat up Alex, because working over Will right in front of him and Savannah would provide all the scare a young man needs."

Millbrae drank again. Then he picked up the cigar and lit it, settling back into a blue-gray cloud.

"That was when I looked at Carl and he looked at me and we read each other's minds. And I looked at Warren and Blazak and they were right there too, right exactly on the same wavelength as Carl and me. Dan Alter was talking to this alleged personal astrologer who I must say was one strikingly beautiful woman. Talking about God, no doubt. So he missed it, but we didn't. No one had to say anything, but in about five seconds, roughing up Will turned into something else. And that's exactly when I said no. I said count me out. And Carl said he thought roughing up Will a little was a good idea, and you, you little fuck—that meant me—are going to talk to John Gaylen about it."

This was Millbrae's out, and I let him have it.

"How much did you offer him?"

"Nine thousand dollars."

I don't know if Dana Millbrae saw my disbelief. He was drunk and confessing to a conspiracy to commit a murder that he wouldn't admit was murder, so he might have been a little distracted. And I shouldn't have been surprised. I know of contract murders set up for anywhere between three and ten thousand dollars. But just the idea of Will's life being bought away for nine thousand dollars brought everything home to me in one instant: the ugliness and smallness of what these men had done, their greed and their cowardice, their arrogance. I couldn't shake the image of Daniel Alter talking up the astrologer while his friends planned the murder of my father. Add ignorance and vanity and lust to the list.

"And you have to understand, Trona, that nine grand was to rough Will up."

"Rough him up? Were those your words to Gaylen?"

"Yeah, and he said what's that mean? What do you want done?"

"And I said break his knee, because in the movies they always talk about breaking knees. And break some of his ribs, too. But don't mess up his face or his teeth, I said, because that seemed like a low blow."

"That was considerate."

He glanced at me, then looked away. He sighed loudly and drank more. Then choked down another big hit of blue smoke.

"Mr. Millbrae, how and when did John Gaylen's work order get upgraded to murder?"

"I don't know. I don't know that it did. It didn't come from me. Ever. Nobody ever said anything about murder."

"Gaylen never said anything about a beating. To him, it was a contract on a life."

"The word murder was never used."

"No. Men here at the Grove don't use that word."

Millbrae tilted up his glass and finished off the martini. His eyes widened a little and he wiped his face with his hand. His lank hair was damp and clung to his forehead.

"I didn't know."

I stared at him but said nothing.

He looked away. "Am I off the hook?"

"You're finished." His mouth opened and his eyes wavered back up to mine.

"Finished?"

"For now."

"Oh, yeah. Finished for now."

I drove long and hard that night, out the 241 and onto the 91, then the 55 and the 5 and the 133 to the 241 again, then off on the 261 and back to the 5, then down to the 405 to Jamboree to Pacific Coast Highway then back up the 55 to the 91 toward home.

During that windows-down, one-hundred-and-forty-mile-an-hour run I thought about Will's life sold for what you'd find in a rich man's pockets. And I thought about what he'd said that last night, *Everyone,* and I realized he was telling me right then who had done it, everyone had done it. Will knew that much. And I also thought about what Millie had said about history lining up to take out Will, the way a dozen things had to quietly conspire in order to get those bullets into him: the Blazaks and Bo Warren, the Reverend Daniel Alter and Luria Blas, Gaylen and Alex, Jaime and Miguel Domingo, Pearlita and Jennifer, Rupaski and Millbrae. Even Joe Trona. Joe, who should have seen it coming, should have smelled the betrayal in the fog that night, should have questioned the sweat on his palms and the tingle of his scar, should have listened to the voice of warning deep in the clamor of his heart.

Everyone.

I got some fast food and parked outside June Dauer's apartment for a while. I didn't go in. I ate. I looked at her windows and her door and didn't know why I was there, except that The Unknown Thing had brought me back again, just like Will had told me it would. I wanted to be baptized but it wasn't practical unless I rousted Reverend Daniel Alter from sleep and forced him into the Chapel of Light. I imagined the Reverend Daniel at the Grove, talking to a beautiful astrologer while the bureaucrats and captains of industry plotted the death of Will. If I was an old master I would have painted the scene. I didn't think a baptism from him would do the job.

I eased down, set my hat on the seat and leaned my head back, looking out at the apartment and the power lines and the stars.

I closed my eyes and pictured June. And imagined that first day I'd walked into my new home in the Tustin hills, the sunlight hitting the red hibiscus and the white roses in the Trona garden.

I imagined Shag and the last of his herd retreating from the plains and into the chill of Yellowstone, to be safe from the men who had tried to exterminate them. There was snow dusting their big drooping manes and their eyes were small, bright and full of soul.

My cell phone rang at two-thirty.

"This is your old friend Bo."

I didn't say anything.

"Things are in the wind, Joe."

"What wind?"

"I talked to Millbrae. Then I talked with the guys, you know who, and we came up with a solution. It involves quite a lot of money."

"I'm not interested."

"Don't be in a hurry. Think about what that tape is worth."

I hung up and thought about it for five minutes. I shut my eyes again.

The next thing I knew it was hours later and the first rays of the sun were shooting off the rearview mirror and into my eyes.

Chapter Twenty-Six

Early that morning I played Millbrae's statement to Birch, Ouderkirk and Phil Dent. There was silence when it ended. Birch muttered, *"Wow."*

Dent started pacing, looking down at the floor.

Ouderkirk laughed. "Worthless shits," he said. "Let's arrest them all on murder one and conspiracy. That's a special circumstance. That's the death penalty."

"Slow down," said Dent. "We have to do this right. Joe, you want to tell us how you got him to talk like that for you?"

I did. I was vague about the "Gaylen" tape and never mentioned Ray Flatley, but I suggested that I could have "improvised" some evidence to get Millbrae's statement. I also told him that I had "collapsed the timeline as to how recently we had talked to Gaylen." And I said that I never told Millbrae that the evidence was genuine.

"You improvised, then collapsed a timeline? You're talking like a lawyer," said Ouderkirk. He turned to our district attorney. "I mean that as a compliment, Phil."

"Thank you, Harmon," said Dent. "With a conspiracy, you just have to pry one away from the group. If you can do that, you're golden. Then you can peel the rest of them off like sections of an orange, try them separately, eat every last one of them."

"I implied to Mr. Millbrae that he might be rewarded if he continued to be helpful," I said. "I didn't promise him anything."

"Look," said Birch. "We've got plenty here to interview Rupaski, Blazak and Bo Warren. Even Alter, if we want to. Blazak's going to be getting it both ways, with the beating of Blas. And as soon as one of them thinks another guy's rolling over, they'll roll over, too. I've seen it a thousand times."

"Gaylen's the key," said Dent. "Gaylen can finger any or all of them as hiring him. That's one thing they'll never admit. They'll all do what Millbrae did—say it was a big misunderstanding, and Gaylen got carried away and Joe here surprised them and we're looking at a jury being asked to believe that public servants and the forty-first richest guy in America are murderers. Tough sell for us, at that point. We start with Gaylen. I think we've got enough for a probable-cause arrest. Take him down. I'll put together a package for an arrest warrant. Joe, what I need from you is a couple of pages summarizing what you've got on Gaylen, and a transcript of Millbrae's statement."

"I'll have them in one hour."

"We closed out our surveillance on Gaylen two days ago," said Birch. "But we'll pick him up fast." He reached for the phone.

Dent kept pacing. Ouderkirk cleaned a fingernail with his pocketknife.

"You did some good work, Joe," he said. "You're going to make a good cop someday."

"Yeah," said Birch, looking at me over the telephone mouthpiece.

"We'll see," said Dent. "Not to spoil the party, but it's a

long swim between a confession made under questionable circumstances and a murder conviction."

"That's why we got you," said Ouderkirk. " 'Cause you're so good at the breaststroke."

Ouderkirk rubbed his chest.

Birch asked for the patrol commander.

"Rick, tell 'em all to be careful with Gaylen," said Ouderkirk. "Creeps can feel when the shovel's over their necks. Dangerous as rattlesnakes then."

"Approach him with caution," Birch told the patrol commander. "Consider him armed and dangerous. Harmon, let's go see if he's someplace obvious, like at home in bed. Get on that report, Joe. Make sure it's something a judge would like to read."

I was more careful with that report than with anything I'd ever written in my life. I documented my suspicion of Gaylen, the long trail that led from Savannah Blazak to Dana Millbrae, the admission from Del Pritchard that he'd placed a transmitter on Will's car. One of Dent's legal secretaries typed a transcript of Millbrae's confession, then I excerpted the most effective parts. *No one had to say anything, but in about five seconds roughing up Will turned into something else.*

Phil Dent asked me to rewrite some parts. He told me to describe my recognition of John Gaylen's voice during his interview with Birch and Ouderkirk, but to play down the fact that I didn't positively identify him as the gunman. He ordered me to delete a reference to staking out Gaylen's home. He asked me to delete the phrase "over drinks," in describing my talk with Millbrae.

When he had read it through a second time, he looked up at me and nodded. "Get ready for a shitstorm," he said. "And be careful with the press. If you look too much like a revenge-hungry son, it could backfire on us in court. Millbrae's confession is going to be hard enough to get into evidence. Without it, we've got our work cut out."

I spent the afternoon at my old home in the Tustin hills, cleaning some things out of Will's closet. Mary Ann came and went, clearly upset, unable to spend more than a few minutes in the big master bedroom while I took down suits and arranged them on the bed. Some I was planning to keep for myself. With a little altering I could wear them. The others I'd decided to donate to the Salvation Army on Fourth Street, which is where Will had always taken his older clothes.

"Please leave some of the light linen ones, Joe. I always liked him in the lighter colors. And the tuxedo that's in the back, in the clear plastic bag—that was for our wedding."

Her eyes welled with tears and she walked briskly out of the room, shoulders back and head up.

Reverend Daniel dropped by in the early afternoon. I'd missed his sermon that morning, because I was busy trying to put friends of his in jail. Daniel looked haggard and worn. He wore his usual chinos and golf shirt and he seemed so eager to help, but so helpless. He hovered behind me as I brought shoes out of the depths of Will's big walk-in.

"I worry about you, Joe."

"I'm doing better."

"Do you enjoy travel?"

"I liked the family vacations when I was a boy. My favorite was all of us in the white van, going to Meteor Crater and the Petrified Forest in Arizona."

"That sounds splendid."

"You see everything when you drive."

Daniel then invited me to visit the Holy Land with a special group from the Chapel of Light. It was a twenty-day "spiritual junket," with time in Egypt, some Greek islands, Paris, Rome and London.

"They're leaving this evening," he said. "But all you need is a passport. Everything else would be complimentary, Joe. A gift to you from the Chapel of Light. First class all the way, the best accommodations we could find."

I looked at him and set a pair of loafers into a box.

"I can't do that."

"Why not?"

"Business, Reverend."

"I thought you were still on administrative leave, because of the shooting."

"I am. There are other things."

He smiled shyly at me, his eyes slightly magnified by his thick glasses. "You know, you'd be welcome to bring a friend to the Holy Land. Anyone you want, Joe. Perhaps the radio woman."

I turned and looked at him. He was holding one of Will's two-tone golf shoes, running his fingers over the spikes.

"Who told you?"

"No one told me anything, Joe. I listened to her show! You told her more in one hour of radio than you've told me in fifteen years as your minister. And I was happy that you did tell her about yourself. I felt, just listening, that you were very open to her. And that she was very open to you. That's all. Maybe she could accompany you, do some interviews, and make a working holiday out of it."

"No."

"Just an offer, Joe."

"Thank you, sir. I appreciate it."

Daniel stayed on while I finished packing the shoes and

belts. He sat on the side of Will and Mary Ann's bed, legs crossed and hands folded over his thigh.

I started going through Will's neckties. They were hooked to a small wooden carousel with brass spokes. I set aside the ones I wanted to keep. The others I laid out on the bed by Reverend Daniel.

"Do you remember that conversation we had, about your father doing things for a larger good?"

"Yes, sir."

"How he always thought he was, even when his actions were damaging or venal? How he thought right and wrong were defined by circumstance?"

"He raised me to believe that."

"Do you understand it?"

"It's not hard to understand. It's hard to live."

"All my faith and all my learning tell me that Will's way is not enough."

"You have God."

"I prayed long and hard to that God, just a few hours ago. Because earlier this morning I heard some things, Joe. Terrible things about good men. And I realized I had to do something. I didn't know what. Thus, my prayers to God. Long prayers, Joe. Long and full of question marks."

"Did you get any answers?"

"Yes. He said, Reverend Daniel, do the right thing. And He said, Reverend Daniel, tell Joe Trona to do the right thing."

"We're going to take them all down, sir."

His face was gray, his expression flat. "I understand. I would appreciate you leaving my name out of it for as long as possible."

"You were there, talking to the astrologer."

He colored then, and looked away. "Yes. And other than the astrologer, there isn't much I can say about that night."

"You might be called, Reverend. That's the DA's decision."

Daniel stood. "And if called, I will answer. I've tried to live my life that way."

He looked out the window for a moment, then sighed and turned back to me. His voice was soft and his eyes were moist.

"Joe, let me ask you to do something, as a man of this sad and painful world. Let this go. It's what Will would have done. Learn from it. Use the knowledge you've gained to further the interests of good. You can do so much good, Joe, if you participate in the world of men as a man. Will brought this upon himself. Salvage from Will's sacrifice something good for yourself. For your family. For your friends. He would have told you to. I promise you that."

"I don't let murderers go."

"Punish them, by all means. Punish them as a man. Don't turn them over to the law. The law will sap all the good that can come of this. All the good your heart can do. All the good *their* hearts can do, if given the chance. The law sees nothing but itself. It can only add sadness to sadness, tragedy to tragedy. Your concerns are larger than the law. Will's were."

"You remind me of Lucifer in the Bible."

"No one has ever said such a hurtful thing to me. Ever."

"I think it's a good comparison, sir. Besides, it's too late. A lot of people know what I know."

He faced me and took my shoulders in his hands. He squeezed and I could feel his fingers begin to tremble as he reached the peak of his strength.

"Joe, this is the most important decision of your young life. Everything that follows will depend on what you do. Not just for you but for many others. If you reconsider, please call me. I have some ideas on how justice can be done, and how good can be advanced. I have some ideas on how all of us can become wiser and benefit from this tragedy. And how Will's name can remain clean and his family provided for, very handsomely. I have commitments from men who can make these things happen. Mr. Millbrae in particular is eager to reconsider his words and his memory. These men are willing to bring their treasures and their power and their loyalty to you. They all put their sins at the feet of Jesus."

"Tell them to go fuck themselves, sir."

"I've never heard you say that word before."

"It's the first time in my life I've ever said it out loud. But I appreciate the warning. And the free trip to the Holy Land."

June allowed me to sit in the producer's booth and watch her do *Real Live* at five. I had the same uneasy feeling I'd had that night with Will, that something was trying to go wrong. I felt the guns against my body. The near dark of the studio seemed threatening, as if bad things were hiding in the shadows.

But June was brilliant and relaxed on-air, talking to a seventh-grade teacher who'd been shot in the head by one of his students two years ago. He had survived with minor injuries. He had some very forgiving and generous things to say about the boy who shot him. Since then, the teacher had spent many hours befriending the youth in lockup. He said that the boy had changed, and was now growing like a beautiful tree transplanted from bad soil. I wondered if the teacher was closer to God than I was. I decided he was, and I was glad there were people like him in the world, especially working with young people.

When June's workday was over, I held her hand and walked her quickly to her car. The early July heat was on us by then and the air was dirty and close. I kept an eye on the hedges and planters on the campus, and on the cars in the parking lot.

A black Mercedes with tinted windows pulled into the lot and parked crookedly in a space.

"You okay, Joe?"

"Just watching."

A woman got out of the Mercedes, then swung open a back door and began unfastening a baby from its car seat.

"What's wrong?"

"Get in your car, please. Turn on the engine and the air conditioner."

She eyed me, but did what I asked. I took the passenger seat beside her, felt the hot air come blasting from the vents.

"Talk to me, Joe."

"I've gotten a hotel room for you. It's a nice one, a suite, they call it, down on the beach in Laguna. I'd feel better about things if you'd live there a couple of days. People know about you and me. Some things are happening and I don't want them to happen to you."

"Shit, Joe, are you serious?"

"Yes."

"Are you going to be there?"

"No."

She stared at me. I watched the air lift her curls and saw the moisture on her temples. Her eyes were dark. I leaned over to kiss her and she turned away.

"Am I in danger?"

"I don't think you are. I'm just worried about you."

She touched my good ear. The air conditioner was getting colder and I felt the sweat tingling on my face.

"But you're worried enough about me to get me a hotel room."

"Just for two days." I continued to watch the parking lot, the cars on the boulevard, the sidewalk. I felt like one big eye with a couple of ears attached to it. I was aware of my hands and my guns and where the door handle was and how long it would take me to push June down to the floorboard of her car.

"That's one of the sweetest things a guy ever did for me. I

mean, it's right up there with flowers, coffee, chocolates and two million rubies on a first date."

"It's for safety."

"Yeah, I know. I have to go home, get some things."

"I'll follow you if that's all right."

She sighed and shook her head. Then she moved her hand to my chin and turned it toward her, grasping tight. She pulled me down into a kiss that lasted one minute and forty-two seconds, according to her dashboard clock.

"Damned air conditioner can't cool me off when you're around, Joe."

"The coolant might be low."

She shook her head and I scanned the lot and street again, before getting out, locking the door and swinging it shut.

I escorted June into her apartment, made sure all the doors and windows were locked, then waited outside in my car. No company that I could see. I climbed the stairs again and we made love before she packed, while she was packing, and after. My heart was so full I could feel it beating in every part of my body. And I could feel her heart, too. It was as if we were a single animal—a tangled, impractical being—but a complete one. I told her I loved her between twenty and thirty times, losing count at eighteen when June gasped and quaked and dug her fingernails into the back of my head so hard that I had to bite a mouthful of her hair to keep from yelping.

The suite at the Surf and Sand was larger than my house and had much better views and furniture. Through the windows you could see the shimmering Pacific. The sky was pale and streaked with clouds on top, wispy blue in the middle, and a darker blue down by the horizon. When you went to the patio and looked down at the beach you could see the children playing in the water and the surfers intent on their rides.

I checked the door locks and deadbolt and the phone line to security. Then I made sure the manager—an acquaintance of mine, through Will—knew she was checked in. He had been kind enough to put June between honeymooners and a family of four. I set a sweet little Browning .22 automatic on the table but June turned white when she saw it. I gathered it up and forgot about giving her basic handgun instruction.

We made love again and it was a slower and different kind of love than before. It occurred to me that we might never feel these things again, and she told me that she felt that way, too. She cried in my arms. I'd never felt another person's tears on my scar before and it was a strange thing. Like being dabbed with something that was cool and warm at the same time, liniment, maybe, or rubbing alcohol. I told her that when this was all over and I felt safe for her, maybe we could take a vacation. She laughed but I didn't ask her why because we were two separate animals again by then and I was getting ready to go.

Back home I talked to Rick Birch on the phone. He said tomorrow Dent was going to charge Jack Blazak with conspiracy to commit murder, leak the story to the media and hope that this would light the fuse under Rupaski and Bo Warren. Birch was going to give Rupaski and Warren a day or two of surveilled "squirm time" before interviewing them about the death of Will. Savannah was sleeping a lot at Hillview, and she had added some details to her earlier accounts of the kidnapping. The Hillview director had allowed her a supervised visit from her mother. Birch said that Savannah had broken into tears when Lorna walked into the visitation room. Alex Blazak was still in jail and Dent's office was going to file charges the next day unless he cooperated a lot more than he had as yet. Pearlita attacked two jail guards and took a dose of pepper spray in the face. Birch and Ouderkirk had gone to Gaylen's house with arrest and search warrants and found it abandoned.

"No car, not many clothes, not many personal items," said Birch. "Thermostat off, three days of mail in the box. No phone. No answering machine. He's gone. But we've got two men on his house, twenty-four, in case he comes back for his toothbrush."

"Has anyone at Bamboo 33 seen him?"

"They don't talk to guys like me. Joe? Watch yourself. If these people would kill Will they'd kill you, too."

I sat in my darkened house with a twelve-gauge Remington 1100 across my lap and watched part of a romantic comedy. I called June and we talked for one hour and fifteen minutes. She said the sunset from the patio had been totally unbelievable and the room-service dinner was the best food she'd ever eaten. The martini had knocked her on her "fanny."

"I'm kind of hammered right now, Joe, but I had this thought that I love you and I miss you and I want to marry you and give you children after we screw around and have fun for a couple of years."

"Okay."

"That was easy."

"What about *Real Live*?"

"I'll keep doing it for as long as I want. It's easy and fun. I mean, all I do is talk."

I looked around my little house, at the simple furnishings wavering in the blue TV light and imagined June Dauer inside it.

"No room service here," I said, running my finger over the shiny stock of the Remington.

"We'll ditch both our places, put the money into something

bigger. I have to tell you, even though we've been behaving like weasels, I do require large spaces and privacy sometimes."

"I do, too."

We were quiet for a while. I listened to her breathe. I could hear the waves splashing onto the beach.

"This is June Dauer," she whispered. "Saying you're real live. If you can't be happy be quiet."

"I'd like to be both," I whispered back.

We hung up a while later.

Bridget Andersen called around ten. Her voice was calm and low and she sounded scared.

"Millie came in late today," she said. "Looked like he'd had a rough night. On the phone a lot, door shut. Had long talks with Carl and a guy named Warren Somebody or Somebody Warren and I got it all on tape. Details about the night Will died. Something about a guy named John Gaylen. They talked about you, Joe—how you were the only one who put it all together about Will. They talked about getting you out of the loop. They talked about Millie recanting something he told you. He said he'd claim it was bullshit to cover his own ass. They talked about me and that original recording—they think I was helping Will. They talked about shutting me up, but I'm not sure if that means fire me or kill me. I left work usual time, and a white Impala followed me to the store, followed me to the health club, followed me home. Carl's jerks. They parked across the street, two houses down. Like I wouldn't see them."

"I thought you pulled out that recorder."

"I put it back when Will was killed."

"Are you all right?"

"Yes. Of course."

"Where's the tape?"

"Up in my closet."

"Stay there."

"You don't have to worry about that."

She gave me her address and hung up. I propped the shotgun in the corner. I called Rick Birch to tell him where I was going and why. Then I threw on my jacket, locked the place up and headed out.

I backed out of the driveway and had to slam my brakes to keep from hitting Bo Warren's red-and-white Corvette.

I got out and he got out.

"Watch where you're going, Joe!"

Four men in long coats appeared from the darkness on my right, weapons extended and trained on my chest. They closed around me and the steel of their guns pressed hard into my body. They stripped off one of my .45s and my ankle .32. A white Impala pulled up behind Warren's car. John Gaylen got out.

"Ah, Joe Trona. Let's talk."

Chapter Twenty-Seven

They moved me forward and into the white sedan—backseat, middle. Two of them got in around me. The one on my right took a rope from the floorboard, set the loop over my head and cinched it tight. I could hear the footsteps of the others as they hustled through the dark to another car. The door locks thunked down. Carl Rupaski turned in the front passenger seat and looked at me. Bo Warren's Corvette grumbled down the quiet street and Gaylen punched the Impala in behind it.

Cologne. Sweat. Gun oil.

"You were stupid to play this kind of game with me," said Rupaski. "I offer you the world, you piss on it. Well, this is what you get."

"What did Bridget get?"

"Acting lessons," said Rupaski. "I wrote out her script and we rehearsed it. I figured you'd come flying out for that alleged tape. We made the call two hundred feet from your front door."

"Where is she now?"

"In the trunk with her lips glued shut."

Gaylen hit the 91 east and drove it fast. Near the county line he got onto the 241 Toll Road. On the long grade toward Windy Ridge I looked at the stars twinkling over the hot dark hills and felt the weight of the .45 automatic that they'd failed to take. Nobody checks for three. Right side, for a left-hand draw, seven shots.

The man to my right rested a revolver on his leg and had the end of the rope wrapped three times through his left fist. The one to my left had some kind of handgun pressed into my kidney. He jammed it harder and looked at me with a challenging smile.

Rupaski turned again. In the faint light his face was etched in black and gray. Under his bushy eyebrows I could see his vulture's eyes, small and gleaming.

"They won't get five feet with that confession of Millie's," he said. "You faked Gaylen's voice somehow, and Gaylen himself will testify to that. So we're going to hold tight, Joe. Me and Jack and Millie and John, here. With you out of the chain, there's nothing. Birch can ask us questions 'til hell freezes over, but he's only getting the answers we want to give."

"He'll find a way."

"He's older than I am. We'll still be shaking our heads and taking the fifth when they put him in the grave."

I could see the lights of the Windy Ridge toll plaza coming into view. They were the only light for miles around, just darkness in every direction, all the way up to the stars.

"The service road's coming up, John," said Rupaski. "Just past that sign."

"I know where."

Gaylen stayed on the gas, then braked hard and aimed the car onto the shoulder. I could hear the gravel and sand popping under the chassis and feel the grip of the brakes. The wind shivered the stout low branches of the sagebrush and manzanita. A few yards beyond the sign he eased the car over a low curb, through an open gate in a chain-link fence clogged with tumbleweeds and onto a dirt service road. He turned right hard, killed his headlights and drove slowly back the way we had come.

A hundred yards. Two hundred. Then Gaylen turned left and followed the dirt road up a long gentle rise. I could see the dust swirling in the pale orange running lights. The hillsides were deep black and you could only tell where they ended by the stars. I looked down at the toll road and saw the cars following their headlights. Then the road leveled off and descended. Once we were over the top I couldn't see anything but the black hills and dull valley of light where the road cut through them.

"You can turn your lights back on," said Rupaski. "Turn left past the water tank."

The sagebrush and wild buckwheat looked silver in the headlights. The dry grasses looked gold. They quivered in the wind, then stopped, then quivered again.

A moment later the tank came into view, one of the big ones with the pump and riser for filling water trucks, an OCTA decal on the side. Gaylen bore left and the road got rougher.

Over another hill, then down into a meadow. You could tell it was a meadow because the stars came down lower and the breeze was weaker. The road went to washboard and the big Impala shocks took up the bumps. Rocks pinged off the bottom and every few seconds a blast of sand hissed against the body.

"You'll like this, Joe," said Rupaski. "I came out here this morning after Millie called, must have been about three A.M. Dark. Quiet. But I fired up one of the backhoes and rode out on this road with it. Used to make summer money running a backhoe for my old man. Always loved them. Anyway, I got out here in this meadow and I lowered that big old toothed blade, and guess what I did with it?"

"You dug me a grave."

"Yep. It's about eight feet deep, a little wider than your

shoulders. You'll have lovely Bridget to keep you company. So it won't be too cold."

The man to my left laughed, jammed the gun hard into my side. "I think we should bury him alive."

"Shut up," said Rupaski. "We're not savages. We're the Authority. The Transportation Authority. We're going to transport Joe and Bridget to a better place, that's all. We serve the public. It's our job and our passion. You know what the funny part is, though, Joe? I'll tell you. Ten acres of this meadow is going to be leveled and paved next month. The TA needs a new south-end service yard for all the maintenance on the new toll roads. It's not cost-effective, trailering the machines out from the Irvine hub. So anyway, you and Bridget get to look up at the bottom of our new yard. You'll be the cornerstones. I think it's funny—Will Trona's adopted freak of a son, and one of his many love bunnies, buried under a TA property. It's like something that would happen in Chicago. John, park it here. The ground's a little soft by the hole, and I sure don't want this car stuck. We'll walk it."

Gaylen stopped the car and shut off the lights and the engine. Rupaski looked back at the man on my right. "Both of you stay with him. Don't bring him out until I tell you to. How many guns you get off him?"

"Both," said the right-side man.

Rupaski smiled and got out, shut the door quietly with his hip.

With the boss gone, the left-side guy drilled the barrel into my kidney again.

"Bury you alive."

"I heard you the first time."

I heard the trunk open, felt the weight change. I saw them walk Bridget along the left side of the car, her hands stuck together behind her, each man with a grip on one of her arms.

"Bring him out," said Rupaski. "This side."

Kidney Man opened his door and got out, aiming his gun into my face. I felt the man behind me cinch up tight on the rope. I climbed out, keeping my arms close in to my body. My best hope was tucked neatly under my right armpit and I didn't want the world to know it.

I straightened and looked at Bridget. She was humming softly, like it hurt. Hair a mess, blouse out from her work skirt, mouth tight and unmoving, tears running down her cheeks.

"Don't worry," I said.

"Don't worry," said Rupaski. "Joe here's got it all under control. All right, girls, march. We've got a ways to go and I gotta be at work early tomorrow."

Rupaski took the lead with a flashlight. Bridget next. Behind her was Gaylen, with a lock on the waistline of her skirt. She wobbled in the low heels and her bright white hair stood out against the dark. She was humming harder. Kidney Man came behind Gaylen, walking backward a few steps, then forward, then backward again, watching me the best he could. Behind me was the cowboy with the rope and the six-gun.

The ground was level and sandy. An old wash, I thought, maybe a stream or spring. I could hear the distant swoosh of the cars on the toll road, and the crunching of feet on sand and dry grass. A plane droned overhead on its way into John Wayne Airport. Far out ahead of us I heard the *chick-chick* of quail as we approached their roost. It's their sound of alarm, the sound they make before they burst into flight.

"Hey Joe," called Rupaski. "How's Mary Ann these days?"

I listened to the quail out ahead of us, but I didn't answer. When Kidney Man turned his back to me to walk a few steps forward I slid my left hand up to my holster and unbuckled the strap.

"I always thought she was a real piece, Joe. I always thought that for a liberal, do-gooder, PC, bottom feeder like Will, she was quite a catch. Not to mention that she's a millionaire ten times over. Of course, he loved himself too much to just stick with one beautiful woman. He had to have a whole bunch of them."

I heard the *chick-chick* again. Then again. The faster they repeat that sound, the more afraid they are. Same place: up ahead and to our right.

I looked for the roost. High bushes. Trees. Maybe even prickly pear cactus, if the patch was wide and high enough. And if we walked close enough to it, they'd break hard and loud, and five human hearts would leap in surprise.

Calm washed over me. My eyesight sharpened. I could see the outlines of the brush up ahead, far from the jittery beam of the flashlight. And my ears heard things I normally would not: the left-right pattern of Cowboy's footsteps behind me, the rustle of Kidney Man's coat as he pivoted backward to watch me. My head felt steady and my legs felt light.

"Yeah, Joe. Besides Will always fighting us on every god-damned thing he could think of, the thing I hated most about him was Mary Ann and her money. To get that pretty and rich a woman just galled me. My wife's ugly. Always has been and always will be. But I am, too, so I didn't expect to marry Raquel Welch or something. Raquel Welch. That just shows how old I am. I should have said some young movie star but I don't know any of them anymore. Don't even go to the movies. All I do is work."

I listened to him and looked past him to the stand of manzanita off to our right. Maybe a hundred and fifty feet ahead.

Chick-chick. Chick-chick. Chick-chick.

"Say something, Joe."

"I think my mother is pretty, too, sir."

He chuckled.

"Bury alive!" said Kidney Man.

"Maybe I will. Maybe I'll just do that, Joe."

Bridget's humming got louder. The manzanita trees were about a hundred feet away. I could hear Rupaski breathing heavily and Cowboy's footsteps behind me and the birds stirring in their roost.

Chick-chick-chick. Chick-chick-chick. Chick-chick-chick.

Bridget stumbled and Gaylen held her up by her skirt. Her white hair flashed in the dark. She was still crying against her sealed lips.

"You should have known better, too, Bridget," said Rupaski. "Blackmailing me. Christ."

Fifty feet from the manzanita. The quail shuffled in the branches. Kidney Man turned back to face me and walked along backwards. I took a deep breath and two more steps.

Chick-chick-chick-chick. Chick-chick-chick-chick.

A flutter of wings.

Then the birds exploded from the roost and Kidney Man swirled away from me and ducked like he was under fire.

"What the hell?" called Rupaski.

I shot Kidney Man twice. Turned and shot Cowboy twice. Kneeled as Gaylen's arm swung my way and I shot him twice, too.

Bridget dropped and Rupaski ran.

I went after him, rope still around my neck. It didn't take me long to catch up. He was slow and heavy and I was ready for him to turn and fire. When I got into range I flew into him with a double jump-kick and sent him sprawling into the brush. I landed hard on him, knocking out his breath, then frisked him, flipped him over and frisked him again. He was gasping and trying to curse and his language was so offensive I put him out with a short left hook to his chin. I tied his hands behind him with the rope and zigzagged back to Gaylen. He was sprawled on his back, breathing fast and shallow. Tears on his cheeks, blood on his lips. His gun was beside him so I kicked it away. Neither of the others was breathing. Cowboy had a faint pulse that died under my fingertips.

I stood over John Gaylen and looked down at the man who had taken Will. I wished there was more I could do than just this. Blood and tears. Short breaths. Fingertips digging into the earth. Then Gaylen's neck strained and his throat rattled and his fingers relaxed in the dirt. None of it made any difference at all to Will.

Bridget was sitting upright in the dirt, hair in her face, legs crossed, silent. Glued hands behind her.

"Mmm," she hummed quietly.

"Yes."

"Mmm-hmm."

"I'm going to help you up."

"Mmm."

"Can you walk?"

She nodded.

I gently pulled her upright. She fell against my chest face-first and I hugged her while the crickets started up again and the moon peeked over the eastern ridge. My eyes and ears had gone back to normal. My heart was beating fast. I broke into a sweat so cold and heavy I could feel it in my socks. I felt victorious and bad.

Chapter Twenty-Eight

Three days later I drove down to a town called Fallbrook, in San Diego County. It was green and hilly and hot. A sign said "Welcome to the Friendly Village." I had lunch in a Mexican restaurant and read the local paper. The front-page news was that Fallbrook had been designated a "Point of Interest" in the new AAA guide to Southern California. It didn't say why. Another article said that Fallbrook's biggest industries were nurseries, citrus and avocados.

I followed a map out of town. The further you got, the bigger the houses were, most of them tucked into the shade of avocado or eucalyptus. There was white fencing, horses and barns, and magnolias with shiny leaves and huge white blossoms.

I found Julie Falbo's last known address, drove past it, then turned around and parked fifty yards from the mailbox. I couldn't see much of the house from where I was, just a swatch of white plaster and part of a chimney, lost in green trees. I drove around to the side and got a better view. There was a driveway leading up. The house looked old and well kept, with a clay tile roof and windows with happy blue trim. Bright violet bougainvillea climbed the columns of a portico that shaded the west side.

To the right of the driveway was a yard with a white post-and-rail fence around it. There was a swimming pool with huge Canary Island palm trees along one side and patio furniture along the other.

A woman sat on the pool deck with her back to me and her feet in the water. A small girl sat beside her. A boy rocketed off the diving board, flew with a squeal and landed with a distant splash.

I got out and pulled on my jacket and put on my hat, in spite of the heat. I walked to the gate. The boy climbed onto the diving board and spotted me and pointed. "Mom? Look!"

She turned and looked at me, then stood. She pulled on a white blouse and buttoned it while she walked toward the gate. Ten yards from me she stopped abruptly, as if an invisible hand had blocked her way. She looked mid-thirties, though I knew she was older than that. Nice figure, lovely face, thick dark hair with a red highlight in it. I could recognize her—just barely— from the one photograph I'd seen, when she was leaving the courthouse and lighting a cigarette.

She came closer, six feet away from me, and stopped again.

"I'm Joe Trona," I said.

"I know."

She stared at me and I saw some of the same hardness in her eyes that I'd seen in the photograph. For a moment the hardness disappeared, then came back again, like she could turn it on and off.

"I don't mean to disturb you, but I wanted to ask you a question."

"These are my children. This is my life. It doesn't connect with yours."

Her voice was soft and pleasant.

The girl came over and leaned against her mother's leg. She studied me, then turned and ran back to the pool and jumped in.

Her brother was in the water, looking at me, elbows locked over the deck. He screamed when she jumped over him.

"They're happy," said Julie Falbo. "I'm satisfied. My husband is caring and devoted. I'm a good wife."

"I'm pleased for all of you."

"What do you want?"

"Thor told me why he threw the acid. He told me about the money he was paid. I want to know who my father is."

She looked at me for a long moment. I could hear the children whispering in the water. Something about a monster with a hat. My half brother and half sister peered at me over the edge of the deck. Julie looked past me toward the house, and called the name Maria. The three syllables came out loud, rough and throaty.

Almost instantly, a stout dark woman appeared, hustling down the steps toward us. She gave me one quick glance, then looked down.

"Maria, watch the children."

Maria barreled past me and swung open the gate.

Julie stepped out and started down the driveway toward my car. The drive was lined with jacaranda trees that gave us a cool, mottled shade and littered the concrete in limp purple blossoms. We walked fairly far apart for people walking together. I looked at her and saw something in her face that I recognized beyond the photograph. I didn't know what it was. It was familiar but I'd never seen it before.

"This conversation won't last long," she said.

"It doesn't have to."

"I was never a nice girl. That's the most important thing you need to know about me. Never nice, always angry."

"At what?"

"I don't know," she said. "I ran away from home when I was fifteen because I saw that I could manipulate my father for whatever I wanted. I will say no more about that. I became a meth freak because I always liked fast things and when my brain was racing I was happy. Ran with bikers until I was seventeen. Got popped for pot, pills, drunk in public. Committed an aggravated assault, once. The assault was against my man, Fastball, they called him. He deserved it. I hit him with a galvanized steel pipe. The trouble was it knocked him out and he was bleeding a lot. I panicked, called 911 and they came and got him. This was up off the Ortega Highway, by San Juan Capistrano. I told the cop that Fastball had fallen down drunk, hit his head on the bench vise out in the garage. The cop didn't believe me. He came back a few hours later, asked me more questions. He still didn't believe me. But he was cool and said he thought Fastball probably deserved it, no matter what happened. So they didn't pop me for that.

"I got pregnant a few months later. It wasn't Fastball. I was trying to stay clean, kicking the speed, staying low, waiting tables. I was eighteen. I met Thor. He was forty. He rode but he wasn't ganged up, just a guy who liked bikes and drugs. He had a job for a while and he liked me a lot. It wasn't like I had a lot of time to find someone better. I started up with him and a month later, told him I'd missed my period, was going to have his baby. He was happy and stupid. It wasn't until after you were born that he started to get suspicious. I might have said something, I don't know. We were always drunk and fighting. He checked the dates and the calendar and said I'd tricked him—you couldn't have been his. I said, so what? Who cares? You're changing his diapers and feeding him out of your lousy gas station job, so what's the difference? That night it got bad. We drank and fought again and did some crank and the next thing I know there's this coffee mug of sulfuric acid he got from one of his meth friends. You were in an orange crate in the kitchen. He tossed the stuff in and it went all over the side of your face. He saw what it did and freaked. Like he was surprised he'd done it, surprised how bad it was. He picked you up and stuck your head under the sink faucet to rinse it off. Didn't work. Tried newspaper, but that didn't work either. The stuff just kept eating away."

I looked at her and she looked at me. Her eyes were dark brown, like mine. No amount of time or makeup or the natural beauty of her face could take away the coldness in them.

"What did you do?"

"I split. I didn't want the next dose on *my* face."

I looked at her, but she wouldn't look back. Her eyes were turned downward and she was focusing in, not out. Something thick rose in her throat.

I could see the basic shape of my head in hers, the same fundamental structure of my face, the same angle and set of the ears and nose. And something of me in her posture too, the way she held herself.

"I called one of my cop friends from a pay phone down in Elsinore. I found out later he went to the house, but Thor had already taken you to the fire station. He rode you on his hog, tucked in his arm like a football. That's because I'd taken the car. I never could figure how he shifted gears. Maybe he just used first or second. It wasn't that far a drive. Anyway. That's what happened. There's worse things, worse stories. When I look back I think it was bad, but then I read the papers and realize it wasn't such a big deal, compared to what happens today. I look around me and I realize you can change and improve yourself and get rid of the past. That's what I did. I don't think about it anymore."

In her profile I saw again what I'd recognized but couldn't define. Even in the photograph, a little of it had shown. I still couldn't put a finger on it. But it was there and I knew it and I knew what it was. The Unknown Thing. Julie Falbo had it. Charlotte Wample had had it, too.

We walked through the fallen jacaranda blossoms. Through the trees the sky was blue and streaked with clouds. I looked at her and a purple blossom fell and stuck in her red-black hair. She carefully rolled it out then flicked it to the driveway like you would a cigarette butt. I realized she was beautiful. She'd become that way since her picture was taken twenty-three years ago. She had looked sharp and hungry back then. Now, she looked filled and strong. It was like some gentle carpenter had taken a sharp young stick and shaped a smooth, beautiful thing from it.

And I understood. Fastball had seen The Unknown Thing in her. Thor had seen it. Even the cop who'd answered Charlotte Wample's 911 had seen it in her, too. He'd seen it very clearly and it had cost everyone.

"The cop who rolled on the 911," I said. "He wasn't a cop. He was a sheriff's deputy."

"He was ten years older than me, married, two kids. He was fabulous to look at. He could talk. Man, could he talk. Energy you wouldn't believe. He made my speed jags look like naps. He loved me. Deputy-Two Will Trona, Orange County Sheriff's, at your service, little missy."

She stopped walking and turned to me. The hard eyes peered at me from the soft face and it was like two women were there.

"I thought it was good when he adopted you. I know he and his wife couldn't conceive. I knew him well enough to know he could give you all the love I couldn't. He kept paying Thor, to protect the rest of his family from his little indiscretion. I'm glad you had a decent place to grow up. And got to go to college and get on with the sheriff's department. I'm sorry you didn't get to know you were his until now."

"Thank you for telling me the truth."

"Is that your car?"

"It was Will's."

"I drive the big Lexus. It's the fastest production sedan in its class."

"They say that on the commercials."

"Please go."

"Wait. If Thor's payments stop, he'll want to talk about what happened and why. It's bothering his tiny soul. And he'll realize it will make him famous all over again."

"I'm taking over those payments. Good-bye."

"I want to know one more thing. You said you couldn't love me. Why?"

Her face was soft but her eyes were hard. "God didn't put my heart in right. It only beats for my own benefit. Everything I do is to get something else."

"Then why not abort me?"

"I thought you'd be worth some money from Will. After Thor did what he did, I didn't think you were worth the trouble."

I thought for a moment. She looked back toward the pool. I could see the boy arching through the air, arms out, legs pumping, a whirl of brown against the blue sky.

"I understand the emptiness in your heart," I said. "I have some, too."

"Not as much as I do, I hope."

"No."

"Will had a full heart. Maybe in you there's the right amount of both."

"I met someone and it feels full now."

Her face went red and tears came to her pale eyes, but they didn't melt the hardness. Her eyes looked cold and wet as quartz at nine thousand feet.

"Good-bye, son. Go."

"Good-bye, Mother. I'm pleased to have met you."

Chapter Twenty-Nine

I still dream poppies. Fields of poppies stretching up into the hills. Sometimes they turn to flames on a man's face, and I realize that face is mine. But sometimes they're just flowers and those are mine too, bright and fragile and brave.

I dream beautiful faces. One face comes back again and again. It's slender and straight and the eyes are a deep brown that sometimes holds laughter and sometimes shatters into lightning. The skin is moist copper and the mouth is small. My heart beats hard. Sometimes the face wakes me up and I reach out and find it beside me, really there, lost in the pillow, locked in sleep. I'll brush the outline of it with my palm and feel the tickle of hair and ear and cheek.

And there's another face, too, not too unlike the first. But it's a man's face and I can see the strength of the jaw and the whiskers on his skin and the hunger in his eyes. Sometimes the hunger is regret and he tries to tell me something but can't get all the words out. He makes the same beginning over and over: *I think you should know . . . I think you should know . . . I think you should know. . . .* And when I dream that face I always tell it the same thing: *I know, I know, I know.* And he leans back and his eyelids droop but his eyes are sharp and he looks at me with pride of ownership, and with a critical coolness that says I can be improved.

And I dream a woman who is full of The Unknown Thing. Her face is lovely but her eyes are hard, and she is always turning away so I have to circle her to see her and even then she turns a little faster and I can never quite catch up, never quite get the view of her that I want. Finally, she's nothing but a whirling blur that slowly vanishes. Good-bye. I'm pleased to have met you.

Baptism won't work anymore. The desire is gone. Instead, I feel a powerful craving to stand in moving water. I tried the beach, but it was too crowded, and the water I need has to flow only one direction. I stood in the gutter on my street one day when one of the neighbors was overwatering her lawn, and let the dark trickle move past my feet. I could feel the beginning of true cleansing but I needed more volume. It was like a song on a distant radio I couldn't quite hear.

So I found a river to stand in. Actually, it's just a creek. There are crawdads and frogs and turtles and small gray fish, and all sorts of shorebirds, both exotic and common. It's not far from my house and it runs even in the summer. If I stand there in the middle, with the shore just yards away on either side, I can feel the gentle movement of the water against my ankles.

A rush of water would be better—a massive, mile-wide surge filled with riffles and rapids and pools and history. My creek is only a few inches deep. But if I close my eyes and let the sin and the scar and the ugliness run out of my heart, the water of the creek takes it away.

I've made a list of the great rivers of the nation, and want to stand in each one before I die. In a blue notebook I've written out a loose schedule that spans five decades and thirty-one rivers. I'm going to start with the Colorado, which is a nice drive from Orange County if you pick up the southern end of it, along the California-Arizona border. After that, the Russian, the Eel, the Sacramento, the Columbia, and so on. By the time I hit the Hudson I'll be an old man. I wonder if sitting in a rocking chair in a river would work. Maybe you could lie on the bank and dangle a foot or a finger.

A week later, they released Savannah to her mother. I talked to her a couple of times each day, usually by phone, and Savannah seemed stronger as the week went by. She told me that she and her mother were going to stay in the Aspen house for the rest of the summer. I visited them once at Pelican Point. Lorna looked alert and sober. Savannah had gained weight. I was surprised when Lorna handed me a check for $100,000 and told me she knew about her husband's offer to me for Savannah's safe return. I took it.

We released Alex in exchange for testimony against his father. And because Phil Dent didn't think the kidnapping charges would hold up if Alex's lawyer put Savannah on the stand and she explained that she had gone to Alex, not the other way around, and had always been free to leave. Alex vanished, as he's so good at doing.

Jack Blazak stayed in jail, of course, in protective custody in Mod J, facing charges of manslaughter for beating Luria Blas and of murder with special circumstances in the death of Will Trona. Melissa in the crime lab has typed his blood against the flesh sample found beneath Luria Blas's fingernail, and established that that flesh once belonged to Mr. Blazak. Her fingernail—that little scratch—will sink him, even if Savannah's tape is eventually ruled inadmissible as evidence.

When we searched Gaylen's car after his death, Rick Birch came up with $35,000 cash, hidden where the spare tire should have been. I think that money was Jack Blazak's way of upgrading a beating to an execution. Even a murderer like Gaylen has his pay scale. I think Bo Warren passed it along to Gaylen before the hit, maybe that night in the parking lot of Bamboo 33. I'm hoping Warren sheds some light on this, when Dent starts to tighten the knot around his neck.

Old Carl Rupaski was also in Mod J, charged with conspiracy in the death of Will, and with forcible kidnapping and attempted murder of Bridget Andersen and me.

Bo Warren got ad-segged—administrative segregation—in Module F because we didn't think he had a high enough public profile to be housed in Mod J. He's facing the same charges as Rupaski. They put him in cell twenty-four, between a white supremacist killer who likes to sing to himself and a talkative armed robber. My friends tell me that Warren feels snubbed in Mod F, which we were hoping he would. Pride might loosen his tongue. The guards tell me that he hates the jail more than any man they've ever seen.

We're using Millbrae to make our case against the three other conspirators. Of course, they're all pointing their fingers at our frightened little rat and at the now defenseless John Gaylen. Their lawyers are leaking stuff to the press every hour, it seems. Millie is *this* close to being arrested. That will be Dent's call. I don't care one way or another whether Millbrae does time. He's a coward and he's ruined and that's enough. He was one of the gophers, anyway, not the Brutus. He was our slippery, reluctant little key.

Bernadette Lee and Pearlita Escobar and Del Pritchard are cooperating with us too, for self-serving reasons of their own.

No one has mentioned the close proximity of the Reverend Daniel Alter to all of what happened. Just wait, if the media gets wind of that. His sermons have been impassioned lately, filled with humility and prayers for redemption and forgiveness. In an act of atonement that few understood, Daniel established a fund for the family of Luria Blas and Miguel Domingo. I thought of donating Lorna's $100,000 but June said this was foolishness. Together, we looked up Enrique Domingo, Luria's little brother. We took him to lunch and when we said good-bye we gave him a new backpack with the hundred large. I put one of my cards and one of Mary Ann's lawyer's cards in one compartment of the bag, in case he was stopped and questioned. So far, no call from Enrique.

I was surprised to get a call from Jennifer Avila. She told me that she'd been used by Pearlita. Pearlita, she said, had been furious at Will for refusing to help her accused brother. This, after Pearlita had led Will to the Ritz-Carlton in Dana Point, which was where he'd found Alex and Savannah. *I'll do what I can do, but I still can't turn coal into a diamond.* Jennifer had called Pearlita from the HACF that night to confirm that Will was there, believing that the shot-caller wanted one more chance to plead Felix's case to Will. Then Pearlita had called Will later that night—with the number that Jennifer had given her—in order to confirm for Gaylen that Will was on his way to the pickup. Jennifer speculated that Pearlita's fury had inspired her to hit Ike Cao on Gaylen's behalf, though certainly some money was involved—the cash in the trunk of Gaylen's car took on a new possibility. Jennifer said she hadn't understood all of this until later. She'd never heard of John Gaylen until after it was over. I believe her. She's too proud a woman to apologize to me for such a huge foolishness, but the crack in her voice apologized for her.

Then she answered a question that I thought would never be answered. I'd wondered about it, but hadn't known who to ask until then. Of all the people on Earth, Jennifer would have been the one that Will would tell.

"Why did he leave me out?" I asked.

"Because he was ashamed," she said. "He was using a girl

to get to her father. He argued with himself about whether he should go through with it or not. He kept changing his mind. He kept wondering what you would think if you knew the whole story. I told him from the start to just turn Savannah over to Child Protective Services. But Will couldn't let go of his opportunity to ruin Blazak. He hated himself for it, but went ahead with it, just the same. It killed him. He told me he wanted to take you up in the world, not down in it. So he didn't include you until the very end. When it was supposed to end happily. He took you along that night so you could see him be a hero."

I had to think about that for a long moment. "In twenty years, he never once asked me for an opinion about himself."

"He adored you. I think he loved you more than his own sons, even though you were adopted."

With a mental health clearance from Dr. Zussman, Sergeant Delano reassigned me out of Men's Central and Module J. Too much potential for conflict, since so many inmates are tied to Will. I'm over at the Musik Honor Farm now, which is out in the country, kind of, and more relaxed. I miss the regimentation, the order, the strictness of Men's Central and Module J.

Last week they did a surprise shake of Sammy's cell, and they turned up a clean little zip gun made from a Cross ballpoint pen, some aluminum from a soft drink can and the spring from a rat trap. He'd used the steel temple rod from his glasses as a firing pin, and had put the thing together using some tiny screws from his eyeglass repair kit. They never found the rest of the trap. Likely, he broke it down and flushed it. No one has any idea where Sammy finally got it. Maybe the same way he got his dog nail clippers, which I now understand he wanted for the powerful spring. The zip gun was outfitted with a .22 rimfire cartridge and would have been fully lethal. Sergeant Delano has launched an intense investigation as to how Sammy got his hands on live ammunition inside Module J. The gun was small enough to conceal and carry in a body cavity or slipped in between the layers of a tennis shoe sole.

A day later, they intercepted a kite from Sammy—intended for Bernadette—specifying an escape plan. It was to begin with Sammy faking convulsions in order to be sent to the Western Medical Center. Once there, Sammy planned to shoot his keeper with the zip gun, disguise himself as a doctor and meet Bernadette in the parking lot. It said right in Sammy's kite that he hoped that the keeper wouldn't be me. Sammy stands to do more time for this felony, though he's likely to draw death for shooting Patrolman Dennis Franklin.

Still, I miss him. And Chapin Fortnell and Frankie Dilsey and Giant Mike Staich and the other murderers, rapists and sociopaths of Mod J. I miss the quiet tension of the mess hall, the wood car and the black car, the Mexican car and the Asian car, this highway of criminals waiting in line to be fed. Hands in your pockets. No talking. Seat left-to-right. Somehow, it all reminds me of me.

I miss my mechanics' sled and the long hours hidden in the plumbing tunnel, listening to the plans and dreams and desires of men in cages. June told me that the fresh air of the Honor Farm would do me good. It should, and I believe almost everything she says, but I'm waiting to see. I've got another year of jail—whatever branch they put me in—but then I'll be eligible for reassignment to patrol.

Patrol.

I'll be a real cop.

I thought long and hard about whether or not to tell my mother about Will and Charlotte Wample. Should I add to the miseries of her grieving heart? Should I let the lie stand and work its slow poison, as lies always do? Was it possible that she would be strengthened in some way, knowing that Will's blood flowed in me—regardless of the way it had gotten there?

One Sunday evening, sitting under the umbrella beside the pool of our home in the Tustin hills, I told her the story.

When I was finished she sat there and sipped her drink and looked out at the green, smog-softened hills.

"Well. Well, Joe. I'm not sure what to say to that."

"You don't need to say anything."

"Will, Will, Will. His lies go on and on."

"This one just stopped. I love you. And I always will. You're my mother."

We stood and she hugged me long and hard, and I hugged back. We said a lot with that hug. A lot about loyalty and betrayal, silence and secrets, pain and strength, forgiveness and love. Mostly about love.

June and I took our first trip together at the end of July. It was just for the weekend—two nights in a place called Bullhead City. Bullhead City is right on the Colorado River and the hotel I booked promised a riverside room with a patio overlooking the majestic Colorado.

We started our drive from her house at nine on a Saturday morning. I drove my Mustang because the county took back Will's car. I was sorry to give it up because it was a good car and it was his. The Mustang is loud and fast and punishing, and after an hour of it you feel like you've been on a carnival ride that won't let you off. We stopped to make love in Riverside, Barstow and Needles, which that day was the hottest city in the nation at 122 degrees. In Riverside we had a large, late breakfast. In Barstow we got hamburgers and root beer floats. In Needles we bought a foam cooler and a six-pack of beer, which we drank on the road. The four-hour drive took nine.

Bullhead City wasn't as beautiful as the brochure made it

out to be. But it was right on the Colorado and our room was cool and quiet and spacious. The downside was that the river was filled with zooming speedboats, careening water-skiers and jet skis driven by seemingly suicidal drunks. But at night they disappeared and the dark water flowed quietly from right to left on its way to Mexico.

Late that night we walked out into it, up to our knees, and felt the cool power moving through us. I held June's hand and closed my eyes and let all of what I didn't want inside me flow down into that water. I imagined the faces of the men I'd killed, and they flowed out of me into the river. I imagined my mother's pain and it flowed into the river, too. I imagined Will and all his secrets, all his hatreds and rivalries and seductions, and they flowed out of my blood and into the river. I imagined my own face and Thor, they passed into the river. I imagined all of these things spreading into the world, moving farther and farther away. I knew they would come back. The important things always come back. Even if they're ugly and you never wanted them inside you in the first place. The river wasn't going to keep anything. It was just going to take the things I had to offer, care for them a while, then give them back to me. Because I was where they belonged.

Will was back inside me before we even made the bank. I carried him back to the hotel with us and he was right there with me on the patio as June and I sat there and looked out at the moonlit water.

I took hold of June's hand and thought about The Unknown Thing, and how June seemed to me to be made of it. I thought about the women I had seen it in, and I realized that it has something to do with goodness and something to do with wickedness but much more to do with what is irresistible. It can lead a man to shame as easily as it can lead him to love.

"What are you thinking about?" June asked.

"You."

"Good things?"

"Good things."

I could have told her the fuller truth, and tried to explain how powerfully her Unknown Thing was pulling me toward her and how it could easily make a fool out of me or us.

But I'm my father's son. So I took his advice again, for the millionth time and counting.

I said nothing more. I held her hand and watched the river glide by, silver on black, bearing sins and secrets, laughter and light.

Eyes open, mouth shut. You might learn something.

I have spoken to you from memory. There are gaps. There is more. I have learned just a few things.

Save your friends, spend your enemies.

Who did it?

Everyone.

What do you say when you're a man with a face like mine, blood on his hands, and a heart that burns hot enough to love and runs cold enough to kill? What do you tell the person next to you?

Look at me. Because I'm looking at you.

Love Merci Rayborn?

Want More?

READ

BLACK WATER

The scene is gruesome: The lovely young wife, shot dead in the bathroom, wearing the purple satin robe her husband had just given her for her twenty-sixth birthday. The handsome husband, a promising young cop, found with a bullet in his head on the threshold of their home. An attempted murder-suicide— the murder in the bathroom was successful, the suicide on the threshold wasn't.

A sharp, twisting new thriller from the Edgar-nominated author of *Red Light* and *Silent Joe,* bringing back Detective Merci Rayborn, and proving yet again that there is no better suspense writer than T. Jefferson Parker.

Chapter One

A rchie pushed the gear shift into third and set his hand on her knee. Coast Highway, southbound. Man in the moon big and close, like he was tilting his head for a peek down into the convertible. Archie glanced up, couldn't tell if the guy was smiling or frowning. Didn't care because Gwen's skin was warm through the dress, a few degrees warmer than the breeze gusting through the car.

He looked at the speedometer then at her. Saw her hair moving, her face sketched in the orange glow of the dashboard lights. A silver champagne flute in one hand, a smile.

Archie pretended he'd never seen her before. Pretended he was trying to look at something else—the squid boat off of Crystal Cove in a pool of white light, say—only to have this Gwen creature drop into his world like some special effect. There she was. What luck.

He lifted the hem of her dress up over her knees and slipped his hand under. She eased back in the seat a little and he heard the breath catch in her throat. He caught the faint smell of her, windblown but unmistakable. Archie had a sharp nose and loved what it brought him. Like right now, the milk-and-orange-blossoms smell of Gwen, bass scent of his life. All the other notes that came to him—coastal sage and the ocean, the new car leather—were just the riffs and fills.

She smiled and tossed the plastic champagne flute in the air, the darkness stealing it without a sound. Then she slid her hand under there with his, popping up the cotton dress and letting it settle like a bedspread while she trailed a finger up his forearm and over his wrist.

"Long way home, Arch."

"Five whole miles."

"What a night. It's cool when we mix our friends and they get along."

"They're all great. Priscilla drank a lot."

"The cops put it away, too. Thanks, Arch. You spent a fortune for all that."

"Worth it. You only turn twenty-six once."

Gwen's curls lifted in a random swirl and she pulled his hand in a little closer. She didn't speak for a long moment. "Twenty-six. I'm lucky. Will you love me when I'm thirty-six? Eighty-six?"

"Done deal."

"I'm really sorry about earlier."

"Forget it. I have. Damned temper."

A serene moment then, as the roar of the engine mixed with the comfort of forgiveness.

"I can't wait to get home, Arch. I'll be outrageously demanding, since it's my birthday. It is still my birthday, isn't it?"

"For about three minutes."

"Hmmm. Maybe you ought to pull over."

Archie downshifted and looked for a turn off the highway. There was one at the state beach, one for the trailer park, another one back by the juice stand. They'd used all of them, just one of those things they loved to do. She'd sit on his lap with her back to him. Up that high she looked like a tourist craning for a view of something, one hand on the arm rest and the other on the dash. The great thing about the new convertible was he could look up past the back of Gwen's head at the stars, then at her again, put his nose in her hair or against her neck and wonder what he'd done to deserve her. For a young man, Archie Wildcraft was not a complete fool, because he understood, at thirty, that he'd done nothing at all to deserve her. Dumb luck, pure and simple.

"There's the turn," she said, pointing.

"I love you," he said.

"I love you, Arch. You're always going to be my man, aren't you."

It wasn't really a question so he didn't answer. He braked and steered off the highway and into the darkness.

Four hours later, Deputy Wildcraft jerked awake when he heard something loud in the living room.

Gwen slept right through it, so Archie cupped one hand firmly over her mouth as he raised her from sleep. Her eyes grew large as he whispered what he'd heard. He prodded her out of the bed and toward the bathroom, which was where Archie had told her to go if something like this ever happened. All the time Archie was trying to listen but he heard nothing from the living room, the house, the whole world.

He watched as she pulled her new purple robe off the floor and moved through the room shadows toward the bath. Archie got a thirty-eight autoloader from under the bed. He set it on his pillow while he pulled on his underwear—comic, "Happy Birthday—I'm Yours" boxers with a big red ribbon printed around the opening. They'd made her laugh. Him too, and they'd made love again and fallen asleep damp and tangled in the sheets.

He put on his robe and picked up the gun. Then he got the phone and carried it toward the bathroom, where a thin horizon of light shone under the door. He opened it and gave her the phone and whispered *don't worry this guy picked the wrong house to burgle maybe just a bird flew into a window if something goes wrong call 911 but let me check it out first.*

I'll call it now, Archie.

Don't call it until I tell you to call it. Turn out the light the twenty-two's under the sink with a full clip and one in the chamber. The safety's down by the triggerguard, push it 'til the red shows.

Be careful.

I'll be careful.

Archie got his flashlight and walked out of the room and into the familiar hallway. Carpet, bare feet hardly making a sound. There was a light switch at the end of the hall, where it opened to the living room. He flipped it on but didn't step in, just stood there scanning—right to left then back again over the sights of the automatic: wall, sofa, window blinds with a big hole in them, chair, wall with a painting, Gwen's birthday presents on the floor. Then the same things again, but in reverse.

He looked down at the big rock in the middle of the living room carpet. Size of a grapefruit. Saw the shards of glass twinkling near the slider. Saw where the wooden blinds had been splintered when the rock came through. Offed the light and listened. The refrigerator hummed and car tires hissed in the distance.

Archie moved quietly into the kitchen and hit another light. The kitchen was empty and undisturbed. Breakfast nook the same. Little family room with the TV and fireplace looked fine, too, just the VCR clock glowing a steady 4:28 A.M.

He checked the bath and the laundry room. Went back to the living room and shined his flashlight down on the rock. Kind of a rounded square, red and smooth with clear skinny marbles running through it like fat. Schist, thought Archie, veined with quartz. Common.

He wondered who'd do something infantile and destructive like this. Kids, probably—don't know who lives here, just want to bust something up, video it, have a story to tell. Maybe some forgotten creep he'd shoved around in Orange County jail when he started work eight years ago. Cops make enemies every day and Archie had made his. They all came to his mind, though none more than any other. The crime lab could get latents off that schist.

All of this sped through Archie's brain as he unlocked the front door, slipped outside and quietly pulled the door shut behind him.

The moon was gone so he turned on the flashlight, scanned the porch and the bushes around it. A rabbit crashed through the leaves and Archie's heart jumped. He stepped across the porch then down to the walkway. It was lined with Chinese flame trees and yellow hibiscus and bird of paradise. The drooping branches of the flame trees made a tunnel. Archie followed the walk around to the back, moving his light beam with his left hand, dangling the thirty-eight in his right.

He stayed on the walk and it led him around the swimming pool. The water was flat and polished and Archie remarked for maybe the millionth time what a beautiful home they lived in now, big but plenty of charm, on a double lot in the hills with this pool and a three-car garage and palm trees fifty feet high leading up the driveway. An extra room for his viewing stones. An extra room for Gwen's music. An extra room for the baby someday.

He continued along the curving walkway then stopped in front of the window where the rock had come through. The beam of his flashlight picked up the big ragged hole and the gleam of fissures spreading in all directions. He saw no footprints, no disturbance of the grass.

Archie stood still and listened, clicked off his flashlight. Never did hear a getaway car. Kids, he thought again: they would throw the rock, haul ass giggling along the west fence, jump it at the corner and be down the hill before he'd gotten Gwen into the bathroom. He thought of her just then, standing in the hard light with her robe on, hair all messed up, scared as a bird and listening to every little sound, the twenty-two probably still in the cabinet under the sink because she didn't like guns. And he thought what a jealous little jerk he'd been for a few minutes at the party. Married to her for eight years and he'd still feel his anger rise when his own friends hugged and kissed her.

He missed her. Wondered what in hell he was doing out here with his happy birthday boxers and a gun and his wife afraid in a locked bathroom a hundred feet away.

He turned back up the walk. Past the pool. Into the tunnel of trees. Then a beam of sharp light in his eyes and by the time he found the flashlight button it was too late.

Up close, an orange explosion.

Bright white light and Archie watching himself fly into it, a bug in the universe, a man going home.

Chapter Two

Sergeant Merci Rayborn nodded at the two deputies standing at the front door of the Wildcraft house. One of them handed her an Order-of-Entry log which she signed after checking her watch. She was a tall woman with a dark pony tail that rode up the orange letters on the back of her windbreaker as she wrote, then down again as she handed back the clipboard.

"Who got here first and where are they?"

"Crowder and Dobbs, Sergeant. In the kitchen area, I believe."

The other uniform looked past her head and said nothing.

In the entryway Merci Rayborn stood still and received. Smell of furniture wax and wood. Smell of flowers. Murmur of voices. She looked at the entryway mirror, the living room furniture, the carpet. She looked at the hole in the blinds, which suggested a hole in the glass behind. She looked at a rock the size of a newborn's head lying near the middle of the floor. At the little pile of gift boxes. No alarm system—kitchen, maybe.

"Merci."

Paul Zamorra came softly down the hallway, light on his feet. And dark in his heart, Merci thought. He had the gentle deliberateness of an undertaker. And the black suit, too.

She turned to her partner. "Paul. Do you know this guy?"

"Not well. You know, just a friendly face. We'd talked."

"Wildcraft. I'm sure we talked, too."

Though she wasn't sure of that at all. The department was sharply divided into people who approved of what Merci Rayborn had done and people who didn't. Some of them wouldn't talk to her, nor she to them unless she had to. This hurt Merci deeply, as if the two halves of her heart detested each other. She had come to distrust all opinions and was trying to get rid of her own.

But Deputy 2 Archie Wildcraft? She remembered nothing about him but his unusual name. Now he was in the hospital with at least one gunshot to his head and little chance of living.

"His wife is the other, Merci. Gwen Wildcraft. She's in the bathroom."

Merci led down the hallway, noting the textured plaster, the black and white Yosemite photographs in brushed stainless steel frames, the way the track lights were aimed to display them. She stopped at the thermostat and noted that it had been set at seventy. She walked past another deputy then down into a large bedroom with French doors and gauzy curtains. Big sleigh bed with the covers messed up. Smell of perfume and human beings.

The bathroom door was open. The door frame was splintered and the lock plate dangled by two screws. Merci leaned over the crime scene tape and looked in.

Here, very different smells—the sharp afterburned scent of nitrocellulose and something faintly metallic and sweet. Gwen Wildcraft lay beside the toilet, back to the floor but her head against the wall at a hard angle, facing down and to her right. Eyes closed, mouth open, arms and legs spread, purple robe almost matching the blood on the wall, the floor, the shower door, the counter and mirror. More from her nose and mouth. Merci noted the cell phone lying face-up in the right-hand sink.

This was Rayborn's 67th homicide scene as an investigator for the Orange County Sheriff's Department. For the 67th time she told herself to see, not feel. Think, not feel. Work, not feel. But, not for the first time in her life, Rayborn told herself she couldn't keep on looking.

"Let's get Crowder and Dobbs."

"All right," said Zamorra.

* * *

The four of them stood in the breakfast nook. Looking into the kitchen, Merci noted the fresh pot of coffee on the maker, unpoured, the machine still wheezing. A timer, she thought, confidently programmed to make coffee that Archie and Gwen Wildcraft would never touch. A red colander filled with oranges sat on the counter and a curved wooden stand dangled a bunch of pale bananas. The word *waste* came to her mind, as it often did.

Crowder was a big man with short gray hair brushed into a severe 1950's flat-top, a little island of scalp showing at the top. He reminded her of a man she'd been in love with many years ago—three to be exact. Crowder watched as Merci brought out a new blue notebook and her good pen, and she wondered if he hated her.

"We were down on Moulton, stopped for coffee. Dispatch said possible gunshot reported in Hunter Ranch. Wasn't a nine-one-one but we rolled right then. It was five-ten. We came in quiet because it's a good neighborhood, wasn't a hot call. Got here at five-fourteen. The house looked okay from the outside. Nobody around, no neighbors, nothing. Houselights showing from a couple of places inside."

"What about outside?"

"No."

"The driveway?"

"No."

She asked twice because two floodlights had been on when she first walked up the Wildcraft driveway. That was just after six, on the cusp of sunrise.

Merci made notes in a loop-crazy shorthand, her subjects separated by slashes like lyrics quoted in a review. CK meant check, always capitals and underlined, sometimes circled if the question seemed extra important. She wrote, *drive lights mo-det? CK/*, then looked up at Zamorra.

"Paul, how many cars in the driveway when you got here?"

"Four."

"Let's have a look where not before we leave tonight. The concrete's new and it could hold a track. Make sure the CSIs examine it before the battalion moves out."

"Yes."

Crowder looked out one of the mullioned breakfast nook windows. Merci followed his gaze to a large fenced yard, patio and orange trees, all sharp with color in the August morning.

Dobbs let out a short sigh. He was young and hard-jawed, with arm muscles that almost filled out his green uniform shirt. Smooth, ruddy face. "Look. We called for backup and paramedics when we found Archie on the other side of the house. We searched the house and found his wife in the bathroom. We taped it off. And by that time the driveway was full, new concrete or not."

Merci looked at him. "Next time think before you open a parking lot."

"I'll stand by my actions, sergeant."

"See where that gets you. You just learned something about your work, deputy. I was thinking you'd done a pretty decent job, considering what you walked into."

Dobbs looked away.

"Anyway," said Crowder. "We rang the bell but didn't get an answer. Porch lights off, but lights on inside. Decided to walk around the house, see what we could see. Wildcraft was on his back on the walkway, about halfway around. Bleeding from the head but still breathing. Wearing a robe. Then, like Dobbs said, we called in, went inside and found the wife. I left two footprints and a kneeprint in that bathroom somewhere. You know, checked her artery, but there was nothing."

"Was there a bathroom light on when you went in?"

"Yeah," said Crowder. "I could still smell the gunsmoke."

Merci smelled nothing of guncotton out here, just the faint sweet smell of wood polish and coffee.

"What did you see driving up?" Zamorra asked.

Dobbs crossed his big arms. "Yes, sir. A black, late model Cadillac made the north turn at Jacaranda when we were turning up. That would be an expected car in this neighborhood, but it was still just a little—past five in the morning. Two white males—early to mid-thirties, plus or minus five. There's a streetlight at the intersection, but it's weak."

"See faces?"

"Very briefly, sir. Passenger was dark-haired, bearded, big face, thick black glasses—you know, I mean the frame part was black and thick. What I thought was, *heavy*. The driver was blond, and I thought *businessman*. I mean, these were instant impressions, sir, just . . . flashes. But they both looked unusual."

"How?" Merci asked.

Dobbs ignored her and spoke only to Zamorra.

"Unusual facial structures."

"What do you mean?" Zamorra asked.

"You know, like when you're down in Laguna on the boardwalk and you can spot the tourists from other countries? Just the faces, you know, the way they formulate. I read in a magazine it's from the facial muscles used to pronounce different languages. You know, like a French face looks different from an American one because their face muscles help make different sounds."

"So, they were French?" asked Zamorra, with a small smile.

Dobbs chuckled. "I couldn't say, sir."

"Take a guess," said Merci.

"I wouldn't guess with so little information," Dobbs said, finally looking at her. "That would be pointless."

Merci felt the blast of anger go through her. After thirty-seven years of trying to stop it she still couldn't, but she'd learned to put her anger into thoughts that could contain it. And sometimes amuse her. What she thought about Dobbs and his condescending arrogance was *give him the guillotine*.

"Since you're big on points, Dobbs, what was the point of parking your car in the driveway of a homicide scene and letting everybody else do the same?"

Merci felt ashamed at harping on this but she had to say something and that was what came out. It was her nature to grab and not let go. If Dobbs disliked her for what she'd done, that was even more reason for him to suck it up, get along, do the job. In her opinion, anyway.

"Look, Sergeant Rayborn," said Crowder. "I'll take the blame for that. I thought about the concrete and figured this was another report that would come down to firecrackers or an engine backfire. I should have said something. I just let him park where he wanted. By the time we found what we found, the backup and medics were here. We were in the bathroom."

"I understand that," she said.

She walked around the quaint little breakfast table and stood in front of Dobbs, got up close and looked straight into his eyes. She saw the uncertainty there and enjoyed it.

"I might have parked there, too," she said. "I don't care about the driveway. The driveway is history. What I care about is you treating your fellow cops like fellow cops instead of something stuck to the bottom of your boot. It's still *us* and *them* deputy. If you don't like me, fine. If you don't like what I did, fine. But keep it to yourself and we'll all be able to do our jobs better. You saw Gwen and Archie. I think we've got bigger things to worry about than our own opinions of each other. What do you think, deputy?"

"Right, sergeant," said Dobbs.

Merci heard a somewhat reduced hostility coming from the man. It was the best she could expect. In the year since her actions had publicly torn apart the department she loved, Merci had basically shut up. She'd taken the oath and told the truth. After that she had little left to say, and no one in particular to say it to. And she'd found that silence confuses the enemy.

But when it came to this, a subordinate officer trying to belittle her in front of fellow professionals, well, this was stomping time. It had happened before. In this last year she'd learned that confrontations were like haircuts—there were good ones and bad ones but none of them changed the essential truth. And the essential truth was that there were many people on the force who would never approve of what she'd done, never forget and never forgive.

So if the man piped down even just a little, it was good enough.

"Thank you," she said.

"I'm pissed off about this, sergeant. Archie wasn't a close friend of mine but I liked him. He was a good guy."

"Then let's work together and get the creep who did this a nice stiff death sentence."

"Yes."

"Okay. Now—French, German, Latvian, Croat, Russian, Finn or Dane? I'm confident that any Orange County Sheriff Deputy could tell the difference in two seconds at five in the morning under a weak street lamp."

Dobbs smiled but still colored. Merci stepped away with a very minor grin.

"Deputies," she said. "Call Dispatch and get us an all-county stop-and-question on that car. Sheriff's Department only. Tell them to use the computers and not the radios, because Sergeant Rayborn doesn't want any gawkers involved. We're one hour cold but it's worth a try. If they're tourists, maybe they got stuck in our famous traffic."

"Yes," said Dobbs.

"Then, go round up the caller. If he won't come over, tell him I'll be knocking on his door real soon and real loud. On the way back, one of you should count your steps between his place and this one."

In her small blue notebook—blue because the man who had taught her to be a homicide detective used blue, and because she had loved him—she scribbled the name and address of the caller who'd reported hearing gunshots, tore off the small sheet and gave it to Dobbs.

"Go ahead, and hear him out on your way back here."

She saw that Dobbs understood her vote of confidence, her encouraging him to informally question the witness. She winced inwardly at what the muscular but not stupendously bright Dobbs might come up with on his informal interview. But in her experience two versions from the same witness were always better than one because contradictions stood out like billboards.

Dobbs nodded and they walked away. At the front door they parted and stood back for District Attorney Clay Brenkus and one of his prosecutors, Ryan Dawes.

Merci swallowed hard, tried to keep her blood pressure from going berserk. Dawes was the DA's most aggressive and best homicide prosecutor and he had a conviction rate of ninety-six percent. He was mid-thirties and looked good in what Merci considered a men's magazine kind of way. An "extreme" athlete, whatever that was, rock surfing or sky skiing or some such shit. His nickname was Jaws and he liked it. He was the only person in the District Attorney's office who'd spoken out when Merci was going through her own public and private hell less than a year ago. Jaws had told the Orange County Journal that what Merci was doing was "a self-serving disgrace."

Rayborn and Zamorra watched the crime scene investigators shoot video and stills of Gwen Wildcraft and everything around her. The coroner's team removed the thermometer and fastened clear plastic bags around her hands, feet and head. Then the CSI's turn again, to measure the distances between body and wall, body and door, body and tub, etc. Then, grunting and slipping in blood, four of them pushed and pulled her into a plastic bag. Rayborn saw two small, round wounds—one at the hairline, just above the left temple; one under, and toward the inside of her left breast.

Rayborn felt great disgust and pity for the human race. She imagined a pink *casita* on a white beach in Mexico. She had never been to such a place but liked to picture it sometimes. She could see it now. She pictured her son, whom she had seen less than one hour ago, splashing happily in the ocean by the pink house. She watched the engagement ring on Gwen's finger, a small diamond caked in dark red, disappear as a tech worked her arm inside the bag ahead of the advancing zipper.

"Rectal temp ninety-seven degrees, Sergeant Rayborn," said the deputy coroner.

"Then she's been dead for less than an hour."

"Maybe longer, if her BT ran high."

A CSI Merci had never worked with handed her two small clear evidence bags. Each contained an empty cartridge case—a thirty-eight or a nine-millimeter by the look of them. One was labeled 1 and the other 2. The CSI stared at the bags as he gave them over. The writing on the cartridge bottoms confirmed her guess: S&W.38 cal.

"I marked the floor tile with circled black numbers, and arrows to show the direction of the openings. Had to get them out of there before—they got kicked around and lost. Both were to her right. One in the corner and next to her knee. I've got a sketch with the relative positions and time. I made sure the video guys got close-ups."

Rayborn glanced at the glass shower door to see if the casings, ejected by an automatic pistol, could have bounced off and left a pit or nick. But the lights glared off the glass and she could see no marks at all. Just the faint outline of herself: square shoulders, strong body, an almost pretty face.

The CSI had placed a small wad of toilet paper in the mouth of each bag to keep it open, keep the moisture from building up and maybe wrecking a print.

"What's your name?"

"Don Leitzel."

"I'm Merci Rayborn. Thank you and good work."

She looked at the dresser in the Wildcraft bedroom, noting the sapphire earrings in a still open box.

They stood in the rock room. Scores of stones, most of them dark in color, all of them elegant in some way that Merci Rayborn couldn't describe. Some small as golf balls, others a couple of feet long. Many of them rested in form-fitting stands. Some of the stands were wood. Others were plaster or clay, some even brushed steel.

"What are these things for?" she asked.

"I don't know," said Zamorra.

"They look Japanese," said Merci. "Maybe Bob would know."

"I'll get him."

She waited in the quiet room. Her gaze went from a rock that looked like a mountain with rivers running down it, to a rock that looked like an island with coves, to a rock that looked like nothing at all. Collections bothered Rayborn because she'd once interviewed a man who kept a collection of hollow, decorated bird's eggs. In a nearby apartment, he kept a collection of hollow, decorated human beings. But as she considered the rock that looked like nothing she thought it was the most graceful nothing she'd ever seen.

Bob Fukiyama and Zamorra stood on either side of her.

"Suiseki," said the assistant pathologist. "Viewing stones."

"What do you do with them?" asked Merci.

"You view them. Appreciate. Meditate."

"Then what?"

"Sergeant?"

"Then what do you do?"

"I think that's all."

Rayborn looked incredulously at the assistant pathologist. She had never meditated. Thought about things, sure, like a tough case she was working, but everyone did that. Appreciated, yes, occasionally. She appreciated her son and looked at him a lot, but Tim, Jr. wasn't a rock.

"Collecting and displaying *suiseki* is an ancient Japanese pastime," Fukiyama said. "My grandfather collected stones. There are societies, shows and displays. Some *suiseki* can be very valuable. Some look like islands. Some look like mountains with snow and streams. Some are more abstract. People in crowded cities keep the stones in their homes, ponder the shapes and what they suggest. The stones take them away from the city and into nature."

"Do they have any left?" she asked absently. She was staring at one that looked like a water buffalo, curled up with its head on its flank, resting.

"Left, sergeant?" asked Fukiyama.

"In Japan, Bob. If it's an ancient hobby and a small island, have they found all the good ones?"

"I don't think so, sergeant. And they're collected all over the world."

"I like the buffalo."

Fukiyama stepped forward and looked at it. "You know, that's a really good stone," he said. "If I remember right, water buffaloes are an entire category in themselves. Hard to find. Grandfather's was a good one, but not as good or as big as that. Or as jade-like."

"See?" Zamorra asked her. "You understand suiseki, you just don't know you do."

"I know a good rock when I see one," she said, still looking at the buffalo stone.

The men laughed quietly but Rayborn didn't. She could still smell Gwen Wildcraft's blood every time she took a breath.

Across the hall was a music room. Merci looked at the keyboards and speakers and mixing board, then at the twisting river of cables, jacks, plugs and cords running beneath them.

There were two CD towers full of discs. Merci looked to see who the artists were, but didn't recognize them.

"How old was she?"

"Twenty-six," said Zamorra. "Yesterday was her birthday."

Merci figured that a musically inclined person ten years her junior would listen to an entirely different kind of music than she did.

"What about Archie?"

"Thirty."

On the walls were bright oil paintings of beaches and hills. They looked like the work of one artist and Merci checked the bottom right corners on three of them: GK. She made a note to confirm Gwen's maiden name.

There were several photographs of Archie and Gwen. Archie had a strong neck, a broad, genial face and big dimples. Straight short hair. Good teeth. Gwen's face was compact and beautifully proportioned beneath a high forehead. Strong eyes. Intelligent and sexual. Eight of the photographs were professional portraits with brass date plates at the bottoms of the frames, going back to 1994. The ninety-four portrait was from their wedding.

Merci looked at the dates and the photographs and watched the Wildcrafts age over eight years. First they looked like a couple on the high school homecoming court. Last they looked like a couple you'd see in a celebrity magazine. In between, six years of gradually evolving handsomeness and beauty.

Dead in her bathroom on the night of her birthday. Shot in the head in his own back yard.

One of us.

Merci stood behind the synthesizer looking down at the keys and controls, then over at the knobs and slide controls of the mixer. She noted the microphone, which was on a stand beside the keyboard. The black paint on the mesh had been worn away by Gwen Wildcraft's lips, and the metal was touched by a red substance that Merci realized was lipstick.

"I'm firing up this tape deck," said Zamorra.

The speakers crackled and Merci watched him turn down the volume. A tentative four-chord intro, then another one, tighter, like the player was figuring it out as she played. The woman's voice was high-pitched and clear. Not strong, but breathy and light:

> We went out and got it all
> Gold and diamonds wall to wall
> And I got you and you got me
> We're who everybody wants to be
> Turn it up loud turn it up high
> Do what you have to
> But don't say goodbye
> Don't even joke about saying goodbye

Rayborn pulled out her blue notebook and wrote, *Dep. 2 30 at $40K base/Wife 26 paints und plays/house a mil plus/pool, furns pricey/CK$*.

Zamorra clicked off the music mid-chord.

Merci stood in the terrible silence for a moment, then turned as a green uniform full of muscles came into the room. "The wit's waiting outside," it said. "One-hundred and fifty-five steps from where he heard the shots to the front door of this house."

"Good work, Dobbs."